Wickham's Second Attempt

Wickham's Second Attempt

By Monika Barbara Potocki

Dedication

With loving gratitude to my Creator, who endowed me with the talent to imagine and write.

To my Heavenly Mother, for her tender care and protection.

To the Saints who never tire of watching over me.

To my earthly parents, my biggest fans throughout my life.

To my friends who put up with me constantly working Pride and Prejudice into our conversations.

May Jane Austen, whose beautiful stories continue to inspire us hundreds of years later, rest in peace.

With special thanks to the actors, actresses, and others who worked on adaptations of Jane Austen's works, bringing them to life for us. May they use their talents wisely.

Chapter 1

Georgiana Darcy looked up from the book she had been perusing, gave a little sigh of contentment, and readjusted herself against the cushions of the sumptuous carriage which was travelling towards London. Another separation from her beloved brother would soon be concluded, and the young girl of sixteen could scarcely wait to be in his warm, protective embrace again.

Five weeks ago, Fitzwilliam Darcy had gone to visit Lady Catherine de Bourgh, their maternal aunt who resided in Kent. Georgiana hoped, rather than expected, the excursion to be a beneficial and pleasant one for him. It was no secret between the siblings that the yearly visit was a monotonous duty rather than a joyful family reunion. But she prayed that this year would be somehow different, for Fitzwilliam desperately needed some sort of diversion; he had been acting peculiarly all winter long.

He had come back from Hertfordshire even more introverted than his wont. On some days it was impossible to extract a word from him beyond a monosyllable and he would pace back and forth in front of the fireplace for hours, seemingly wrestling with a grave moral dilemma. When forced to attend balls, parties, and concerts, Fitzwilliam stationed himself in an obscure corner of the room and scrutinized every lady in it as if mentally comparing them to some spectral ideal. Invariably, the evening ended with her brother stalking to the carriage, unsatisfied.

And then there were brief intervals in which he relaxed, and seemed to taste the sweetness of surrender to his nemesis, whatever it might be. During those times, a whimsical look filled Fitzwilliam's eyes, a contented smile touched his lips, and he gazed at vacant chairs in the London townhouse as if they held some treasured occupant. One morning at the breakfast table he had stared so steadfastly at the seat across from him that Georgiana wondered whether he was quite sane.

Upon that occasion she had timidly inquired of Fitzwilliam if he felt well. When he answered in the affirmative, she doubted him, but dared not press the point further. Her brother always inspired in herself a respect which almost overcame her affection, and Georgiana did not venture to pry into his private affairs any more than she would have meddled with her late father's. And in her innocence and youth, she was unable to deduce that love might be the cause of his idiosyncrasies.

Therefore, she silently prayed that time and the trip into Kent would resolve whatever was plaguing the best brother on earth. If they failed, however, she was sure that their upcoming summer at Pemberley would succeed. That grand country estate was unquestionably Fitzwilliam's favorite place, and it was there that Georgiana would occasionally see the serious gentleman relax and enjoy riding, fishing, and hunting like any young man of eight and twenty. One way or another, this slight scourge would pass, she was sure of it.

Miss Darcy leafed through the volume in her lap, calculating how many more pages there were to read. At the sound of a slight cough which emanated from the opposite side of the coach, she glanced up and looked at the place where Mrs. Annesley, her kind-hearted companion, sat. They exchanged small smiles and Georgiana lifted the book once more. She was about to resume reading when something unusual outside the carriage's windows caught her eye.

On the horizon were the darkest storm clouds she had ever seen. With their broad expanse and navy hue they reminded her of midnight, and were surrounded by a foreboding silhouette of white.

"Mrs. Annesley, pray look!" the girl exclaimed softly. The attendant obliged her charge at once and leaned towards the glass to examine the noteworthy spectacle.

"My, that sky certainly does not look very promising, does it?" the older lady said, glancing at Georgiana. Catching the young woman's anxious countenance, however, she hastened to add, "But do not distress yourself, Miss Darcy. Our coachman is sensible and highly experienced; he will either circumvent the tempest or see that we reach an inn before it strikes."

Indeed, at that very moment an urging cry reached their ears, and the tempo of the horses' tread quickened.

Calming herself with a deep breath, Georgiana concentrated on the written words once more. This phase only lasted for a little less than two minutes before a growl of thunder recalled her attention to the sky.

Her heart skipped a beat as she gazed upwards. The clouds which, but a moment before, had been on the horizon were now blanketing half the sky and were still advancing at a furious pace. Flashes of lightening lit up sections of them. It was clear that

2

complete avoidance of the looming storm was impossible, especially as they were travelling through countryside, with no villages or buildings visible anywhere.

Mrs. Annesley, noticing the same, inspected all the windows to ensure that they were fully closed against the imminent downpour.

"At the rate those clouds are moving, I am sure that it will pass soon," she said to her charge as the first raindrops were heard upon the roof of the carriage.

"Yes, I suppose so," Miss Darcy replied absentmindedly, watching the streaks of lightening grow brighter and listening to the claps of thunder increase in volume. A judicious young woman, she knew that the travelling conditions were fast becoming treacherous and that as a matter of prudence they ought to pray and hope that blue skies would be restored expeditiously. And yet, there was one small traitorous piece of her heart which could not help rejoicing in the adventure of traveling through so memorable a squall. For despite her elevated social status, Georgiana often felt that her life was far too dull.

Most of her childhood had been eclipsed by the early death of her mother. The little Miss Darcy had been raised by a grieving family. With the subsequent passing of her father five years ago, she had been sent to a school whose object was to create proper young ladies, and not to indulge its pupils in youthful play. During vacations, Georgiana came back to see Fitzwilliam. But her brother, as kind and generous as he was, was a rather sedate soul, often weighted down by responsibilities which few carried at his age. And now, he had hired a dignified, decorous lady as her companion. Georgiana liked Mrs. Annesley and felt comfortable discussing many things with her, but often longed for a more animated friend, one who laughed wholeheartedly and had a knack for making life thrilling. Thus, the sixteen-year-old Miss Darcy grasped at whatever scraps of exhilaration fell her way.

Unfortunately, this hunger had recently almost been satisfied by poisoned fare. Ten months ago, Georgiana had been staying at Ramsgate in the society of Mrs. Younge, Mrs. Annesley's predecessor, when, seemingly by chance, she became reacquainted with George Wickham, the son of her late father's steward. She remembered the handsome young man from her childhood, for he had then devoted hours to her amusement. Overjoyed at having a familiar and cheerful personage near, Miss Darcy gladly received his visits and accepted his invitations to walk along the magnificent windswept seashores. Very soon, however, Mr. Wickham began calling during the evenings, and instead of reminiscing about the past, commenced flattering the golden-haired maiden's present beauty and accomplishments. The suitor's devices worked. Mr. Wickham persuaded Georgiana's affectionate heart that it was in love. And then, he suggested the elopement.

Such a radical proposal gave her pause. But the young man was unrelenting.

"I love you," he had said. "And I simply cannot contain my affection! Oh, sweetest Georgiana, do not subject me to the torment of waiting. Why should we delay happiness by a single hour? By going to Gretna Green, we can accomplish in a matter of days what would otherwise take weeks, or even years, considering your age! What a good joke it will be, to return and introduce you as Mrs. Wickham to your brother and all your relatives and acquaintances! And do not worry about Fitzwilliam - he will approve. He and I were always good friends, remember?"

Such reasoning drew her fifteen-year-old mind in, particularly after she confided in Mrs. Younge and received enthusiastic approbation. Hence, she told Mr. Wickham – *George* - that she would marry him. As the accepted suitor fervently kissed her hand again and again, Miss Darcy decided that life was perfect. She was betrothed to a wonderful man, and the prospect of a spontaneous, secretive trip to Scotland, a clandestine wedding, and then the excitement of announcing the same to her connections was before them!

A day or two before the intended elopement, the fairy tale unraveled. Fitzwilliam Darcy unexpectedly arrived to see his sister. Beholding his dear and vigilant countenance again, Georgiana felt her conscience awakening. How could she abandon a brother who had done so much for her, without a word of farewell?

She had gone and confessed the whole truth to him at once. As she did so, an unforgettable expression diffused over Fitzwilliam's face. And she knew. Even before her brother ordered Wickham away from Ramsgate, even before he explained, she knew that her former playmate had mercilessly used her. Fitzwilliam's narrative merely supplied the particulars.

George Wickham and her brother had been at odds for years. They played together as boys, but as the former grew, he advanced far more in vice than in education or industry. During the old Mr.

Darcy's lifetime, the ruthless young fellow had done everything to worm himself into the elderly gentleman's graces in the hopes that a substantial inheritance and easy life would be his. This hope was partially fulfilled when a valuable living and a thousand pounds were bequeathed to him. But Mr. Wickham, having no interest in being a clergyman (since that position still required some trouble and a quiet style of life) quickly requested to exchange his claim to the living for three thousand pounds. Fitzwilliam, knowing the man's unsuitability for any position of responsibility, complied and hoped that he had heard the last of his onetime friend.

For a couple years, it seemed that this wish would be granted. The almost-clergyman disappeared altogether from her brother's notice. Fitzwilliam had nearly forgotten his existence when, one fine day, he unsuspectingly came across a letter from George Wickham.

It seemed that the three thousand pounds had been gambled and drunk away, and their squanderer was now resolved upon taking orders, and expected that the valuable living would be provided him. When Fitzwilliam refused to open the doors of the parsonage to the wastrel, Wickham's letters rose in pitch and burned with threats, but the former stood firm. At last, the abusive dispatches ceased and Wickham disappeared anew. He remained distant until that fateful afternoon, when Fitzwilliam Darcy discovered that the profligate had been consorting with his beloved sister, preying upon both her dowry and the opportunity for revenge.

Of course, the brother's arrival allayed the worst dangers. Mr. Wickham left the place immediately, and Mrs. Younge was removed from her charge. Everything that could be done to hush the entire affair was done, successfully. But the healing of Georgiana's heart – that could not be accomplished as quickly. Her brother soothed and never reproached, as did their cousin, her other guardian, Colonel Richard Fitzwilliam. Still, it took months before she smiled again, and now, nearly a year later, her natural shyness and reserve remained redoubled.

"I do not believe that I have ever seen the sky so dark during the daytime," Mrs. Annesley remarked quietly, cutting into Miss Darcy's thoughts.

Indeed, the early afternoon seemed like an eerie twilight. For a moment, the lightening had ceased, and despite the pouring rain, the wind was quiet as well. The air in the carriage seemed too thick and heavy to draw into one's lungs. The stillness was haunting.

Mrs. Annesley was just opening her lips to break the foreboding silence again when the sky itself shattered it.

CRACK-BOOM!

The strike must have been merely meters away.

For an instant, Georgiana was rendered deaf and blind and had one terrifying second of wondering whether those changes would be permanent.

Thankfully, the stunned senses began to return, but unfortunately were not the only things which recovered their ability to react to the environment.

The horses leading the carriage had also been bewildered by the blast, and when the first moment of astonishment passed, they decided that they had had enough of orderly prancing in the middle of such frightful conditions. Neighing for all they were worth, they dug their back hoofs into the ground, flailed their front ones into the air, and stopped the conveyance dead in its tracks.

Thump, thwack, thump!

A glimpse of the coachman and two footmen falling to the ground as a result of the deceleration was caught through the windows.

"James, Tom -," Georgiana cried out, pressing herself to the glass and vainly trying to see if the servants were alright. But before she could even name Andrew, the girl and Mrs. Annesley had two other lives to worry about: their own.

The horses finished rearing, and throwing their front hoofs down upon the road, bolted.

Carelessly, insanely, down the path the creatures flew, mercilessly hauling the carriage with two human beings behind them. It concerned them not a whit that the women inside could scarcely keep their seats as the wheels of the conveyance fell into craters in the road and were pulled out of them anew with startling rapidity. And then, the stallions hit upon the most atrocious idea of all: they veered, abandoned the road completely, and began dragging the carriage across the neighboring hillside.

For Mrs. Annesley this was the last straw. Striving to be calm for the sake of her charge, she locked eyes with the girl directly across from herself and loudly decreed:

"We have to jump!"

"Are we not safer within the carriage?" Miss Darcy asked, panicked.

Mrs. Annesley hurriedly shook her head.

"No, the horses are uncontrolled, and wild! Only God knows where they will take us! We must get out, at once!" Bracing herself as well as she could against the wall of the jostling carriage, the older woman reached out and unlatched the door. It flew open instantly. Turning back towards her charge Mrs. Annesley shouted over the wind, "Let me see first how best to do this; you follow after!"

"Yes, madam!" the wide-eyed girl managed. Heart pounding, barely breathing, she watched her companion gingerly but hastily cross the threshold and lower herself onto the attached step, clinging to the door frame for dear life. In this precarious position, the woman paused, trying to gauge the impact of the wind and the carriage's speed upon her planned leap. The horses, it would seem, had different ideas. At this, the most hazardous of moments, they pulled the conveyance over a small crater in the hillside.

"Aaaaaaaahhhhh!"

"MRS. ANNESLEY!" Georgiana screamed.

Her hand shot forward as if, within the span of a second, it could cross the three feet of space which were between its mistress and the open carriage door, grasp the older woman and pull her back into the carriage.

The reflexive action failed to do any good. Reaching out in vain, Miss Darcy helplessly watched as her companion lost her grip and footing and, tumbling downwards, disappeared from sight.

Stunned, her locomotion and sense of time greatly retarded, Georgiana leaned forward and prepared to stand. While she was generally an indecisive creature, unaccustomed to acting on her own, the pressing need for self-preservation and the lack of a more experienced guide forced her to attend to and follow the common sense which her own head was issuing:

I must gain the door, carefully look out, gain sight of Mrs. Annesley and join her, albeit in a more deliberate manner! I must!

As her torso moved forward, however, her eyes unwittingly glanced through the window. In an instant, she comprehended that she would have no opportunity to implement any plan.

Directly in the horses' path, only about twenty feet from their present position, was a deep, wide ravine.

Chapter 2

The girl instinctively shut her eyes to prevent herself from seeing what was to come.

There was no time to steel herself further, to think of friends and family who were being left behind, or to mourn all the aspirations which would never be accomplished. She had but one moment.

"Oh, God," she cried aloud, "have mercy upon me!"

CRACK-BOOM!

A shock wave and deafening blast hit Georgiana in the same instant. As if in a dream she felt her body flying forward, then its progress suddenly being halted by something which felt like a stone wall, then dropping down and hitting another hard surface with a sound thump.

She was ignorant of the fact that all these terrors were the product of a lightning bolt which had struck a tree on the opposite side of the ravine, right next to the very path which the horses had been planning to leap onto and traverse. The creatures had reared in fright at the very edge of the ravine, and then turned sharply left and continued their mad race along the banks of the chasm rather than over it. As a result of these maneuvers, the maiden within the carriage had been dislodged from her seat, thrown against the opposite wall, her shoulder bearing most of the impact, and had come to rest upon the floor.

Georgiana Darcy, however, was certain that the loud crash had been produced by the carriage hitting a boulder in the riverbank; the blinding flash was her first glimpse of heavenly glory, and the sensation of rapid acceleration and then deceleration had been caused by the separation of soul from body. Brimming with anticipation, she allowed her lashes to slowly flutter open, fully expecting to see her parents and cherubim, if not the Lord Himself.

Instead, she beheld nothing more spectacular than the ceiling of the carriage. This, and another jolt of the floor beneath her, caused Miss Darcy to realize that for the moment at least, she had been spared. Fear was remembered. The shaky limbs were gathered and hoisted up into a standing position. Grasping the interiors of the coach, she made her way to the windows just in time to see the horses veer once again, this time away from the ravine and into an expanse of fields.

Georgiana's panic was as great as ever. She knew nothing of this countryside. The stretch of soft, green grass could end at any moment, giving way to another abyss or forest, or any number of obstacles which could splinter the carriage and kill its occupant.

I have to exit, just like Mrs. Annesley said!

The carriage's erratic maneuvers had somehow managed to close the door which Mrs. Annesley had opened. Miss Darcy fumbled her way to it and flung it open once more. Afraid that her bonnet would impair her field of vision, she tore it off and tossed it upon the seat. Her blue coat suffered a similar fate lest it make her movements less nimble. Thinking a heartfelt prayer, she concentrated every ounce of strength in the two hands which attached her to the door's frame, and proceeded to back out of the compartment, desperately trying to ignore the drenching rain and the rhythmic nudging of the loose carriage door against her side.

One movement of one foot, and then an identical one with the other. There. She was standing securely on the step. All that remained was to locate a good landing spot and carry out the fateful leap. Soon, very soon, she would be safe.

Her eyes roved the soft, wet grass. Yes, this was the ideal spot if there ever was one. Summoning a last surge from her dwindling stores of energy, she concentrated on pushing off.

The muscles in her arms and legs contracted. Those in her fingers relaxed. Taken together, they equaled one Miss Georgiana Darcy plummeting through the air, clear of the carriage, but, unfortunately, not free from all danger.

Somewhere, somehow, she had miscalculated. Unsurprisingly. After all, a young lady of wealth and breeding had infinitely more practice at the pianoforte than at leaving carriages mid-ride.

Instead of the fashionably shod feet, it was the golden head which contacted the ground first. Even worse, its chosen pillow was one of the few rocks which could be found in that meadow.

The loss of consciousness was instantaneous.

Meanwhile, the coach disappeared from the vicinity as the horses, left to their fancy, circled around and began retracing the path which had taken them into the fields. The rain beat down the grasses, bending every blade down to the same height as those indented by the thoroughbreds' hoofs and the wheels of the carriage. Within minutes, these traces of their onetime presence were completely obliterated.

By mere chance the stallions found their way back to the place, three miles away from the unconscious Miss Darcy, where their wild galloping had convinced Mrs. Annesley that the separation of coach and passengers was mandatory. Deciding to accomplish the jump which lightening had prevented, they raced down the same route they had taken before and scarcely missed trampling Mrs. Annesley, who was still lying insensate where she had fallen. This time no loud noise spooked them. They sprung for the opposite side of the ravine, and made it. The coach was not so fortunate. Gravity pulled it down into the crevice as its leaders' hoofs made contact with the opposite bank. When the carriage attempted to follow its harness, it slammed into the rocky side of the chasm and broke into pieces which fell and met the flowing river on the bottom.

Chapter 3

Lighting stung Elizabeth Bennet's eyes, and the thunder caused her to involuntarily shudder. Standing at one of the windows of Longbourn's drawing room, she watched the raging storm. It possessed the distinction of being the first object that had managed to distract her thoughts from Mr. Darcy, his proposal, and his letter in a fortnight. But it was not just the white luminous streaks in the sky or the earth-rattling noise which drew her attention. Elizabeth feared greatly for her father.

A few days after her return from Kent, Mr. Bennet had gone on a rare business trip to London. At first, his second eldest daughter was glad of his absence, for he would have surely noticed her abstraction, and would have either teased its origin from her or been pained by her refusal to divulge it. The week of relative solitude and confiding in Jane had enabled Elizabeth to look forward to her father's company with equanimity. Thus, she had been eagerly anticipating Mr. Bennet's arrival until that afternoon, when the heavens darkened and opened. Now she prayed that her father's entourage had not left London before the storm, or if they had been so unfortunate, that they would find suitable shelter for its duration.

Crack!

Another lightning bolt hit the earth within a mile of Longbourn, causing Elizabeth to slightly jump. Before her heels came to rest upon the rug again, the air was pierced anew by a shriek.

"O Mr. Bennet! The carriage will overturn in this storm, and he shall be killed, and what will become of us all! The Collinses will be here tomorrow to turn us out because of that foolish entail, and we shall be starving in the shrubbery, and in the mud!"

"Mama, I am certain that Charlotte Collins would never allow that to happen. Besides, Papa is a sensible man, and he would certainly halt at an inn and wait out such a storm," the ever optimistic and gentle Jane soothed.

"No, he would not!" Mrs. Bennet cried. "You know your father's willful nature! He shall insist upon proceeding, and they shall lose a wheel, and-!"

"He is coming! There is the carriage now!" Kitty interrupted eagerly.

"Is he?" Mrs. Bennet inquired, rising quickly from her seat and rushing towards the window. "He *is* coming! Oh, you have a fine father, girls! He braved the storm and did his best to arrive home so that we would not worry…"

Elizabeth looked down to hide a smile of relief and amusement. She had learned long ago that it was easier to laugh at her mother's inconsistent exclamations than to become incensed at their absurdity.

Drawing nearer to the window, she peered out as another flash illuminated the countryside. Longbourn's only conveyance was indeed approaching, and at a rather rapid pace, considering the unsafe roads. Slightly perturbed by this fact, Elizabeth leaned closer to the glass and noted that *something* about the carriage was odd. It seemed…unbalanced. Something was missing.

Apprehensive once more, she hurried to the front door along with her sisters, only to be stunned by the sight of her father opening the carriage door and tossing down the step himself. He descended without aid, and it was only then that Elizabeth realized that there was no footman riding on the back of the carriage.

"Papa, where is Peter?" Jane called out, discerning the same.

Their father, standing in the pouring rain, made no answer other than turning slightly back towards the carriage. The missing footman suddenly appeared at the coach's door, carrying a large, bedraggled bundle in his strong arms. He awkwardly stepped down, taking great care not to jostle it. Obeying Mr. Bennet's curt wave, Peter preceded his master into the house. He was nearly at the threshold with his burden when the Bennet ladies uttered a sudden, united gasp.

Peter was carrying a girl!

The damsel was insensate, draped over the footman's arms in a most shocking manner. Dressed in a gown which had once been white but was now almost entirely colored by mud, her cascading golden tresses likewise soiled, she was a pitiable sight.

"The poor dear!" Jane cried, dashing towards the limp young woman as soon as Peter entered the house, Elizabeth at her heels.

"She is so dirty!" Kitty exclaimed.

"It looks as if she took a swim in a bog!" Lydia sniffed.

"Mr. Bennet, what is *that*?" the Mistress of Longbourn shrilled.

Her husband removed his overcoat and coolly retorted,

"An unconscious young woman."

"Where did you find her, Papa?" Elizabeth softly inquired, tenderly lifting a few blond curls which the rain had plastered to the girl's face.

"We were passing by the small meadow which is about ten miles from here, and I was looking out the window when I noticed a large, whitish form lying in the middle. I thought it odd, so I had the carriage halt and sent Peter to investigate. This is what he found."

"And what did you bring the waif here for?" Mrs. Bennet demanded.

Mr. Bennet glanced sharply at his wife. She had had faults in the past, but this inhospitality surpassed them all! Hiding disgust behind wit, as usual, he replied in an overly-calm tone.

"For the sake of your consequence, my dear. Can you suppose what would have happened had I not retrieved her and someone else from Hertfordshire, perhaps Sir William Lucas, discovered her instead? You could scarcely bear to be outdone by Lady Lucas. We both know that she would immediately advance her status among the gossips in Meryton by announcing this new, mysterious arrival. Now you may have that honor, my dear!"

Before Mrs. Bennet could answer, Elizabeth, mindful that every moment that the young maiden spent in the drenched clothes increased her risk of catching her death of cold, quickly interrupted her parents' conversation to command,

"Peter, take her up to the spare room, quickly."

The servant only had time to execute one step in that direction before Mrs. Bennet shrieked,

"Up to *my* spare room? He certainly shall not! The linens will be ruined the moment that bundle of mud is put upon them."

Jane and Elizabeth exchanged a glance.

"Mama, the sheets may easily be changed afterwards," Jane pleaded earnestly.

"No! I am Mistress here, and I will not hear of my spare room being disgraced with such an occupant! She could be a peddler or robber for all we know!"

"Very well, then, madam," Elizabeth replied, her eyes flashing. "The spare room will remain untouched. Peter, carry her up to my bedchamber. I shall sleep with Jane as long as necessary."

"Yes, do that, Peter," the Master of Longbourn commanded, before the Mistress could get another word in edgewise. The servant obeyed at once, bearing the girl up the stairs. Comprehending that she had been overruled, Mrs. Bennet gave her two most deserving daughters a wilting glare and consented to retreat back into the drawing room, moaning,

"What is to become of us! My nerves cannot endure this! Hill, Hill, where is Hill? Fetch my smelling salts, summon the maids, I feel faint - oh, the pounding in my head!"

Elizabeth and Jane exchanged another painful look, both perfectly aware that their mother's sudden ailment proceeded solely from disappointment and a desire to force them to tend to the young unfortunate without the help of servants. Their father, discerning the same, murmured something under his breath about sending for the apothecary once the dangerous storm abated, and withdrew. The two girls, left to their own nursing assets, dashed up the stairs, joining Peter just in time to open the door of Elizabeth's bedchamber for the burdened man.

He carried the maiden over to the bed, from which Jane hastily stripped the covers, and laid her down gently. Her beautiful, sullied hair fell across the white pillow, but no one in the room had a care for the damage it caused as the eldest lady breathlessly said,

"Thank you, Peter, you may leave us now."

The attendant departed just as the two youngest Bennet sisters, unable to contain their curiosity, skipped into the room.

"Kitty, shut the door. Lydia, get me the scissors from my sewing basket," Elizabeth ordered, determined that they might as well be put to use if they wished to gawk at the proceedings.

Surprisingly, the usually frivolous girls obeyed at once, but Lydia did not scruple to ask as she handed over the asked-for implement,

"Are you going to crop her hair, Lizzy? It shall scarcely make her look any nastier, the little muddied thing."

"Lydia, that is unkind," was Jane's gentle reproach as her nimble hands unlaced the young woman's boots. "We will cut off her wet clothes since it would take too long to undress her in a more conventional manner. She is already seriously ill, and a cold or, God forbid, pneumonia, might complicate her recovery terribly."

During the explanation Elizabeth had inserted the scissors' separated blades at the neckline of the soaked gown, and as quickly as she could without nicking the skin underneath, slit the garment from top to bottom. So intent on expediency were Jane and she that neither of them took note of the quality of the clothes which they were removing, especially as, covered in soggy dirt, they did not give a first impression of fashion. In any case, a thorough inspection of them was far from their minds as Elizabeth commanded,

"Fetch several towels, Kitty, and one of my nightgowns, quickly! Lydia, take these ruined things down to the kitchen and tell the cook to burn them in the stove."

The latter did not take kindly to the firm request, whining as her arms were filled with deformed boots and dissected apparel:

"Why must *I* go downstairs while Kitty can stay here? I want to be here when she wakes up and hear her excuse for lying in the meadow!"

Elizabeth heard Jane taking a breath, doubtlessly as a prelude to another comforting statement, but she was too harried and too satiated by her youngest sister's lack of empathy to permit her another soothing articulation. Before Jane could speak, she retorted,

"Considering that she has remained unconscious during a prolonged carriage ride and has not so much as stirred since we saw her, I doubt that you need to fear missing a dramatic awakening, Lydia. You will probably be fortunate if you *ever* hear her speak. And in any case, the faster you dispose of the old clothing, the quicker you can return and gape at the poor child to your heart's content!"

Muttering indignantly, Lydia consented to obey, but only because she sensed that the proprietress of the bedchamber would not balk at imposing a permanent banishment if she continued to contravene. In the meantime, Elizabeth grasped the nightgown and towels which Kitty proffered, and dried and dressed the badly-bruised lady. Once she had draped the warm covers over the patient, she finally decelerated her ministrations somewhat and glanced at Jane.

"Do you suppose we should wash her hair, or will the attempt hurt her neck in her fragile condition?"

Jane cast a tender look at the still form.

"If we are very careful, I do not think that any harm will come of it. We cannot leave her tresses in such a state."

"Very well." The girls set to filling a basin with water and bringing it over to the bed, where Elizabeth, the stronger of the two, warily lifted the guest's head as Jane slipped the miniature, makeshift bathtub under it and proceeded to gingerly rinse out the mussed curls.

All at once, Jane's horrified voice rang through the entire bedchamber.

"Lizzy!"

"What is it?" Elizabeth exclaimed, tearing her gaze away from the patient to look at her sister.

"Feel the back of her head. Right here, where my hand is."

The other nursemaid obeyed, and presently remarked in a small, frightened voice,

"With a lump like that, 'tis little wonder that she is senseless."

Kitty, who had until now been standing silently at the foot of the bed, leapt forward and craned her neck, trying to see the cause of her siblings' distress.

"What is it?" she pried. "Has she a wound?"

"No, but she has a great deal of swelling," Elizabeth replied. "Her head must have been hit with great force." Miss Kitty's curious hand shot forward, reached into the wet hair and palpated the famous bump. "Gently!"

"Alright, Lizzy, alright," Kitty replied, exasperated, untangling her fingers from the soaked strands. "Will it kill her?"

Elizabeth shuddered.

"Just pray that it does not," she whispered, fearfully looking upon the inanimate girl before them.

Hours passed. The golden tresses were washed and dried, the covers smoothened. The storm ceased, and the apothecary, Mr. Jones, came. He examined the patient and shook his head. Only time would tell, he said. Instructed to keep her warm and the room quiet, the two eldest Miss Bennets divided the approaching night into watches and took turns sitting up with the unmoving form.

Thus the night waxed and waned. As the next day dawned, Elizabeth could be found clasping the hand of the mysterious visitor, gently brushing its knuckles with her thumb, hoping that this sensation would reach the girl's mind and pull her back to consciousness. She also took the opportunity to stroke and admire the blue ring which graced the limp hand.

Lydia had first noticed the ornament soon after they washed the invalid's hair, and unashamedly claimed it as her inheritance if the young woman's injuries proved to be mortal. It was a pretty silver ring of modest size, bearing a circlet of white stones, in the center of which reposed a larger indigo one. While they admired its tasteful design, none of the inhabitants of Longbourn were well-versed enough in the knowledge of fine jewels to properly recognize its worth. Young ladies of great consequence were rarely found abandoned on the side of the road, and thus they assumed that the gems were, like those on their own accessories, made of cut glass.

Elizabeth glanced at the clock with a sigh. It was seven o'clock, which meant that she had been stroking the small hand for an entire hour without effect. Tired by the fruitless effort, she laid the limb down with a sigh, and rising from her seat, walked quietly to the window. Brushing the curtain away from the glass, she gazed out into the morn, little imagining what was happening miles away in London.

Chapter 4

Fitzwilliam Darcy sat languidly in the luxurious study of his townhouse. He knew not that it was the fifth of May, or that his sister had been expected in London on the fourth. The letter which would have informed him of the latter lay unopened in the pile of correspondence which he had not even thought to glance through since his return from Kent.

For the previous fortnight, he had thought of nothing but a certain ten-minute interview in the Hunsford parsonage, and continuously berated himself for all the reasons it had gone astray from his expectations. How often had he imagined their culmination! As he walked to the Collins' residence that fateful day he had dreamed, once again, of what he thought would occur within it. He would present himself in the parlor and Elizabeth would greet him with a faint expression of anticipation, surmising what was about to transpire. During his ardent declaration, her face would take on a joyous expression, and when he finished, her eyes would mischievously flash as she uttered some witty answer which meant '*Yes*' and gave him implicit permission to seat himself next to his beloved, instead of on a chair several feet away. Or perhaps, her happiness would be so heartfelt that instead of her characteristic teasing she would reply with some profound phrases which were worthy of Shakespeare. He would go to her at once, kiss her hands and speak her Christian name aloud, delighting in the pleased blush on her cheeks.

Instead, he had been spurned, accused, and deprecated. Fitzwilliam Darcy had been informed in no uncertain terms that Elizabeth Bennet would wed any man in the world more readily than himself. If that were not enough, he was enlightened as to the horrendous state of his manners and character. By the time he regained the front door of the parsonage, he knew that his darling prized the dirt under her feet more than she did his affection.

Darcy's lot would have been infinitely easier had he truly been the ungenerous man Elizabeth had accused him of being, the illiberal soul which he was beginning to believe himself to be. But despite those unpleasant opinions, he was actually an amiable man at heart, and thus unable to indulge in the sentiments which would soothe many other men under similar circumstances. He could not hate

Elizabeth Bennet for her uncharitable words. Nor could Darcy feel enough resentment to pry away her hold on his heart. The blessing which had been denied had not lost an ounce of its value in his estimation. On the contrary, the young lady from Hertfordshire was cherished all the more, for the rejected suitor could not but admire her for her very refusal. Wealth and consequence were not enough to secure *her* good opinion!

So Mr. Fitzwilliam Darcy remained sequestered in the study, heartbreak compounding itself by the hour, resigning himself to an unhappy future. He knew that the love he harbored for Elizabeth was not one which could be recovered from. The impossibility of overcoming it had been clearly proven the previous winter, when he had spent months reminding himself of what he owed to his station in life and trying to forget her. Thus, Darcy now accepted that he would never have what he had observed between his parents: a romantic marriage, built upon mutual esteem and the warmth of a first attachment. His life would be a solitary one.

The gentleman leaned back in the leather chair with a sigh, pressing his hand against his forehead in a futile endeavor to stop it from throbbing. It was then that he heard the knocking.

In the first startled moment, Darcy thought the sound a product of his headache. It was only after glancing around the room bewilderedly that he realized it had come from the door. Out of long habit, rather than from a desire to see anyone, he straightened up and called out,

"Come in!"

The door opened, and Darcy made an attempt to focus his tired eyes on the figure which appeared in the threshold. It was Mrs. Harrison, the townhouse's housekeeper. Had he been his usual observant self, the young man would have immediately noticed her reddened, teary eyes and her tight grip on the doorknob. As it was, the master barely perceived her presence.

"I beg your pardon, sir. I know that you left strict orders not to be disturbed, but," here Mrs. Harrison took a deep breath to keep her voice from shuddering, "Tom, Andrew, and James have arrived and wish to speak to you, about…it concerns Miss Georgiana, sir."

Darcy gazed at her blankly. It did not occur to his sluggish mind that the return of the coachman and footmen assigned to his sister, with unsolicited news of her, might not be the herald of fortune.

"May I send them in?" Mrs. Harrison asked.

"Yes," Darcy replied, hardly knowing what he was assenting to.

Mrs. Harrison nodded shakily, retreated, and shut the door before going to convey her employer's consent to the aforementioned persons.

When she had gone, Darcy relaxed once more. *Georgiana.* That was the only word of Mrs. Harrison's entire communication which had genuinely permeated his consciousness. For the first time in a sennight, his thoughts turned to a person other than Elizabeth Bennet or himself as a mental image of his little sister's pretty, innocent face floated before him. How strongly he suddenly longed for her presence, for her timid devotion! In the midst of such poignant woe it was a sweet consolation to know that someone thoroughly loved him, even if he did not merit such esteem. And yet, how had he repaid her faithfulness? How much damage had he done by setting such a proud, disagreeable example of what a Darcy ought to be? Georgiana's character, thankfully, appeared to still be full of humility, but it was only too possible that having so ungentlemanly a brother had, in some way, injured her sensibilities.

Waiting for the servants, Darcy made two desperate resolutions. First, he had to undo any harm he had already caused Georgiana. From that day forward, he would involve them both in charitable works, introduce her to every respectable person he knew, even if they happened to be of a lower status, and ensure that *she* never became entangled in vanity. Second, Georgiana would be his reason for living. He would cling to her, love her, and exist in the sunshine of her admiration. In half a decade or so, for Darcy could not bear the possibility that it could be sooner, she would marry a gentleman who would cherish her just as he would have treasured Elizabeth. While Fitzwilliam Darcy would never be a father, he would laugh with and delight in his nephews and nieces. From Georgiana's happiness, he would derive his.

Coming out of this reverie, Darcy became aware of hushed voices at the door. Once again, he resumed a more poised posture, gathered his wits, and prepared to attend to whatever matter of business his employees wished to discuss.

The heavy oak door received an indecisive knock before it swung open. Tom, the coachman, reluctantly stepped in. Andrew and James, the footmen, followed him softly. The threesome stationed themselves before the master's desk, wholeheartedly wishing that they be obliged to do anything but bear such ill tidings to their beloved superior.

Darcy, on the other hand, was much more alert at their entrance than he had been at Mrs. Harrison's. He scrutinized their torn, muddy garments, their bleak faces, and their exhausted eyes with surprise.

"What is the matter?" the master inquired.

Tom glanced at his fellow servants' faces, took a deep breath, and falteringly said,

"There was an…incident on the road, sir."

"Namely?"

"I was driving Miss Darcy and Mrs. Annesley to London yesterday, as scheduled. While we were travelling, a terrible thunderstorm came upon us so suddenly that there was nowhere to take shelter. A particularly close lighting strike spooked the horses and they bolted."

Darcy caught his breath.

"Is everyone safe?" he asked in a measured, forcibly calm voice.

"The three of us were thrown from the conveyance at the very beginning of the rampage, Mr. Darcy, but are quite unhurt. Mrs. Annesley, we understand, soon afterwards attempted to see if it would be safe to jump from the carriage. During that endeavor, she lost her grip and fell to the side of the road, temporarily losing consciousness and breaking her wrist and ankle. We eventually found her and saw her to an inn some miles off, where we entrusted the good woman to a local doctor's care. She is expected to make a full recovery."

As soon as the coachman finished his speech, Darcy's hands began to shake uncontrollably. He had, of course, noticed the omission of Georgiana's status from the narrative, and could not help suspecting that the oversight had been deliberate; it was unlike his servants to accidentally exclude so important a piece of information. Struggling for air, he choked out,

"And…my sister?"

Tom again looked at Andrew and James, whose heads were bent, and silently shook his own before likewise looking down.

"Tell me!" Darcy demanded, abruptly resigning the seat and regaining his feet.

It was James who, after a heavy pause, answered.

"We are sorry, sir," he sadly replied.

Darcy's heart pounded in his chest, and his head swam. His hands found the desk and grasped onto it for support as he mustered the courage to inquire in a terrified, trembling voice:

"What do you mean?"

"Mr. Darcy, very close to where Mrs. Annesley lay, there was a wide ravine, with a raging stream at the bottom. It was in these waters that we noticed the sparse remains of the carriage, enmeshed in some rocks. The horses managed to make the jump, for we found them grazing on the opposite side, but in doing so they apparently broke the harness, sending the coach into the waters. We looked for Miss Georgiana, thinking that she might have miraculously had time to follow her companion's example, but we found no trace of her, sir. Thus, we concluded that she must have…fallen with the carriage."

"There was no reason to conclude that!" Darcy cried out, precipitously becoming incredulous. "But since that was your opinion, did you try to reach the coach, to help her out of her predicament?"

"Sir, when I said 'remains of the carriage', I meant a few pieces of wood and the back wheels. It was not an intact carriage, where someone could possibly be lodged."

"Then she was simply swept away by the water, and probably managed to climb out onto the bank a few yards downstream."

"We hoped so too, at first. But we followed the stream and scoured the banks for several miles. There was no sign of Miss Georgiana."

Darcy shook his head. This could not be happening! It was impossible that so soon after losing Elizabeth, he had also lost the one last person who would have made life worth living.

"You *must* have missed her! She *had* to be walking or sitting somewhere along the way!"

Andrew, guilt-ridden that hitherto his friends had been doing the explaining, began to speak soothingly at this juncture.

"Mr. Darcy…pray believe me when I say that the three of us understand your feelings. We experienced them ourselves but a few hours ago. However, after combing through the area, we were forced to accept the truth. Let us for a moment assume the best, that Miss Georgiana managed to escape the treacherous conveyance before it reached the chasm. If that were the case, we would have surely found her, either wounded and immobile or well and tending to her injured companion. It is implausible that someone arrived on the scene before

23

us and took her away, for the horses ran far off the road to quite a deserted place, and even if someone should have happened upon them, they would have rescued Mrs. Annesley as well. But frankly, sir, I think it unreasonable to believe that Miss Darcy was so fortunate. Mrs. Annesley quit the carriage not seventy feet from the edge of the ravine, and according to her, Miss Darcy was still sitting within at that time. The horses were flying at such a speed that there would only have been two or three seconds for her to stand, gain the door, and execute a jump, and this in a carriage which was bouncing and jostling for all its worth. Then again, the abyss was extremely deep. So great a fall…such a churning river underneath…and as you are aware, Miss Georgiana did not know how to swim."

Yes, Darcy did know, and he felt as if the entire world had been shattered in that canyon and swept out to sea.

"I wish to see the situation for myself. Come, show me what you speak of!" the gentleman feverishly exclaimed, running his hand through his hair before dashing at the study door.

"Yes, of course, sir," Tom replied as he and his friends hurried after their employer.

Chapter 5

Being in a sickroom is always exhausting. Even when the invalid sleeps and requires nothing, the mere act of watching them, most anxiously, for any sign of bettering or worsening is enough to render a nurse fatigued. Then there is the fear of the future; shall the patient leave the bed of their own accord, or will someone have to lift their form from it and lay it in a harder, more permanent cradle? However soft the caretaker's chair might initially be, long hours spent in it invariably stiffen the joints and make them ache.

This was Elizabeth Bennet's experience the day after the injured damsel had been brought to Longbourn. Jane would have gladly borne her share of these discomforts, had she been available; but, alas! The older Miss Bennet had to tend to a much older woman, who writhed and moaned and cried about her nerves and about how little her word counted in the house where she was mistress.

Early in the afternoon Elizabeth rose and took a turn about the room. Seeking some form of distraction from the fact that her patient had not moved in four and twenty hours, and from the subsequent ruminating on what horrid things this might indicate, she began to rearrange the inkstand, small vase, and other items which stood on the bedchamber's writing table. Having shifted these into novel positions, Elizabeth hesitantly unlocked a certain drawer, reached into the desk, and pulled out a letter which she knew would again capture her attention.

She unfolded and skimmed it, even though she knew every line in it by heart. The letter was but four pages long, but it had succeeded in informing Elizabeth Bennet more about herself than twenty years of self-observation.

The missive had been written by Fitzwilliam Darcy the night of his failed marriage proposal, for the purpose of vehemently explaining away the hefty charges she had leveled at him during their dispute. Against her utmost wishes, upon reading the letter Miss Elizabeth Bennet had been forced to admit that the man had legitimate reasons for acting as he did.

While she still regretted that he had inserted his two pence – or two pounds, rather – into his friend's love life, she could now understand and respect the reasons for his interference. Her sister Jane, all goodness and loveliness that she was, was also very serene and private; she had always publicly displayed less affection than she felt. Jane had treated Charles Bingley civilly and kindly, as she did everyone, but had never shown a single symptom of particular regard while in his company. Was it any wonder, then, that Darcy had advised Mr. Bingley to look elsewhere for a bride? Could one blame him for protecting his friend from a loveless marriage, especially one which would have come with a most aggravating mother-in-law and embarrassing sisters who loved to flirt?

But it was the other answered charge which made Elizabeth occasionally bite the inside of her cheek to punish herself for her doltishness. She had been pathetically blind! When Mr. George Wickham arrived in the nearby village of Meryton to join the militia stationed there, she had been one of the first to befriend him and to listen to his tales – nay, his slanders. Having disliked the proud Mr. Darcy since the evening they had met, Elizabeth was only too happy to hear and spread the tragic story told by the handsome new stranger in town. Who would have thought Mr. Darcy as bad as this? To deprive his own father's godson of his rightful inheritance, to withhold the living which he ought to have had! It certainly helped Mr. Wickham's cause that he had intermixed flattery with his yarns, and awoken in Elizabeth a small infatuation. Thankfully, the flirtation went nowhere. Miss Bennet recognized the imprudence of such a match, and Mr. Wickham likewise moved on to court Mary King, an unattractive young woman who had recently inherited ten thousand pounds (a conquest which ended when the maiden's uncle removed her to Liverpool, far from the mercenary officer's grasp). The lack of serious consequences, however, did little to soothe Elizabeth's conscience when she read Mr. Darcy's letter, which contained a through account of the events of Ramsgate and of George Wickham's affinity for idleness and dissipation. Elizabeth had been horrified when she realized where vanity had led her. She tormented herself for a few days, confided in Jane and no one else, and then buried the shocking missive in a locked drawer of her desk.

As Miss Bennet browsed through the handwritten pages, the bedclothes on the other side of the room slightly rustled.

Elizabeth's neck snapped up from the papers to peer at the bed. She found the invalid's arms slightly moving and her eyelashes fluttering. Throwing down the letter, Miss Bennet veritably ran across the room and bent over the girl.

"Can you hear me?" she inquired with bated breath.

With great effort, the mysterious maiden opened and focused her grey eyes upon the face before her. Elizabeth thought that she would try to speak, but after a second of this gaze, the patient's visage flooded with terror. The girl childishly tried to pull up the covers and shrink into the pillows, obviously rendered mute by fright and weakness. Miss Bennet stroked the golden head, pulled down the coverlet, and repeatedly soothed, "It is alright; I shall not hurt you," in vain.

This went on for perhaps a minute-and-a-half, after which the invalid began to show signs of fatigue. She could barely keep her eyes open, despite her panic. After quickly analyzing the benefits and risks of keeping her awake in such an alarmed state, Elizabeth sighed with disappointment and gave permission for the girl's eyelids to adhere together again.

"Never mind, dear, go back to sleep. We can speak later. Relax, and sleep."

The patient obeyed immediately. The nurse smoothened the disturbed blanket and slipped back to her customary chair. For the first time since the maiden had been laid in her bed, Elizabeth whispered a prayer of thanksgiving. Surely, this brief moment of apparent consciousness meant that at the very least, there was hope for some sort of recovery.

But the poor child! How petrified she had been! Then again, was it any wonder? To wake up, perhaps in pain, definitely in confusion, and see a stranger! Hopefully, in a matter of hours if not sooner, the maiden would awaken with a clear mind and a calmer demeanor. Until then, Elizabeth Bennet would refuse to budge from her present position. She would be there to welcome the visitor properly to Longbourn.

Chapter 6

Fitzwilliam Darcy stood at the edge of the accursed ravine, his glazed eyes staring at the swirling, churning waters below. The overcast sky above prevented sunshine from falling on the scene, and the chilly, still air mirrored the lifeless spirit of the grieving man.

Georgiana died here. This was the only thought which steadily pulsated through his mind with every heartthrob. *Georgiana died here.*

The servants had driven Darcy to the exact location where they had discovered Mrs. Annesley and the fragments of the carriage. Man of action that he was, their master immediately began to investigate, despite the fact that nature had destroyed all the evidence. The current had splintered and stolen the remaining parts of Georgiana's conveyance. Even though her brother walked about the area attentively, scouring every inch of soil for any imprints of wheels, or better yet, of a young lady's shoes, he found nothing but smooth, damp land.

Finding this employment to be completely in vain, Darcy at last commenced following the tributary downstream for several miles as it grew into a broad, seabound river. Every stride towards the untamed ocean, every fruitless searching glance made it more difficult to nurse the absurd, yet precious hope that a golden-haired maiden would surface from the waves, climb up the side of the cliff, and dash into her brother's waiting arms.

The prolonged walk brought him to the little outlying village where Georgiana's companion was convalescing. Darcy, at his wits' end, requested, and was granted, an interview with the tearful, guilt-ridden Mrs. Annesley. That lady was only able to enlighten her employer on one new point which had not already been communicated by the other servants: between heartrending sobs, she unwillingly disclosed that her charge had been fully conscious of the severity of their predicament and duly terrified as a result. As she described the scene in the carriage during those final moments, the gentleman jumped up and paced as if wild dogs were snapping at his heels. He could scarcely remain in the room until Mrs. Annesley finished. When she concluded, he somehow managed to find the words to reassure her that the present state of affairs was not her fault and took his leave.

In order to leave no stone unturned, he presented himself before the village physician and inquired if that professional had had any patients resembling Georgiana in the past few days. Receiving a negative answer, Darcy set his face against the wind, and deigned to retrace his steps. On the way back, he no longer sought a living being; instead, he longed to find anything which could serve as a memento of Georgiana's last moments. But even that was denied him.

The ill-fated stream took my sister. Could it not have had enough pity to leave a single shred of white silk from her gown or a piece of her bonnet enmeshed in its rocks, so as to give me something tangible to clasp to my heart?

Growing numb, Darcy eventually returned to the place where the carriage was believed to have left solid ground and begun its plummet into the waters. Ceasing his walk, he neared and now stood at the very edge, gazing below.

The drop was so deep! Georgiana certainly had time to realize that she was dying! What had flashed through her mind when she recognized that her life on earth was ending after a mere sixteen years? Had terror prevailed, or had she made some sort of final accounting of all her sweet, guileless actions? Had she called his name? Did the impact of the carriage hitting the rocks below kill her outright or at least induce merciful unconsciousness as to the rest? Or had she heard the carriage shattering around her, felt the waves seize her body and drag it further and further from the daylight, as her lungs filled with water and the dreadful pain of suffocation?

Shuddering, Darcy turned from the bank and the questions which he would never be able to answer, not at least until his own soul departed for that presently unreachable sphere. Slowly, he focused his eyes on the carriage and the servants which were stationed about an eighth of a mile away, and began to make his way towards them.

Tom, James and Andrew watched the defeated gentleman advance in silence. They had not spoken one word, even to each other, since they arrived. Each was searching his heart and mind, pondering if they could have done anything differently during the storm to prevent the calamity, or whether they could do anything at present to soothe the master during this poignant epoch in his life. They could think of nothing.

Fitzwilliam Darcy reached them, put his hand against the carriage, and leaned on its painted, sturdy frame for support. All sense of purpose suddenly and thoroughly left him. He remained in that attitude for several minutes, staring at the damp ground, perfectly oblivious to all around him. He might have stood so for an eternity had not Tom, in a valiant effort to recall him to the world, inquired,

"Where to, sir?"

Darcy looked up at the coachman and dully considered the question. *Where to?* Where on earth had he to go? He had no sister. He had no wife, nor any hope of one. He had nobody to go to, no darling to return to. In truth, there was but one place he wished to be: in Hertfordshire, in Elizabeth Bennet's arms. It was her form he wished to clasp to his heart as he mourned Georgiana, her tresses which he wanted to rain with tears of grief. Hers was the only voice he could have borne to hear murmuring consolations at such a time. His greatest comfort would have been to look into Elizabeth's loving eyes and comprehend that even without his beloved sister, a future of joy, laughter, and family still existed. But the outcome of their last meetings at Hunsford had rendered such a route wholly unfeasible. And so, the coachman's question was, for Darcy, unanswerable.

For the first time in his long career, Tom found it necessary to give suggestions.

"Back to Town, Mr. Darcy? Or perhaps to Pemberley? Or to one of your relatives' residences?"

His master considered the offers. London was by far the closest choice, but it was swarming with eligible young women who would surely descend on his townhouse the moment Miss Darcy's fate was rumored, and fill it with insincere wails of 'O, Georgiana, the best friend I ever had', and 'Poor Mr. Darcy, thank goodness I happened to be in Town, so that I may comfort him!'. Some of his relations might possess quieter houses and genuine sympathy, but he found that he could not bear the thought of even their company. Therefore, only the option of Pemberley remained. He could retire there, away from the world, closeted only with his affliction and loyal servants who would leave him alone if he but gave the word.

Thus, he muttered,

"Pemberley," before dragging himself up the step and into the solitary interior of the coach.

Chapter 7

The next morning, bright sunlight streamed into Elizabeth's bedchamber for the first time in two days. The cloudless dawn found the room's proprietress still keeping her vigil. Jane and Mrs. Hill had come in several times during the night, begging her to lie down awhile and doze, but their kind suggestions went unheeded. Eagerness to witness a longer period of consciousness and hope that this wished-for event would soon occur kept the faithful nurse awake.

About nine o'clock, Elizabeth watched as the warm, bright illumination lazily crept along the floor. It took about half-an-hour, but the sunlight completed its customary path across the polished wooden planks and began to climb up the side of the bed. Fifteen minutes later, it gently caressed the fair face of the slumbering maiden.

Its mellow touch produced the long-desired effect. The patient's eyelashes fluttered and parted to reveal the grey, introspective pupils once again.

Unlike the previous evening, Elizabeth restrained her instinct to rush at the bed and monopolize the young lady's attention. Instead, believing that a moment of privacy might forward the patient's adjustment to her new surroundings, she sat perfectly still and silent, watching as the girl moved her head about the pillow and looked around the room. Only when the pretty eyes noticed and rested upon herself did Elizabeth quietly draw the chair nearer to the bed and say cheerfully,

"Well, now, someone appears to be much better this morning!"

It was a bit dimmer than the day before, but the same frightened and confused expression sprang into the grey eyes. Hoping to dissipate it, Miss Bennet leaned forward and added,

"I must admit that having a bit of color in your cheeks suits you remarkably well, my dear! Why, I declare that your handsomeness rivals that of my sister Jane! Quite a remarkable feat, for she is known as a famous local beauty hereabouts, with her flawless figure and Grecian profile."

"I…I…that is…I thank you," the girl stuttered. She haltingly brought her hand up to her face and touched it curiously, as if she were feeling the soft skin for the first time.

Elizabeth smiled encouragingly at the verbal communication and continued bantering blithely.

"You gave us quite a fright, madam. You have not been overly eager to acknowledge the world for the past few days. How do you feel now?"

There was a long pause before Elizabeth was favored with a reply.

"I am…well, thank you."

"Are you certain?" was the doubtful response.

"Yes…pray do not trouble yourself…"

Miss Bennet graciously shook her head, and comforted the reluctant girl with a pat on the shoulder. She began to wonder whether the hesitant rejoinders were born of a timid nature rather than of weakness and confusion.

"'Tis no trouble. We shall be much more distressed if we suspect that you are concealing an ailment than if you disclose it and allow us to be of assistance to you." A pause was inserted here, but when it failed to bring about an admission, Elizabeth directly stated, "You have a very large bump on the back of your head, which suggests that you hit it against something. Have you no headache?"

"It…just a little one."

The nurse doubted this assessment, but let the matter be. She offered food and water to the invalid, but both were politely declined. Silence penetrated the room. During it, the patient moved her injured head feebly on the pillow; her gaze, however, roamed the room much more vigorously. At length, the healthy girl deigned to remark,

"In case you were wondering where we are, this is Longbourn, my father's estate in Hertfordshire."

The weak maiden nodded in understanding, and for several awkward minutes, the conversation again ceased. Not wishing to exhaust the patient, Elizabeth leaned back in the chair and observed as the girl nervously clasped her hands on top of the coverlets and absentmindedly stroked the dark blue ring on her right hand. As she watched, a strange feeling of uneasiness seized Elizabeth, but she quickly attributed it to the stress which all of Longbourn had been under.

Soon afterwards, the damsel began to send anxious glances at Miss Bennet, and unclosed her lips several times, as if she wished to communicate something. Three entire minutes by the clock passed in this manner before she finally managed to whisper,

"How did I come to be here?"

Elizabeth raised an eyebrow archly.

"We were rather hoping that you would be able to help us answer that question. All I know is that, two days ago, my father found you ten miles from here, lying in a field during a dreadful storm." Cocking her head, she confided, "As you can imagine, the entire family and the servants have been *most* curious about how that could have come about. We should dearly love to be enlightened!"

The girl stared at the nursemaid, and shook her head.

"I am afraid that…I cannot…enlighten you," she murmured, alarmed.

"You mean that you cannot recall anything about the field, or how you happened to be there?"

"That is correct," the frightened patient whispered, in a manner reminiscent of an innocent child who has wrongfully been asked to confess their part in mischief, and fears punishment as the result of an honest refusal. Elizabeth noticed the trembling lips, and sought to reassure their proprietress by lavishing a tender touch upon her hands.

"There, now, I suspected that such might be the case when you awoke. We often do not remember events which are extremely distressing; it is as if our mind wishes to spare us the agony of reminiscing. But pray tell me: what is the last thing you can remember?"

The young woman blinked several times, glanced at the window, the bookcase, and her companion by turns, and made no response. Her breaths were drawn in more and more rapidly, as if she were greatly agitated, and her fingers pulled restlessly at the bedclothes. Taken aback by these strange affectations, Elizabeth determined to put an end to them at once, lest they endanger the patient in her fragile state. Hence, Miss Bennet leapt out of the chair and gently seated herself on the edge of the bed.

"How thoughtless of me!" she exclaimed. "Here I am asking you all these probing questions, and we have not even been properly introduced! Allow me to repair this horrendous breach of etiquette forthwith! My name is Elizabeth Bennet, but my friends and family call me Lizzy. You may follow their example, if you wish. And what is your name?"

Instead of pacifying the visitor, this commonplace inquiry only intensified the panic in her eyes, and she remained silent.

"What is your name?" the interlocutress repeated after an uncomfortable pause. Again, there was no answer.

Drawing back, the healthy maiden inspected the ailing one's countenance, trying to account for the girl's unanticipated reticence. Eventually, following the only probable explanation which came into her head, Elizabeth took one of the invalid's hands in her own and leaned down towards the poor damsel.

"My dear," she began, pouring sincerity into every syllable, "you need not have any misgivings about confiding in me. If you were running from someone, or someplace, and have a legitimate reason to fear discovery, I will do everything in my power to guard your secret and keep you safe. But I cannot be of assistance unless you tell me who you are and what the matter is."

Despite its kindness, this speech did not produce the desired effect. With a sigh, Miss Bennet straightened up and gathered her patience. While she was perfectly sensible to the shock which Longbourn's guest had recently experienced, having woken up in an unfamiliar house among strangers, Elizabeth was also cognizant of the difficulties which could arise if the same personage refused to divulge her secrets. Reputation was a fragile treasure, and housing a lady with a hidden past could shatter it for the Bennets beyond repair. Hoping that more lighthearted questions would loosen the visitor's tongue, Elizabeth pleaded playfully,

"Will you at least tell me what your age is? We have nearly begun placing wagers on whether you are fifteen or sixteen." The maiden shifted uncomfortably, but said nothing. "Come, my dear, such a morsel of knowledge can scarcely be used to trace you, and has already been estimated, anyhow!"

The appeal fell as if on deaf ears.

"Well, I suppose one cannot fault you for being a bit taciturn, considering what you have endured in recent days. But, if you cannot bring yourself to trust me, is there anyone else whom you can and will turn to? Have you any family or friends whom you should like to inform of your whereabouts?"

This question was, once more, answered with silence. But it was in this particular stillness that Elizabeth happened to notice something extremely peculiar about the expression in the maiden's eyes.

They were not the eyes of a woman who was warily deciding what she should or should not communicate to a new acquaintance.

Instead, they were the pupils of a lost child, who, when questioned by kindly people, is too young to be capable of giving their parents' names and address. Miss Bennet bit her lip as a most troubling idea invaded her thoughts. Wishing to investigate it further, she reached out and arrested the girl's hands in her own, so that they could not grant her succor in answering the following question.

"What is the color of your hair, milady?" she asked, glancing at the locks which were pulled back into a braid, the end of which had been imprisoned under the damsel's back for the duration of her awakening, making it impossible for their owner to glimpse them. "You might as well tell me, for I can see it plainly."

The girl swallowed, desperate to gratify the interviewer after so long and distressing a series of unanswerable questions. Taking inspiration from Elizabeth's own dark chestnut locks, she guessed,

"Brown?"

Elizabeth exhaled tersely, now certain of the dreadful truth. Releasing the young lady's hands and reaching behind her, she brought the braid in front of its proprietress's eyes.

"Gold," Miss Bennet corrected.

As expected, the maiden stared at the tresses as if they were completely foreign to her. Hesitantly, she reached for and took the plait, gave it a sharp tug, and winced, surprised, when the action caused her pain.

Elizabeth, seeing this, took up a small mirror from the bedside table next to them and offered it to the young woman. The golden-haired damsel clasped its handle weakly, and stared into the glass as if looking upon a fascinating picture which she had never seen before.

Chapter 8

The throng was great. Mr. and Mrs. Bennet, their five daughters, and even a few of the servants had crowded into Elizabeth's bedchamber, eager to observe the examination. The patient was propped up on pillows, a shawl over her shoulders. In the chair which Elizabeth had occupied not two hours before sat Mr. Jones, Meryton's bespectacled, middle-aged apothecary.

"You have a ring on your right hand. How did you procure it?" he asked gently.

The girl glanced down at the mentioned ornament, and shook her head for what seemed to be the hundredth time.

"You do not remember?"

"No."

At that, Mr. Jones looked about, and espied a book resting on the nightstand.

"Miss Bennet," he asked, glancing in Elizabeth's direction, "would you mind if we availed ourselves of your reading material?"

"Not at all," the addressed lady said. The apothecary reached for the tome, opened it, and held it about two feet in front of the patient.

"Miss, are you able to see these words clearly?"

"Yes, sir," she meekly replied.

"Good. Can you read this section?"

The shy maiden leaned forward ever so slightly, and commenced:

"'Late have I loved You, O Beauty ever ancient, ever new, late have I loved You! You were within me, but I was outside, and it was there that I searched for You. In my unloveliness I plunged into the lovely things which You created. You were with me, but I was not with You. Created things kept me from You; yet if they had not been in You they would not have been at all. You called, You shouted, and You broke through my deafness. You flashed, You shone, and You dispelled my blindness. You breathed Your fragrance on me; I drew in breath and now I pant for You. I have tasted You, now I hunger and thirst for more. You touched me, and I burned for Your peace.'" Even the difficult words of the passage slipped deftly through the girl's lips, and she spoke them with reverence and feeling, clearly comprehending what she was reading. It was apparent that the thieving accident had not stolen her literacy.

"Very well, madam." Having said this, Mr. Jones closed the volume and put it back in its place. Turning to the observers, he concluded, "That is all. You may step outside; I shall be just a moment."

Mr. Bennet, ever invested in appearing nonchalant, was the first to leave his post and wander out the door. Elizabeth, after seeing that Jane had gone to assist the apothecary in administering a headache-alleviating draught, followed him. The youngest three Bennet sisters departed last, shadowed by their very displeased mother.

"Well, Lizzy?" the master of the house said, leaning against the corridor's wall, in a carefree tone which belied his creased brow. "I am glad that I shall not be paying Mr. Jones's fee completely in vain, no matter how capable he is of formulating a diagnosis for our little friend in there. At the very least, his visit has enlightened me as to the whereabouts of my copy of *The Confessions of St. Augustine.* I noticed it to be misplaced last week, and after a great deal of searching, had almost despaired of ever seeing the book again."

"After having me in residence for twenty years, sir, I should think that you would know that nearly every volume which deserts your library refuges in my realm," Elizabeth rebutted. But the smile which accompanied the witty remark did not reach her eyes.

Her father was prevented from formulating a response by Jane's exit from the bedchamber. The apothecary was at her heels. Mr. Jones softly drew the door closed, straightened his shoulders, and sighed. The family glanced at one another, and even Mr. Bennet unconsciously ceased supporting himself against the plaster.

"She is amnesic."

Worry overshadowed the countenances of Longbourn's master and of his second eldest daughter, while pure confusion covered the faces of the other ladies in attendance.

"Do you mean to tell me," Mr. Bennet began, "that the condition actually exists outside the pages of nonsensical novels?"

"Alas, yes, sir. I am not surprised at your incredulity, for it is very rare. But I have heard of other such cases. And I am convinced that the girl in the room behind me is suffering from the ailment."

"What are you talking of, Mr. Jones?" Mrs. Bennet cried out. "What did you say she has? Amasia? Enesia? Is it infectious? Can it

37

be fatal? And all my daughters exposed to the contagion just now! Oh my girls! To think I shall soon be standing over your graves…"

"Mama, please, calm yourself," Elizabeth cut in as gently as she could. "Amnesia is just a physician's term for loss of memory. Mr. Jones means to tell us that the young lady cannot remember her past due to the trauma to her head."

Mrs. Bennet stared at the elucidator for a few seconds before exclaiming,

"*Cannot remember?* Poppycock! The vagrant does not *want* to remember! This way she can live on your father's generosity all her days!"

Mr. Jones took over the debate.

"Madam, I can assure you that it is a legitimate disability. The injury has rendered my patient incapable of recollecting. Desire has nothing to do with it."

The expert opinion of the apothecary forced Mrs. Bennet to hesitate before she devised her next remark, but she fabricated it without a prolonged delay.

"She reads well enough. Somehow she has not forgotten her schooling!" the lady scoffed triumphantly.

"It is true that her proficiency appears to be unimpaired. Amnesia, however, is known to be capricious in such ways. It can obliterate certain portions of one's mind, and leave others completely intact. A colleague of mine in the south saw a case several years ago where a Cambridge-educated man was thrown off his horse. He lost consciousness for several minutes, but upon awakening seemed to be as healthy and hearty as ever…until he returned home and began looking over the accounts. It was then that my friend's patient realized that he was unable to perform simple calculations. He had to relearn arithmetic over the course of several months. Similarly, your guest has lost her knowledge of her previous circumstances, but her skills and accomplishments are untouched. We do not know why similar accidents are able to produce such a vast range of outcomes, but it may have to do with the manner in which the head is struck."

This extended explanation succeeded in silencing, if not satisfying, the Mistress of Longbourn. She voiced no further skepticism, but pursed her lips and employed herself with wringing the handkerchief she held. Mr. Bennet, after glancing at his wife to reassure himself that he would be able to speak without interruption, asked,

"What can we do to hasten the recovery?"

"Unfortunately, in her case we can only wait. Unlike arithmetic, one cannot teach a person their own memories."

"I mean no disrespect, Mr. Jones, but is there no specialist in London or elsewhere who could give more insight on the topic?"

The apothecary gravely shook his head.

"The truth is, no one thoroughly understands the mind or its injuries. Any physician who tells you otherwise is a liar. I will take no umbrage if you summon someone else, for it is only natural that you want the best for your visitor; I forewarn you, however, not to expect any further progress in the girl's condition as a result."

Mr. Bennet nodded, slightly defeated, and said no more.

"How long will it be before she remembers?" Jane asked softly.

Every inch of the apothecary's countenance was suddenly covered with sobriety.

"I cannot say," he said slowly. "The amnesia might resolve itself in days, weeks, or months. The process may be gradual, where she will remember a random memory every few days. Then again, it may be sudden, and the recollections of her entire life might unexpectedly burst upon her. Generally, if there are no signs of improvement within the first week, it is probable that the recovery will be a very drawn out one. But, I must warn you, it is possible that she might never remember anything. To her dying breath, she will think of yesterday as the first day of her life. The Good Lord will inform her of the other details afterwards, I am sure."

He paused, looking at each family member in turn. Seeing that no one was equal to commenting on his last piece of information, Mr. Jones cleared his throat and much more confidently, instructed them,

"Keep the young lady warm, quiet and comfortable. Give her something light to eat. If the headache does not wane completely during the next two days, send for me. And most importantly, do not agitate her. I was forced to inquire about her memory in order to formulate my diagnosis, but you saw for yourselves that it was not a pleasant experience and it should not be repeated. She should not be pressed to remember," the apothecary's eye trained itself on Mrs. Bennet for the slightest instant, "or teased about her condition." Lydia and Kitty were glanced at as he uttered the last. "Such actions will only cause unnecessary distress and impede improvement."

"Mr. Jones," Elizabeth thoughtfully interjected, "we have spread word around Meryton that Longbourn harbors an injured young woman. Suppose that her family or friends were to come seeking her. Under the circumstances, should we allow them an audience?"

"By all means, let them see and identify her, if possible. But never, *never* present them to her as people from her past whom she should remember. Introduce them as if they were any new acquaintance. If their company rouses her mind so much the better; if not, she will be spared the agony of vainly trying to recall memories of them, as well as the consequent awkwardness and embarrassment of her inability to do so."

Having finished saying all that he had set out to communicate, the apothecary bowed and began to take his leave. Mr. Bennet made an unprecedented offer to see him to the door. Although clearly surprised, Mr. Jones accepted and descended the stairs with the Master of Longbourn. The ladies were left with the doleful moaning of their matriarch.

"Oh, that father of yours, girls, girls! Because of that silly entail we have not a shilling to call our own, and other troubles enough, but does he care a whit? No, he brings home another mouth to feed! If only he cared for my nerves the way he cares for vagabonds!"

Elizabeth shifted her weight from one foot to another impatiently. Did the woman she called mother have no heart or sense at all? If someone unfamiliar with their situation were to hear her protestations they would conclude that the Bennets lived in a dirt-floor hut and knew not when their next meal would come from, instead of presuming them to be the landholding family that they were. Of course, an income of two thousand pounds a year placed them nowhere near the top tier of society, but it certainly assured a comfortable lifestyle, as long as their father lived. Upon his death, matters would be slightly complicated unless one of them made a good marriage in the meantime; the entail would take Longbourn out of the hands of his widow and daughters and bestow it upon Mr. Collins, their distant cousin. But still! She and her sisters were educated, respectable young women, and starvation would be kept at bay. Servitude as housekeepers or governesses would be rather unpleasant, considering the sort of life to which they were accustomed, but it could scarcely be more horrid than listening to Mrs. Bennet anticipate it for years in advance.

Where is Papa? she sighed drearily to herself as her mother droned on. He was taking an inordinate amount of time to bid farewell to the apothecary, and she longed for his reentrance, which would probably be the only effective means of turning the conversation into a more agreeable channel. She only hoped that he would not go directly to the library after closing Longbourn's front door and leave them to fend with Mrs. Bennet themselves.

Thankfully, their introverted father did them the favor of reappearing at length. He looked around at the circle of women gruffly, and asked,

"What are you standing around here for? You heard what the man recommended; go to it. Or do you suppose that a light dinner will order itself and walk into the sickroom?"

The Mistress of Longbourn took a step towards him and said in a gentler and wily tone,

"My dear, when are you going to make arrangements to send the girl off?"

"What girl?" the gentleman replied promptly, irritation already apparent in his voice. Elizabeth, who knew him best, noticed that his countenance was wearing an expression which was different than its two favorite robes of cheerfulness and detachment. The elderly man looked disgusted, angry and indignant. Being all too familiar with her parents' disputes, she knew that Mrs. Bennet could but rarely rouse her husband to such affectivity, and thus she suspected that his prolonged leave-taking of the apothecary had something to do with his state of mind.

"O, Mr. Bennet, how can you be so tiresome? You know that the peddler in Lizzy's room must be gotten rid of one way or another, for we cannot keep her here. The sooner this business is concluded, the better, I say!"

The brow above the master's spectacles clouded over and wrinkled.

"And why, exactly, can she not remain here?" he asked in a tone of exaggerated doltishness.

Mrs. Bennet's mouth dropped slightly ajar; she had, reasonably, thought that her prolonged wailing had made her position clear enough. But rather eager to refresh her spouse's memory, she began,

41

"My dear! She could be part of a band of robbers, and one night she will give them a signal, and we will all be murdered in our beds! Or, she could be a lunatic, escaped from Bedlam. After all, what sort of person cannot remember their own name - the moment she touches a candle Longbourn will be burnt down into smoldering ashes. We - ,"

"Madam, that will do!" the gentleman thundered, in a voice which none had heard him use since the day that a five-year-old Lydia had snuck into his library and paged through one of his favorite volumes with fingers that had been occupied with mud pies directly beforehand. "A lunatic, you suggest? Well, Mrs. Bennet, I highly doubt that any person from Bedlam would have the self-possession to remain as collected and composed as that young woman, especially under such trying circumstances. Indeed, I suspect that if any of you, with the possible exception of Lizzy or Jane, woke up in a strange household without memory, there would be enough shrieking to break a few ears and turn more than one head grey. Since we have not had anything even akin to that from our little invalid, I am forced to conclude that she has more sense than the four of you put together, and I always felt that we could use more reason hereabouts. Save your breath to cool your porridge, my dear, for I have decided: the girl stays." He turned and was about to descend the stairs when he looked back and caught the distressed damsel's stunned expression. A familiar smile slowly commandeered his lips, and he continued gaily, "Is that truly so dreadful? I admit that we Bennets are an odd lot: a matron who is continually affected by nerves, a patriarch who exists for the sake of his books, an eldest daughter who sees no fault in the inhabitants of Newgate, another daughter who studies Socrates for pleasure, followed by two girls who swoon at the mere sight of officers. And then there is Lizzy, who takes delight in anything ridiculous. Longbourn scarcely is the ideal home for a sensible young woman, but since fate was so unkind as to put her in my path rather than in Sir William Lucas's, we will have to do the best we can until she recovers!" He began proceeding down the stairs, commanding with his parting breath: "Feed her."

Kitty and Lydia, unwilling to see or hear the rest, scurried away to their room as quickly as their feet could carry them. Mary, foreseeing that Jane's hands would be full of a hysterical matron in a matter of seconds, rose to the occasion and offered to inform Mrs. Hill that a meal suitable for an invalid was wanted. Elizabeth, for her

42

part, hurried back to her own bedchamber, delighted by the outcome of her father's intervention and enthusiastic about making the mysterious maiden's closer acquaintance.

Chapter 9

Elizabeth reentered the room to find a most pitiable sight. The invalid sat up in bed, contorting the coverlets between her hands. The grey eyes were wide with terror, and the slender form was trembling violently.

"My dear!" the older girl cried out, hastening to her side. "Are you cold? Shall I fetch another blanket to put around your shoulders?"

"N-No…," the frightened damsel stammered, casting a glance down upon the coverlets. "No, I am not cold."

"Then what is the matter?" Elizabeth inquired, seating herself in her usual bedside chair and taking the delicate hand in her own.

"I…it…I…," the agitated girl took a deep breath, and with a courage born of desperation, suddenly lifted her eyes to Elizabeth's and whispered, "Am I mad? Is that what Mr. Jones said? Shall I be sent to Bedlam?"

These questions would have been amusing had they not been uttered with terrified earnestness.

"No, he said nothing of the sort!" Elizabeth hurriedly soothed, pressing the thin hand reassuringly. "You are perfectly lucid, dearest. Your only serious ailment is the injury to your head, which according to Mr. Jones, has caused you to forget certain things. But he holds out hope that you will recall them, perhaps as early as this week. In the meantime, you are not to worry about anything except getting enough rest!"

"You speak in earnest? You are not trying to pacify me…humor me?"

"I give you my solemn word that I conceal nothing."

Relief swept into the girl's face, and with it, her customary shyness.

"Thank you…I am so sorry…I should not have demanded an answer…in such a manner…it is not my place to…"

Miss Bennet gently reached out and touched the poor child's lips, silencing the unwarranted apology.

"Hush, now, enough of that," she kindly ordered. "It *is* your right to know your own condition. Never hesitate to ask about your own affairs. I cannot imagine how frightening all this must be for you. Pray believe me; you are far more composed than I would be under such circumstances."

The mysterious lady shook her head at the last remark, as she wholeheartedly doubted it, but found the former ones encouraging enough to dare to reiterate,

"I may remember?"

"Yes."

"And…if I do not?" she whispered as her eyes filled with tears. Abandoned by particular memories, yet haunted by her tarrying knowledge of propriety and normalcy, she knew that it would be terrible to never have a name, or a home. What would people call her? What place in society could she possibly fill?

Elizabeth rose from the chair, advanced one step, and seated herself upon the edge of the bed. Twining her arm around the guest's shoulders, she smiled and replied,

"It has already been settled that you shall remain here indefinitely."

Rather than relieving the maiden, this piece of information only seemed to make her even more uncomfortable.

"That is too generous. I would be too great a burden…"

"Indeed!" Elizabeth cut in, laughing. "In what way shall you be a nuisance, pray? Are you planning to sing *fortississimo* at three o' clock in the morning? Or will you develop a habit of contradicting everything my mother says?"

"No, of course not," the girl murmured, alarmed.

"I did not think so," Miss Bennet smiled. "Therefore, you shall just be another young lady at Longbourn, and much less trouble than the last two that took up residence here, I daresay!"

The maiden shook her golden head.

"Thank you…for your kindness…but it is out of the question."

As exasperated as one could be with so gentle and unassuming a soul, the nurse feigned resignation and matter-of-factly asked,

"Since you will not hear of staying here, my dear, may I ask what you are planning to do, or where you are planning to go, if we turn you out-of-doors as soon as you are able to get up?"

"I…," the girl's voice faded away, and she fell silent, perfectly aware that she had no reasonable rejoinder to Miss Bennet's inquiry. Unsympathetic, Elizabeth firmly informed her:

"Until you *are* able to answer that question sensibly, we will keep you here, whether it be your will or no. My father is not in the habit of saving young ladies from the elements only to turn them loose to perish from hunger." Seeing that the young lady had finished her protestations, and had assumed a worried look in response to her attendant's uncompromising tone, Elizabeth smiled and became playful once again. "And now that that small matter of business has been settled, we must start tallying everything which must be done in order to properly introduce you into Hertfordshire society. First of all, we must come to a consensus on what name you should take until your own comes to light. While *I* have no qualms about forever addressing you as 'my dear', I believe that it would be rather unseemly for the servants and the young men hereabouts to speak to you thus!"

The blush which rose to the girl's cheeks was very faint, and the smile she suddenly bestowed very wane and brief, but they were there, and were enough to give a glimpse of her good-natured character. Elizabeth privately reflected that when their guest got over her love of speaking in monosyllables and stutters, she would almost definitely make a cheerful, lively friend. For now, however, Miss Bennet contented herself with asking,

"Do you have any particular preferences in regards to a name?"

Again, the sunny-colored curls moved back and forth.

"Then suppose I offer suggestions, and you tell me whether you like the name or no. Would that be a satisfactory arrangement?"

The invalid replied in the positive very eagerly.

"Well, then, I personally like the name 'Elizabeth', but I fear that having two people of the same name living in Longbourn might cause a bit of confusion!" The tiny smile briefly reappeared. "In the same vein, we had better avoid the names 'Jane', 'Mary', 'Catherine' and 'Lydia', as well as 'Fanny', for that is my mother's name." Miss Bennet cocked her head to one side and gazed intently at the face before her. "Then we must assure that the title suits you. Hmmm…I would say that you look like a 'Rosemary', but I am afraid that there are already two or three girls by that name in the nearby village of Meryton. By the way, do you like names derived from flowers, such as 'Heather' or 'Violet'?"

"Yes," was the frank answer.

Mischief crept into Elizabeth's head. Suppressing the mirthful mien which threatened to imprint itself upon her features, she leaned towards her companion and declared,

"In that case, I believe that I have the perfect alias." She paused for dramatic touch, then queried: "What do you think of the name Miss Honeysuckle Bluebell Nottingham?"

Rather than bolstering the shy smile which Elizabeth had meant to encourage by the ridiculous suggestion, repressed horror flooded the girl's face. Plainly, Miss Bennet realized anew, the child was unaccustomed to deciphering masked jests. But she also proved herself an easily swayed personage, since her next words completely belied the feeling in her eyes.

"If…if you think the name best, I shall be glad to take it," she said, even as she repressed tears at the thought of being called something as ludicrous as 'Honeysuckle' forevermore.

Instantly penitent for having caused such distress, Elizabeth gathered the poor soul into a compassionate embrace, exclaiming,

"No, I do not think it the best; far from it! In fact, I doubt that anyone with a speck of taste could find that appellation appealing! I was only teasing you. Pray forgive me."

As best as it could while encased in Elizabeth's arms, the girl's head shook.

"Please…you…need not...apologize. It was my fault…I was so silly to think you in earnest!"

"And I was unspeakably cruel to make you think I was serious." Miss Bennet's hand made a few comforting circular motions upon the maiden's back. "Now, then, returning to my saner suggestions, would you like to be called Heather or Violet?"

"I…."

"Speak freely," Elizabeth urged.

"I like both, but…somehow…cannot imagine responding to either."

"Very well, then. What about Louisa or Sara?"

The invalid considered, and softly rejected both.

"Anne?"

The grey eyes widened, and a small smile crept over the timid face.

"I…I do believe that I…would like 'Anne' very much."

Elizabeth clapped her hands.

"It is settled then; Anne it shall be! All we need now is a surname." For a fleeting instant, she considered endowing the sweet child with the name of 'Bennet', but abandoned the idea when she considered her mother's future reaction to the title. "Any preferences there?" When she received confirmation that there were none, they went through a list of patronymics. Neither lady liked 'Anne Cooper', 'Anne Anderson' was far too droll, and 'Anne Morris' sounded too flat to them. They almost despaired of finding a suitable surname when Elizabeth exclaimed,

"What of 'Anne Edwards'?"

"Anne…Edwards," the patient murmured. "That is pretty!"

"Truly?"

"Yes."

Miss Bennet repeated the name, and the decision was final.

Chapter 10

The tray which the Master of Longbourn had ordered soon arrived. After a half-hour of eating and quiet conversation, Miss Anne Edwards, as she had been renamed, obediently heeded her new friend's suggestion to lie back and try to sleep. She quickly succeeded in this undertaking, and Elizabeth was left to listen to the even sounds of her breathing as she perused the volume which had been 'misplaced' from her father's library. This time, however, her vigil was cut short. Only a few minutes after Anne had drifted off, the door opened and Mary walked in, carrying a stack of philosophical texts.

"If you are tired, Lizzy, I will gladly take over your watch, and share with you the duty of looking after our less fortunate neighbor."

"Thank you, Mary. I was hoping for a respite, but expected that it would be Jane who would relieve me."

"She has given mother the draught of laudanum which the latter called for, and is with our father in his library," the younger sister replied softly, seating herself in a comfortable chair and setting down her burdens on a nearby table.

"Then I will go and join them, if you are wholly certain that you will manage without me," Elizabeth said, rising and casting an anxious glance at the slumbering patient. She had never witnessed Mary volunteering in a sickroom before, and doubted that any of her sister's extensive reading had covered the arts of administering food to a weakened individual or catching slight signs of distress.

Ironically, while pondering thus, she missed a rather strong sign of indignation and hurt upon her own sister's face, as well as the slight staccato in Mary's answer:

"Yes, I can."

Still uncertain, but feeling that it would be extremely beneficial for her to take a turn around the house and spend a few minutes in a room where there was no need to drop one's voice to a soft whisper, Elizabeth yielded. Instructing Mary to call for help at the first sign of crisis, she left the sickroom and bounded down to the library.

As reported, Mr. Bennet and his eldest were closeted together; the gentleman seated at his desk, the gentlewoman standing leisurely in front of it.

"Is there any news?" Jane inquired anxiously.

Elizabeth closed the library door and leaned against it.

"Yes and no," she replied. "There has been no change, but we decided that until there is, the title 'Miss Anne Edwards' will suit her admirably."

"Humph!" Mr. Bennet grunted by way of approbation. "Thank you for getting to it before Lydia and Kitty saddled her with some ludicrous moniker which half the neighborhood would find difficult to pronounce."

"We did debate giving her a fancier name, but in the end decided to be sensible," Elizabeth admitted with a sly smile.

Her father returned the smirk. His superior knowledge of his favorite child allowed him to accurately imagine the scene which had just occurred upstairs.

"I take it that she was none too pleased with your suggestions, Lizzy?" he asked laughingly.

"Not at all!" Elizabeth exclaimed, shaking her head dramatically. "She seems so sweet a girl, but I am afraid that her sense of humor leaves something to be desired. Never fear - I shall teach her to laugh yet!"

"Lizzy!" Jane murmured reprovingly. "It is unjust to designate our visitor humorless simply because she refused to share in your jokes. Think of what she has gone through, and whether you could be lighthearted in her place."

Far from being repentant, her sister gaily rebutted,

"Depend upon it, if I could forget that my mother has some of the most fragile nerves in England and that two of my sisters have a talent for making themselves ridiculous wherever they go, I would be sprightlier than I am now, weighed down by all these cares."

"Elizabeth!"

"Alright, alright, dear Jane," was the younger girl's capitulation. In reparation, she drew nearer the gentle maiden, took the fair hand in her own and stroked it consolingly. "I solemnly acknowledge that if I were presently lying in a bed, bereft of you and all my memories, I would be very cast down. Forgive me, but after spending so much time in a sickroom and worrying about our guest – *Anne* – I naturally tried to find some relief in banter."

She was, of course, handsomely forgiven. Having now turned Lizzy's mind in a more serious direction, the eldest Miss Bennet took the opportunity to inquire into Mr. Bennet's opinions about a certain matter.

"Who do you suppose she could be, Papa?"

"Why do you ask me?" the Master of Longbourn retorted. "Do you suppose me to be a mystic who is capable of looking into the past and ascertaining the child's name and connections?"

Far too accustomed to her father's manner to be nonplussed by it, and far too respectful to reprimand this glibness as she had Elizabeth's, Jane calmly rejoined,

"Not at all, sir. But I am sure that you must have formed some theory about her origins by now, and since I am having trouble doing the same, I should certainly like to hear your thoughts on the subject."

"And who gave you leave to appoint *me* as the mastermind of conjuncture? Ask Lizzy. She has more wit than the rest of you silly girls, and has assuredly pieced together a brilliant hypothesis. Is it not so, Lizzy?" he demanded, turning to his favorite daughter.

The dark-haired maiden shrugged.

"Considering her literacy and the hand ornament she wears, it is indisputable that she or her close associates must have had some education and a little bit of pocket money sometime or other. To speculate much beyond that would be irresponsible. She could be a shopkeeper's daughter, an orphan, any number of things. Hopefully some friends or relations will come seeking her soon and offer more information."

Mr. Bennet put down his glasses on the desk deliberately, leaned back in his chair, and shocked his daughters by flatly declaring,

"I would not depend upon it."

Both sets of beautiful eyes in front of him instantly widened in horror. Despite the assurances which Elizabeth had conveyed to their visitor, they had been convinced that they would soon prove to be unnecessary. After all, who would not miss and seek so sweet and innocent a girl? It was Jane who cried out,

"Why, Papa? It is true that it has been two days, but tracing a person takes time! Especially when they have been transported several miles from their last known location!"

"I will tell you why, Janet," Mr. Bennet replied harshly. "It just so happens, that when I escorted Mr. Jones to the door this morning, he quietly informed me that his examination had revealed the girl's shoulder to be badly bruised."

His daughters glanced at each other and then jointly gazed at him, uncomprehending.

"We noticed the same when we clothed her in the nightdress," Elizabeth replied matter-of-factly, "but we paid the injury little attention after discovering the one on her head."

"Medically speaking, it is of small consequence. Curiously, however, the apothecary informed me that the nature of the bruise suggests that she was thrown with great force against something, and that in his professional opinion, it is impossible for her to have fallen upon the road in such a way as to have injured her head and the shoulder simultaneously. He is of the opinion that she sustained the trauma to her shoulder before she struck her head against the rock and lost consciousness. I am at a loss to explain how she could have possibly hurt it herself walking in that meadow. Except for that one square foot where a boulder peered out from the earth, the field was covered with the softest grass for miles around."

Jane regarded her father warily.

"What, exactly, are you suggesting, sir?" she murmured.

"I believe," Elizabeth said slowly, "that he means to imply that someone might have dealt rather roughly with Anne in the hours before she lost her memory."

Jane's neck rapidly flicked her head in Elizabeth's direction, and then turned it back to face her father. Instead of allaying her dismay, Mr. Bennet increased the feeling by remarking,

"Precisely."

"No, Papa! Forgive me, but you must be mistaken! Who would wish to harm so young and gentle a creature?"

Sighing, the Master of Longbourn rose from his chair and stretched his limbs before replying somewhat flippantly,

"Not all young ladies are as fortunate as you two, to possess a father or guardian whose chief faults consist of indolence, great fondness for privacy, and an overzealousness for satire." Disregarding Jane's vehemently shaking head, he continued, "There are unscrupulous men and women who will mistreat their charges, my dears. And when the charges are lost, they celebrate the loss of their burdens rather than hastening to find and take them up anew. Considering Anne's inexplicable injuries, she might have been subject to such a past, and advertising her present whereabouts any more widely than we already have will probably be useless. If she does not remember of her own accord or, if upon remembering, has no wish to

52

return, she will stay at Longbourn forever, to vex your mother. I can always use an apprentice in that trade!"

Elizabeth's pretty face twined itself skeptically.

"Of course, pity for her situation plays no part in this decision to extend your hospitality to her indefinitely," she slyly suggested.

"Certainly not! Do you take me for a softhearted fool?" Mr. Bennet harshly retorted. Rising, he strode to them, gently took Elizabeth's right arm with one hand and Jane's left arm with the other, and commenced walking them towards the door. "Now, off with the two of you! A man ringed by seven women needs at least one room in the house to call his own, and I stake my claim on this library. I am not to be disturbed, is that clear?" Seeing them over the threshold, their father released them. But before he closed the door, Mr. Bennet thoroughly undermined his act by softly adding, "Let me know if there are any important bulletins from the sickroom."

Chapter 11

The carriage slowly wound its way around the vast park, passing a dozen striking vistas which were completely unappreciated by all of the human beings sitting on or within the coach. Not even the magnificent sight of the largest mansion in Derbyshire standing beyond a glimmering lake was sufficient to rouse their spirits.

At long last, the wheels of the conveyance scraped against the gravel of the drive, and finally ceased to turn in front of the palatial building. Andrew nimbly jumped from his perched position, opened the door, and briskly set out the step before respectfully standing aside. He stood thus for a full three quarters of a minute, but no passenger alighted. Moreover, not the slightest rustle or movement was heard from within the coach.

Wondering if the traveler had been lulled to sleep, the footman glanced inside. What he saw wrung his heart. Mr. Darcy sat lost to the world, not in sleep, but in abstraction. The gentleman stared blankly at the cushions on the opposite side of the coach, shoulders sagging. His usually carefully arranged brown locks were disheveled; frenzied hands had surely torn at them for at least part of the journey. The perpetrators were now more peaceful, clasped in a peculiar attitude which suggested that after foregoing the former employment, the man had commenced wringing them only to forget himself in the middle of the occupation and fall into the present stupor.

"Sir?" Andrew eventually managed to choke out. "We are home."

It took a moment, but the words roused his employer. Mr. Darcy's shoulders slightly straightened, and he glanced about. Noticing the open carriage door and Andrew, he turned to the window beside him, and with some surprise, recognized the view. He was at Pemberley. But despite the footman's pronouncement, it would never truly be a *home* again.

Holding back uncommon tears, Andrew watched the passenger look around helplessly for his hat and walking cane instead of reaching for them immediately, as he did when he was cognizant of where he had laid them down last. The items were located and collected at length, and only then did Mr. Darcy slowly emerge from the coach.

Eyesight blurred by moisture, Andrew did not observe how pale the master became as he stepped down, nor how the hand adorn with the signet ring clutched the door for support longer than its wont. Fortunately, James and Fredrick, Darcy's valet, who had also made the journey, and kept Tom company for its duration, had both regained the ground by this point. The distress signals which escaped the other footman were seen by them. Then, when the proprietor of the building looked up at it, and the hazy idea that he was the very last of the ancient family who had owned it for centuries permeated his mind, these two servants also marked the sway in his form and the swift bending of his knees, and not a moment too soon.

"Sir!" Fredrick cried out, leaping to his employer's side. He threw an arm around the gentleman's waist and ducked so that Mr. Darcy's right arm fell upon his shoulders for added support. James simultaneously grasped the master's other coat sleeve, bracing him from the opposite side. Between the two of them they managed to keep the taller man upright. After a moment and a deep breath, Mr. Darcy regained enough strength to bear most, but not all, of his own weight. Thus, exchanging a desperate glance, the valet and footman retained their firm hold and began to guide their employer gently towards the front door of the house.

As they advanced through the archway and into the courtyard, Darcy dimly and bitterly reflected that less than three weeks ago, he had been so determined to preserve his image as a vigorous, authoritative master that he would have concealed even a headache, lest such a trifling ailment cast upon him a light of weakness. And now, he was returning to Pemberley from a prolonged absence, supported by servants, barely able to walk, and he cared not. It would not have concerned him a whit had they dressed him in a beggar's garments and carried him in overtly.

At length, the threesome reached the front steps. James and Fredrick patiently attended Darcy as he dragged his heavy legs up slowly, one at a time, and felt an onrush of relief when their charge safely crossed the threshold.

But their entrance affected the man between them quite differently. The silence inside the house was, to Darcy, deafening. Pemberley was generally a tranquil place, with its efficient staff going about their duties quietly and soberly, but there had been one exception to that rule: whenever its master returned from a journey, his younger sister would, without fail, dash out of her chambers or the music room, hasten to close the distance between the siblings, and throw herself upon his neck with a cry of 'Fitzwilliam!'. Now, there was neither the tussle of feet flying down the steps, nor a warm embrace.

There was the sound of footsteps, however, but they were much more sedate than the ones Georgiana's brother longed to hear. They heralded the approach of the housekeeper, Mrs. Reynolds, and indeed, within the span of a few seconds, that lady made her appearance in the entrance hall.

She had heard the carriage, and was naturally coming to investigate who the new arrival was. About sixty years of age, respectably attired, she took great pride and joy in minding the impressive house, and was ever ready to demonstrate it to visitors. Thinking that the coach bore such callers, she donned a smile and promptly moved towards the front door.

The unexpected scene in the hall instantaneously wiped the joyous expression from her countenance. The gentleman whom she had known since he was a generous-hearted child of four, who had never been affected by anything more than a trifling cold, was draped over his valet's shoulders in the most shocking manner, looking very ill indeed. Mrs. Reynolds' lower lip dropped in shock, but only for a second; the next, she was hurrying towards the men with all due haste, her mind already formulating strategies for dealing with the crisis at hand.

"Master Fitzwilliam," she began authoritatively; in her distress, formality was unwittingly cast aside, and her tongue reverted to calling the dear boy the name of his youth, "you must be put to bed at once! Fredrick, James, help him upstairs! I shall send for the doctor without delay, sir, and before he arrives you will take some tea…"

Mr. Darcy, with an effort, focused on the poor woman's maternal, fearful eyes. His heart wrenched even harder than before. If a presumed illness of his was capable of causing Mrs. Reynolds such pain, what would the news that Miss Darcy was dead and gone do to her?

He knew he could not bring himself to voice those fateful words, or any of their derivatives, to the housekeeper before him or anyone else. Such an attempt would kill him. During a brief rest on the road, he had sat at a writing desk for half-an-hour, trying to compose a letter to Georgiana's other guardian. Words generally flowed easily from his pen, at least, much more easily than they fell from his lips. But faced with the duty of recording the words 'Georgiana', 'carriage accident' and 'deceased' on the same sheet of paper, skill had utterly failed him. His hand had commenced quivering so fiercely that drops of ink sprayed forth from the pen and covered the paper with unsightly patterns.

"Fredrick," the Master of Pemberley said, withdrawing his arm from the servant's shoulders and holding himself upright by sheer force of will, "tell Mrs. Reynolds. Mrs. Reynolds," he lowered his voice, unable to maintain a louder tone, "pray write of…it…to Colonel Richard Fitzwilliam. Forgive me for giving you such a charge! And…if anyone should call, be it Richard or Charles Bingley…I am not at home."

That said, the servants watched Darcy stagger toward his study, little dreaming that he would not give another command for months to come.

Chapter 12

Back at Longbourn, the days flew by and in almost every aspect, Anne recovered remarkably well. Her headaches vanished and Mr. Jones soon gave her permission to sit up on the bedchamber's window seat, wrapped in a warm dressing gown. The bruises faded. Her appetite improved.

There was one area, however, where no progress whatsoever could be discerned. Her memory remained absent. The curtain which covered it never fluttered; it was perpetually drawn tightly shut. No shadowy images or ghostly voices ever intruded upon Anne's consciousness or dreams. Nothing, except that and those whom she had come to know since her awakening, felt familiar to her.

This interruption in the otherwise seamless recovery naturally kindled much consternation in both the patient and attendants. Disregarding Mr. Jones' opinion that it would be useless, there were a few days where they zealously altered her nourishment, encouraged hours upon hours of rest, and kept the bedchamber aired, hoping that these adjustments would encourage the strayed recollections to wander back to their proper places.

The happy event had been at last despaired of, but after a little while, it hardly seemed to matter. Despite widespread reports in Meryton about Miss Edwards' existence and ailments, no one came forward to claim her. Anne was content at Longbourn, and everyone, save Mrs. Bennet, grew exceedingly fond of her. Mary, at last, found an eager listener for her philosophical musings, one who shyly punctuated her lectures with short sentences of admiration. Likewise, Kitty and Lydia soon discovered the joy of pelting Anne with amusing stories of their escapades, for unlike Jane or Elizabeth, she never reproved them for dressing up one of the officers in Mrs. Forster's gowns or for slipping a mouse into the Colonel's pocket. For his part, Mr. Bennet was caught at least twice in Elizabeth's bedchamber, a chessboard between himself and its current tenant. Anne warmed to Jane and her solicitous attentions, as anyone would. But it was Elizabeth, the one whom she had beheld first upon awakening, whom she truly loved as a sister.

They complimented each other perfectly. Elizabeth's powers of observation were often useful in detecting the slight changes of countenance and loquaciousness which signaled Anne to be distressed about her intrusion on Longbourn or her amnesia, and Miss Bennet's vivacity was instrumental in bringing the younger girl out of the same dejection. Lizzy, as Anne called her, spent many agreeable hours describing the people who lived in and about the neighborhood for the newcomer's benefit, so that when the time came to venture outside Miss Edwards would be able to integrate into society with very little effort. And the ladies soon found that they shared the same taste in literature. Many an evening would find them huddling over the same book, and the following morning would discover them sleeping side by side, the interesting volume open between them. After a few of these episodes, Elizabeth abandoned her original intention of sleeping with her elder sister, and returned to her old dwelling and new roommate.

Chapter 13

Elizabeth gently pulled the brush through the golden locks one last time. Now that the tresses which cascaded down Anne's shoulders and back were perfectly straight, she paused in her work and smiled at the reflection in the mirror.

"Have you any preference as to how you would like it arranged?" she asked.

Anne shrugged quickly and nervously shook her head.

"Do as you think best, Lizzy," she whispered in reply. After a short pause, she murmured, "I do not even know whether I should wear it up or down."

Elizabeth laughed softly.

"Oh Anne! While it is true that we do not know whether you were out a few weeks ago, at Longbourn you will certainly be so. If *Lydia* is allowed to flirt with every officer in the county, there is no reason for you not to do likewise!"

"Lizzy!" her friend blushed, mortified at the mere thought of trifling with anyone, let alone a gentleman.

"Come now, dearest! It cannot be so difficult. A flutter of the eyelids, a sly smile; nothing that you cannot accomplish if you but try!"

"Please, I really do not…," the girl's voice became more and more distressed and unnerved. Miss Bennet caught a glimpse of the terrified countenance in the mirror and instantaneously repented.

"Forgive me, Anne," Elizabeth earnestly begged as she gently stroked the blond tresses. "Of course I do not expect you to follow my younger sisters' example and expose yourself to ridicule. You should know by now that I only mean a fraction of what I say." Her mind unaccountably wandered, and smiling a little, she found herself demurely murmuring, "I am afraid he was correct after all."

"Who, Lizzy?" Miss Edwards piped up curiously, rather surprised at her roommate's unusually inattentive tone.

"Oh, just a onetime acquaintance of mine," Elizabeth replied, a little too lightly, as she pinned up the golden locks. "He once told me that I found great enjoyment in professing opinions which in fact were not my own. At the time I thought it quite ungenerous of him, but I have since learned to give credence to that remark. It is true that in teasing I often exaggerate my statements in order to provoke a reaction in my interlocutor, and I derive much amusement from overthrowing their guard. Notwithstanding his faults, he was a very astute man."

The other maiden in the chamber was too innocent in the ways of the world to properly interpret the overly carefree tone with which Elizabeth made the speech, or the lowering of her voice towards the end of it. Miss Bennet, suddenly aware that a little bit of regret had slipped into her words, quickly returned her attention to the hairdressing, and said no more on the subject.

"There, all is finished," she announced at length after slipping one last pin into the soft strands. "You look very distinguished, Miss Edwards!"

"Thank you," the girl murmured. As Elizabeth reached for her hand to help her up, Anne suddenly paled.

"What is it, dearest?" When the maiden gave no answer, Miss Bennet continued, "We are simply going to take a turn around the house; I promise you, there are no dragons lurking outside the door of this bedchamber."

Anne mustered a slight smile, and although still uneasy, allowed Elizabeth to lead her across the room, and then across the threshold.

Miss Edwards craned her neck this way and that, peering first at the ceilings, then at the floors, then at what lay between them with the interest and curiosity of a small child who is in the process of learning the basic principles of the world. Old drawings and small paintings which had hung in Longbourn's halls before anyone could remember and which no one noticed anymore each attracted Anne's attention for a minute or two. She toured Mary's room as if it were a queen's bedchamber and every object in it was linked to a pivotal moment in English history. Elizabeth watched her charge's shy explorations with a smile, and occasionally interjected brief explanations.

They finished walking through the upper part of the house and at length descended the staircase. There, Elizabeth showed Anne around the dining parlor, Mr. Bennet's library, and eventually led her into the drawing room.

It was in that apartment that Longbourn's newest occupant demonstrated the most spontaneity which she had ever displayed. The pianoforte in the center of the room drew the girl like a magnet.

Without express invitation, Anne walked over to it, spent a minute looking at it, and then actually reached out and gently caressed its top.

"Would you care to try?" Elizabeth asked eagerly.

The girl snatched away her hand like a guilty child.

"No...thank you, but...no," Anne replied, certainty clearly lacking from her tone.

"Why not?"

"I...I do not...I fear I shall break it," Miss Edwards admitted, at length.

Elizabeth laughed.

"Is that all? Let me assure you, my dearest, that you could not injure this instrument if you tried. Its keys have been known to survive blows from Lydia's fists during fits of rage. And when Kitty was little, she would climb up and stand on the top, claiming that the position afforded the best view of the room. You may experiment with this indestructible instrument to your heart's content." Seeing that the girl still seemed unsure, Miss Bennet took her by the shoulders and pressed her down onto the piano bench. It took several moments of further coaxing and reassuring, but eventually, Anne consented to touch the keys. Noticing the sheets of music before her, she scanned the first few bars of a Mozart masterpiece. Suddenly, just like the words which Mr. Jones had had her read, the dots and lines took on meaning. They issued instructions to the obedient fingers, which, one-by-one, began to apply pressure to the polished ivory underneath them. The melody came to life, tentatively at first, but grew bolder by the measure.

Elizabeth stood behind the performer, listening in silence and following the music. About halfway through the page, she noticed that a particularly difficult passage was approaching, one that neither she nor Jane nor Mary had been able to master, despite repeated trials. Miss Bennet drew in her breath and held it, waiting for the unscripted slurring and discord which was sure to come.

She waited in vain. Anne's fingers simply accelerated their flawless dance. Every note rang out crystal-clear. An uneducated listener would have thought the passage as easy as any other.

Elizabeth exhaled slowly. Still and mute, she vastly enjoyed the remainder of the piece. Only when the decrescendo had faded did she open her lips to speak.

Astonishingly, however, she was not given a chance to voice her sentiments. Without seeking permission, Anne launched into a sonata whose music was unfolded just to the right of Mozart's symphony. Elizabeth's mouth opened in shock. Cautiously, she stepped to the side of the piano bench in order to gain a better view of the musician's countenance.

The usually tense and timid girl was radiantly smiling. Her breath was coming in small, excited bursts. For the first time since arriving at Longbourn, she seemed to have thoroughly forgotten her troubles, as well as herself. Instead of trudging through the moments, wondering what the past and future held, her soul was floating, frolicking upon air.

Seeing that Anne had no need, or even awareness of her, Elizabeth quietly retreated to a nearby sofa. Drawing up her knees, she clasped her arms around her legs and, in that comfortable position, listened to the exclusive concert.

At length, the sonata too was completed. This time, Elizabeth did not attempt to speak. Instead, she concentrated on paralyzing every muscle, hoping that the enduring stillness would propagate the miracle of the little Miss Edwards confidently plucking away at the old instrument. Her prayers were granted. Anne recommenced playing.

Unlike the previous ones, the next piece was very simple. It was composed of no more than ten different notes, but they were so magnificently threaded together that it seemed a masterpiece. Elizabeth listened to the pleasant, tinkering aria only to discover that its melody was completely foreign to her. Attending more closely, she realized that Anne was not looking at any of the sheets of music before her. Instead, she gazed down leisurely upon the keys, watching her fingers as they practically moved themselves. There was no effort of composition or improvisation whatsoever. The piece went on for several minutes, with occasional variations on the same, sweet theme. Then, it slowly ascended to a crescendo, and ended on a slightly dramatic note.

Miss Bennet dared not applaud, but this time, even the lack of interruption failed to entice any more sounds from the instrument. Anne's fingers slipped from the keys, and in a deep preoccupation, she reached for the blue ring on her right hand. The thumb and second finger of her left hand began to stroke and then nudge the circlet clockwise a few millimeters at a time.

As Elizabeth watched this tranced performance, she again felt an inexplicable, suffocating sensation.

Why is it that every time the girl touches her ring, I feel as if all the air has suddenly left the room?

Being a creature who disliked feeling irrational emotions, Elizabeth Bennet leaned forward and, staring at the musician for all she was worth, tried to find a reason for the tightness in her chest. The strange impression deepened, teasing her, and then, ended as quickly as it had come on.

Elizabeth exhaled in frustration, and attempted momentarily to recapture the feeling. Soon recognizing the effort to be useless, however, she decided to turn into an alternative path of thought and broke the silence by asking,

"Wherever did that lovely song come from, Anne?"

Miss Edwards precipitously ceased toying with her ring and looked again at the ivory keys.

"Lovely? You mean revolting."

Elizabeth started and stared, wondering for a moment whether the shy maiden was trying her hand at satire, until she noticed the abashed and uncomfortable expression upon her face.

"It was lovely, Anne," Miss Bennet insisted. "Your taste in music can stand some amendment if you can honestly call it unpleasant. Where did that dear tune come from? I was not aware that we had the sheet music for anything akin to it."

"I…I did not read anything. I truly do not know…I must have improvised it. Clearly, I am a poor composer."

Elizabeth warmly replied that Anne was Bach's equal and ought to stop deprecating herself, but was getting nowhere when a most unlikely reinforcement arrived. The drawing room door was precipitously thrown open, and Mrs. Bennet strutted in, saying,

"I do not mind saying so, Mary, that was a very pretty piece! You will never play as well as Jane or Lizzy, but I must say that - ," noticing who was actually seated at the pianoforte, the Mistress of Longbourn broke off her compliments sharply. Narrowing her eyes, she gave the performer a look which made her shake in her shoes, and then focused them on her own daughter. "I did not know, Lizzy," Mrs. Bennet recommenced in a much harder tone, "that your father agreed to purchase a new instrument for you girls. But he must have, if you let street tramps pound on that one."

Having had her say, the middle-aged woman made a dramatic exit, slamming the door behind her.

Chapter 14

The girls sat in silence and mortification for a short eternity. Just as Anne was regaining enough animation to start withdrawing from the piano bench, the stillness was broken by her companion's voice.

"Sometimes," Elizabeth burst out angrily, "I wish that Mama had kept her promise, and had never spoken to me again!"

Anne looked appropriately shocked and scandalized at the eccentric exclamation, but remained silent despite the strong lines of curiosity which appeared on her forehead. Her companion, however, was astute enough to notice them and generous enough to explain,

"She threatened to never speak to or see me again after I persisted in refusing Mr. Collins's offer of marriage."

Miss Edwards managed to repeat,

"Mr. Collins?"

"Yes. Our cousin who holds the entail on Longbourn." Seeing that Anne was interested, Elizabeth decided to perseverate upon the topic in order to abolish the memory of Mrs. Bennet's rudeness from both their minds. "He currently lives in Kent, and was apparently counselled by his wealthy patroness to marry, and he set off to do so in a hurry. I happened to be the first fortunate maiden who received his proposals. Mama zealously demanded that I accept, for then we would be safe should something happen to Papa, and I must confess that it would have been a most prudent match, but…the man, Anne! Not only did I not love him, I found him positively appalling. As for the offer itself, well – a mere summary would never do it justice!"

"Was it that good?" Miss Edwards asked naively, hoping to hear more about her friend's romantic experiences.

"Good!" Elizabeth cried out. "I suppose that it had a few merits, if one likes rehearsed, pompous - ," she broke off. Seized by a playful thought, she jumped up from the sofa, practically skipped to the pianoforte, grasped Anne's hand, and gently pulled her from the bench, across the room, and into the dining parlor. "I truly believe that a demonstration will serve us better. Here, my dear, is where the infamous proposal took place! Sit down in this chair, like I had the privilege of doing as Mr. Collins lay bare his heart. Pretend that you have sensed what was coming, and tried to flee the premises only to be halted by your mother and ordered to stay and hear the man out. Have you an accurate picture of the circumstances?"

Anne nodded.

Elizabeth hurried to the other end of the room, adopted a stiff posture, and clasping her hands before herself began in an unnaturally deep voice,

"'Believe me, my dear Miss Elizabeth, that your modesty, so far from doing you any disservice, rather adds to your other perfections. You can hardly doubt the purport of my discourse, however your natural delicacy may lead you to dissemble; my attentions have been too marked to be mistaken. Almost as soon as I entered the house I singled you out as the companion of my future life. But before I am run away with by my feelings on this subject, perhaps it will be advisable for me to state my reasons for marrying - and moreover for coming into Hertfordshire with the design of selecting a wife, as I certainly did.'"

Anne began to smile broadly, struck by Elizabeth's vocal mimicry and the humorous last line, already imagining what sort of gentleman was being impersonated.

Raising her nose into the air at a ridiculous angle, Elizabeth continued,

"'My reasons for marrying are, first, that I think it a right thing for every clergyman in easy circumstances (like myself) to set the example of matrimony in his parish. Secondly, that I am convinced it will add very greatly to my happiness; and thirdly - which perhaps I ought to have mentioned earlier, that it is the particular advice and recommendation of the very noble lady whom I have the honor of calling patroness. Twice has she condescended to give me her opinion (unasked too!) on this subject…she said, 'Mr. Collins, you must marry. A clergyman like you must marry. Choose properly, choose a gentlewoman for *my* sake; and for your *own*, let her be an active, useful sort of person, not brought up high, but able to make a small income go a good way. This is my advice. Find such a woman as soon as you can, bring her to Hunsford, and I will visit her'…You will find her manners beyond anything I can describe; and your wit and vivacity I think must be acceptable to her, especially when tempered with the silence and respect which her rank will inevitably excite.'"

A small giggle escaped Miss Edwards.

"'Thus much for my general intention in favor of matrimony; it remains to be told why my views were directed to Longbourn instead of my own neighborhood, where I assure you there are many amiable young women. But the fact is, that being, as I am, to inherit this estate after the death of your honored father, I could not satisfy myself without resolving to choose a wife from among his daughters.'" Elizabeth paraded through the room, stood before the tittering damsel, and boomed out, "'And now, nothing remains -,'" she threw herself upon her knees before Anne, "'but to assure you in the most *animated* language of the *violence* of my affections!' O, they were violent indeed, my dear Miss Edwards, for when I refused them, they were bestowed within the week upon my friend, Charlotte Lucas!"

She got no further, for Anne was laughing! Not smiling, not simply chuckling, but laughing aloud musically as her shoulders shook and copious tears ran down her cheeks! Where amusing books and teasing had failed, the recounting of Mr. Collins' proposal had succeeded. The typically withdrawn child was laughing!

Miss Bennet attempted to increase her friend's pleasure by continuing, but the hilarity of the moment was too much. Deciding that all the best material was spent anyhow, she surrendered and joined in the merriment. The two continued thus for some minutes, until their laughter rendered them exhausted.

Wiping her eyes, however, Anne seemed still eager for more, for she uncommonly pried,

"Have you had any other ridiculous proposals, Lizzy?"

Elizabeth collected herself, pondered, remembered, and was on the point of stating that she once had a suitor who told her that she would be a degradation to himself when she was checked by the creak of the door hinges.

"O, Miss Lizzy, I do apologize," the housekeeper exclaimed. "I did not know that there was anyone here."

"It is quite alright, Mrs. Hill," the brunette replied, rising. "You are here to prepare the room for dinner, I daresay?"

"Yes, but I do not wish to disturb you and Miss Edwards - ,"

"Think no more of it, I beg you. We have been downstairs for a long time, and from the looks of Miss Edwards, she should lie down for a while before the meal. Pray go about your work."

Going over to Anne, Elizabeth asked for her approbation of this plan, and of course received it. The young ladies left the dining parlor, and went to rest without Miss Edwards being informed of the existence of Mr. Darcy or his proposals.

Chapter 15

"Miss Sophia Long, Miss Anne Edwards," Elizabeth said, clasping the quivering arm intertwined with hers even more tightly. To everyone else in the house, the luncheon party at Lucas Lodge was a small, unceremonious affair. But for Anne, whose encounters with society until now had consisted of a few awkward meetings with Lady and Maria Lucas in Longbourn's drawing room, the event might as well have been an assembly at St. James' Court. The frightened child had duly attached herself to Elizabeth since the moment they stepped through the front door and had not released her for an instant. "Sophia is one of Mrs. Long's nieces, Anne."

Miss Edwards' neck twitched up and down. Miss Long's response was far less nervous, and she spoke very prettily about how much she had heard about Hertfordshire's newest arrival and how glad she was to meet her at last. Several minutes and a few embarrassed smiles from Anne later, the three young ladies parted with a promise to call on each other soon.

"There, there. The worst is over," Elizabeth promised, patting her companion's arm comfortingly as they slowly walked across the room. "You have just made the acquaintance of most of our neighbors and some of the more popular members of the militia. Henceforth, the majority of the faces you will see will be familiar rather than foreign. Dare I ask what you think of your new friends?"

Miss Edwards smiled shyly.

"I like them very well indeed."

Unsatisfied, Elizabeth teased,

"Is that all the reply I am to expect? Might one ask for a little elaboration?"

"All the ladies have been too sweet to me, and…and…"

"And?" Miss Bennet demanded.

"And I…can certainly see why Lydia and Kitty are so fond of the officers. They are such a merry and…handsome…lot!"

A hearty laugh escaped Elizabeth, causing Anne to blush painfully.

"Upon my word, you *did* notice the young men whom we introduced you to! You gave a first-rate imitation of ignorance when I was speaking to them. I was certain that the only thing you noted during my conversation with Captain Carter was the pattern on the rug!"

Overcome with embarrassment and distress, Miss Edwards murmured anxiously,

"O, Lizzy, did I really seem so rude?"

"Rude, no. Abashed? Yes."

"Forgive me, Lizzy. I did not mean to cause you any mortification…"

"Believe me, dear heart!" the dark-haired girl exclaimed, "I was far more discomfited by Lydia's eagerness to have the Captain snatch the lavender sprigs from her hair. Cast your eyes down all that you will if it keeps you from flaunting your golden curls and tempting the officers' fingers!"

This answer seemed to pacify Anne for a moment, but soon she drew nearer to Elizabeth, and in a low, anguished tone said,

"But surely I *have* done something wrong! Lady Lucas looks quite severe. How have I offended her, Lizzy? Pray tell me!"

Elizabeth stole a glance at their hostess. She was glowering indeed, but not in their direction. Her irate eyes were observing the other end of the room, where her husband was bustling, overseeing several servants who were bringing in baskets and little crates. Smiling anew, she turned back to Anne.

"Be easy, my friend. In this case, it is Sir William who is the insufferable eradicator of propriety. My mother informs us that the last time he made such a display as the one you are about to see, Lady Lucas did not speak to him for a fortnight together. She believes that his antics completely ruin the elegance and grace of her affairs. I suppose she is right, but am still quite unable to condemn Sir William for this vice."

Miss Edwards was too self-conscious to inquire into what sort of human imperfection they were about to witness, but she did not need to speak in order to have her curiosity satisfied. The two young ladies stood side-by-side watching the unfolding scene. The servants set up miniature corrals in the far end of the parlor before turning to the baskets. Carefully pulling back the soft white blankets which covered the tops, they reached in, and commenced pulling out squirming, darling balls of fur and placing them behind the short fences.

"Ohhhh!" Anne softly cooed when she realized what they were. "What sweet, adorable little puppies!"

"Sir William is exceptionally fond of dog breeding," her amused companion explained. "Whenever a superior litter is born he will stop at nothing to show off his fine new stock, even if it means bringing a dozen unwelcome guests into the house."

The knight of whom they were speaking at that moment looked in their direction, and cried out jovially across the room,

"Miss Lizzy, Miss Anne! Come and see the capital animals I have here! They truly are miracles of nature and boast of the finest parentage. Come, come!"

Unable to resist such a public, eager invitation, the two girls made their way across the room quickly enough to satisfy Sir William's vanity but slowly enough to hide their secret enthusiasm from Lady Lucas. They approached the yelping bunch and knelt by the kennels. One was filled with young English foxhounds, and the other with pugs.

"Just look at them, ladies," Sir William boomed, hovering over the animals with pride. "You shall never see two better litters of pups in your life, depend on it! This is Maggie," he continued, pointing to one of the pugs, "and this is Max and that one closest to yourselves is Waldo." Walking over to the other enclosure, the gentleman recommenced, "Bailey sits in the corner there, this one is Daisy, the smallest one is Sadie, and the one trying to jump up on Miss Anne through the fence is Farley. What do you say now, my dears?"

The two girls obediently peered in and carefully inspected the adorable little creatures, making certain to look at each and every one for an adequate amount of time.

"I cannot deny that they are some of the strongest, most handsome dogs I ever had the privilege to see," Miss Bennet sincerely replied after a few moments. "You certainly have a way with them, sir."

"It is a gift I have had ever since I was a young boy, Miss Lizzy. Some men, like my young son-in-law Collins, tend gardens, but I prefer dogs. One cannot race cucumbers or derive the same sort of exhilaration from watching melons grow."

Elizabeth replied with a small laugh, and began stroking the pups. For once, Anne needed little encouragement to join her and was soon rubbing Farley's ears, much to the foxhound's pleasure.

"That one will make a superior hunting dog," Sir William informed them.

Shocked into speaking, Miss Edwards exclaimed,
"Farley?"

"Yes," the middle-aged man said, looking down at the golden head. "Why should you be surprised? Look at his build! Besides, he is the most obedient of them all, and will be a joy to train."

Anne gently grasped the little pup's torso with her two hands, lifted him out of the pen and held him directly in front of herself. His tiny paws moved energetically, his tail wagged, and his big, expressive eyes blinked. Feeling called upon to explain her wonderment, the timid young lady stuttered,

"I just…I find it so hard to believe…that something so innocent…will one day aid in killing…," her voice trailed off.

Sir William shrugged. As a sportsman, he had grown insensate to the unpleasantness of depriving beautiful birds or other small creatures of their existence, particularly as his own wife and daughters were far too practical to ever remind him of it by bemoaning the fate of game. Frankly, he considered Anne's statement rather silly and childish, but relying on his good manners, replied kindly,

"I am afraid that that is the way of the world, Miss Anne. In order to keep ourselves fit and amused, we gentlemen must occasionally go hunting, and necessarily train our dogs to do likewise. Fear not; Farley will not be rendered an ounce less friendly by his out-of-door pursuits."

The reassurances did not affect any positive change in Miss Edwards' countenance, and she soon lowered the puppy back into his temporary residence and made as if she wished to withdraw. Her desire went unnoticed by Elizabeth, who was still cooing over Sadie. Feeling unequal to going back to the rest of the company on her own, Anne remained by the small corrals, and after a few moments tried to take an interest in the pugs. Unfortunately, Farley possessed a jealous streak, and unleashed a valiant campaign to bring the nice young lady back to his side. Anne withstood his begging pose, endearing yelps, and big brown eyes for a short spell, but the pup's offensive was soon too much for her. She drew back towards the foxhounds' pen, and began stroking the white and brown coat, utterly forgetting what the small dog was destined for. The pleased creature rolled over, had her scratch his stomach, and held her attention for over a quarter of an hour. Elizabeth, finishing Sadie's playtime, rose and was on the point of beckoning to her friend when she noticed Miss Edwards' occupation. Thinking better of the summons, she quietly withdrew a short distance away, hoping that Anne's ease with Farley might embolden the girl to sit for a few minutes on her own without a guard in the immediate vicinity. Anxious that the experiment be not cruel, however, she kept an eye on her friend and was prepared to hasten back to her side at the first sign of agitation. To the ignorance of both young ladies, Mr. Bennet did likewise, albeit from his station near the windows.

The surveillance was in vain. Anne eventually realized that she had been abandoned. But, just as her grey eyes began to fill with dismay, Farley let out a sweet little yelp. Miss Edwards broke into a broad smile, appeared to shrug off her knowledge that Elizabeth had removed to a different part of the room, and turned back to the puppy.

Chapter 16

Like all pleasant affairs, the one at Lucas Lodge seemed to end far too soon. Despite this, six cheerful young ladies followed Mrs. Bennet out-of-doors. Anne, in particular, seemed brighter than her wont and possessed a distinct spring in her step. The air outside was refreshing, for it had rained while they partook of the midday meal, and although the precipitation had stopped, a few clouds and the lovely smell of dewed grass tarried.

The matriarch was approaching the carriage when she happened to glance at the surrounding throng.

"Girls, where is your father?!" Mrs. Bennet exclaimed, noticing that her husband was absent.

"He stayed behind to discuss a matter of business with Sir William Lucas," Jane immediately answered.

"Oh, why does he dawdle? He had three hours during the party to discuss anything he wanted. Now we are to stand out in the wet drive and breathe in damp air because Mr. Bennet suddenly remembered some trifling thing he needed to tell his friend. We shall probably all die of pneumonia, but what is that to him? What *can* he be saying to Sir William?"

Jane stroked her mother's arm soothingly.

"When he told me that he would be a moment, he smiled and mentioned something about bringing home a visitor," she replied.

"Visitors?" Mrs. Bennet screeched so loudly that the horses harnessed to the carriage behind her startled, snorted, tossed their manes and stamped nervously. "He wants to bring the Lucases to dine with us this evening, and without telling me? I have no concern over the meal itself, for I am certain that my everyday dinners are better than whatever they usually have at home. But Hill was to rearrange the drawing room furniture today, and if Lady Lucas gets one glimpse of the disarray it will be all over Meryton on the morrow!"

"Mama, I am certain that - ,"

"And I am sure that they will want to drive down in our carriage, but their rickety old coach will have to do for them for once. There is not enough room for a fly in ours. It was tight enough when there were just seven of us, before your father started picking up orphans or stowaways from the streets."

Anne appeared crestfallen. She turned away to hide her discomfort, trying to reason away her injured feelings.

Elizabeth, for her part, was furious. It had been weeks. One would think that the Mistress of Longbourn would have acclimated to the new *status quo*, or at least seen the futility in uttering baneful remarks which solely pained Anne and increased Mr. Bennet's determination to retain her.

Being far too mindful of filial respect to cross swords with her mother over the matter, but seeing that lady angry and apt to pour more ire upon Miss Edwards' innocent head, she quickly moved to evacuate the girl from the vicinity before further disparagement could take place.

"You shall have more room in the carriage than you suppose, Mama," she replied. "For Anne and I are going to take advantage of the freshened air and walk home." Having said this much, and without waiting for Mrs. Bennet's approbation or disapproval, she pulled Miss Edwards away from the others and hurried them both down a grassy path in the general direction of Longbourn.

Once they were advanced far enough into the countryside to be out of sight and earshot of the others, Elizabeth noted that Anne still seemed a tad dejected, although she was valiantly trying to hide her emotions. With the intention of distracting the girl, she commented,

"The sun is beginning to peek through the clouds, and will soon conquer them completely, making for a very nice stroll. By the by, my dearest Miss Edwards, do you *really* find overcast days preferable to sunny ones?"

Anne looked down, abashed.

"I see that you overheard my brief conversation with Sir William Lucas," she murmured apologetically.

"I confess I did, and was very surprised by your opinions, but not by your willingness to please him."

"But when Sir William inquired about my ideas of pleasant weather, he seemed so certain that I liked cloudy skies that he even commented that the brightness of daylight was often adept at producing headaches, and listed not one redeeming quality of sunlight."

"And you agree completely with that assessment?"

Anne continued gazing at the grass as a small, ashamed,

"No," escaped her lips.

Her walking companion laughed teasingly.

"I suppose we should consider ourselves fortunate that Sir William refrained from mentioning that he prefers pugs to English foxhounds? If he had, would poor Farley have been thrown down instantly, and all your caresses redirected at Waldo?"

"Oh no! I could never be so affectionate to one of those peculiar creatures! But, I confess - had I been aware of Sir William's preferences, I would have spent much more time by the pugs."

Still laughing softly, Elizabeth sided up to her friend and twined her arm through Anne's. As they fell into step together, she said smilingly, yet seriously,

"This incessant desire to appease all is your worst fault, Anne. It is a very poor habit to foster. First of all, you will never fully succeed, for humanity is very fickle; what pleases one will invariably offend another. Imagine what would occur if I constantly attempted to humor both my mother and father!" Anne bit back a smile at this idea. "Besides, frequent fluctuations of opinion give the appearance of a weak mind. Furthermore, it is possible that someday you shall meet someone who it would be dangerous to please. A subset of mankind, unfortunately, takes delight in and approves of evil." Giving the thoughtful, contrite Anne a comforting little nudge, Elizabeth concluded, "Therefore, my dear, seek above all to please God. That way you will not go astray, no matter what your company. Afterwards, if you have good reason to think that your options are equal in His Sight, please yourself. Play with the foxhounds rather than the pugs, even if their owner cherishes the latter more. Or, as I did only the day before you came to us, defy fickle fashion trends and trim your new dress with bows rather than with lace!"

Anne murmured in apparent agreement.

They relapsed into silence. Enraptured by the beauty of the walk, the elder girl let go of Miss Edwards and executed a sprightly pirouette to take in every aspect of the delightful landscape. About to encourage her protégé to do the same, she turned back to Anne, only to notice a frightful expression which she had not witnessed since the day Mr. Jones had questioned Anne as to her memory, or lack thereof.

"Anne?" whispered Miss Bennet, instantaneously alarmed.

The maiden met her friend's eyes and calmed her somewhat by uttering an attentive,

"Yes, Lizzy?"

75

"What are you thinking of?"

Anne turned away and surveyed the view with an uncomfortable eye, wondering whether disclosing the true nature of the thoughts which were consuming her golden head would make her appear disobedient. After all, she had been begged not to entertain such ideas! But knowing full well that Elizabeth would question, badger and plead until she extracted a replete confession, Anne swallowed nervously and began,

"Do you remember how you just said that you decided to trim your new gown with bows the day before I came to Longbourn?" At Elizabeth's nod, Anne confided shyly, "I was simply…that is, I could not…help wondering…what *I* was doing that day. Oh, Lizzy, do not think me thankless! I am aware of how much you and your family have done to save me from thinking about the past! But it is so difficult whenever…unavoidably… someone mentions a date antecedent to the fifth of May…and I have not the slightest inkling of what my activities were! Was I wandering through the fields alone, or was there someone with me? Did I have a home? Who did I belong to, if anyone?"

"My dear," Elizabeth murmured, reaching out and smoothing a few golden curls upon Miss Edwards' head, as she had often done during the time when the latter was an invalid, "how could I condemn you from engaging in something which I myself would be prone to do? While we wish that you would not fixate on it for your own peace of mind, I am certain that, if I were in your situation, scarcely would an hour pass by without my wondering about the bygone. And even though I cannot answer those questions for you, I can from the bottom of my heart assure you that in any case, you now belong to us."

Anne started, blushed, and then paled.

"Please refrain from saying that. There are very few who would share that opinion."

"What hateful person, pray, would recuse themselves from it? Other than my unreasonable and prejudiced mother, that is."

Dismayed, Anne turned upon her friend.

"I was thinking of your mother, but I was not going to classify her quite so harshly. Really, Lizzy, you ought to cease speaking about your caring mother in such a fashion - ," Here, the unusually animated Miss Edwards remembered that she was a shy creature, turned a very bright red, and stopped abruptly.

"Speak on," her friend urged.

Anne's color deepened, and her head shook slightly before she bent it towards the ground.

"I do not think I had better. It is not my place to question the way your family -,"

"You are entitled to your opinion," Elizabeth cut in. "Especially if it is not malicious. Indeed, I gather that you were about to defend my mother, a rare enterprise for anyone, even Jane. Therefore, speak on – it is my dearest wish to hear anything which might make me view the woman who gave me life in a better light!" Drawing nearer to her friend, the older girl joined her arm with Anne's, and nudged her affectionately as a prompt to begin. When this failed, she murmured comfortingly, "Anne, I promise you: whatever you say, I shall not be resentful."

Unable to withstand so ardent a plea, with quivering lips and faltering voice, Miss Edwards consented to say,

"I think…that is, I believe…from what I have seen of Mrs. Bennet, that most of her statements towards myself originate from fierce love towards yourself and your sisters." Had a more confident person made this assertion, Elizabeth would have contradicted and challenged it straightaway; as it was, she bit her tongue and consented to listen in silence. "As…impertinent…inappropriate it is for me to state it aloud, your family's situation *is* precarious. One bad cold caught by your father, and all your mother's dire predictions can easily come true. And I am an extra expense upon the overstretched coffers, taking up funds which ought to be used for yourself and your sisters." Elizabeth longed to observe that if the Mistress of Longbourn was truly concerned about money matters, it was in her power to change their financial state substantially, considering that at least a quarter of Longbourn's yearly income was squandered by that lady and her two favorite daughters. Remembering, however, that Miss Edwards had yet to learn to be confident in the face of a challenge, she checked herself. "And…Lizzy, be not angry with me for saying this to you…for I sympathize with you completely…but even her insistence that you marry Mr. Collins was born of love. For your mother, a life of comfort is more important than a life of romance and mutual understanding. Look…look…at the choice she made for herself. And, Lizzy, do consider…imagine how difficult it would be if you and your sisters were forced to support yourselves. You would have to be obedient, not to a husband, but to an employer who could discharge you whenever it suited his fancy. At least, by marrying Mr.

Collins, you would be secure. You would have a home, a carriage, and servants."

Elizabeth considered. She had been perfectly aware of the material benefits of accepting Mr. Collins, of course, but was forced to admit,

"I never thought of my mother treating me as she had treated herself. I always imagined her singling me out as the daughter whose happiness was to be sacrificed so that she and her other children would be provided for and the latter able to marry for love." Elizabeth inhaled, exhaled, and continued, "While I am not fully convinced that I was wrong, you have presented a very interesting alternative method of viewing the matter, one which I would be glad to adopt if I thought there was any chance of it being accurate. You ought to express your opinions more often, Anne. You will surely teach me something valuable if you do. But returning to my previous point, regardless of what Mama says, you are now and forevermore a part of Longbourn."

"Even if its master is none too pleased with having me there either?"

"You are a strange soul, Anne! Shielding my mother's outright incivility from scrutiny, but failing to recognize my father's overtures of goodwill! Let me assure you that Papa is just as fond of you as I am, if not more so. Remember how he came upstairs and played chess with you during those early days of your recuperation? And how he constantly invites you to borrow books from his cherished library? Believe me, when Mr. Thomas Bennet dislikes someone, he will go to great lengths to relieve himself of their company, instead of seeking them out."

"I know that he has been most generous to me," Anne freely admitted. "But there are moments when he mentions how tired he is of having so many women at Longbourn, and how much trouble young ladies are."

"That is just his way, Anne!" Elizabeth exclaimed. "Have you not seen how brusquely he sometimes deals with me and Jane? Would you have it that he dislikes us all? He finds joy in teasing his favorites."

"Lizzy…I presume far too much, to even mention my…hope…nay – fantasy…of such a moment, but I have never heard from Mr. Bennet's lips any sort of direct assurance that he does not mind having me at Longbourn."

"And you probably never will," Elizabeth acknowledged. "But I can promise you that he said just as much, albeit out of your hearing, the day you awoke. Papa thinks you intelligent enough to decipher his sarcasms and witticisms and to come to the conclusion that he is indeed fond of you. But I know – sometimes we women want to be told tender things directly, instead of being left to suppose them on our own. Papa's subtle cues of affection are as inadequate to you as my mother's chosen method of looking after us is to me. But try. Do your best to read into his actions more than you listen to his words."

Miss Edwards agreed to do so, and pensively fingered her watch, an accessory which had been handed down to her by Kitty when that girl bought herself a superior timepiece on a mad spending splurge. She flicked it open in the same absentminded manner. Glancing at it, lazily at first, and more attentively immediately afterwards, she exclaimed,

"Gracious, Lizzy, how we have been dawdling! We have yet to cover half the distance between Lucas Lodge and Longbourn, and we are supposed to be at dinner in less than twenty minutes!"

Elizabeth checked her own watch, found that it collaborated Anne's claims, and snapping it closed, merely shrugged.

"Well, then, we must be grateful that there are means by which we can hasten our progress homeward. Come!" she cried, breaking into a run. She dashed forward about ten feet, but slowed and then stopped when she realized that Miss Edwards was not following suit. "What is the matter? Do you not yet feel well enough to race back?" she asked.

"No, I…," Anne murmured, biting her lip indecisively. "I…I am sure that I am able to run, but it…I mean, I thought that…running was rather frowned upon for young ladies."

Elizabeth chuckled.

"And so it is. But my dear, do you see anyone about who could possibly frown at us?"

Miss Edwards dutifully glanced about, but, as Elizabeth had expected, could locate no observers except for a handful of squirrels and birds.

"No," she admitted. "I do not."

"Then why should we be late for dinner when we can gain Longbourn with time to spare, as well as derive exercise and enjoyment from the process?"

The apparent sagacity of this question won Miss Edwards over. When Miss Bennet recommenced her canter, she hurried to join her, and kept up relatively well; Elizabeth was only obligated to slow her pace by the least little bit in order for them to be dashing side-by-side. They sprinted across the grass, and down the side of a hill, picking up more and more speed. The air rushed in their faces, their frocks fluttered in the wind, and the ribbons which secured their bonnets tightened against their chins as the strong breeze valiantly tried to knock them off their tresses. All this only served to drive them on faster, and laugh out loud like a pair of carefree, elated children. They veritably flew over the next ridge, and the next, and the one after that.

In this manner, they reached Longbourn's gate in a record amount of time, hair undone, shawls askew. Finally they halted, and realized that they were quite out of breath.

"That…was…," Anne exclaimed, between gasps of air, "the most delightful…thing I ever did! Now I know what it must feel like to be a bird!"

"See?" Elizabeth returned triumphantly, despite her own panting breath. "And because…of a stringent attachment to propriety…you almost missed the experience!"

Anne nodded in agreement, finding that she liked Elizabeth's way of thinking very much indeed.

"That is why I am doubly glad to have a wise advisor like yourself, Lizzy, to correct me when I am being overly scrupulous!"

"Quite. Remember, propriety has its season, and so do its breaches. It is unsuitable for a single woman to travel unchaperoned, for instance, but what if she is alone at home with her father and he takes seriously ill? Should she not take the fleetest mare from the stable and ride to fetch the doctor? If you can do someone a good turn by sacrificing a little detail of propriety, so long as you preserve righteousness, by all means, come to their aid! For what is right is not always fashionable."

They entered the house and divested themselves of their bonnets and gloves before moving towards the drawing room. Little did Anne suspect that within moments, the assurance which Elizabeth had given on the road, that of her being wanted at Longbourn, would be validated in a most unheralded manner. For, when she opened the door and advanced three steps into the room, a barking flash of white and brown charged directly at her. Its pounce nearly knocked the startled girl to the floor. A most unladylike shriek broke from her lips as she struggled to retain her balance.

Mr. Bennet, who was seated by the hearth reading a newspaper, looked up and seemed completely unconcerned by her trouble.

"Miss Edwards," he said tersely, "now that you are returned from your wild romp with my daughter, would you kindly control your dog? His antics have just about driven me to distraction. How is one to read about the ongoings in Parliament when your puppy is running circles around the coffee table?"

Anne fell back a step and gaped at the master of the house.

"I… am afraid that I misunderstood you, sir," she replied, faintly. "What was it you wanted?"

"I wished for the quiet which has, for the last hour, been completely obliterated by your pet, Miss Edwards!"

The girl shook her head, beginning to comprehend but not to believe.

"*My* pet, sir?"

"Yes, yours! Now, could you do something about that ball of fur?"

Anne's hands flew to her mouth. Her eyes filled with tears. As Mr. Bennet unfolded his newspaper and pretended to attend to it, she slowly allowed herself to sink to the floor. Once she was sitting upon the carpet, Anne cast a quick glance in the old gentleman's direction, fearing that he might have changed his mind during the preceding seconds, and then, taking a deep breath, called,

"Farley!"

The gregarious puppy obeyed the summons at once. Anne clasped him in her arms as he wiggled, barked, and licked away the tears of overwhelming joy which had begun to streak down her cheeks. A few moments passed in this happy manner, during which Elizabeth laughed openly and Mr. Bennet smiled furtively from behind the newspaper. Collecting herself after a minute or two, Anne looked at the Master of Longbourn and prepared to voice her thanks.

His attitude, again, fazed her. He had anticipated her, and in preparation for her attention on his person had assumed a deep frown and sullen stare at the columns of the publication. Miss Edwards' eyebrows knitted together at the incongruous sight. Why should the man look so vexed at her happiness? Had he not purposely initiated it? Surely, if he thought Farley so undesirable a presence, he need not have obtained the canine, particularly as nobody had requested the favor.

Putting together all that Elizabeth had told her and this newest occurrence, the intelligent girl at this moment came to comprehend the enigma that was Thomas Bennet. Like Elizabeth, he often verbally expressed opinions which he did not truly hold; it was in actions that he communicated love. Due to her talk with Elizabeth and her joy at having Farley, Anne's courage was high, and she ventured to express her thanks in a manner which was far more gratifying to the benefactor than conventional expressions of obligation would have been.

"I wholeheartedly apologize for my dog's behavior," Miss Edwards replied softly as she rose and hoisted the puppy from the floor. She gave Mr. Bennet an apologetic glance and promised, "In the future, I will be sure to keep him out of your way whenever you are reading, sir." She and Elizabeth then made their exit from the room, leaving behind a very eccentric, but pleased gentleman.

Chapter 17

Taking up a glass of lemonade from the refreshment table which had been set out on the lawn, Elizabeth surveyed the merriment around her. It was unusual for Longbourn to be so lively, but Mrs. Bennet had insisted upon hosting a farewell party for the militia, much to Lydia and Kitty's delight. And so, the garden was filled with neighbors and red coats. Jane and Mary conversed with a large group of young ladies under the shade of the oaks. Mrs. Bennet was engaged in some profound discussion with Colonel Forster and his wife, while her second youngest flirted with Lieutenant Chamberlayne a few feet away. But, wonder of wonders, Lydia was not engaged in a like manner. *She* was speaking quite passionately to an old man, instead of a young one. Edging a bit closer to this unlikely duo Elizabeth was favored with scraps of their exchange, and instantaneously recognized it to be a very close duplicate of the one which she had been treated to at breakfast every day for a week.

"But when Mrs. Forster first asked me, you said that I might go to Brighton!" Lydia wailed.

"That was before the bridge was washed out and before the militia decided to use one of the most dubious roads in England as an alternative route to their destination."

"Mrs. Forster is going. She is not afraid of highwaymen!"

"Mrs. Forster must accompany her husband, but I, who have the power of selection, have chosen not to offer you up as prey to robbers and convicts."

As if she had not heard, Lydia stamped her foot impatiently and tossed her head.

"Why?" she continued to whimper.

Mr. Bennet, who had been on the point of departing, turned back to her with an incredulous look.

"Why? Considering my last statement, I should have thought it obvious. But since you clearly lack the ability to surmise the reason for my cruelty, I shall have to be more explicit: even if you are the silliest girl in His Majesty's realm, you are still my daughter, and I do not relish the thought of you being brought home broken and bruised, like Anne, or worse. Thus, you will remain at Longbourn, crushed in spirit but at least whole in body. Now, run off and make the most of today, for you will not see another red coat all summer!"

The disappointed girl unleashed a most unladylike, frustrated sound, and indignantly stormed away. Unmoved, the old gentleman shrugged his shoulders and went off to seek the company of Sir William Lucas. Elizabeth, too, wandered away, and sipped her lemonade as she pondered the scene that she had just witnessed. Since Anne's arrival, Mr. Bennet had been more of a father to all five – or six - of them than ever. He spent a greater part of each day in the drawing room, took an interest in their whereabouts, and occasionally even scolded the two youngest for their more blatant breaches of propriety. Perhaps the presence of another rational mind at Longbourn was enough to attract him out of the recesses of the study, or Anne's condition was a somber, perpetual reminder of how easily a young daughter could be lost to her family. Either way, it was a welcome change.

Reminded of her protégé by these musings, Miss Bennet's eyes sought the child out. Anne sat upon a white bench located in the periphery of the garden, Farley draped over her feet. It was encouraging that she had needed no coaxing to attend the event, but had proceeded out-of-doors and commandeered her present seat of her own free will. Moreover, whenever a young woman or Sir William Lucas paused in front of her and offered a greeting, she shyly responded and managed to carry on a conversation for several minutes. Her timidity was still far from conquered, however, for Miss Edwards did not solicit these attentions; unless addressed by one of the aforementioned persons, her eyes steadfastly trained themselves upon the sketching pad she held and slowly traced upon. Noticing that there was no one near her friend at present, and wondering what subject had the artist so engrossed, Elizabeth started for that section of the garden.

"Good afternoon, milady," Elizabeth said when she arrived at her chosen destination.

"Good day, Miss Bennet," Anne retorted playfully, glancing up. This unexpected, sweet impertinence caused the older girl to burst into delighted peals of laughter as she seated herself upon the bench and slipped her arm through Miss Edwards'.

"Rather spirited today, are we not?" she asked with a smile. "Oh, wait and see, my dear - I shall make a mischievous creature of you yet! But in the meantime, show me what images you have been delineating with your pencil."

Once again demure, Anne slowly handed Elizabeth the pad, saying,

"They are not very good. I was simply sketching some of the views I had from this vantage point."

Carefully, Miss Bennet turned and studied the pages. On the first was a beautiful drawing of Longbourn House, as it appeared in the afternoon light. The second leaf bore the profile of Sir William. The third was graced by a faithful representation of Kitty and Lydia running across the lawn, as they had been doing not an hour before. The illustrations were so lifelike that Elizabeth was taken aback. Glancing at her companion, she exclaimed,

"You and your modesty, Anne! How dare you disparage your ability? I have rarely seen such fine work. Why, this likeness of Sir William looks as if it would speak to us, and I am almost ready to believe that in another moment, my sisters' running will cause them to fall off the edge of the page. Having never been able to draw myself, I am all admiration, dearest."

Miss Edwards was unconvinced. Casting down her eyes, she murmured,

"You flatter me, Lizzy, in the hope of raising my self-esteem. Is that not the case?"

Elizabeth's head turned sharply towards Anne.

"No, it is not. It would be prodigiously unfair of me to inflate your self-worth on false premises."

She handed back the drawings to Anne, and was formulating further reassurances when the sound of shod feet moving through soft grass caused her eyes to shift upwards and meet a most unwelcome sight.

Lydia, accompanied by Mr. Wickham, was making her way towards them. Elizabeth had not caught a single glimpse of the aforementioned gentleman for the duration of the afternoon, and thus had supposed him to be absent from the party, much to her relief. She certainly had no desire to see him or speak with him, now that she was aware that at least half of what came from his lips was the grossest falsehood. Refusing to exert herself on his behalf, she remained seated as the pair approached. Anne, her hands full of paper and a pencil, followed her example.

"Lizzy, I have been telling Mr. Wickham about Anne, and he wishes to become acquainted with her," Lydia said impatiently as soon as they were within earshot. The pouting, fifteen-year-old face betrayed that its proprietress was very put out by the fact that the young man desired to converse with anyone besides herself.

"Miss Bennet, it is wonderful to see you again," Mr. Wickham added, much more civilly. "As your delightful sister was saying, I would be forever grateful if you would do me the honor of introducing me to your seatmate, of whom I have already heard much."

Extremely displeased by the prospect of acquainting an innocent soul with the scoundrel before them, but seeing no alternative, Elizabeth curtly stated,

"Miss Anne Edwards; Mr. George Wickham." No gesture accompanied these words, and she kept her dark pupils cast down as she uttered them, as if fascinated by the methodical motion of Farley's tail. She thus missed the slightly anxious air which leapt into Mr. Wickham's pupils as he looked upon Anne and waited for her to speak.

"A pleasure, sir," the fair damsel dutifully murmured.

"A very great pleasure, indeed, madam," Mr. Wickham rejoined, more boldly. "I saw you sitting at Miss Bennet's side when I entered the garden, and immediately inquired as to who you were. Forgive me for intruding upon your quiet little niche here, but as an unworthy moth is drawn to a brilliant lamp, so was I drawn hither by your beauty." Taken aback, breathless, flustered, and blushing, Anne made no answer. Elizabeth likewise remained mute. Undaunted by the cold reception which his comments received, Mr. Wickham continued smoothly, "And so, Miss Edwards, I beg you to put up with this meddlesome soldier for just a few minutes, and allow him to bask in the sunshine which reflects off your golden locks."

Unable to think of any other civil reply, Miss Edwards finally managed a most embarrassed,

"Of course."

"I see that I have interrupted an earnest artist at work," Mr. Wickham said, leaning towards the pad on Anne's lap and attempting to look at its contents. "Might one ask to see the newest masterpiece in England?"

Miss Edwards looked as if she would like to dissuade him from thinking so highly of her work before he saw it and became grievous disappointed, but lacked the courage for it. She silently handed over the booklet with downcast eyes, averse to seeing the officer's disillusionment.

"Upon my word!" he burst out, after taking in a few of the pages. "What outstanding talent you have! I have seen many pictures drawn by young ladies, but none were as true to life as these."

"You see, Anne?" Elizabeth added, deciding that if the man was to keep intruding on their privacy, his remarks might as well be put to good use. "This should prove that I was earnest in my accolades."

The younger maiden lifted her head and, turning it fully to Elizabeth, said softly,

"All it proves is that you are both too kind."

Miss Bennet glanced up at the sky with a crooked smile in a demonstrative show of exasperation, and said nothing. Mr. Wickham, on the other hand, was far more forthcoming.

"Your reaction is rather typical of virtuosos, Miss Edwards. They always strive for greater feats than their audience demands. But perhaps your dissatisfaction is caused by the unworthiness of the original rather than of the copy. An artist ought to always draw the prettiest thing in sight. By the by, have you ever attempted a self-portrait?"

Anne took on the hue of beets and shook her head. Elizabeth, for her part, gave a barely audible huff. To think that a few months ago, she had been drawn in by such flat, elementary flirtations! Honestly, she had behaved worse than Lydia: listening to slander, helping spread rumors, and at almost one and twenty, she did not even have the excuse of youth to lean back upon.

"Well, Miss Edwards, what shall you draw next? I warn you, however, that if you take up my suggestion and sketch your own countenance, I will surely be begging for the finished product!"

Anne's tongue twitched many times within her mouth before it formed the barely coherent words,

"No…I…I was thinking of drawing Farley." She bit her lip, unsure of whether to continue, but seeing an interested and friendly face before her, she managed to add, "He has been rather uncooperative. I should like to capture him from the front, but every time I try to position him he immediately lies down anew."

Mr. Wickham seemed astonished at hearing three sentences come from her lips together, but recovered himself very promptly and, bending down, scooped the naughty puppy into his arms.

"Fear not, mademoiselle, reinforcements have arrived! I shall subdue this wild animal for your good pleasure!" Holding the foxhound so that Farley's two front paws rested on his forearm and the dog's head was erect a few inches above them, the self-appointed warrior proffered the reluctant subject to the artist. "Hold still, ye ferocious beast, for all your struggle shall be in vain; I shall not release thee until the damsel commands me to restore thy freedom!"

This dramatic proclamation caused Miss Edwards to break into a timid giggle. Thanking the young man in a scarcely audible tone, she repaid him more substantially for his trouble by turning to a clean sheet of paper and applying herself to copying Farley's furry head.

Mr. Wickham remained in front of the two seated ladies for above half-an-hour, keeping the canine in position and wearing out his welcome in both Lydia's and Elizabeth's minds. The former soon tired of standing next to a man who was more interested in complimenting Miss Edwards on her fine taste in animals than in addressing herself, and she turned on her heel with a huff and walked away to seek more agreeable companions. Elizabeth, on the other hand, found his very person loathsome, but found that all the more reason to stay where she was and keep watch over Anne. Since Mr. Wickham rarely included her in the conversation, Miss Bennet kept busy by observing the man before them. Mentally peeling away his good-humored expression, she noted in his face an aura which suggested that he had seen more gambling and bottles of gin than most men, and wondered that it had escaped her before.

Anne was putting the finishing touches on the sketched Farley's paws when Colonel Forster called to Wickham. Seeing the other red coats grouping together and getting ready to depart, the dog bearer quickly replaced his charge on the soft grass and took his leave of the young ladies, sparing many precious moments to dwell on how happy he was to become acquainted with Miss Edwards. Then he uttered a final goodbye to both, and, to Elizabeth's great relief, went away.

Chapter 18

When they prepared to retire that evening, Elizabeth noted that one part of Anne's nighttime toilette was greatly protracted. Although they were en route for bed and anticipated to meet no one but Sleep, Miss Edwards' locks nearly shimmered as a result of the hundreds of brushstrokes which had been pulled through them. Now that her arms had finally grown weary of their prior occupation, her fingers endlessly twirled one of the curls which was wont to fall over the fair forehead. In the meantime, her lips and eyes both smiled dreamily at the reflection in the dressing table's looking-glass.

Miss Bennet, for her part, observed these novel proceedings in silence for a long while, but at last began laughing.

"Anne, you have been peacocking in front of that mirror for above half-an-hour. If you remain there much longer, I shall be forced to declare you one of the vainest women of my acquaintance!"

The younger girl immediately pulled away from the pretty picture in the glass and flushed; in her romantic abstraction, she had forgotten that a vigilant roommate was present. Glancing at the clock, she hurriedly began to plait the golden tresses.

"Forgive me, I did not notice the lateness of the hour. It was inexcusable of me to keep you from your rest for so long. Pray allow me just one more minute to finish this braid, and I will extinguish the candles straightaway."

"The plethora of light and the lack of sleep trouble me much less than the fear of seeing you become pretentious, Anne! But in all earnestness, I am not overtired, and will gladly wait for your toilette to be completed at its usual pace."

Miss Edwards expressed her thanks, and slowed the deft movements of her fingers. They had made their way about halfway down the long locks when Anne pensively commented,

"Mr. Wickham is a very pleasant man, is he not?"

Elizabeth instantly looked up from the book she had just taken up to peruse.

"Mr. Wickham!" she cried, stunned. "Is *his* flattery the seed of these new airs?"

Anne's cheeks reddened, confirming the worst.

"Pray do not scold me, Lizzy. I know that his kind remarks this afternoon were completely unmerited, but I found them so very pleasant nonetheless. It is one thing to hear praise from your lips, and another entirely to hear it slipping from those of a handsome young man." The speaker gave her reflection in the mirror an uncharacteristically coy smile.

Closing and putting down the tome she held, Elizabeth walked directly to the dressing table and placed her hands upon Anne's shoulders.

"Again, you are too severe upon yourself, my dear. You are a lovely young lady, and you merit every happiness and compliment which comes your way. However -," Miss Bennet paused, and took a moment to frame the ensuing statement. "However, you must not take a mere flirtation so much to heart. There are men who…take pleasure in toying with our emotions."

"Oh, I know *that*, Lizzy!" the fair maiden protested. "I never dreamt Mr. Wickham to be serious. Was I forward during our encounter with him, that you say this?"

Elizabeth shook her head.

"No, not at all! I just…feared that his coquetry might have caused an unfounded infatuation."

Anne shook her head so forcefully that her braid nearly became undone.

"Oh, no, no, Lizzy!" she cried. "How poor your opinion of me must be! To suppose that a few kind words could make me fall in love with their elocutionist! No, my dearest friend, I have not gone mad yet. Mr. Wickham shall live in my memory as a pleasant gentleman who was generous enough to spare a few minutes of his time to put me at ease, and no more."

Elizabeth found Anne's vehement exclamation vastly comforting. Truth be told, she was still slightly irritated that Mr. Wickham had been the first man to pay attentions to Miss Edwards and would always live on in her recollections as such; she would have much preferred that the honor belong to a more respectable man. But it was done, and all things considered, it was not the pinnacle of tragedy. The officer in question would be far removed from Meryton on the morrow, and therefore, his dose of flattery would harm Anne no more than it had injured Lydia and Kitty. Let her reminisce and relive the scene in the garden for the next few days. Soon enough her mind would turn again to other matters, but until then, she might as well smile at her reflection a little more readily and feel herself beautiful and admired.

Having resolved to be unconcerned, Elizabeth returned to the bed and slipping between the covers, watched Anne blow out the candle. The sweet girl then joined her, and after exchanging a quiet 'Goodnight', both surrendered to sleep.

Chapter 19

The next morning, Anne and Elizabeth awoke to the sounds of Kitty and Lydia's lamentations. Wails of "I cannot believe that we shall never see a red coat again!" and "The summer shall be so dull, I am certain that I will die of boredom!" filled the entire house and reached the ears of the stable hands. With a sigh, Elizabeth rolled over to face her adopted sister and gave her a wry smile.

"This, I suppose, is the price we pay for the comfort of not seeing the two youngest Miss Bennets cast aside every shred of decorum during our visits to Meryton."

Anne laughed softly.

"Their inducements to be overly lively shall be greatly reduced when the last officer departs the village today, I cannot deny. Still, I pity them, the poor dears. After all the amusement the militia afforded, life *will* seem quite dull to them, for a spell."

"One which I can scarcely wait to pass," the chestnut-haired girl mercilessly said, sitting up and throwing back the covers. "I strongly prefer to wake of my own accord, or to the sound of birdsong, rather than to the chorus which we presently hear. But would you listen to me? Both of us have been roused by the same cacophony, yet you pity my sisters while I complain. Sometimes you and Jane make me feel positively wicked, angels that you are!"

Anne strongly protested this appraisal of their relative virtue as she likewise rose and dressed. Neither had convinced the other by the time that they were ready to descend the stairs, and therefore the subject was eventually dropped. They went down into the breakfast room to find the heartbroken Lydia and Kitty gorging themselves on blueberry scones, still whimpering about their wish to go to Brighton between bites. As expected, Mrs. Bennet was sympathizing, Jane soothing, and Mary sermonizing. Mr. Bennet greeted the two newcomers with an amused smile, and stealthy whispered to them his hope that the next time a young lady from Longbourn was left desolate, she would have the goodness to express her sorrow mutely. Elizabeth and Anne took their places, and had managed to consume about half of their respective breakfasts when Mrs. Hill entered the room.

"A letter has just come to you by express, Miss Lizzy," the housekeeper said, dropping a curtsy and handing Elizabeth the missive.

Instantly anxious, particularly when she recognized her Aunt Gardiner's hand on the envelope, Elizabeth wasted no time in breaking the seal and unfolding the letter. Everyone looked at her in silence; the mention of an express had managed to silence even Lydia and Kitty. After half a minute of rapid reading, she looked up at her family, relief and worry warring in her countenance.

"Mrs. Gardiner writes that all four of our little cousins have contracted scarlet fever. The apothecary has assured her that their illnesses are not serious, but she will need abundant nursing help, and asks that I come and tend my cousins as I have been previously exposed to the sickness. May I go, Papa?" she pleaded, turning to her father.

"Yes, so long as you give me your solemn word that you will not take scarlet fever a second time," the Master of Longbourn replied.

"Dear father, I promise," Elizabeth said seriously, as if it were completely in her power to safeguard her health. She remembered how much anxiety her first attack of the fever, at five years of age, had caused the poor man who presently sat on her right. Reaching out, she placed a comforting touch upon his hand. "I promise that I shall do everything to come back home as hale and hearty as ever."

The old gentleman sighed.

"Then you may go, my child. But I am afraid that I cannot offer you the carriage, for the horses are needed on the farm. I hate to send you all the way to London by post but -,"

"It is of no consequence," Elizabeth cut in, forestalling the remainder of his apology. "I should dislike taking the carriage as far as London in any case. It would be a completely unnecessary expense, particularly as the coach would have to return to Longbourn empty; for who knows how long my aunt will have need of me? And this will scarcely be the first time I have traveled by post. I beg you, sir, think no more of it, and pray excuse me." This said, she rose from the table and left the room with the intention of going upstairs and packing her things. But she had barely gained the hall when she heard the sound of the breakfast parlor's door unclosing once more, and realized that Miss Edwards was following her. Pausing, she turned and asked,

"What is it, Anne?"

"I am so sorry about your cousins, Lizzy," the young girl sorrowfully replied. Elizabeth smiled, and reached for her friend's hand.

"Thank you, my dear, but I do not think that you need to be doling out such mournful condolences just yet. From Aunt Gardiner's letter it appears that they are all suffering with rather mild cases. I suspect that her sole purpose in sending for me is to have someone to ensure that her little ones remain in bed during their convalescence, for it is difficult enough to deal with *one* bedridden, pouting child, let alone four!"

"It sounds like quite a task," Anne acknowledged. Biting her lip, she hesitantly added, "I know that I have not been invited, but…do you think that I could…come along to help? I do not know much about nursing…but I can try to amuse your cousins. And, I must own that…I do not know what I shall do without you if you are gone from Longbourn for several weeks."

"Oh Anne!" Elizabeth murmured comfortingly as she stroked the soft hand she held. "I should love to take you with me, and I am certain that my relations would have no objection to having you as well, but as we are unaware of whether you have ever had scarlet fever it would be a very foolish undertaking. As for amusing yourself in my absence, do whatever pleases you. I only ask that you and the others do not write any letters – my aunt's house will be under quarantine, and getting someone to bring us the necessities will be difficult enough. But Papa will certainly need someone to play chess and discuss his reading material with, and as I shall be unavailable I am afraid those tasks will fall onto you. And when he is engaged with other pursuits, do not hesitate to walk about as we so often do – there is no need for you to remain in the drawing room all day and bear my sisters' idiosyncrasies and my mother's…tender concern for us, as you call it," she concluded, laughing.

Miss Edwards shook her head.

"I have no qualms about spending more time with the other residents of Longbourn, Lizzy. It is just that…"

"You shall not have anyone to hold you by the hand and lead you down a path every time there is a fork in the road, a decision to be made. So much the better! This separation will benefit you greatly in that regard. Do you remember what I told you?"

Anne smiled and sighed exaggeratedly.

"When all things are equal on the scale of right and wrong, I should please myself."

"Exactly!" Elizabeth clapped her hands in an enthusiastic show of approval. "Now that that is settled, would you be so kind as to come help me prepare for my journey?"

"Of course!"

Within the span of two hours, Elizabeth was standing on the main street of Meryton awaiting the post-carriage, her trunks beside her. She was alone, for expediency had negated the possibility of an entourage, and forced her to bid farewell to Anne and her family at Longbourn House.

Miss Bennet was far from the only person leaving Hertfordshire that morning. Just past the buildings which she had known all her life, the fields were bursting with last minute preparations for another exodus. Horses neighed, men's boots trampled the ground, and officers called to their soldiers and to each other. These sounds reached the lady's ears, and it was with great satisfaction that she overheard the most important order of all:

"Forward, march!"

And, immediately, a thousand pairs of boots fell into step, heading towards Brighton.

Elizabeth heaved a sigh of relief as the post-carriage rolled up and her own trunks were loaded. How sweet it was, to know that this epoch of her family's history was closed! To be certain that all temptation of officers was expunged for the time being!

But there was still one officer in Meryton. *He* had no intention of leaving. Had Mrs. Gardiner's niece looked to her left as she boarded the coach, the brilliant red coat would have surely caught her eye. But, preoccupied as she was with safely ascending the step and securing a comfortable seat, the young man standing across the street went unnoticed by Miss Bennet. Nor did Elizabeth glance out the window as the carriage began its journey. If she had, she would have observed the unexpected sight of Mr. Wickham walking in the direction of Longbourn.

Chapter 20

Three weeks later:

Elizabeth energetically alighted from the coach, bid the driver farewell, and gratefully stretched her limbs. The carriage had been exceedingly cramped, but she did not regret the decision to return to Meryton via one of Mr. Gardiner's delivery coaches. Sitting among a shipment of fabric was a small price to pay for the happiness of returning home earlier than expected and being able to personally bear the good news that the quarantine had been lifted and that all the little Gardiners were well on their way to recovery.

Because her mode of transportation had left London before daybreak and travelled expeditiously, the morning was still very young as Elizabeth gaily ran towards home. She smiled mischievously, plotting to put her unannounced arrival to good use by slipping into the residence unnoticed, waiting surreptitiously in the library while Longbourn's occupants awoke and came downstairs, and then presenting herself nonchalantly at the breakfast table. What a nice surprise it would affect!

But it was not to be. Certain members of her family were far forwarder than expected; Mrs. Bennet's strident tones reached Elizabeth's ears before she even gained the house's drive. Intermingled with that lady's wailings were the rambunctious voices of her two youngest daughters.

Rising early was not among her mother's habits. Anxious to ascertain what sort of problem could have drawn the Mistress of Longbourn out of bed at such an hour, Elizabeth abandoned any idea of a memorable entry and hastened over the threshold. Pulling off her bonnet and gloves, she put them on a side table in the entry hall and hurried into the clamorous drawing room.

She did not have time to inquire as to the cause of the upset, or even to greet her mother and sisters. As soon as the creak of the door announced her presence, Mrs. Bennet cried out without the slightest preface or welcome:

"There she is! Well, Miss Lizzy, what have you to say now? First you refuse Mr. Collins, and now this! I told your father that Anne, as you call her, was no good! But did anyone listen to me? No! And now the sly, two-faced creature has stolen him away!"

Elizabeth was eyeing her mother with unrestrained bewilderment and mortification.

"Mama, I have not the slightest notion of what you are referring to - ,"

"Do you not?" her mother interrupted. "He liked *you* well enough once, but did you do anything to secure him? No, you just meandered about the garden aimlessly, talking of everything and nothing! And now Miss Edwards has ensnared him!"

Her second eldest took a deep breath and checked her exasperation before asking,

"Who is *he*, Mama?"

The Mistress of Longbourn was far too incensed to favor her daughter with a reply. She turned away in a huff. It was Kitty who did her elder sister the favor of translating.

"On Thursday, Mr. Wickham made Anne an offer of marriage, and she accepted him."

Elizabeth's eyes widened, her mouth unclosed, and she involuntarily took a step backwards as if the news had physically struck her. A moment passed in complete silence, before she somehow found the strength to cry out,

"*Our* Anne? Engaged to Mr. Wickham? Absolutely impossible!"

"Ah, *now* do you feel remorse over your lack of effort, Miss Lizzy? Why should it be impossible, especially for such a conniving imp?" Mrs. Bennet recommenced.

"In the first place, Mr. Wickham is in Brighton…"

Lydia merrily shook her head.

"No, he is not! He took a leave just as his regiment was about to leave Meryton. He has called here nearly every day since!"

"But…but...," Elizabeth sputtered. She had not felt so undignified, so ineloquent since she was five years old. "But…Mr. *Wickham*…?"

"Has been taken in by that tramp which Mr. Bennet brought here, and whom you insisted on keeping. *She* shall be taken care of, while the rest of us are starving on the roadsides."

Catching her breath, jolted by the constant insults directed at Anne, Elizabeth realized that recovering at least some of her equanimity was crucial, lest her discomposure be interpreted as regret. By sheer force of will, she cut through the chorus of questions playing in her mind in order to defend Miss Edwards.

"No one is going to hunger, Mama," she interjected. "Our inheritances may not be very large, but they will be enough to buy bread. Furthermore, Mama, I have no personal injuries to resent in regards to Anne and Mr. Wickham. I have not thought of him as a potential suitor for quite some time, I assure you. And nothing shall convince me that Anne acted in a cunning manner!"

That said, she quitted the room, unwilling to hear any more on the topic from her frustrated mother. As soon as she had done so, all her strength drained out of her, and she was forced to lean against the recently-closed drawing room door.

Anne and Mr. Wickham to wed? There must be some mistake!, every ounce of her reason cried. What on earth could Anne, of all women, offer Mr. Wickham, one of the most mercenary blackguards in England? What had possessed him to make an offer to her? Certainly not Miss Edwards' scheming; the girl was too shy to use arts and allurements to capture one of the opposite sex. And he had to know that Mr. Bennet could give her nothing.

Suddenly, a horrible, suffocating idea rose up and clutched Elizabeth. What if the engagement was not a voluntary one? What if the profligate had assumed Miss Edwards unprotected and friendless, acted accordingly, only to find otherwise? Poor Anne was innocent enough for anything. It was too easy to imagine the sequence of events: Mr. Wickham arriving at Longbourn for a visit, feeling rather sportive, happening upon Miss Edwards alone in the parlor, mystifying her with a few flirtatious expressions, drawing near to the confused countenance, and before Anne knew what he was about, commandeering her lips with his own. All it would take then to complete the unhappy match was someone to discover them in that attitude and to threaten to inform Colonel Forster of the lieutenant's conduct. Perhaps Mr. Bennet himself had taken issue with the visitor's indiscretion and demanded satisfaction.

The poor, dear child!, Elizabeth cried out silently to herself, convinced that she had come upon the only logical explanation for the current state of affairs. It mattered not that her mother had said nothing as to the origins of the match; as a general rule, Mrs. Bennet concerned herself much more with the ends of a courtship rather than its means. All that troubled the Mistress of Longbourn was that a guest would be married, while her daughters remained maids. In the meantime, little Anne Edwards was being forced into a most undesirable match under the threat of disgrace.

98

Gathering her skirts with both hands, up and out of the way of her feet, Elizabeth detached herself from the drawing room door and dashed up the staircase, her compassionate heart longing to offer whatever meager comfort it could to her unhappy friend.

Chapter 21

Foregoing the knock, as was their custom, the second eldest Miss Bennet pushed open the bedchamber's door, half-expecting to find Anne curled up in a pitiable ball on the bed, sobbing.

But the room contained no distressed, doleful maiden. It harbored no one but a reading, smiling Anne, who, upon Elizabeth's arrival cried out,

"Lizzy!" and flung the tome of poetry away so carelessly that it nearly flew into the fireplace. Then she dashed across the room to fling her arms around her returned roommate.

"What a start you gave me!" she exclaimed merrily, pecking Elizabeth's cheek. "For an instant I thought I was seeing visions! I was certain that you would write of your impending arrival, after the quarantine was lifted. Your cousins are alright, I trust?"

"They will be well," Elizabeth answered. She pulled away, and with astonishment took in Anne's blooming cheeks and bashfully fluttering eyelashes. Despite the juvenile ebullience of her greeting, there seemed to be much more woman than child in Miss Edwards' sparkling eyes. Completely confused, not knowing what to think, the older girl cautiously added, "And you? How are you?"

Anne's smile grew in breadth.

"I have never been happier," was the declaration, given in the midst of another excited, strong embrace. "Never!" Loosening her arms and thus allowing some air to flow into Elizabeth's lungs anew, she grasped her adopted sister's hands, laughing. "I have such cause for joy, Lizzy! Prepare yourself for some astonishing news, my friend." Giving her confidante the shortest of seconds to brace herself, the young woman blithely continued: "George - Mr. Wickham as you know him - *he* loves *me*. He *loves* me! We are engaged, and even though it has been several days, I still cannot believe it. That an educated man like him, who has lived in and seen so much of the world, should love me, is incredible. Well, what do you say? Are you not stunned?"

Elizabeth ineloquently returned,

"I...yes, I am stunned."

Then, taking yet another look at Anne's overjoyed face, she swallowed and asked the difficult question.

"How did the engagement come about?"

Anne giggled with delight, making it apparent that she had longed for the pleasure of hearing and answering that very question.

"He simply kept calling and calling, each and every day. For two weeks, I did not suspect that interest in me was the originator of his visits! Frankly, I did not allow myself to thoroughly consider the possibility that he might love me until he spoke! And when he did! Oh, Lizzy, I have never heard such dear, tender words. I thought that my heart would burst for joy!"

Elizabeth looked down at her hands and massaged her fingers together, vexed.

"Is that so?" she muttered.

"Lizzy?" Anne paused and truly noticed the other's subdued manner for the first time. "You are not pleased!" An instant of bewilderment came, and went, and was succeeded by an expression of horror. "Oh, no, Lizzy - had I known I would have never accepted his attentions! Your mother spoke of it often, but Jane gave me the most fervent reassurances that Mrs. Bennet was in error and that you were indifferent to him! I - ,"

"Anne," Elizabeth cut in, regarding her friend with an affable look, "Mama was mistaken, and Jane was correct. A very long time ago I was as charmed by Mr. Wickham's manners as any young lady in Hertfordshire, but I never felt anything akin to deep love for him. I would never consider marrying him now." *Even if he were the Prince Regent himself,* she added in thought.

Relief flooded Anne's grey eyes.

"Truly, Lizzy?"

"Yes, dearest."

"But then why did you look so grave just now when you heard of my engagement? Are you sorry to see me leave Longbourn?"

Elizabeth reached down, took the small hand in her own, and led Miss Edwards towards the edge of the bed in silence. Reaching it, she made them both sit, and turned to her friend.

"Undoubtedly, my heart writhes at the mere thought of losing you, Anne. But I have other, less selfish, concerns about the match. It is your future happiness which troubles me the most. You know Mr. Wickham so little, Anne. It is but three weeks since you first laid eyes on him! Surely, you cannot become well-acquainted during so brief a time, let alone determine whether the gentleman shall make a worthy companion for the next fifty years."

Anne heard this objection with the attitude of one who has already thought of and carefully considered it sometime previously, but who appreciates the concern of the objector nonetheless.

"Our courtship has been contained in a very short period; that I am powerless to deny. Its brevity troubled me too, but then I spoke to your father of it. He did not feel that my ability to make a wise decision had been impaired as a result. Mr. Bennet said that usually, when a young woman and man first meet, they spend very little time together - they might exchange a greeting in passing on the street, or share a dance at a ball. Thus, they need months before they are able to piece together enough scraps of conversation to form a complete picture of one another and decide whether they had better spend their lives together. But George has spent every day here, nearly from dawn to dusk, for three weeks. We have talked a great deal. If one should calculate the number of hours I have spent in his company, they would surely surpass similar tallies of other engaged couples. For instance, think of the courtship between your friend Charlotte and your cousin Mr. Collins. From what I recollect, they knew each other for barely a week before she accepted his proposals."

Elizabeth sat as a stone statue. Of all times for her father to start giving advice on matters of romance! Mr. Wickham's attentions and Anne's inquiries had clearly worked the wonders which no amount of her own prodding had managed to produce. If it had been the handiwork of any other man, she would have clapped her hands and laughed with joy. But no - the man who had excited Mr. Bennet's confidence was England's worst blackguard! Regrouping with effort, she pounced on the vulnerable end of the argument.

"I would scarcely call theirs a happy marriage, Anne," Elizabeth stated unequivocally, gazing at the young woman beside her. "Had Charlotte half your sensitivity she would be mad by now. She is fettered for life to a man who embarrasses himself and his wife at every turn, in any society."

Anne smiled mournfully with compassion for the poor young woman whom she had never met, but nevertheless rejoined,

"Thankfully, I shall not be so afflicted; George is liked wherever he goes."

Elizabeth took a deep breath before she reminded Miss Edwards:

"Not by all. Mr. Darcy is not particularly fond of him."

"Who?"

102

"Mr. Darcy. The man who Mr. Wickham claims denied him the living."

"What living?" Anne asked, her brow creasing in confusion.

Elizabeth gaped openly at her friend.

"Surely, your fiancé has told you the story of his great misfortune!"

Bewilderment and concern for Mr. Wickham immediately flooded Anne's countenance.

"Misfortune? What happened? I was unaware that my poor George suffered under adversities and tribulations!" she cried.

"You need not distress yourself," Elizabeth replied dryly. "The circumstance to which I alluded took place five years ago, and Mr. Wickham has certainly survived it. To make the complicated tale as succinct as possible: Mr. Wickham's godfather, a gentleman named Darcy, conditionally bequeathed a living to him in his will, hoping that he would make the church his profession. But your betrothed alleged that his patron's heir unjustly denied him the living. However, I have it on *very* good authority that sermon-making was not palatable to Mr. Wickham at the time, and that he declined the living. The younger Mr. Darcy, who had serious reasons to question Mr. Wickham's suitability for the position, compensated him accordingly."

There, she had said it. It pained her to break Anne's heart and newfound spirit, but it had to be done. She reached out to caress Miss Edwards' hand, hoping that the affectionate gesture would manage to ameliorate the crestfallen expression and tear-laden eyes which were sure to presently appear.

Alas, Elizabeth grievously underestimated the innocence of her with whom she was conversing! The statement which would have appeared as clear as fresh stream-water to anyone else proved to be as murky as the bottom of a pond to the fair maiden. Unaware of the sinful ways of the world and therefore unqualified to grasp the part that her fiancé played in them, Anne cried out,

"Why, of course!" She merrily leapt from the bed and pranced toward the window, playing with her blue ring. "Anyone with a grain of sense could recognize that George would be completely miserable as a clergyman! Imagine so lively a man conducting a funeral or holding a long, distressing vigil by a sickbed regularly. Mr. Darcy must have recognized the incongruity and saved poor George from himself. My darling was probably jesting when he said that he had been unjustly denied such a life."

"I assure you most solemnly that he was perfectly serious."

Anne shrugged, a little puzzled, but not alarmed.

"Then he must have had a difficult day with the regiment and experienced a few wistful moments reflecting on all the different ways life might have treated him."

"But he spent the first weeks of his stay in Meryton speaking of little else," Elizabeth urged.

"His first weeks?" her friend pounced eagerly. Miss Bennet nodded. "See, then, Lizzy? It was simply the product of a hard transition to military life."

Elizabeth fought against the instinct to bury her face in her hands. She had left behind a child barely capable of articulating her preference of strawberry jam over currant jelly, and come home to a young woman who, to a close friend at least, doggedly defended a man she had known but three weeks. Feeling unequal to further debate on Mr. Wickham's meaning, fearing that her insistence was doing more harm than good, Miss Bennet changed tactics. Giving the golden-haired beauty an earnest look, she said,

"You said that he loves you, and you seem very eager to marry him. But I have not yet heard you say that *you* love *him*. Do you?"

Miss Edwards blushed heartily at the forwardness which she was being asked to display, but immediately said,

"I had thought that my feelings would be quite apparent to you, of all people, Lizzy! But if you hanker for solemn assurances of attachment, I am able and willing to provide them. Lizzy," she gazed confidently into the brown eyes of her friend, "I love George Wickham. He is the gentlest man of my acquaintance. I love the way he can make me laugh. He is so wise; he knows me better than I know myself. Very early on in our courtship, George asked me what flowers I prefer. You know how much I like lilies of the valley, but as my wont, I was hesitant to admit my preference lest he think it unworthy. Seeing my restraint, George then proposed that he would guess my favorite bloom, and, what do you think? Of all the flowers that grow in England, his first guess was lily-of-the-valley! When I, in amazement, validated the selection, he declared that he had known that it had to be so, for the fragrance of the lilies strongly mirrored that of my own sweet air. And the very next day, he made it a point to bring me a small bouquet of the little white bells." Miss Edwards paused, smiled coyly, and then continued, "Furthermore, while I am aware that it is not the most important of considerations, I must confess that I find George Wickham terribly handsome. Yes, I love him, Lizzy."

Elizabeth rose. Plainly, there was nothing to be gained by questioning Anne further. She needed someone else's perspective on the matter, if she was to acquire fresh material with which to dissuade the misguided and smitten girl. Ending the nonproductive conversation, therefore, with a flat and neutral remark that it would be very peculiar indeed if a fiancée found her intended grotesque, Miss Bennet excused herself and stepped out into the hall.

Chapter 22

As soon as the door of her own bedchamber closed behind her, Elizabeth practically ran to Jane's. Giving the wood an impatient knock which awaited no answer, she burst into her sister's room.

Jane was still abed, albeit awake, relishing the warmth and softness of her pillows and coverlets before rising for the day. Startled by the relatively noisy intrusion, her beautiful head turned towards the door, and after a brief moment, her eyes widened with surprise and pleasure.

"Dearest Lizzy! How glad I am to see you! Are our cousins recovering satisfactorily?"

"Good morning, Jane. All our relations in London are in perfect health, or soon will be," Elizabeth said, leaning down to kiss the older girl's cheek by way of greeting. Wasting no time after the affectionate gesture, she allowed her heart to flood her face with its earnestness, and asked directly in quite a severe tone, "Jane, how has this happened?"

The elder Miss Bennet studied the serious, concerned countenance before her and, knowing Lizzy as well as she did, immediately comprehended what was uppermost in her sister's thoughts.

"I see you have heard of Anne's betrothal," she said, slowly sitting up in bed.

"Is it possible for anyone to set foot inside Longbourn and *not* hear of it?" Elizabeth asked, a tad bitterly, motioning towards the door which, while thick, was not perfectly adept at muffling every shriek that emanated from the drawing room downstairs. "I have spoken to Anne already, but of course, with her I had to phrase my queries tactfully. Jane, tell me the truth: was there any impropriety in the case?"

"No, of course not!" Miss Bennet cried out.

"Are you certain?"

"Utterly and completely. Lizzy, how could you even think such things of Anne?"

"I was thinking of Mr. Wickham," Elizabeth replied as she seated herself on the edge of the bed. "Jane, you are the only person in Hertfordshire besides myself who knows what he is. I cannot believe that the case is as plain as you and Anne would have it!"

The older girl paused, and reaching for her sister's hand, took and held it comfortingly.

"I see what you are feeling. I, too, was surprised…nay, shocked, and very uneasy at that. I confess that I attended very carefully to Mr. Wickham's conduct as a result. But Lizzy, after all these weeks, I did not witness a single incident or hear a syllable which betrayed him as anything less than honorable and gentleman-like. You may believe me. I knew he could not be as undeserving as we thought him. Indeed, if anything, Mr. Wickham has been too scrupulous in ministering to propriety."

"Has he? How?" Elizabeth inquired provocatively. As much as she loved Jane, she was terribly afraid that her sister's generous nature had softened her perception of Mr. Wickham's manners.

"For the first ten days or so, he never even attempted to speak to her alone. He paid long calls at Longbourn, sat in the parlor with Mama and everyone, and valiantly tried to draw Anne into the general conversation. It was then that I, and our entire family, began to notice his partiality. One fine morning, he finally suggested that they take a walk in the garden; with his next breath, however, he invited me and Kitty and Lydia to come along, which we did. This pattern was repeated daily. They hardly ever strayed from earshot, and never from sight. And it was only in the last week that he commenced offering her his arm during these outings!"

"Did you, Lydia and Kitty listen to the proposal?!"

"No, not exactly," Jane admitted. "But we watched it. He called on us Thursday morning, and asked Papa if he could have a private audience with Anne. When Papa agreed, Mr. Wickham took her to the garden directly and seated her at once upon the white bench which is plainly visible from the drawing room window. He placed himself a respectable distance from her and began to speak. Anne seemed vastly surprised, but pleased, and blushed very prettily during the professions. When the suitor finished, she timidly nodded her acceptance, allowing Mr. Wickham to take her hand and place a gentle kiss upon it. They spoke for a few minutes longer, before returning to the house."

Elizabeth quit the bed, marched to the window, and looked out for a brief second before turning around and demanding,

"They have never been alone together?"

"Never."

Elizabeth exhaled and let her shoulders relax slightly, relieved that at least nothing unsuitable had taken place. But much perplexity remained unquenched.

"And what says Papa to all this, Jane?" the younger sister asked after a thoughtful pause. Anne had strongly implied that Mr. Bennet approved of her unexpected fortune, but Elizabeth longed for a second opinion on every circumstance surrounding the shocking engagement.

"Mr. Wickham went to him as soon as he and Anne crossed Longbourn's threshold after their betrothal, and, as I understand it, asked for his consent. Papa did not officially give it, saying that while he earnestly wished he could take credit for begetting so sensible and quiet a daughter as Anne, he had not been so fortunate, and therefore she was not his to dispose of. After a protracted amount of wittiness, however, Papa condescended to inform Mr. Wickham that if Miss Edwards wished to leave Longbourn as his bride, its master had no objection. In addition, throughout the courtship Papa teased Anne mercilessly. We both know that that is our father's way of showing his approval, Lizzy."

"Yes it is," Elizabeth murmured, dissatisfied, as her eyes sought the floor pensively. "But Papa is ignorant of Wickham's history, and thus his judgment in this case might not be perfectly sound."

Jane quietly rose from the bed, threw a shawl over her shoulders and went to the lady who was leaning back against the windowpane. Gently placing a soft hand on her sister's shoulder, she inquired,

"What exactly do you fear, dearest?"

Elizabeth raised her eyes to Jane's and answered in a determined and uncompromising voice,

"I am petrified that he is planning to have a bit of sport with Anne, in one way or another."

"But Lizzy," Miss Bennet murmured in a comforting tone, "consider. Is it not ridiculous that Mr. Wickham would go through such a great deal of trouble for a bit of amusement? He has taken a leave from the regiment, openly courted Anne, and publicly published the engagement, even to having the banns read! Why would he do thus, if he only wished to toy with our friend's feelings? The eyes of all are upon him now, and should he behave wrongly his reputation will be tarnished throughout Hertfordshire, and news of it will certainly reach Colonel Forster. Simply put, the temptation is not adequate to the risk!"

"I must admit that it makes no sense, but neither does his wish to marry her. Mr. Wickham has made no secret of the fact that he means to wed for money and connections. Two months ago he was still pursuing Mary King for her inheritance of ten thousand pounds! And what can sweet, simple, penniless Anne offer a man who is a fortune hunter and profligate in every sense of the word? Mr. Wickham has flirted with a vast array of women, and possesses manners which would win him favor with more than one wealthy lady. What charms has Anne, other than youth and a sweet temper, which could cause such a man to throw away all his hopes of wealth and an easy life?"

"Lizzy!"

"Do not be so horrified, Jane. I do not wish to demean Anne or her accomplishments, but we must look at the case through Mr. Wickham's eyes, not our own."

Miss Bennet edged even closer to Elizabeth, and rebutted with a small smile,

"I see that you have not considered the idea that he might have reformed, dearest."

"You do the charitable side of my nature a grave injustice. The happy thought of such a miracle did cross my mind, but its unlikelihood soon drowned my fantasies," Elizabeth replied, fiddling with her necklace. "But then again - is it true that Mr. Wickham has ceased maligning Mr. Darcy? Anne claims to have no knowledge of their dispute, and yet, I could scarce believe that he has refrained from dwelling on his favorite topic for so long."

Jane's brows contracted, and she stared intently at the floor beneath their feet for a protracted moment, reviving every memory of the past few weeks. When they were all before her, she said slowly,

"I had not considered it before, but now that you have mentioned it Mr. Wickham has not so much as pronounced Mr. Darcy's name, much less spoken ill of him. There, you see? Men do change, Lizzy."

"Or perhaps lack the incentive to commit slander when their nemesis is long removed from the county." She paused for a moment, and then continued stubbornly, "His current silence absolves him of nothing; nor should *we* feign oblivion to his past defamation!"

Jane studied Elizabeth's face closely. Years of experience had taught her to interpret the glimmers which flickered in her sister's dark eyes, and it was with consternation that she translated them now. Desperate to forestall the fruits of Elizabeth's contrivance, Miss Bennet turned on her heel so that she faced the younger girl directly, and grasped both her hands with tremendous earnestness.

"My dear, dear Lizzy, I see what you are thinking, but I ask you - I beg you, have some faith in humanity! Do not dismantle Anne's happiness by telling her and Papa of things which are now history, and might have been born of a misunderstanding in the first place! You have not even seen Mr. Wickham and Anne together – when you do, I am certain that you will recognize the artlessness of his affection straightaway. How heartless it would be of us, to destroy their beautiful future simply because the bridegroom *might* have committed an indiscretion or two in the past! Wait and see for yourself before you form conclusions!"

It had been a long time since Elizabeth had seen Jane so impassioned, and it gave her pause. And, truth be told, despite her own seeming resolve, her heart wavered. The reports of Mr. Wickham's singular conduct tempted her to believe that the impossible *could* have happened. And, then again, Anne had been happy...so happy.

Gently pulling her hands out of Jane's, Elizabeth walked towards the door. With a palm firmly against the knob, she looked back and offered a partial surrender:

"Very well. Against my better judgment, I shall refrain from the most reasonable course until I have had an opportunity to observe them together. But I warn you that I will be very cynical, and will not look upon Mr. Wickham with your understanding eye. At his first lapse, Anne and Papa shall be informed of everything. Now, do not shake your head at me and tell me that it is too rigorous a trial. The man has made a fool of me once; Heaven forbid that the same happen to Anne as I stand idly by! This one chance I give him is already one more than he deserves." And she was gone before Jane's soothing voice could talk her into any more injudicious ideas.

What mattered now was to see Mr. Wickham and Anne – together.

Chapter 23

Her opportunity to observe Mr. Wickham's new habits came without delay. As Elizabeth exited Jane's bedchamber, she beheld Anne hurrying towards it anxiously.

"Lizzy," the fair girl said, "I was just going to look for you. Mary is not dressed yet, and George has already arrived and is in the drawing room as we speak! If…if it is not too much trouble, and if you are not too tired from your journey, could you come down with me and sit with us, just until Jane or Mary can come and relieve you?"

Casting a scrutinizing glance at every line of Miss Edwards' countenance, Elizabeth slowly replied,

"I would willingly come for much longer than that. But why have you need of me? Are you afraid to be with him alone?"

Anne laughed merrily at what she supposed was one of her friend's witty speeches.

"Of course not, you silly Lizzy o' mine! How can a fiancée fear her intended? It is far more on George's account that I ask your presence, than for my own purposes. He says that we should always have a chaperone about until we are married, as my stainless reputation is more precious to him than polished gold, and that he cannot bear to think that he should be the means by which the slightest spot is put on it!"

"What grand speeches," Elizabeth muttered. "Then again, he always did have a flair for them."

"Yes, indeed he does, and I love to hear them," Anne replied gaily. "You are coming, Lizzy?"

Elizabeth nodded, and they went downstairs directly.

Mr. Wickham was indeed in the drawing room, and he leapt to his feet when the two ladies entered, greeting Anne before she had passed the threshold. Crossing the gap which separated him from Miss Edwards, he took her hand and pressed a tender kiss upon it. Then, leading her by the same, he guided her to the sofa while remarking how particularly resplendent she appeared that morning. Anne was carefully deposited on the couch, and only then did Mr. Wickham turn towards Elizabeth.

"Good morning, Miss Bennet." That was all. No mention of her absence, or return, or a polite inquiry into the health of the

Gardiners. Furthermore, the officer scarcely waited for Elizabeth's tongue to finish forming the words 'Good day' before his back was to her again and he was seating himself on the sofa.

Even as she silently rebuked the officer's rudeness, Elizabeth's conscience could not help remembering that in days of old, in reference to matches which she approved of, she used to say that general incivility was the very essence of love.

Shaking off the troublesome recollection, Miss Bennet determined to be as ornery a chaperone as possible, and moved to sit in an armchair directly across from the sofa; Mr. Wickham would soon suspect that there were people at Longbourn who were unwilling to accept his surprising conquest!

She was halfway there when another thought occurred to her: if he and Anne were left to themselves, with an attendant who appeared to be inattentive, the lieutenant might be more readily tempted to some action or words which would expose his true intentions and allow her to disband the imprudent match once and for all. Therefore, she veered right, and went to a seat at the opposite end of the rather long room. To complete the illusion, she picked up a book from a nearby table and pretended to be engrossed by the love story within its pages, while in reality both her ears and eyes were surreptitiously trained on the unlikely one unfolding before her.

The engaged couple first spoke of the weather, of Mr. Wickham's walk to Longbourn, and other trivial matters. Despite this, the young man managed to find at least two or three openings in the uninteresting conversation to inform Miss Edwards how much he had missed her since their parting at ten o' clock the previous evening and how the singing of the larks paled in comparison to the voice of his beloved.

When they finally stilled their tongues and allowed a comfortable pause to hang between them, the lieutenant leaned towards Anne, reducing the distance between them from three feet to two-and-a-half.

"I have a little something for you," Mr. Wickham said, in a lower tone, but one still within Elizabeth's range of hearing. Reaching into his pocket, he brought out a small silver ring.

"Mr. Wickham!" Anne exclaimed softly. "It is absolutely covetable!"

The officer smiled.

"As if it were in your celestial nature to covet anything! I am glad that you like my meager purchase, however, for I was going to ask you to wear it on your finger until our wedding day, when I can finally replace it with a more enduring symbol of my fidelity and love."

Miss Edwards nodded shyly. Mr. Wickham reached over and, taking up her right hand, made as if he were going to slip the ring upon it, when he suddenly paused.

Anne, who had been looking at his shining eyes rather than at their hands, glanced down, hoping to discover his impediment.

She found it in the form of the blue ring which had been on her hand since before she could remember. Mr. Wickham's ring had been forced to pause because the spot which ought to have been its own was occupied.

"Oh!" she exclaimed laughingly. She tried to free her right hand as she offered the officer her left one. "Perhaps this would be a better arrangement, sir."

The young man only clasped her right fingers tighter.

"I would much rather have my ring on the hand which I kissed during my proposal, milady, if it is all the same to you."

The girl flushed at his sentimentality, and said,

"Well, I suppose that it can be done." She twisted the indigo adornment off her extremity, and proffered the latter to her fiancé anew. He took it, and with a smile of extreme triumph, slipped on the simpler silver ring. Next, the alabaster fingers were raised to his lips, before finally being released.

When Anne finished blushing, she began to slip the blue ring onto her left hand, when another hand caught and arrested hers again.

"Pray do not do that," Mr. Wickham murmured in the deepest of tones.

Anne's, and Elizabeth's, attention was captured.

"Might...might I ask why?" Miss Edwards inquired hesitantly.

The lieutenant leaned forward, and continuing in his deep voice, answered,

"When a man loves a woman very much, he naturally becomes jealous. Be it rational or no, I want your hands reserved for my ring, and mine alone." Drawing back slightly from a very hued lady, Mr. Wickham added in a lighter tone, "Besides, unless I am much mistaken, you have not the slightest idea where that ring came from. Marriage is all about starting anew."

Miss Edwards looked down at the piece of jewelry she held and hesitated for a second longer than anyone expected her to. Elizabeth thought that, for once, she might actually protest and go against his advice.

Soon enough, however, a smile covered Miss Edwards' face and she said,

"You are perfectly right." She looked across the room. "Lizzy, should you like to have the blue ring? I believe that you admired it once or twice?"

Elizabeth glanced up from her book.

"I think it a very nice piece of jewelry," she said slowly. "But I do not think that I could feel conscientious wearing it. In my mind, it is such a part of you, that if I were to don it, I am certain I would feel like a species of thief. And anyhow," here Miss Bennet glanced sharply at Mr. Wickham, "why should you try to part with it permanently? I am sure that your fiancé can have no objection to your stowing it away as a keepsake, even if he would rather have a monopoly over your hands."

Mr. Wickham nodded and interposed without delay,

"Of course, my dear Miss Edwards. If it pleases you to retain the ring, by all means do so. I only want your happiness; and if joy for you means wearing both rings concurrently, then put them on and forgive me for my selfish request!"

But the young woman's mind was already made up, and she shook her head.

"No, you are correct. It is a pretty ring, but it does cause me distress. It is nonsensical to drag mementos from an unremembered time into our married life. Take it off my hands, I beg you, Lizzy. Or, if you are not inclined to have it, I will see that Lydia gets it. I know that she will accept it."

"On second thought," Elizabeth replied, yielding at the unsavory idea of the spoiled Lydia having yet another of her whims granted, "if you are resolved, then I will take it."

Without the slightest hesitation, Miss Edwards rose and walked across the room with the doffed ornament. Far more tentatively, the older girl plucked it from her fingers. Anne had barely regained her comfortable perch on the sofa when Mr. Wickham's voice again broke the silence.

"Miss Edwards, would you play something for me? Let us check and see that my little gift does not impair the ability of your fingers to move with ease across the keys."

"I should be glad to," the maiden replied promptly.

They rose and approached the pianoforte. The lieutenant pulled out the bench for his lady, all gentlemanliness. The fair maid sat and asked what he would like to hear. Since the soldier had no ready answer, he commenced paging through the music books which lay on the instrument, looking for a suitable piece. As she waited for his selection, Anne turned her attention to the keys and began to play the little improvisation which she had stumbled upon that day when she first tried the pianoforte. Elizabeth listened eagerly, for she had been longing to hear the tune again; in Miss Bennet's opinion, nothing in their music books could hold a candle to the simple melody. But unfortunately, this time she was not to hear it to completion, for Miss Edwards terminated it in the middle with an uncharacteristic, frustrated blow to ten keys at once.

"Anne?!" Elizabeth exclaimed. "What in the world are you doing?"

"I am sure that I do not know," the younger girl returned bitterly, as both her friend and fiancé regarded her with dismay. Drawing a deep breath, she collected herself within the span of seconds, and continued in a much more contrite voice, "I am sorry for misusing the instrument, Lizzy. I have no excuse for my action. All I know is that I have rearranged this piece a dozen times in the last few weeks, and I like each version less than the original. And yet, I feel compelled to keep practicing, until it is perfect."

"It already is perfect, Anne," Miss Bennet insisted.

As expected, Miss Edwards shook her head. Elizabeth sighed, and prepared to do battle over her protégé's outlandish tastes, when Mr. Wickham diplomatically placed another piece of music in front of the younger lady.

"I wholeheartedly wish that, in time, the quaint piece will be altered to suit both the artist and the audience. In the meanwhile, what do we say about playing this lovely concerto, Miss Edwards?"

Anne, of course, agreed and immediately began to play the music set before her. Mr. Wickham stood beside the instrument and fastened his eyes upon his intended's face. Elizabeth, for her part, sat quietly in the comfortable armchair and looked at the couple and the sparkling object in her palm by turns.

She decided to put the latter in her jewelry box for safekeeping at her earliest convenience. But what to do with the other scene before her eyes was far more important. Mr. Wickham was changed; he was gentler and attentive. Miss Bennet longed for a private audience with him, to ask questions which could not be uttered in Anne's presence, but suspected that it would take weeks to pry the two lovers away from each other's company.

Chapter 24

Miraculously, a marvelous chance to interrogate Mr. George Wickham presented itself the very next day.

The morning dawned grey and cloudy, the sort of morning which causes people to pull the covers over their heads and sleep longer than their wont. Miss Edwards fell prey to the warm coverlets like the rest of the ladies at Longbourn, and thus was wholly unprepared for the announcement that Mr. Wickham had been spotted a quarter of a mile from the front door, and was fast approaching.

Closet doors were thrown open; a gown was flung on; a sash was seized. Boots were laced in an absolute fury. In short, everything which could be done to ensure that a certain gentleman would be received at the soonest possible moment was done. In culmination, Anne veritably ran out of the room, and began to move in a similar manner down the stairs.

That was when the mishap occurred. Kitty, too, had been in a hurry: she had wagered with her youngest sister that Lydia would not be able to complete her toilette and overtake Kitty before the latter reached the breakfast table. A few farthings functioning as an added incentive, Kitty was determined to win the challenge. She rushed out into the hall a quarter of a second after Miss Edwards, and began following her at an extremely close proximity. The two girls reached the stairs at almost the same time, with Anne in the lead. They were halfway down when Miss Edwards, ever mindful of others, came to her senses and realized that Kitty wished to pass her. As a prelude to stepping aside, Anne slowed. Naturally, her trailing gown also decelerated behind her. The Bennet girl, however, realized not the intent of the leader in time, and continued at her mad pace. This resulted in Kitty's foot miscalculating when Anne's gown would vacate the step before it, and shooting forward a fraction of a second too soon, it pinned the muslin to the wooden planks.

Anne lurched forward. The only thing which saved her from flying through the air was a loose grip on the banister; this was instantly tightened, and it kept Miss Edwards secured to the staircase. The young woman behind her had not taken any such precautions before the crash, but desperately sought them as she commenced tumbling forward. One hand caught the railing, the other Anne's shoulder, and her lips uttered a shriek loud enough to summon Elizabeth from her bedchamber.

After a few seconds of wild grasping and struggling, Kitty too managed to regain equilibrium. The two ladies then parted, caught their breaths, and took inventory of the damage. Bones and flesh of both were sound, but Anne's hem was torn.

"Are you alright?" Elizabeth's concerned voice called from above.

"Yes," Miss Catherine Bennet answered, preparing to go down without any further ado.

"Kitty, what should one say if they collide with another and tear the hem of their dress?" Mr. Bennet's voice sternly asked. The Master of Longbourn had been passing through the hall, and, resultantly, had witnessed the entire fiasco.

Kitty, still unaccustomed to her father's new ways, stared at him for a moment before turning to Miss Edwards contritely.

"I am sorry, Anne. It was wrong of me to give you so close a chase. Particularly on the stairs."

Miss Edwards, as usual, was all understanding and forgiveness.

"That is quite alright, Kitty. You ought to apologize to Jane, rather than to myself; this is her gown, after all. I also was remiss in hurrying down so."

"Anne," Elizabeth said, leaning over the banister at the top of the stairs, "I believe that there is one more of Jane's gowns in our closet, and you had better go and put it on. I will intercept Mr. Wickham in the garden and inform him of the reason for the delay."

The younger woman thanked her profusely as she dashed up the stairs to comply. When she reached the top, however, Elizabeth arrested her progress by laying a firm but gentle hand on her elbow. Casting a glance downward to ascertain that the other family members had dispersed and would not hear, Miss Bennet met her friend's eye and lowered her voice as she spoke.

"My dear, while it is only natural that our feet hasten to be where our heart is, it is unladylike to gallop to a man's side at such a pace. It makes you appear forward. Any devoted suitor will gladly wait the additional half-minute it takes you to descend the stairs in a more genteel fashion."

Abashed, Anne glanced down at the floorboards.

"You are entirely correct, Lizzy. I promise that my affection for George will be expressed in a more dignified manner henceforth."

Contented, Elizabeth smiled and allowed Miss Edwards to go without further admonishment on the subject. It was painful to have to ask for more decorous behavior from Anne, particularly as that personage had finally managed to acquire a spring in her step and a sparkle in her eyes which had been sorely lacking during her first few weeks at Longbourn. But there was no help for it. Mr. Wickham scarcely needed more encouragement than he was already getting, and Miss Bennet was determined that if anything should go awry, no one would be able to pin the blame on Anne's conduct.

With the future bride safely ensconced upstairs, Elizabeth made straight for the part of the garden which Mr. Wickham was then traversing.

"Good day, sir," she said warmly as she approached.

"Good day, Miss Bennet. Where is Miss Edwards?" Mr. Wickham inquired, glancing behind Elizabeth a tad anxiously.

Any other suitor of Anne's would have received a straightforward answer from Elizabeth to this simple question. Despite her penchant for teasing, it was not her way to seriously toy with the feelings of others. But in this case, she doubted the lover and his pledged affections so much and found them in such great need of examination that she assumed a somber countenance and allowed herself to say, in a very low tone,

"I am afraid that there has been an accident."

The strength of his reaction both astonished and gratified her. Mr. Wickham positively started, regarded her with a terrified gaze, and gasped out:

"What happened?"

"She and Kitty were walking - nay, *running*, down the staircase together, when the latter bumped into Anne and caused her to lose her balance."

"Mercy! Is…is she seriously injured?"

"Kitty escaped unscathed. Anne was not so fortunate - her gown caught, and the hemline tore."

Mr. Wickham, who had not ceased staring at Elizabeth, trying to anticipate her for the entirety of the aforementioned dialogue, incredulously inquired at this juncture,

"Is that all? She did not fall down the stairs, or hit her dear head again, or anything of the sort?"

Elizabeth smiled and shook her own head mirthfully.

"As soon as she dons another gown, she will be as well as ever, and will come out. I promised to keep you company until then."

The lieutenant exhaled sharply, relieved. After taking several deep breaths, as if to calm himself, he straightened his shoulders and rewarded Elizabeth with a resentful gaze.

"I must say that you have surprised and disappointed me, Miss Bennet. I did not think that you were the sort of woman who would sport with a man's feelings for your own amusement," he retorted, turning and resuming his walk. Elizabeth, left behind, stared at the distancing figure in amazement.

During that short exchange, he demonstrated more feeling than I have ever seen him display before! He seemed truly concerned for Anne...but then again, he once seemed to be the most wronged gentleman of my acquaintance. Now, it is of utmost importance that I wheedle my way into his good graces once again quickly, and pretend to be his friend as of yore - for it has always been in front of a sympathetic listener that charming falsehoods glide from his lips.

This resolution formed, Elizabeth broke into a gentle trot and soon caught up with the offended lieutenant. Siding up to the red coat, she boldly began carrying it out.

"It was unkind of me to tease you so, I do not deny it," she admitted by way of apology. "But surely your surprise at my insensitive jest cannot compare with the shock which I suffered upon arriving at Longbourn yesterday."

Mr. Wickham appeared to accept the meager olive-branch, for he slowed his pace somewhat and, turning towards her, replied in a more composed and amiable tone,

"Yes, I foresaw that you would be. It has been a very short courtship, and one which has overthrown many of my former expectations of matrimony. But what are dowries and connections to beauty and affability? When I look at Miss Edwards, I see how foolish all my bygone seeking was! Your friend is as pure and lovely as the fragrant roses which grace Longbourn's garden in the springtime, Miss Bennet. "

Elizabeth was all agreement.

"Yes, she is indeed. I confess that I am quite jealous of the officer who shall deprive us of her company. I can understand your haste to take her away, however. It is but rarely that one meets a woman like Anne Edwards."

"And finds her unmarried, still!"

"Certainly." Elizabeth glanced in the direction of the house, and ascertaining that the object of their conversation was nowhere yet in sight, commented casually, "I suppose that ample confidences are exchanged between the two of you?"

"Of course. How else can matters stand between a pair of young, enamored persons?"

"Assuredly I know of no alternative modes of courtship, sir. I have always been under the impression that betrothed couples speak openly to each other about any topic which suits their fancy. Which is why I was surprised yesterday when I realized that Anne has never before heard of Mr. Darcy, or been informed of his great cruelty towards you!"

Mr. Wickham stopped short, and wheeled around to face the lady who was accompanying him.

"Did you enlighten her?" he asked, desperate to appear nonchalant.

"Not as to all the minute particulars," Elizabeth replied lightly. "But I must mention that your fiancée's eyes widened at the notion that you might have been a clergyman! Should you ever wish to incite her wonder, I suggest that you expand upon the topic."

The officer lowered his gaze to the green grass and fiddled uneasily with his walking cane. After a protracted moment, he replied in a bland tone,

"I do not think that I will." Raising his eyes to Elizabeth's, he continued, "And I would be much obliged, madam, if you would refrain from mentioning the affair to my betrothed again."

"But why?" the young woman inquired, both eye and tongue heralding perplexity. "Doubtlessly, it cannot be considered a matter of confidence, for all of Hertfordshire is aware of the nature of your falling out with Mr. Darcy. *You* have never been reluctant to speak of it before. Is it not unseemly that the woman whom you are to marry is in ignorance of what the rest of the county knows?"

Mr. Wickham considered for what seemed like half-an-hour before finally responding to Miss Bennet's wise question.

"Perhaps." At first it seemed that he would offer no other rejoinder, but when he sensed his companion was highly dissatisfied, the lieutenant slowly recommenced strolling and haltingly, apologetically, began expounding upon his astonishing request.

"I have been reflecting on my past behavior a great deal of late, Miss Bennet. And I find that I am not quite satisfied with the manner in which I acted towards Darcy. If a gentleman considers himself aggrieved by another, he ought to settle score with that man directly, and, in the spirit of charity, refrain from publishing his grievances in public. I am afraid that bitterness sunk its claws into my heart deeper than I realized, and my tongue pronounced a few things which ought to have remained unsaid."

Elizabeth fervently wished that they were a bit closer to one of the garden benches, for she suddenly found it nearly impossible to support herself as her stunned heart silently cried:

He has admitted fault! He has acknowledged the impropriety of his slander! He has done what I considered impossible! Is not regret the first step of reform? Can it be that for once my sweet, naïve Jane is correct in appraising a sinner so leniently? But halt, Elizabeth Bennet! Ere you pronounce a blessing upon his conquest of your dearest friend, probe a bit further…see how deep the vein of repentance runs!

Regaining her strength and archness, Jane's skeptical sister baited George Wickham with a sympathetic smile and the following impassioned speech:

"You are gallantry itself, Mr. Wickham!" she cried with feeling. "But I must contest your present stance. You are too severe upon yourself! If Mr. Darcy was truly as bad as you said, it was only right for you to warn the neighborhood of his character, lest someone else be taken in by him. It is very possible that you protected at least one of our acquaintances from much grief by warning everyone to keep their distance from your former friend. In the same bent, think of Anne! Imagine that she comes to visit us in Hertfordshire one day, leaving you behind to your duties, and finds that Mr. Bingley has reinstated himself at Netherfield with his friends. She should be forewarned against beginning an acquaintance with Mr. Darcy! If you dislike the trouble of opening so painful a subject, I will be glad to tell her all that you told me."

The young man shook his head resolutely.

"Miss Bennet, I thank you for your concern, but I entreat you - pray let the matter rest!"

Elizabeth remunerated this statement with a raise of her eyebrows.

"Again, the natural question is *why* we should allow so reprehensible a man to continue unchecked in society."

With a sigh that spoke of subtle exasperation, Mr. Wickham struck the ground with his cane. Several profound breaths and looks around the lawn later, he tersely answered,

"As I have already said, I was bitter, Miss Bennet. Frustrated men are often intemperate. Darcy might have had his reasons for denying me the inheritance, but in my indignation, I refused to explore the case from his point of view."

"I think that you have been spending too much time in the company of Anne and Jane!" Elizabeth cried out straightaway, hiding her true admiration for this declaration in hopes of obtaining a further confession. "What justifications can there possibly be for forcing the playmate of one's youth into poverty and blatantly disregarding the dying wishes of one's own father?"

The former slanderer looked her full in the face. Truth in all his looks, embarrassment in his eye, pleading in his accent, Mr. Wickham murmured,

"Miss Bennet, I do believe that you are less innocent in the ways of the world than my dear Miss Edwards, which is why I will dare to say the following to you. However, I must beg that what I am about to disclose go no further than yourself." Without waiting for a confirmation from Elizabeth, he quickly continued, as if he wished to say the horrid words and be done with them. "Darcy…he is the sort of man who holds, and who has always held, very strict standards regarding behavior. Even in Cambridge, where there were no parents to pester him about keeping the Lord's Day, he could unfailingly be found in a pew on Sunday morning. Likewise, he never took more than a small amount of liquor. On the other hand, I, like most young English fellows, was not so steady. I enjoyed port or brandy a tad too often, and engaged in the other casual errors of youth. Darcy may have witnessed my conduct after I had taken a drop overmuch of wine, and in his gravity, concluded that I was unfit for a position of responsibility. I hope that your own opinion of me will not be injured by this admission, for I assure you, madam, that you would be hard-pressed to find five men amongst your acquaintance who did not employ themselves similarly during their schooling." He concluded his remarks with an apprehensive look, clearly frightened of her reaction.

Elizabeth painstakingly scrutinized her companion's face for the entire duration of his speech, and carefully considered his words. Despite herself, she found her opposition to the hastily-formed union between Mr. Wickham and Anne abating. Miss Bennet was not yet completely resigned to the match, but she was no longer impatient to see it undone.

During the entirety of their acquaintance, not once had the man before her ever owned up to the possession of a single fault, but now he had incriminated himself in drunkenness, other irreligious habits, and, most importantly, exhibited shame. While Elizabeth Bennet was cynical, she was also gracious. Perhaps Mr. Wickham had sunk into vices temporarily, but, as he had declared, she knew that it was unfortunately not an uncommon occurrence among the gentlemen of the day. At least, he now seemed to be regretting them profoundly.

"I can see why you are anxious to ascertain that no word of this will reach Anne," the lady commented quietly. "For she would indeed be greatly grieved. Like every woman, Anne deserves an unstained man, and it is a pity that so few exist nowadays. But there are many like you among us, and we can never be certain which gentleman fully kept the Lord's ordinances and which occasionally slipped into the devil's snares, for most are far less forthcoming about their faults than yourself. I do hope, however, that you are truly repentant, and are not planning to resume your former pursuits before or after the wedding."

"May I be stricken down instantly if I ever so much as think of it!" the officer fervently exclaimed. "No, Miss Bennet, I have forsworn such ways forever. Fear not, your friend shall be safe with me - I will guard my virtuous lady with every fiber of my being!"

This proclamation was somewhat reassuring to Elizabeth, but before she could either commend him or quiz him further, the soft swish of muslin against grass was heard. Looking up, both beheld a smiling Miss Edwards strolling towards them. Elizabeth was the first to speak.

"See here, Anne!" she cried. "I have kept my promise, and I now return Mr. Wickham to your protection. Inspect him, question him, and reassure yourself that he did not sustain any damage during the time he was under my care."

The approaching girl laughed.

"I knew I could entrust my betrothed to you, Lizzy! You have my sincere thanks." Bestowing one last smile upon her friend, her

124

attention was then promptly absorbed by another. Mr. Wickham took the hand she extended, bestowed a tender kiss upon it, and placed it on his arm.

"Will you join me in taking a turn about the garden, Miss Edwards?" he asked in a low, sentimental tone.

"Of course, sir," Anne answered warmly.

The gentleman glanced over his shoulder at Elizabeth.

"Will you do us the honor of accompanying us, Miss Bennet?" he inquired.

"It would be my pleasure," that lady confirmed.

And they started off. As she trailed the lovesick couple, Elizabeth relived her conversation with Mr. Wickham several times, and found it vastly comforting. He had not mentioned that his profligacy had continued for some time after Cambridge, nor disclosed the fact that he had been compensated for the living by Mr. Darcy and had squandered the money; but then again, one could not expect a man who was trying to reestablish his character to unabashedly announce every single violation he had incurred in the past. Only one consideration still pestered her: while the lieutenant had acknowledged the impropriety of his prior conduct and stated his intention to live wholesomely hereafter, she wondered if the commitment would outlast a serious temptation. Despite these lingering doubts, however, Elizabeth sought Jane out after the threesome returned to the house and confided that Mr. Wickham was rising every hour in her esteem.

Chapter 25

That night, hundreds of miles north of Hertfordshire, in a pitch-black drawing room, sat the broken man who had once been the perceptive, imperious Fitzwilliam Darcy. It concerned him not that he could see nothing of the chamber, or that it was well past three o'clock in the morning, a time when all prudent folk ought to be abed. Such trivialities had long ceased to interest the Master of Pemberley.

From his limp posture in the armchair one might be tempted to deduce that the room's sole occupant was asleep, or on the verge of being so. Nothing could be further from the truth. His mind was crowded with thoughts. Very occasionally they sorrowfully relived some old sweet memory of Georgiana, or remembered a treasured moment spent in Elizabeth's company. But almost always, his ideas fixated on other things: self-deprecation, guilt, and despair.

The number of pence in the Darcy fortune was miniscule when compared to the number of times their owner had reviewed his life, and probed into every recess of his character. Guided by Miss Elizabeth Bennet's words at Hunsford, the Master of Pemberley had come to decide that despite all the flattery thrown by society and servants, he was one of the meanest, cruelest, most selfish souls ever to inhabit the earth. This somber conclusion had been born from careful consideration of the possible origins of Elizabeth's refusal and Georgiana's demise. What were the odds that two such tragedies had randomly occurred together, and effectively demolished every bit of joy and hope from his world? The chances were very, very small. No, in all probability, these events had been purposely orchestrated in order to force Fitzwilliam Darcy to the admission that he was far from the stellar, honorable gentleman his conceited head had conceived. A Higher Power had finally lost patience with the man who routinely looked down upon his poorer brethren and slighted those lower in society, forgetting that his own happy situation in life was but an accident of birth.

How differently now did everything about the past year seem! It had been one long attempt by the Almighty to call him back from the sin of the fallen angels, pride. But instead of realizing it, he, Fitzwilliam Darcy, had sunk deeper into the mire.

Warnings had dotted his path from the minute his horse's hoofs dug into Hertfordshire soil. All the inhabitants of that county freely aired their disgust at his pride, but instead of reconsidering his loftiness he likened them to savages. Mrs. Bennet, during that long-ago Netherfield visit, implied quite openly that she deemed him lacking in gentlemanlike behavior; he had silently berated the woman's stupidity. A few months later, in Kent, he witnessed Lady Catherine disparaging her lowly visitors at every turn. He had sometimes felt ashamed at his aunt's ill-breeding, but had utterly failed to realize that her attitudes perfectly mirrored his own. Why had he not listened with a more liberal mind, and seen himself as he truly was?

The tender love for sweet, dear Elizabeth Bennet which the Lord mysteriously seeded in his heart had been the greatest call to conversion of all. It had been planted to show him where true treasure lay: not in aristocratic roots or in a pocketbook, but in a kind heart and joyful smiles. So strong an affection would have elicited gallantry from any decent man! But in his vanity, he had considered the woman he loved as an evil which had to be grudgingly borne so as to avert the greater scourge of a life without her. And he had told Elizabeth so, frankly and openly!

What alternative could the Almighty have then, but to allow him to hear the truth from the lips of her whom he loved, in blazing phrases which were sure to burn into Fitzwilliam Darcy's memory? And lest he use Georgiana as a distraction from reflection upon his shortcomings, she too, had been taken from his grasp. Or maybe she had been snatched away before he could corrupt her innocent sweetness with his pride?

Anyhow, the two events seared deep! There no longer existed seconds in which Darcy was ignorant of his character. Every moment, he was painfully aware that he was a despicable human being whose actions had righteously drawn down the hatred of the world's most wonderful woman, and had cost his sister her life.

Sleep was the worst nemesis. In it, Georgiana died a thousand terrible deaths, and Elizabeth accused him of everything from conceit to singlehandedly being the reason that Rome fell. He dreaded repose, and resisted it as much as humanely possible. Every forty or fifty hours, however, Darcy's body betrayed him, his knees buckled, and he fell back upon a sofa or into a chair, dozing against his will. Invariably, he woke in a cold sweat, gasping for air. Shaken, he would rise and pace back and forth, trying to forget a nightmarish vision of famished sharks snapping at the drowning Georgiana or of Elizabeth lashing out: 'You could not have made me the offer of your hand in any possible way that would have tempted me to accept it!'

During the early days of his hopelessness, Darcy's hand would occasionally reach for brandy, but unfailingly, would withdraw before it even touched the decanter. How could he even think of adding drunkenness to his already outstanding bill of sins? Besides, Georgiana's death and Elizabeth's enmity had been his doing, and he ought to feel them.

Even Pemberley failed to save him. Had its steward possessed a dishonest bone in his body, he could have easily made away with most of the estate without rousing its master's attention, or concern. But Mr. Aldridge fully respected the trust which had been laid at his feet and kept things going as smoothly as could be expected. Darcy, to his credit, occasionally reflected on the matter of Pemberley's management, but invariably arrived at the same conclusion: the less he had to do with it, the better. A brute such as he had no right to decide about the livelihood of others. Any compliments which the tenants had ever offered about his generosity were certainly just the usual flattery, perhaps elicited by fear.

The servants at first left him alone to his grief, as they filled the corridors and rooms of Pemberley with the sound of theirs. But days passed, and then weeks, and slowly, they realized that time was not working its healing powers upon the wound in Mr. Darcy's heart. The sobs which bemoaned Miss Georgiana were eventually replaced by silent tears which mourned the master's alteration.

Very, very gradually, they realized what had to be done, and heartbroken, they began to do it. Mrs. Reynolds learned that sending an unsolicited tray into the master's study was insufficient to tempt him to take nourishment. It was necessary to go up to him and press a piece of food into one of his hands and a cup of tea into the other, and then sit oneself down upon a nearby chair and refuse to budge until the sustenance was consumed. This she did without fail thrice every day, and never closed the door behind her afterwards without wiping a tear from each cheek. Fredrick likewise discovered that Mr. Darcy had lost all interest in how thick his beard was or how long his hair grew. Unable, however, to come to terms with his once impeccable employer looking perpetually unkempt, he devised a pitiable routine. Every morning, he would seek out Mr. Darcy, coax the haunted man upstairs into a bath, shave him, and dress him in a fresh outfit before allowing him to roam back down towards the empty drawing rooms.

Through it all, the Master of Pemberley showed no resentment at being treated like a child or invalid by his own servants; his muddled mind scarcely recognized what was happening about him.

A few rays of light infiltrated the formerly dark room. Focusing on the windows opposite his chair, Darcy realized that another unwelcome dawn was at hand.

Dragging his numb form up from the armchair, Darcy stumbled across the room and drew the curtain, shutting out the light. Then, in the gloomy chamber, he fell to his knees, clasped his hands together, and silently made the only two petitions which he dared, or cared, to make.

He prayed that Elizabeth Bennet would be happy. Then he asked for death.

Chapter 26

"Well, I suppose that from now on we shall all be in an uproar preparing for Anne's wedding? I daresay that I will not emerge from my bookroom whatsoever for the next few weeks!" Mr. Bennet said jovially at the breakfast table one morning, about a fortnight after Elizabeth's return from London.

It was an unusual day. Mr. Wickham, having business in Meryton, had not arrived before the morning meal. Thus, only the Bennets and Anne sat around the breakfast table.

"A wedding? Whatever for?" Mrs. Bennet retorted from the opposite end of the table. "It is just Anne marrying Mr. Wickham. Surely there is no occasion to put ourselves through such an inconvenience! Besides, I am certain that Anne does not wish for a fuss to be made. You do not want a *wedding*, do you, Anne? All those people staring at you, observing your every move, when you are too shy to even bear Lady Lucas's attention during a morning visit!"

Miss Edwards cast her eyes down upon the tablecloth to hide the faint glimmer of disappointment which had sprung into them. Her timidity had not prevented her from dreaming of processing down a decorated church aisle, to the melody of the organ, in the midst of her dear acquaintances and friends. But ever conscious that she was a mere guest at Longbourn, she dutifully replied,

"Oh, no, Mrs. Bennet. I would not wish to ever inconvenience you. I will be more than glad to quietly walk to the church with George on my wedding day…with perhaps the company of Lizzy and Jane, if you can spare them, madam." She added the last quite guiltily, ashamed of being unable to silence this one remaining shard of hope.

Mrs. Bennet was about to assure Anne that she was quite welcome to Lizzy and Jane for a morning, so long as that was all she desired on her wedding day, when Mr. Bennet, who had been watching Miss Edwards' face with an uncharacteristic expression of concern, exclaimed jovially,

"Anne, you are truly a sensible girl! I was so frightened that you would insist on a grand ceremony, and we all know the trouble that would cause! I am an old man, and adjust very poorly to new circumstances. It would be exceedingly painful to suddenly be bereft of all my daughters and be left alone with an empty house, with only my dear wife to fill the silence! Although I am sure that she would faithfully do her utmost to dispel the quiet."

"Bereft of our daughters! What nonsense do you speak of, Mr. Bennet?" the Mistress of Longbourn cried out. "Anne is the only one who shall be leaving the house. Our girls will remain here, just the same as they have always done."

"Yes, but if Miss Edwards was to have an elegant nuptial, we could not retain them long at Longbourn, Mrs. Bennet. There is nothing like a romantic wedding ceremony to create a furor of engagements!"

His wife started abruptly, and her eyes widened with interest.

"My dear Mr. Bennet," she replied in a much more subdued and attentive tone, "what exactly is your meaning?"

Mr. Bennet leaned forward ever so slightly in his chair and put down his teacup in preparation for an unusually long and plain speech.

"Let us assume for a moment that Anne should have a large wedding. Naturally, we would have to invite all her acquaintances from Hertfordshire out of politeness. You must know, my dear, that many of the landholding families hereabouts have unmarried sons. And then Mr. Wickham would undoubtedly bring along many of the officers to act as groomsmen, assuming that they could be spared from their duties. The church would simply be filled with young eligible bachelors. Now, Anne, tell me: if the size of your wedding warranted bridesmaids, who would you ask to fulfill that important role? My daughters, perhaps?" At Miss Edwards' nod, the gentleman took a deep breath and continued, looking directly at his wife.

"And so, Mrs. Bennet, at this hypothetical function our beautiful daughters would be required to proceed slowly down the aisle, attired in their best finery, in the midst of a sea of young men. Then, for the duration of the actual ceremony, they would be stationed in the front of the church, where they could be readily observed by the same gentlemen as biblical passages extolling the virtues of love and matrimony were read aloud. If all that were not enough to turn the youngsters' heads, I am sure that a wedding breakfast or ball would complete the mischief. I would not be at all surprised if I had five suitors paying a visit to my library by the end of the evening. Next, we would have the chore of planning a quintuple wedding, and then one fine evening, perhaps one or two months after Anne's departure, you and I would find ourselves all alone in this dining room. But,

131

thankfully, Anne has retained her wits, and will not hear of having a grand affair made over her nuptials. So our girls shall remain at our hearth, instead of scampering all about the country with their husbands. Is that not something to be grateful for, my dear?"

By the time her husband finished, Mrs. Bennet's eyes were as big as saucers and her lips were trembling with agitation. The elderly gentleman, seeing that his explanation had had the desired effect, sat back with a carefully formulated careless air and braced himself for the ensuing eruption. He had not long to wait; his wife only took time to fill her lungs with air before shrieking,

"You call Anne's refusal to oblige us and have a large wedding retaining her senses? *I* certainly do not! It will make us the laughingstock of the neighborhood. Anne," here Mrs. Bennet turned upon that young lady indignantly, "you will *not* disgrace Longbourn by strolling to the church with Mr. Wickham on your wedding day! I do not want to hear another word out of you. I am the closest thing you have to a mother, and I insist upon your having a wedding. Now, you will go into town with the girls today, and you will all order new dresses. Kitty, do make sure that you pick out some nice blue fabric, as the officers have not seen you in that color yet. And Jane, do not even dream of buying anything in green, for it casts quite a shadow upon your complexion…"

Mr. Bennet threw his linen napkin down on the table, feigning annoyance. He abruptly rose, and while his wife was instructing Lydia in the merits of a particular type of lace, he stationed himself behind Anne's chair and put his hands on both her shoulders.

"Well, Anne? I suppose you shall have to endure a nice wedding after all," he said. One wink from him, a knowing smile from Elizabeth, and a grateful glance from Anne, and he was gone to his bookroom, barricading himself from the commotion as best he could.

Chapter 27

On the way to Meryton, Elizabeth remembered that she had recently seen a book of very pretty dress patterns in the bookshop, and decided to try to rediscover it. The other young ladies left her to this errand, as they hurried along to the dress shop to fulfill the much more exciting task of choosing fabrics. Walking into the bookstore and greeting the proprietor, Elizabeth inquired about the tome she sought. Mr. Russell was unable to understand exactly which piece of his merchandise Miss Bennet spoke of, but he invited her to browse the shelves and see if she could locate it again.

As a result, Elizabeth wandered about the store, reading titles and occasionally pulling down a volume to examine its contents more thoroughly. There were few places where she felt more content than in a bookshop, surrounded by new, penned adventures which had yet to be vicariously lived. Everything, from the colors of the covers to the subtle scent of ink, rejoiced her heart. One of the volumes caught her eye, and removing it from the shelf, Miss Bennet leaned against a bookshelf and became engrossed. Bookshelves surrounded her, and as she was standing towards the back of the store, she was out of sight. Elizabeth remained there for a good fifteen minutes before being roused by the sound of the front door opening and closing. Curious to see who the new patron was, she peered through a small space in between bookshelves, from where one could observe without being seen.

Miss Bennet felt as if ice cold water had been poured upon her.

The girl who had entered the shop was the very opposite of extraordinary. She was a very pale, freckled redhead who was dressed in a pale blue outfit and carried a parasol against the sun. There was nothing in her features or bearing which made the new customer particularly striking. But Elizabeth knew that those were not her only advantages. This maiden was Mary King, proprietress of a fortune of ten thousand pounds, and had been Mr. Wickham's favorite young lady but a few months before.

What was she doing in Meryton? She was supposed to be miles away, permanently!

A great battle commenced in Elizabeth's heart. She could not decide whether to embrace the girl's coming or to mourn it. On one hand, Mary King's unexpected presence in town would be a better test of Mr. Wickham's honor than any exam which she could devise. On the other, Miss Bennet had begun to hope that the lieutenant had truly changed for the better; it would be painful to have those hopes dashed, not to mention how Anne would suffer at being cast aside for another.

Miss King, unconscious of being observed from behind, walked up to Mr. Russell and asked for a particular book. He retired to the backroom to procure it. Mary stayed by the counter, twirling her parasol.

Just then, the front door opened, and a man entered.

Judging from her countenance, his appearance pleased Miss King very much. She immediately called out,

"How do you do, Mr. Wickham?!"

The officer started, but then bowed and said,

"I thought you in Liverpool, madam."

"Compared to Meryton, Liverpool was exceedingly dull, so I convinced my uncle to let me return. But alas! As soon as I set foot in Hertfordshire yesterday I was informed that the militia was removed to Brighton for the summer. At least they left one friend behind for me!" As she uttered the last, Miss King tapped her fan flirtatiously against Mr. Wickham's forearm, much to Elizabeth's ire and grief.

Her heart was already breaking for Anne. Surely, it was all over; Mary King was a hundred – no - ten thousand times more in line with Mr. Wickham's idea of a good wife than Miss Edwards, and she was practically throwing herself at him.

"The Gouldings asked me to the small dinner they are giving tomorrow. Will you be present?"

Mr. Wickham cleared his throat and shook his head.

"No, Miss King. The Gouldings were kind enough to extend their invitation to me, but I declined. Having arrived just yesterday, you have not heard, I presume, that most of my time nowadays is engaged in a very agreeable manner?"

"Oh?"

"A few weeks ago, my hand had the privilege of being accepted in marriage by the finest young lady in England. She, and plans for our wedding, are now my constant companions and sole vocation."

Mary King's eyes widened in shock. She wondered if she could have misheard. Eight weeks ago, the man before her had been courting her so earnestly that the entire neighborhood had presumed them practically engaged, and now, when she had abandoned her family and friends in Liverpool to return to him, she was informed of his engagement to another? It was nearly beyond belief.

On the other side of the bookcase, Elizabeth Bennet's eyes also dilated, but for an entirely different reason. While she was mindful of the pain which Mr. Wickham had just caused Miss King, she was far more stunned at his constancy to Anne. How quickly he halted Mary's flirtations by proclaiming himself betrothed to a girl of no consequence! How well he was conquering the temptation of faithlessness!

An embarrassed blush tinting her cheeks, the rejected maiden managed to politely state,

"I wish you every happiness in the world, sir." She would have dearly loved to conclude her remarks there, but curiosity overrode pride, and she found herself asking, "Might I inquire who the fortunate lady is?"

"Miss Anne Edwards."

Miss King reciprocated this confidence with a confused gaze.

"I am afraid that I do not recall her."

"She arrived in the county after your departure, madam, and is staying with her friends at Longbourn. The first time I laid eyes on her, I knew that she was the one I wished to wed. Until that moment, I had never given credence to the idea that one could lose their heart at first sight."

"How romantic," Mary murmured. "If you will excuse me, sir, I will be on my way. I have a pressing appointment which I cannot miss."

The lieutenant lifted his hat respectfully.

"Of course, madam, good day."

"Good day," the lady mumbled under her breath, and left the store expeditiously, forgetting Mr. Russell and the book which she had sent him to fetch.

Mr. Wickham spared the retreating damsel no further glances, and leaning against the counter, awaited the shopkeeper's return. A minute passed before that man reappeared, a thick tome in hand. He looked around the shop thoroughly before addressing the officer:

"Pardon me, Mr. Wickham, have you seen Miss King?"

"Yes, she left a moment ago," the officer answered nonchalantly. "She mentioned that she had an important engagement."

"Well, then, I suppose that I may put this aside for a moment," Mr. Russell jovially replied. "And I assume that you are here to take possession of the book which you ordered for Miss Edwards?"

"Your presumption is correct, sir," the red-clad man replied, pulling out a few coins from his pocket. "I would be much obliged if you could wrap it for me in a bit of paper."

"Gladly." As Mr. Russell busied himself with folding the thick, crinkling brown paper around the piece of literature, a few chuckles escaped his lips. "Pardon the impertinence, sir, but I must remark that you are fortunate indeed in your choice of wife. Most men embroiled in a courtship would have to exert themselves and their pocketbooks a great deal more than yourself in order to please the lady of their choice. Even though I understand that my friend on the opposite side of the street sold you a silver ring of late, for most women that would be merely a beginning."

Mr. Wickham laughed and nodded.

"Indeed it would. But most men do not have the good fortune of engaging the affections of a creature who is as disinterested as she is tender."

"True, true," the shopkeeper agreed, passing over the parcel. Its recipient tipped his hat once again, and with a cheerful goodbye, departed. Elizabeth, leaving her post, slipped up to the window and watched him walk away, in the direction opposite that in which Miss King had gone.

Chapter 28

Elizabeth exited the bookshop and walked down the street as if treading air instead of dusty road. For the first time since she had returned from London, her heart was as light as a feather. She scarcely restrained herself from skipping down the street in a most juvenile manner. Over and over, she replayed the scene in the bookstore in her mind, rejoicing.

Reaching the dress shop, she pushed the door open and went in. As expected, Lydia and Kitty were frantically digging through a mound of fabrics, squealing their opinions about the various colors and arguing about who would look best in a particular shade. Jane and Mary were also employed in seeking out materials, albeit in a much more civil and subdued manner. But surprisingly, the bride-to-be was nowhere near the fabrics. Approaching her sisters, Elizabeth inquired sternly,

"Where is Anne? It is for her sake that we are here; not for yours."

Kitty sacrificed a moment to wave at a corner of the shop before plunging into the muslins anew.

Looking in the indicated direction, Elizabeth saw Miss Edwards standing at a small table, poring over large pieces of paper which were spread out over it. Walking over, she put her hand on her friend's back and joined her in studying the curiosities. Finding them to be sheets of music, she softly asked,

"I take it we are choosing hymns for the ceremony?"

Anne lifted her head hastily and then shook it.

"No, not exactly," she admitted. "I was just looking through the sheet music which Mr. Dawson has in the store, hoping to find an inspiration for the betterment of that tune which keeps vexing me." She sighed. "But so far, I have been unsuccessful."

Elizabeth sighed in turn, her exhale containing far more notes of frustration than Miss Edwards'.

"Anne, for the thousandth time, that song of yours needs as much improvement as Jane needs charity. And even if it did, you have more important things to think of at present. Do you want to face Papa and Mama this afternoon without a thread of fabric for your wedding dress? Come, leave the music be, and join my sisters."

Miss Edwards obediently turned from the table, but asserted,

"I already have chosen the material for my dress, Lizzy."

"Oh? Well, let us see the cloth!"

The fair maiden walked to a bolt of white fabric, and taking one of its edges, handed it to Elizabeth. Miss Bennet took it, and rubbed it between her thumb and index finger. Glancing up at Anne, she inquired in a peculiar voice,

"And what will be used for the veil?"

"This," her friend said, indicating a certain material stationed very close to the coarse white muslin which Elizabeth held.

The dark-haired lady took one look at the indicated bolt, dropped the corner of the muslin, and deciding to dispense with equivocalness, demanded,

"Did the low price affect your choice?"

Anne blushed at being found out so readily, but as she possessed too much integrity to fib outright and too much humility to risk being dissuaded from purchasing the cheap material, she attempted to circumvent the question.

"Truly, Lizzy, they are most suitable. The fabrics might seem different when fashioned into the wedding garments."

Unfortunately for her, the second eldest Miss Bennet was too well-acquainted with the process of dressmaking to believe such rigmarole.

"The best seamstress in England would not be able to make a proper veil out of that cotton-like stuff, nor a decent dress out of that pathetic muslin. At this rate, you shall look worse on your wedding day than you do every day in Jane's hand-me-downs! Even my father, as disinterested as he is in gowns and lace, would be horrified to see any woman of his house attired so, to say nothing of what your fiancé will think when he sees you processing down the aisle!"

"But - ," Anne began anew.

"No protests," Elizabeth interrupted flatly. Seizing Anne's hand, she marched her over to the part of the store where silks and satins were displayed. Without inquiring as to the bride's preferences, she grasped a roll of snow-colored satin, and called to Mr. Dawson,

"Cut seven yards of this, if you please!"

The shopkeeper came forward nodding eagerly.

"Yes, Miss Bennet."

"Lizzy!" Anne cried out, aghast. "Lizzy, I implore you –,"

Ignoring Miss Edwards, Elizabeth continued,

"And kindly give me two yards of that white lace for the veil."

Mr. Dawson, who had never expected the Bennets' visit to his store to be so profitable, was quick to comply. As he removed the bolts from their places and spread them out on the counter in order to commence scissoring, Anne made one last desperate attempt to halt the purchase.

"Dearest, pray listen to me. I-,"

But she was stalled immediately by Elizabeth's demand,

"Do you find fault with the material?"

"Oh, no, of course not."

"Are you unhappy with the color?"

"No, I think it very pretty. But -,"

The intense interrogation ended with an unsympathetic conclusion of:

"Then your only qualm concerns the price."

Outwitted, Anne finally conceded,

"Yes!" Lowering her voice, she continued, "Lizzy, in your goodness you forget that I am nothing more than a beggar plucked from the side of the road. I cannot in good conscience charge Mr. Bennet's account with such enormous expenses! It is already difficult enough for your family to not exceed its income!"

"And in your self-abasement, you forget that everyone considers you part of the family," Elizabeth retorted. "But fear not, I never had any intention of burdening my father with this transaction's bill." She pulled out a few folded notes, and handed them over to Mr. Dawson. This action was unsurprisingly noticed by Lydia; the youngest Miss Bennet was exceedingly adept at noticing the contents of her sisters' pockets. And she did not scruple to call out,

"Lizzy, where in the world did you get all that? Did Papa give it to you? It is unfair of him, considering that he refused me a pound just last week when I wanted to buy that charming bonnet the milliner had in the window!"

"Calm yourself, Lydia," her sister replied. "I practice something called economy, and have saved this out of my own pocket money, a little at a time."

"Which is one more reason why you should not spend it on me!" Miss Edwards stubbornly muttered behind her.

Elizabeth turned and took the mortified girl tenderly by the arms.

"I want to," she said sincerely. "It is not every day that one of my best friends gets married, let alone to a man of whom I approve. If you cannot be reconciled to this purchase in any other way, consider it my wedding present to you and Mr. Wickham."

Miss Edwards was astute enough to know that further argument was futile. She surrendered, and quietly rejoiced, but not only about the prospect of being properly attired at the altar. Elizabeth's restraint about the upcoming marriage had been a bitter drop in her cup of joy, and if it had not been for multiple endorsements coming in from other quarters, she would have broken the engagement. Hearing the wholehearted approbation was like having a barrelful of balm poured out upon her soul.

Chapter 29

Mr. Bennet was proven correct. Longbourn passed the next few weeks in absolute upheaval. Meetings with the Reverend, fittings, and debates about the wedding breakfast's menu dominated life. A great number of wedding tour destinations were suggested. And one afternoon, the entire family found themselves in the drawing room, putting together an extensive guest list. They invited every member of the four and twenty families with whom they regularly dined. Many names from Meryton found their way onto the inclusive list. Far more officers than could possibly be spared from their duties in Brighton were invited. Then, once her own memory was exhausted, the wedding planner turned upon the bridegroom.

"Would you like to invite anyone particular, Mr. Wickham?" Mrs. Bennet asked, eagerly poised to hear the names of a few dozen unmarried gentlemen. But she was to be disappointed.

"I think not, madam. I do believe that you are already in the process of asking everyone who is dear to me."

Mrs. Bennet was quite displeased.

"But are there not one or two people who we might have overlooked, sir?" she nearly pleaded. "I am certain that you must have some friends who we know nothing of! We should be glad to make their acquaintance."

The fiancé looked as if he were about to reaffirm his previous assurances when his eye fell upon Anne, who was sitting next to Jane and gaily reviewing the lists before them. Something about the sight of her caused him to pause and spread a slow, peculiar smile over his lips. Still gazing at Miss Edwards, he answered the Mistress of Longbourn,

"Now that you have mentioned it, Mrs. Bennet, there is one person whom I should like to witness our nuptials: an old friend who, I am sure, will derive much delight from the occasion."

"I knew it!" the woman cried triumphantly. "Simply dictate their name and address, and we will see to the rest."

"With all due respect, madam, I would much rather communicate the joyous tidings and extend the invitation myself. It has been far too long since I corresponded with my friend, and I would welcome the opportunity."

Mrs. Bennet assented; as long as the personage was invited, she scarcely cared if Mr. Wickham dispatched a cavalry regiment to bear the summons. The remainder of the evening passed uneventfully. With the coming of night, Anne's betrothed left them to return to his temporary dwelling, and to write his letter.

When the center of her universe departed from Longbourn, Miss Edwards neatly stacked the papers she had been working on, stretched her stiff limbs and going to the tea service, poured a cup of strong brew. This refreshment she brought back to the sofa, and settling in close to her favorite adopted sister, commenced sipping it slowly.

"I never dreamed that planning a wedding could be so laborious," she murmured.

"Neither did I," Elizabeth mused. "But then again, I never thought to see a guest list numbering a hundred or more, at least not for the wedding of anyone amongst my acquaintance. Consequently, I believe that your nuptials will be the talk of the neighborhood for decades to come. Will you be able to bear it, my shy little friend?"

"I believe I can!" Anne returned, brimming with joy. "Normally I would say no, but I am so happy that anything is possible. Although," she continued in a graver tone, beginning to tinker with her engagement ring, "I was somewhat surprised by George's restraint in contributing to the guest list. I expected that someone with a manner as warm and charming as his would have too many friends to count. Perhaps he does, but simply does not wish to exacerbate the financial and logistical burdens of the festivities. What do you think?"

At this inquiry, the words of her former suitor ran unbidden through Elizabeth's mind:

'*Mr. Wickham is blessed with such happy manners as may ensure his making friends—whether he may be equally capable of retaining them, is less certain.*'

It had been a very fitting description of the man Mr. Darcy had known, but, thankfully, the characterization no longer applied to Mr. Wickham. Anxious to spare Anne pain, as always, Elizabeth decided to answer with a vague, softened truth.

"I think…," Miss Bennet started, eyeing the maddening, monotonous turns of the silver ring. These, again, nearly drove her to distraction, and she was compelled to break off and begin anew. "I

142

think that it is possible that a man who is relatively young, and has travelled a great deal through England, may have made many acquaintances, but few true friends. However, I have great hopes that during his marriage to you, he will adopt a style of living which is more conducive to intimacy."

"So do I," Anne smiled. The excited grey eyes darted around the room, drinking in every detail of the homey scene as their proprietress imagined a similar one in her own little parlor in years to come. But they dimmed significantly when they came to rest upon a young woman who was still sitting at the table and meticulously writing out invitations. Anne considered her silently for a moment, and then shifted her form very close to Elizabeth's.

"Lizzy?" she whispered.

"Yes, dear?"

"Do you suppose…that Jane does not approve of my marriage to George?"

"Jane?!" Elizabeth softly exclaimed, careful to modulate the volume of her voice so that only Anne would hear. "Whatever put such a notion in your head? She has been one of the match's biggest proponents!"

"Yes, she has been most kind and helpful," Miss Edwards put in hastily, "but, in comparison to you, Kitty, Lydia, and even Mary, she has been rather…dispassionate…about the entire wedding. While I do not expect her to squeal over the prospect of seeing the officers again, she does not seem to be particularly looking forward to the day."

The older girl stole a glance at the slightly stooped shoulders of her somber sister. With a sigh, she turned back to Anne and said,

"I fear that she is indeed unenthusiastic about the event, but you must not take that to mean censure of your case. Anyone's wedding would probably affect her spirits for the worse." After a brief pause for effect, Elizabeth asked, "What have you heard of Mr. Bingley, the absentee tenant of Netherfield Park?"

"A few things. I understand that he is single and handsome, and most of your neighbors consider him remarkably well-mannered. However, Mrs. Bennet does not seem to be very fond of him. She calls him an undeserving young man."

"She liked him well enough when he was paying attentions to Jane," her friend retorted.

Anne's eyes widened.

"He courted Jane!" she murmured in amazement.

Clandestinely scanning their immediate surroundings to ensure that their conversation was still private, Elizabeth leaned closer to Anne's ear and whispered,

"There was no formal courtship, but his attentions were overt enough to spark expectations of marriage. But he left suddenly on buisness, without a proper farewell, and has not returned to Netherfield since. And Jane still pines for him, though she is loath to admit it even to herself. It is a great pity, too, for he was a wonderful young man and I am convinced that he cared for her a great deal, but was unduly influenced by relations and friends who thought our family's position beneath him."

"How dreadful! Poor, poor Jane!"

Miss Bennet nodded.

"That she is. But now, I think we had better draw apart, before someone observes us and begins to tease and attempt to draw us out. Papa is looking over this way."

Anne immediately took the advice to heart, slid a few inches from her confidante, and fell to stroking the puppy who had traipsed up to her slippers. The glint emanating from behind Mr. Bennet's spectacles announced that the old man was absolutely plotting some cunning remark, and all of Miss Edwards' pains to forestall his inquiries would have been for naught had his wife not interrupted.

The Mistress of Longbourn had been sitting restlessly for several minutes, becoming more agitated by the moment when she considered how astray her plans regarding Mr. Wickham's guests had gone. The shrewd mother had counted on at least twenty more eligible men being present at the already populous wedding. With so many new gentlemen, she could have undoubtedly gotten husbands for all her daughters. But now, she would be forced to work mainly with officers who had already seen her girls countless times, and had unfortunately not yet demonstrated any particular regard for them. Longing to voice her misery in some way, she began moaning,

"Oh, what pains in my head, what flutterings in my side! This wedding will be the death of me yet!"

Abandoning his premeditated schemes to tease Elizabeth and Anne about their whispered conversation, Mr. Bennet rolled his eyes unsympathetically and addressed his wife instead.

"That is the price, you see, of having a member of one's household married. It must make you more satisfied that all five of our daughters are still single."

"It does no such thing!" Mrs. Bennet vehemently returned. "If anything, it only increases my agony! Oh, you do not know what I suffer! I will get no rest tonight, I am sure!"

"And neither shall Mrs. Hill, I daresay," her husband coldly retorted, turning back to his newspaper.

At this signal of complete apathy, yet another moan escaped his wife. She fell back in her chair, fanning herself with a handkerchief for all she was worth.

"Ohhhh. My poor, poor, *shattered* nerves!"

Kitty and Lydia withdrew their eyes. Mary took a deep breath and flipped open her book, and even Jane went back to writing in silence.

There was one person in the room, however, who was attending to every lament which passed the matron's lips. Shockingly, Anne had never before witnessed one of Mrs. Bennet's nervous attacks; she had been insensate during the last one which had occurred, just having been brought to Longbourn, and since then, the afflicted woman had chosen to manifest her disapproval of various situations and persons with angry words rather than with illness. The cries which had no effect on Mrs. Bennet's kin tore into her heart. Glancing around the room and marveling at the insensitivity of all those present, Miss Edwards rose to her feet and hesitantly took two steps forward. In a trembling voice and with eyes filled with tears, she addressed the Mistress of Longbourn,

"Madam, is there nothing you can take for your present relief? A glass of wine or a cup of tea, can I get you one?"

This simple offer had the extraordinary effect of hushing Mrs. Bennet immediately. Startled out of her wailing, she slowly sat upright and stared at the young woman, her lower lip displaced a full inch from its higher partner. It had been decades since someone had *offered* her aid or attentions. Usually she was required to scream for the smelling salts and the maids. It took a half-minute before Mrs. Bennet's two lips came together again, and she said in a very affable tone,

"Yes. Yes, a cup of tea would do me good. Fetch it."

Anne trotted to the service, hurriedly poured a cup of tea, taking care to add two big lumps of sugar and cream, just as the

Mistress of Longbourn liked, and delivered it. Standing by as the older woman brought the cup to her lips, she anxiously asked,

"Would it help if I opened the windows?"

The teacup's progress upward was halted, and Miss Edwards was regarded with another profound stare. At length, Mrs. Bennet stammered,

"A little...fresh air would be just the thing."

The girl dashed at the windows, threw them open as urgently as someone breathing in suffocating smoke would have, and returned to the poor woman, perfectly ignorant of the amused glances which the others were exchanging at her taking the fictitious ailments seriously. Sinking down upon her knees at the side of Mrs. Bennet's chair, she murmured feelingly,

"Forgive me, madam, this is all my fault! I should never have allowed you to make so great a fuss over my wedding; it is unconscionable that your health should be compromised because of it. If there is anything in the planned festivities which you wish to dispose of, pray do it, if it will take some strain from you!"

Highly gratified, beaming with triumph, possessing the air of someone who has sought a particular reaction for years and finally attained it, the Mistress of Longbourn actually smiled and said,

"No, no, dear, do not concern yourself about me so." Her hand reached out, and maternally patted Anne's cheek. "It is better this way. I can find and work out all the pitfalls of the ceremony and celebration during your wedding, so that when my daughters' come along they will proceed flawlessly."

Miss Edwards nodded, not particularly convinced, but unable to think of any protests which would override the older woman's reasoning. She contented herself with saying,

"Is there anything else I can do for you, Mrs. Bennet?"

Mrs. Bennet paused, considered, and then nodded.

"Yes, my dear. Go and play something on the instrument. You play very well, Anne. Amuse us with that lullaby you were practicing the other day. It is so soft and soothing. I am certain that it will take what remains of my headache away directly."

Unsurprisingly, the maiden did as she was bidden. When the lulling chords filled the room, Mrs. Bennet closed her eyes and swayed back and forth in time with the music, a most satisfied expression on her face. The rest of the family pretended to continue their respective occupations. In reality, all were attempting to accept the idea that one of their matriarch's fits had ended without her having to be helped upstairs and waited on by every servant in the house.

Chapter 30

Elizabeth sat imprisoned behind the whist table. She had very little desire to play, but her Aunt Phillips had insisted upon her joining the party, and it was impossible to refuse the hostess. Had the reluctant participant had her way, she would have taken a seat at Anne's side instead, upon the sofa which was stationed at the opposite end of the room. With the wedding a mere week away, there were fewer and fewer hours which could be spent together, and Elizabeth yearned to get her fill of Anne before Mr. Wickham whisked his bride miles away. Moments such as this one, when Miss Edwards sat alone without her fiancé's company, were especially precious. But there was a game to be played, and so instead of enjoying a dose of sisterly conversation, she was forced to attend to her cards and the moves of the other players.

Halfway through the game, the sound of the doorbell announcing some latecomer could be faintly detected over the voices of the thirty people gathered in the Philips' parlor.

Miss Edwards' seat afforded her a good view of the door, and she naturally looked up as the newest additions were admitted into the parlor. Elizabeth happened to be giving Anne another wistful glance at that very moment, and was stunned by the surprise, consternation, and even jealousy which suddenly covered the usually placid face.

Concerned and curious about what could have affected the transformation, Miss Bennet's eyes darted to the threshold. They found Mr. Wickham crossing it. His arrival had been expected, and therefore could not singlehandedly account for the peculiar expression upon her friend's face. The mystery was solved, however, when the dark pupils descried the presence of a strange lady upon Mr. Wickham's arm.

Promptly forgetting the game of whist and everyone else, Elizabeth stared at the officer's unexpected companion, trying to determine as much as she could about the unanticipated visitor.

She was respectably dressed. The cap and black muslin gown she wore gave her a matronly aspect and suggested that she was a widow. A close scrutiny would reveal her to be about five years Mr. Wickham's senior, but her bearing and rather handsome face gave a first impression of her being his equal in age.

The couple approached Anne, who in the meantime had schooled her features into a more neutral expression and rose to meet them. With perfect composure, Mr. Wickham disengaged his arm from the woman and addressed his fiancée. Elizabeth was too far away to hear what was said, but it appeared to be an introduction, for during his speech Anne and the mysterious lady curtsied to one another, and after its conclusion exchanged a few short remarks. Directly following these proceedings, the lieutenant seized Anne's hand, pressed a tender kiss upon it as was their custom, and moved to seat himself on the sofa at the side of his intended, leaving the matron to sit in an armchair next to it.

"Miss Bennet?"

The voice of her fellow whist player startled Elizabeth out of her observations. She uttered the necessary apology, tore her eyes away from the threesome and refocused them on the cards she held. As soon as the immediate need for her attention to them was dissipated, however, she recommenced casting sly glances across the room, and continued to do so for the remainder of the evening, even though there was not much to see. The engaged couple and Mr. Wickham's friend kept up what seemed to be a steady and pleasant conversation. Throughout it, the lady in black sent many maternal smiles Anne's way. For the most part, Miss Edwards appeared comfortable with her presence and attentions, except for a few rare instances when a certain spark of jealousy again appeared in the recesses of her eyes. Elizabeth was at a loss to determine whether it proceeded from her feelings towards her new acquaintance or from her disappointment at not having Mr. Wickham to herself for the evening. It could certainly not be attributed to the conduct of the lieutenant. *He* was as attentive to his fiancée as ever, and five minutes by the clock could pass without his loving eyes leaving her fair face.

There was but one incident which gave a small measure of discomposure to Miss Bennet. During a pause in the generally lively conversation, Anne looked away from her companions in order to search for a handkerchief in her reticule. While she was thus employed, the officer and the matron looked at one another and exchanged a smile. It was the nature of that unspoken communication which slightly perplexed Elizabeth, for it seemed to be much more than a nicety to fill the silent void. It was strongly reminiscent of a smile which two adults might surreptitiously share in the presence of a child who has just uttered a most naïve and amusing speech.

Considering that the youngest member of their group was sixteen instead of six, such an expression was very out of place. It lasted on both faces for only a fleeting moment, however, and was expunged before Anne lifted her eyes anew. Elizabeth thought about it for a little longer, but as subsequent glances showed Mr. Wickham and his friend to be respectfully conversing with Miss Edwards, she eventually concluded that the peculiar smile must have been related to some aspect of the discussion which she had been unable to hear.

Finally, the card game was completed and the guests began to take their leave. Miss Bennet fully intended to approach Anne's party and ask for an introduction at the soonest possible moment, but lo! First one neighbor, and then another, came up and commandeered her company. By the time she managed to free herself, Mr. Wickham and the ladies with him had risen from their seats and moved into the hall. Elizabeth followed suit, hoping to overtake them. She saw their group near the front door of the house, and managed to get within earshot of them when she was once again detained by her Aunt Philips. Remembering her manners, she thanked her relation for her hospitality with as much grace as could be mustered. Jane joined them and did likewise. For a moment, Elizabeth hoped that her sister's arrival would allow her to excuse herself; but unfortunately, Mrs. Philips took her hand and showed no sign of relinquishing it even as she waxed poetic over Jane's new cloak. Elizabeth nobly attended to their banter as they debated the merits of the wrap's color, but by the time they had taken to discussing its seams curiosity had fastened her eyes and ears upon the trio by the door.

The mysterious lady took Anne's hand in her own with a warm smile, and in a confiding tone, said,

"Well, my dear, I cannot fully express how wonderful it was to make your acquaintance. You have made my old friend very happy. I speak honestly when I say that seeing you on his arm," the speaker glanced at Wickham with a small smile, "is the most delightful vista which I have viewed in quite a while."

Anne nodded, looking pleased, and replied,

"Thank you. I was likewise honored to meet you."

"And I," Mr. Wickham put in, "am ecstatic that you two ladies have taken a fancy to one another. You will be the best of friends, just as I hoped you would be. Now, my fairest maiden, if you consent, I shall walk our wedding guest to the Inn, since it happens to be on the way to my quarters."

"Of course," Miss Edwards said, detaching her arm from his. "'Till tomorrow, then?"

"'Till tomorrow, milady," the gentleman confirmed.

Anne then turned to the widow, who during the preceding farewells had stood in silence, watching the lovers with an abstracted air, and bid her goodnight. The bride-to-be's voice appeared to bring the woman out of her preoccupation with a start, judging by the slight twitch of her neck and the disjointed manner in which she returned the adieu:

"Oh…goodnight, Georgi – Anne," she stumbled. Recollecting herself, she promptly added, "Goodnight, Anne. I also look forward to seeing you on the morrow."

Unfazed by her new acquaintance's slip of the tongue, the young lady nodded. Dropping another curtsy, she watched as her intended and the older lady departed via the front door and disappeared into the darkness of the night.

Elizabeth, still eavesdropping, noted the lisp, but likewise paid it little mind; she was at present far more interested in the lady's identity than in the fluency of her speech. After all, it was to be expected that a middle-aged woman who had been travelling and then subjected to an evening of social interaction with new acquaintances would be exhausted and lack perfect presence of mind.

Bereft of her own party, Miss Edwards joined Elizabeth's. At long last, Mrs. Philips finished her numerous remarks and allowed them to take their leave. The three young ladies stepped into Mr. Bennet's carriage and listened to Lydia and Kitty laughing all the way to Longbourn.

Meanwhile, on the other side of the village, Mr. Wickham and his friend parted ways immediately upon entering the Meryton Inn. The mysterious matron, whose name happened to be Mrs. Mabel Younge, retreated to the room which was her own, shut the door, and burst into the fit of laughter which she had been repressing all evening. Mr. Wickham had forewarned her about the delicious circumstances, but to witness them with her own eyes was past satisfying. A thousand years of scheming could not have granted her fuller vengeance upon the gentleman who had dismissed her from her post at Ramsgate without a reference. She only wished that George Wickham could have joined her in front of the fireplace for a glass of whiskey and a few good sneers at Fitzwilliam Darcy's expense. But

151

since he was bound to avoid any semblance of impropriety until the wedding, she would have to rejoice alone for that evening, at least. As a substitute, Mrs. Younge withdrew from her pocketbook the letter which had first informed her of their upcoming triumph, and skimmed the writing, which ran:

My dearest Mabel,

You will laugh when I tell you what a stroke of fortune has fallen my way since we last met. Congratulate me, my dear: I am to be married. She comes with thirty thousand pounds, and an elder brother, who, when informed of our nuptials, will eagerly furnish me with thousands more to save his precious girl from want, should I lose a substantial portion of the original dowry at cards.

From those clues alone, can you guess who the bride is? In case you cannot, I will not hold you in suspense any longer. The brat is Darcy's darling little sister. I must say that it was a profitable day for me when the tattletale got a bump on the head which caused her to forget me and all the seeds of wisdom which were doubtlessly planted in her mind last summer. She gave me no trouble; the greatest hurdle was convincing the town and her new friends of my devotion. They, unfortunately, still remembered my former declaration that I had to have something to live on when I married. But it is done at last, and I flatter myself that my imitation of a virtuous and sincere lover as I paid court to shy, destitute 'Anne Edwards' was a performance worthy of London's best theater.

Come to the wedding, Mabel! There is no danger of the imp remembering you, I am certain. Her memory is fully erased. Come and watch me become a man of leisure. And if you should think of any clever ways to present my bride to a certain Mr. Fitzwilliam Darcy of Pemberley, tell me and I shall be forever grateful!

George Wickham

Chapter 31

"It was a splendid party, was it not, Anne?" Elizabeth inquired of her roommate later that evening as they prepared to retire. "I did not expect it to be such a large affair, but Mrs. Philips can hardly bear to be outdone by Mama in anything, and I am certain that the entertainment was meant to counter the upcoming festivities at Longbourn. But fear not - Mama will prevail in the end, even if it means inviting the whole of England to your wedding!"

"Yes, indeed," Anne murmured inattentively.

Elizabeth turned from her mirror to glance at the maiden who perched on their bed, fiddling absentmindedly with her shawl's fringe. An amused smile crept into Miss Bennet's features, and she deigned to tease,

"You are not going to be jealous, I hope, and be troubled by Mr. Wickham's choice of wedding guests?"

"No, I will not…that is, I *wish* not to be," Anne admitted, guilty glancing down at the coverlets.

Elizabeth shook her head slightly and turned back to the mirror.

"I am sure that there is no reason to be worried, my dear. Many gentlemen have intimate acquaintances with women which are not of a romantic nature. I own that I, too, was expecting a gentleman to be Mr. Wickham's particular friend, but our expectations signify nothing. I suppose your fiancé has known her long?"

"Yes, indeed. George mentioned that they met through her husband before she was widowed, an unhappy event which took place several years ago."

"There you have it, Anne. She is nothing but an old friend, most likely invited for the sake of her husband's memory than for her own importance. And besides, she appeared to be prodigiously kind and attentive to you. An unsuccessful rival would never have been so benevolent."

"Yes, that is true," Miss Edwards murmured.

"I see you are still dissatisfied, my poor friend. It is a pity that I was not properly introduced to her and did not partake of your conversation. I am certain that I would have amassed plentiful evidence as to Mr. Wickham's impartiality for his old acquaintance, and resultantly I would be much better prepared to laugh you out of your ludicrous envy at present. But no matter; I shall meet her soon enough, I dare say. By the by, what is her name?"

Anne was resigning her position on the bed at this juncture, but she deigned to reply as she donned a pair of white slippers,

"Mrs. Younge."

The woman seated in front of the dressing table started so violently that she nearly tore out several brown curls along with the hairpin which she had been removing. Instantaneously, Elizabeth's breathing and heartbeat became disordered, and pivoting in her seat in Anne's direction, she gasped,

"What did you say?"

"I said that her name was Mrs. Younge, Lizzy," Miss Edwards repeated. Catching her companion's peculiar look, she added, "Is there something the matter? Have you heard Mr. Wickham ever mention her before?"

"No," Elizabeth managed. "No, I have never heard...*Mr. Wickham*...mention a Mrs. Younge before."

The bride-to-be accepted this answer without examining the breathless tone in which it was delivered, for she was once again sinking into preoccupation. She wandered to the center of the room before pausing in her walk. Fixating her eyes upon a couple of burning candles which were situated on the dressing table, Anne continued her leisurely pondering.

Miss Bennet's thoughts, however, were much more energetic. Mrs. Younge's name brought up many associations, none of them particularly pleasant. According to Mr. Darcy's letter, Mrs. Younge had been the corrupt companion of Miss Darcy, and had ruthlessly promoted a dishonorable elopement for that poor child and Mr. Wickham. Why then, had Anne's bridegroom invited her to *this* wedding? After all, it was in very bad taste to introduce an innocent soul like Miss Edwards to so unprincipled a woman! Did Mr. Wickham hope to transform Mrs. Younge's heart by asking her to witness his own amendment and subsequent happiness?

"Lizzy," Anne's quiet voice cut into Elizabeth's speculations, "I believe that I have managed to identify what exactly had me so vexed this evening." Forcing a smile, as if she knew the forthcoming confession to be quite a silly one, and giving into the soothing habit of fiddling with her engagement ring, she continued, "It was because Mrs. Younge seemed to *understand* George so well. One passing glance between them seemed to communicate more than half-an-hour

154

of our conversations. I am to be his wife, and yet I still have need of spoken or written words to comprehend his meanings, to know his thoughts! How I long to understand George completely, like she does! But I suppose I shall simply have to be patient, and learn to read my darling gradually…," her voice trailed off. She continued playing with the hand ornament, however, and staring at the lit candles.

There was something striking about Anne Edwards in that moment. From Elizabeth's seated position, she appeared taller than usual, and the shadows cast by the nonuniform candlelight dimmed and darkened the sunny-colored curls. The sharp, observing glance which she directed at the flickering luminosity caused the girlish face to settle into lines which were quite unusual for it. And most importantly, the slow, methodical movement of the engagement ring around and around Anne's finger awoke in Elizabeth those same feelings which had clutched her intermittently for the past three months. But this time, they did not merely tease her and subside. Instead, they intensified.

Her mind primed by the references to Mrs. Younge and reminisces of Mr. Darcy, his letter, and the circumstances of Ramsgate, sudden, disjointed waves of recollection began to sweep over Elizabeth.

She remembered another unembarrassed observer, one who had watched people rather than flickering flames, standing and staring at Netherfield, at Lucas Lodge, in Longbourn's own parlor. She saw the same, dark-haired personage towering over her as she played on a pianoforte at Rosings Park. And in all these scenes, the subject also spun a ring…not an engagement band, but a gentleman's signet ring…round and round his finger.

Why, Anne looks just like…she is the very image of Mr. Darcy!

Scarcely able to collect her faculties, but mindful of the unique opportunity for comparison, Elizabeth fixated her shocked eyes upon the young maiden and somewhat more methodically, began to contrast her features with those of her former suitor.

Yes, those were his cheekbones, and his ears. The other parts of Anne's face were much more feminine, and of course, she was much fairer than the gentleman. But the steadfast gaze, the displeased expression, were the same. Identical, in fact.

How can such a thing be possible? Elizabeth silently cried, reeling.

Had she met the girl anyplace else and seen the same, she would have wagered that it was a family resemblance. But this was *Anne*. Anne Edwards, her friend, her roommate. Anne who had been picked off a deserted meadow, Anne who had no recollections of the past.

Could that past have held more consequence, more wealth, more education, than any of us dared to assume?

Spontaneously, the scene of Mrs. Younge parting from Anne flew through her head. The woman's lisp rang in Elizabeth's ears.

Goodnight, Georgi-Anne.

Had that been an innocent stutter, or had it been the product of the widow checking herself at the very last moment before she revealed something of great import? What could she have started out to say?

Georgi...Georgi...Georgi-Anne...Georgiana! Georgiana Darcy!

No. No! It cannot *be true. Dearest God, please do not let it be true!*

"Lizzy?"

Elizabeth's mind was forced back to the present, and she gasped out,

"What?"

"Is anything wrong?"

"Wha-..no! No! Whatever gave you the notion that...anything was amiss?" a nervous and breathless Elizabeth exclaimed in an obtuse manner.

"For one, you were staring at me as if I were a species of ghost," Miss Edwards smiled. "And for another, you are panting." Frowning at this realization, she advanced and laid a hand upon Elizabeth's forehead. "Do you feel ill?"

"Not at all," Miss Bennet hastened to reply. "I am simply...tired. Aunt Philips forced me to play far too many hands today, against my will."

Still touching her friend's face with the back of her hand, Anne murmured reassuringly,

"You are a little warm and flushed, but you have no fever. However, you should not overdraw your good fortune. Come to bed at once and rest, Lizzy!"

Am I mad, or did that order possess a hint of Mr. Darcy's authoritative tone?

"In a moment, Anne. You go and lie down, and I shall join you directly. Go now, like a good girl."

Miss Edwards withdrew her hand, and sighed, exasperated.

"Sometimes you can be positively impossible, my friend. You are quick to give advice, but are none too hasty to accept it yourself. Fortunately for you, I, too, am tired and have no strength to properly admonish you into compliance, and thus will attempt to influence you by example. Goodnight."

Leaving a small, sisterly pat on Elizabeth's head, Anne went to the bedstead, doffed her shawl and slippers, and placed herself between the sheets, girlishly remarking that she hoped to dream of George. Being truly exhausted, only a few minutes passed before her form completely relaxed and her breathing became perfectly even.

Taking advantage of this sound sleep, Elizabeth took up a candle and stole quietly to the bedside. Partially shielding its rays with her hand so that they would not fall full upon the girl's face and awaken her, the anxious young woman studied her friend's countenance by the meager light. The resemblance was less glaring than when Anne had assumed Mr. Darcy's mien, but it could still be traced. Perturbed, Elizabeth slipped back to her seat, set down the light, and began to think rapidly.

If it was so, how differently did everything about the affair appear! Wickham's attentions to Miss Edwards were not the fruit of admiration for the young lady's intellect and beauty, but based on the opportunity of having an unknown heiress, far from the protection of her brother and cousin, at his disposal. His sudden unwillingness to speak of the falling out with Mr. Darcy was probably not the result of a change of heart after all, but of fear that reminiscing about the incident and multiple repetitions of the name 'Darcy' might awaken a part of Anne's consciousness which had to remain latent if his scheme was to succeed. She remembered the lieutenant's horror when he discovered that she and Anne had discussed the subject. His openness about the secrets of his past did not stem from a wish to condemn and turn away from them; rather, she had caught him off-guard with her questions, and manipulating the truth was far simpler than inventing a

157

novel excuse as to why Miss Edwards ought to be kept in the dark about his history. Likewise, his strict attachment to propriety was designed to make the girl comfortable with his advances – Georgiana's conscience had been so disturbed by the idea of an elopement that she had broken with him entirely and told her brother all. And of course Mr. Wickham had evaded Mary King's attentions! Why would he trouble himself with pleasing an eligible maiden with ten thousand pounds when he was weeks away from leading one with thirty thousand to the altar? As for his selection of wedding guests, if Anne was Miss Darcy, Mrs. Younge was the natural choice. Their mutual scheme had been overthrown by Mr. Darcy and his honorable sister at Ramsgate, and now Anne's marriage to Wickham would be their shared victory.

Elizabeth remembered the strange expression of glee which had crossed Wickham's face when he deprived Anne's finger of the indigo ring and replaced it with his own. Had that ring belonged to Georgiana Darcy? She also recalled what Wickham's fiancée had said: '*He knows me better than I know myself*'. Naturally, he would know that Georgiana Darcy preferred lilies of the valley – he had courted her just last year, and had played with her in the fields of Pemberley when she was a little girl. Was that why he had managed to woo the shy and uncertain Anne in just three weeks? Had Wickham been using his former knowledge the whole time, tricking her into thinking that he understood her as a kindred spirit?

Of course, Wickham was moving through slightly dangerous waters: with this much deceit in the matter, Mr. Darcy would have every legal right to withhold his sister's dowry from him. But legalities were one thing, and feelings of the heart another. Elizabeth knew enough of Mr. Darcy to be certain that he was far too fond of Georgiana to allow her to sink into poverty if it was in his power to prevent it.

Shutting her eyes tightly, Miss Bennet tried to recall all that she knew about Georgiana Darcy. She remembered Mr. Darcy saying that his sister was a little taller than herself and very good at playing the pianoforte; those facts matched. Miss Darcy was sixteen, and Anne certainly looked to be about fifteen or sixteen. Mr. Wickham had once described the lady as very proud, but he had proven to be a poor historian before, particularly where the Darcys were concerned.

Frightened almost out of her wits at the hypothesis, Elizabeth shook her dark head energetically, forcing herself to break the peculiar train of thought.

It simply cannot be!

Jumping up from the chair, she removed her dressing gown and hung it up as she mentally chided herself. What utter nonsense she was thinking! Supposing dear, sweet, timid Anne to be Georgiana Darcy, a woman who probably exuded pride and confidence with every movement and speech! And on what scant evidence: a proficiency at the pianoforte, a fancied resemblance, a common habit which was probably shared by thousands of people throughout England, a silly slip of the tongue. Mr. Darcy, whatever his faults might be, was certainly not the sort of man who would lose his sister in a meadow without ever seeking her again! No, she, Elizabeth Bennet, was just being overly imaginative of late. It appeared that despite her best efforts, some of the old insecurities about a match between Mr. Wickham and Anne still lay dormant in the recesses of her mind, and were inventing ridiculous excuses to surface. However, she was a reasonable woman, and she firmly resolved to never dwell upon anything but the plain facts of the case forevermore. Anne was simply Anne: a penniless girl of unknown origin, who had somehow stirred Mr. Wickham's heart into repentance and love. She had been claimed by no one, and thus she was most likely unwanted by her own family, if they were living. With George Wickham lay Anne's greatest chance of future happiness, and her friends would do well to cease questioning Mr. Wickham's motives because of preposterous fantasies.

This settled, Elizabeth slipped into bed, pressed a gentle kiss upon her friend's brow, and forcefully banishing any remaining questions about Anne's identity far from her mind, drifted off to sleep.

Chapter 32

Mr. Wickham and Anne, apparently newlywed, were driving in a buggy. As it made its way down a long drive, the gentleman leaned towards his bride and whispered earnestly into her ear for a prolonged length of time, recounting his version of the circumstances regarding the living which he had been denied. As he spoke, Anne's face became quite indignant, and uncharacteristic anger distorted her features.

Wickham, at last, ceased murmuring to her and, with a satisfied air and smirk, leaned back against his seat as their journey continued. Before long, the buggy halted before a mansion. It was much larger than Netherfield, and a thousand-fold grander. Mr. Darcy's tall, distinguished figure was pacing back and forth in front of the said edifice. Hearing the wheels of the conveyance, he turned as if startled.

Anne's husband climbed out. His face was the perfect study of sadistic glee and anticipation. He mockingly executed a bow in the other gentleman's direction and began to advance slowly and deliberately towards his former friend.

Mr. Darcy, however, was not looking at him. Mr. Wickham's removal from the buggy allowed him an unobstructed view of the lady seated therein. Mr. Darcy audibly gasped, and was about to hasten towards Anne when Mr. Wickham reached him and precipitously stopped him by grasping his arm.

"If you wish to speak to my wife, it will cost you," he sneered.

Comprehending his old enemy at once, Mr. Darcy retrieved the deed to Pemberley and a pencil out of his pocket without the slightest hesitation. He quickly signed it, bequeathing the land and house to Mr. George Wickham, and thrust the legal document into the hand of the new proprietor. Then he rushed towards the buggy.

But Anne, her mind poisoned by her husband's slander, knew not that the approaching gentleman had, in forgotten days, cherished her as only a devoted brother could. When Mr. Darcy reached the conveyance and extended his hand to help her alight, she drew back, aghast at his forwardness.

Poor Mr. Darcy did not know what to make of her reaction. "Come to me," he gently coaxed.

Anne glared at him, and lifting her hand, savagely slapped Mr. Darcy's cheek. As he fell back a step, in shock, an expression of deep heartbreak etching itself upon his countenance, the formerly amiable young woman snapped,

"You are the last man in the world with whom I should wish to become acquainted!"

In the background, Mr. Wickham's laughter rose to a crescendo.

Elizabeth's eyes flew open as terror propelled her to sit bolt upright in bed. Her linen nightgown was soaked through with cold sweat, and she gasped for air. Another frightful moment passed, and then, as she took in the sight of the still, moonlit bedchamber, it occurred to her that the scene which she had just witnessed was the product of dreams, not reality. A hurried glance to her right confirmed that Anne was sleeping peacefully and had not the slightest intention of abusing respectable young men. Unspeakable relief washed over Miss Bennet, and her rational faculties began to return.

"It was just a nightmare," she whispered to herself in the darkness.

Realizing that it would be prudent to quit the bed before her still-agitated breathing woke Anne, and knowing that sleep would probably not call upon her again that night, Elizabeth made an effort to rise. It was anything but easy. Her hands shook violently as they threw aside the covers, and her trembling legs were so undependable that she was forced to lean against the side-table for a moment before transferring all her weight onto them. Once she had attained their support, she tottered to the window seat and sank down upon it.

"It was just a nightmare," she murmured again, more firmly than the first time she had attempted to console herself with those words.

Notwithstanding, a shiver escaped the disquieted girl. What if it were not an empty dream, but a harbinger of events to come? What if the impossible had somehow happened, and Anne truly was Georgiana Darcy? Probabilities aside, what exactly would that mean?

It meant that Mr. Wickham cared naught for Miss Edwards. It meant that he would consider Anne a route by which he could exact revenge. It meant that Anne would be entering into a loveless and maligning marriage, one in which Mr. Wickham would not hesitate to

161

openly inflict pain upon her, knowing that every sharp stab would resonate in her brother's heart.

Elizabeth buried her clammy face in her hands as she, despite her better judgment, surrendered to doubt and resigned herself to troubles and efforts yet unknown. The terrible vision she had endured in her sleep was burned into her consciousness, and she knew that it would not give her a moment of peace until she discredited its underlying assumption entirely. She could not live through the next week with such burdening uncertainty. Whatever inconvenience the pursuit of truth occasioned, it would be abundantly repaid by her ability to observe Anne's wedding without fretting about her dearest friend's future. And if there was indeed something troublesome in the matter, it would be best if it surfaced before the marriage vows were spoken, not after. Otherwise, the guilt of her inaction would haunt her for a lifetime.

That decided, it was next necessary to think of how to go about her purpose: namely, how to ascertain that Anne was *not* Georgiana Darcy in less than a week.

She contemplated simply confronting Mr. Wickham when he came on the morrow. It would be the easiest way, to maneuver him into the library or the parlor alone, directly ask the vital question and watch for any semblance of alarm in his features. But, unfortunately, if her fears were true, Mr. Wickham was an accomplished liar. If he had something to conceal, he would unflinchingly deny it. Worse yet, if he had hidden designs on Anne, it would be sheer foolishness to inform him that he was suspected. Such a move might provoke some desperate scheme on his part. And even if his intentions were of the most honorable sort, Miss Bennet's distrust of him so close to the wedding day would only occasion embarrassment and awkwardness for all involved. No, interrogating Mr. Wickham would not do at all!

Racking her intellect, Elizabeth rose from the window-seat and commenced pacing back and forth in the bedchamber. She needed to promptly contact someone who was acquainted with Georgiana Darcy! But who? A few people with the necessary qualification came to mind: Lady Catherine de Bourgh, Colonel Fitzwilliam, Mr. and Miss Bingley, and, of course…Mr. Darcy. Writing to the first would be the most proper option, but Miss Bennet strongly doubted Her Ladyship's ability to remain tactful under such provoking circumstances. Either she would send a disdainful reply which proclaimed Miss Darcy to be safe and scolded Elizabeth for daring to imagine that poor, nameless Anne was her niece, or she would travel to Longbourn post-haste and inflict indiscreet advice on how to restore the girl's memory. Colonel Fitzwilliam and the Bingleys would probably be more prudent, but Elizabeth had not the slightest idea where any of them could be found. As for Mr. Darcy…even if she could somehow bear the embarrassment and incongruity of writing to a man whom she had viciously refused but a few months before, Mr. Darcy could likewise be visiting friends or attending to business anywhere in England or beyond. And there was no time for trial and error, for a flurry of sent and returned letters. A definite, reliable answer had to be procured in less than five days!

To and fro, to and fro, Elizabeth's thoughts far outpaced her steps. Was there anyone to whom she could turn? The answer, continually, was no.

Chapter 33

Two hours later, at the end of all ideas, the exhausted maiden sank down once more upon the window seat and turned to the moonlit view outside. Her tired eyes roved across the fields and groves. What a staggering contrast their peaceful silence was to her disturbing thoughts! If only these powerful misgivings had never entered her head, if only the most distressing schemes of her existence centered upon how to keep her two youngest sisters from flirting with every man they encountered on the streets of Meryton!

Meryton!

Elizabeth pulled back from the window and reflexively tightened her grip on the edge of the seat. Her mind raced. Meryton. Everyone in the little village knew her family and every landowning family in the area, and every piece of gossip which these social superiors produced. It was entirely possible that some small hamlet in Derbyshire complied news about the Darcys as readily as Meryton collected tidbits about Mrs. Bennet's latest antics. Here, another set of fortunate recollections met her. Such a town *did* exist, for certain; Aunt Gardiner had spoken much of it and had lived in it. According to her dear relation, the village of Lambton was but five miles from Pemberley, and the residents were privy to many of the general ongoings of the estate. And what was to prevent her from going there and seeking what she sought? Even if some old acquaintance happened to see her there, she could always attribute her visit to a wish to see her favorite aunt's birthplace. Of course, whatever information she managed to gather would be second or thirdhand, but it would surely be enough. She was not after a flawless account of all the dishes which had appeared on Pemberley's dining table during the past week or a precise tally of the horses in its stables. All that she longed for were a few rumors about Miss Darcy's current location and well-being, and then it would be into a carriage and away!

Having struck upon this golden idea, the only predicament which remained was how to take a journey to Derbyshire without awakening Mr. Wickham's curiosity or her father's concern for her sanity. For, unless she acquainted the latter with a most mortifying and protracted tale, she would necessarily have to fib…or better yet, avoid telling him anything altogether. Even if she did tell Mr. Bennet the full truth about her past acquaintance with Mr. Darcy and her present suspicions, there was no guarantee that he would not laugh at her and refuse to let her go.

Yes, that was how she would do it. She would leave Longbourn before anyone but the servants was up, and she would leave word that she was going on a little journey.

As quietly as possible, she retrieved a satchel from a corner of the room and began to fill it with the utmost necessities of travelling. Taking along all the money she owned, which was a modest amount, particularly after the purchase of the wedding gown and veil, she made ready for departure. The bright clouds of dawn were already visible on the horizon when Elizabeth reached for one last item: she brought out a small jewelry box, took the blue ring, and put it in her pocketbook.

Putting on a light coat and taking up the small bag she had prepared, Elizabeth walked to and crossed the threshold of the room. Looking back once more at the sleeping form upon the bed, she drew the door shut.

She stole softly down to the kitchen, where, as expected, the cook and Mrs. Hill were already present. The housekeeper was the first to notice the young lady.

"Why, Miss Lizzy! If I may take the liberty of saying so, you are up extraordinarily early this morning, even for yourself! Is there anything we may do for you?"

"Good morning, Mrs. Hill, Mrs. Lane," Miss Bennet replied, nodding to each woman in turn. "Will you allow me to steal a couple of those warm muffins for my breakfast?"

"Of course, but would you not prefer a more substantial meal, miss? I would be happy to fix something for you," Mrs. Lane offered.

"Thank you, but I will not be taking a true breakfast at Longbourn today, or for the next few days, and I would be grateful if you both could inform my family of the same."

The housekeeper gave the maiden a sharp look. Elizabeth, a dutiful and obedient daughter, usually informed her parents of her intentions personally before absenting herself from home for any amount of time. Thus, the current request was quite uncharacteristic. Hoping to gain further enlightenment on what had spurred it, she respectfully inquired,

"Is everything well, Miss Lizzy?"

Elizabeth busied herself with wrapping the baked goods in her handkerchief. Not only did this action save Mrs. Lane the trouble of packing the breakfast; it also allowed Elizabeth to look down at the platter rather than straight into the perceptive women's eyes as she gave a response designed to lead their presumptions astray.

"Have you ever bought a gift which seemed appropriate at the time but later on came to realize that it might be seen as too thrifty?" she asked with a self-conscious smile. "Some in the neighborhood, I am sure, would say that I acted miserly. Papa would have bought Anne a nice wedding dress anyhow, so I did her no great favor by purchasing the material, and yet, she is my dearest friend, and everyone else is giving her such nice things. One has to shop in London to find gifts of comparable quality." At this juncture, the striking of the clock in the drawing room reached their ears, and Miss Bennet immediately took the opportunity to conclude with, "Oh, dear me - how late it is! I must hurry if I am to catch the post. Good day, Mrs. Hill, Mrs. Lane," before dashing out of the kitchen, accompanied by their adieus.

Unaccustomed to fibbing, Miss Bennet felt conscience-stricken as she departed. While she had not lied outright, she had purposely misguided two loyal servants, and through them, the entire family. But she was determined to keep all troubling suspicions locked solely in her own mind until they were, hopefully, disproved.

Chapter 34

With each passing mile Elizabeth felt more foolish. The hours rushed by, eroding the impression left by the frightful nightmare as well as her sense of purpose. When she reached Lambton, she would undoubtedly be informed that Miss Georgiana Darcy was at Pemberley or visiting friends, in perfect health, and preparing for her coming out. At every station, Elizabeth deliberated the merits of disembarking and boarding a coach traveling in the opposite direction; the only thing which prevented her from undertaking that course of action was the conviction that since she had come thus far, she might as well see the thing through.

The sun had already dipped below the horizon on the second day of her journey by the time her conveyance drove into Lambton. They stopped in front of the inn. A footman helped her down and unloaded her trunks. Elizabeth entered the edifice and found the innkeeper, a portly man in his fifties who tactfully concealed his surprise at having an unaccompanied young lady patronizing his establishment, offered lodgings, and introduced her to a servant named Harriet. With the greatest politeness, that girl asked Miss Bennet to walk upstairs with her. When the latter assented, she was shown into an apartment featuring a comfortable sitting room and a small bedchamber.

Elizabeth walked over to the windows which provided a fair prospect of the quiet, cobblestone street and looked out, imagining a younger version of her aunt playing or running about below. It was a quaint village, and she wished that she had time to explore it at leisure.

"Is this satisfactory, miss?" the maid asked, causing Elizabeth to turn around.

"Yes, I thank you."

"Will you be requiring anything else?"

"A simple supper would be lovely."

"I shall bring it up directly," Harriet said, and turned to go.

During the servant's brief absence, Miss Bennet paced up and down in the sitting room, formulating inquiries which would hopefully draw out the desired information without requiring her to ask about Miss Darcy's whereabouts outright. Fully conscious of how odd a young lady travelling alone must appear, Elizabeth was desperate to avoid any more attention than necessary. Thankfully, by the time the maid reappeared with a tray, a decent strategy had been invented.

"That was very prompt, Harriet, thank you!" the young lady exclaimed, hoping that a compliment would charm the servant into loquaciousness. The adulation was answered with a warm smile and small curtsy before the supper tray was set down upon the table. As Elizabeth advanced to take a seat and do justice to the sustenance, she casually asked, "I was wondering whether there are any sights worth seeing hereabouts?"

Harriet helped Elizabeth with her chair, and considered for a brief moment before replying,

"I doubt that there is anything in Lambton which would be of great interest to a traveler. We have several shops and such, but nothing which could really be called unique or unattainable elsewhere. But then, of course, one person's idea of amusement may vary greatly from another's."

"Very true. For my part, I find scenic walks, fine trees and grounds, and even great houses richly furnished extremely noteworthy. Do you think that I will find *any* sources of diversion in or around Lambton, Harriet?" The last sentence was accompanied by an expression of exaggerated desperation.

Harriet allowed herself the liberty of a short laugh at Elizabeth's mien before unknowingly falling into the carefully set trap.

"If handsome grounds please you, ma'am, I believe that you might find visiting Pemberley worthwhile. It has some of the finest woods in England."

Feigning ignorance, Elizabeth echoed,

"Pemberley?"

"'Tis a great estate less than five miles from here, Miss Bennet. The house is the largest in Derbyshire, and the surrounding countryside is remarkable. It boasts of numerous streams, a lake, and a park that is more than ten miles around."

"Dear me, that does sound grand! What fortunate family owns the aforementioned domain?"

"Pemberley belongs to Mr. Darcy…Mr. Fitzwilliam Darcy."

"Does he share his vast realm with his wife and children? Or is he a hermit who leads a solitary life inside his provincial castle, and cares naught for the company of others?" Elizabeth quipped lightheartedly as she helped herself to a piece of cold chicken, blissfully unconscious at how closely she was approximating Mr. Darcy's current circumstances.

The maid giggled anew. Without a doubt, the young lady before her was the most entertaining guest that the inn had hosted for a twelvemonth, and after a busy day, Harriet was enjoying the witticisms prodigiously. Her mirth loosened her tongue, and she began to chatter a bit more indiscriminately.

"To the best of my knowledge, Mr. Darcy is not exactly a recluse, but he is fond of privacy, and is unmarried." An impish smile diffused over Harriet's face, and she added, "Pemberley's servants often say that they do not know who would be good enough for him!"

Miss Bennet hurriedly reached for the napkin and pretended to wipe her lips, which were, in reality, stained with a diverted smirk. Evidently, the attendants were just as conceited as the master. She wondered how many duchesses and countesses they had deemed unworthy of their employer's hand and home. How aghast would they be to discover that their high and mighty master had offered for a county girl of no consequence! At last, she felt equal to lowering the cloth and giving a repartee.

"Considering his unwed state, Mr. Darcy must share that opinion, or at least be unable to find a woman who does."

The servant girl burst out laughing.

"I never thought of it before, miss, but it must be so!" she exclaimed.

Elizabeth also chuckled, partially at her own cleverness, and partially because she was glad to be able to furnish some diversion for the hardworking girl. Realizing, however, that the hour was growing late, she felt compelled to finish the conversation, finally have the assurances she sought, and then lay her relieved, weary head upon a pillow. Reaching for a freshly-baked roll, she therefore flippantly added,

"It appears that I was not far from the truth when I supposed Mr. Darcy to lead a solitary life. I suppose that the man has friends or relations, at least, who are permitted occasional access across the moat?"

Harriet smiled.

"There is no moat at Pemberley, Miss Bennet, unless one were to count the trout streams as such! But you are correct. Sometimes Mr. Darcy does have long visits from gentlefolk, his aunts and uncles and cousins among them. And then he often has his sister by his side…or had, I should say."

Elizabeth's neck turned so quickly that it nearly creaked from the rotational stress put upon it. Fixedly staring at the servant with dismay, she asked,

"Had? Has the young lady gone away to friends for a while, or been wed to a duke?"

Harriet's answer sent chilling shivers down Elizabeth's back.

"Neither, ma'am." Suddenly serious, she paused. "Miss Darcy is reputed to have been drowned several months ago. I know none of the details, nor can I fathom why she would be in the water during mid-spring. The month of May is generally too cold for sea-bathing. Perhaps she was standing near water or on a boat and fell in. But those are my own conjectures, and nothing more."

The month of May?!

Forcing herself to remain rational, Miss Bennet solemnly asked,

"I suppose the funeral was a very fine affair?"

Harriet shrugged.

"I know not, miss. Neither I, nor anyone I know, saw or heard anything of the burying."

Appetite thoroughly destroyed, Elizabeth put down the roll and wiped her fingers on the provided white napkin. Motioning for the repast to be removed from the table, she swallowed the lump in her throat. There was one last fact which she had to extract from Harriet before the girl departed for the night, even though she prayed that it was a piece of knowledge which would be harvested needlessly.

"The drowning of a young woman is always tragic, no matter how it occurs," she said to close the subject. "But let us return to Pemberley and its fine grounds. I may have time to view them, but naturally do not wish to disturb their proprietor. Do you know if Mr. Darcy is down for the summer?"

Harriet immediately shook her head.

"I doubt it. I know for certain that the house is open to visitors, for a couple staying at this inn toured it two days ago and were very impressed. Customarily, the moment Mr. Darcy steps upon his land the house is closed and all unknown callers are turned away. As aforementioned, he values privacy. Therefore, I am relatively positive of his absence. Besides, whenever he is in residence, he frequently comes into Lambton to tend to one business or another – he owns and lets about half of the buildings in the village - and no one has caught a glimpse of him hereabouts for quite some time."

"I see," Elizabeth murmured. Collecting herself, she rose from the table and said in an even, gentlewomanly tone, "Thank you, Harriet, that will be all. I plan to rise early tomorrow. Please see to it that a small breakfast is available by seven. Goodnight."

"Goodnight," the maid returned, curtseying as best she could with a tray in her hands, and left the nice young lady to herself.

As soon as the door-latch clicked, Miss Bennet commenced pacing and muttering under her breath, trying to convince herself that there was no need to become overwrought. True, Georgiana Darcy was absent from Pemberley, but she was said to be drowned, not missing.

Elizabeth Bennet, this is answer enough! Georgiana Darcy is dead. It is a different, sadder reassurance than the one you expected, but it is an answer nonetheless. You have made a fool of yourself long enough.

In spite of this earnest internal monologue, Miss Edwards' friend could not be pacified by Harriet's vague information. If she, or Jane, or Lydia, or one of the Lucas girls had drowned, all of Meryton would know precisely where they had been standing as they fell in, what they had been wearing, and how many people had attempted to pull them to safety. But even if distance had diluted the facts of Miss Darcy's death, the lack of funeral details could not be as easily dismissed. If she had been buried nearby, the intelligent maid would surely know of it. On the other hand, why would Mr. Darcy wish to inter his precious sister far away from Pemberley and the resting places of their parents? Maybe he could not bear to see her grave, or…perhaps there was no grave?

Wringing her hands, Elizabeth made the only decision which could be considered sensible at that late hour: to retire for the night, and hope that her mind would be sharper in the morning. And going into the hired bedchamber, she executed it at once.

171

Chapter 35

The creak of Longbourn's library door interrupted the steady crackle of the fire and caused Mr. Bennet to glance up from his book. He had certainly not been expecting visitors, considering that the clock on the mantel showed it to be well past two o'clock in the morning. But an instant later he heard the soft rustling of a dressing gown and saw a white-clad figure slip into the room and advance towards the shelves.

The Master of Longbourn smiled slyly to himself before abruptly halting its progress across the library by exclaiming,

"Well, well, so the bride-to-be cannot sleep?"

"Mr. Bennet!" Anne, startled, softly cried out. "I beg your pardon. I did not expect to find anyone here at this time of night."

"Neither did I, but this volume turned out to be far more engrossing than I anticipated."

Anne only hesitated for a second before inquiring,

"Is it the new one which just came from London?"

"The very one. But do not try to redirect the conversation, young lady. What is your pretext for wandering around the house at such an unconventional hour?"

"I…I was unable to sleep and decided to borrow a book from the library."

"And what is the cause of this restlessness? Are your thoughts haunted by a remarkably handsome man named Mr. Wickham, or do you simply miss my second eldest daughter?"

"Both, I imagine," Anne replied, but in rather too quiet a tone.

"The first is to be expected, but the second is quite vexing to me as well, I assure you, Miss Edwards. I am afraid that my Lizzy is becoming rather flighty. It seems that every time I blink she is off to Kent or London. But I do admit that the purpose of this latest excursion appears to be most noble and generous," Mr. Bennet said, concluding with a wink.

"Yes, indeed. She is truly too kind to me…there was no reason for her to go through all that trouble just to procure another gift…," the young woman's voice trailed off absently.

The gentleman's brows drew together as he watched the girl, who had become as dear to him as one of his own daughters, gaze bemusedly into the flames. He suddenly knew that she was not merely excited, but preoccupied. Thus, he resolutely closed his enthralling book and putting it aside, addressed her gently.

"Annie…come sit by the fire."

His paternal tone immediately pulled Miss Edwards out of her reverie, stupefied her, and then exacted her obedience. She stepped forward and seated herself in a chair facing Mr. Bennet.

"Something is troubling you, is it not?"

"No," was the answer. But her mirthless countenance betrayed her.

"Annie, you are not very proficient at uttering falsehoods. You *are* unsettled, my dear. Now, considering that Lizzy is from home and Jane is fast asleep, do you think that you could make use of me as a confidant? I should be happy to attend you."

"Thank you, Mr. Bennet, but it is nothing, truly," Anne replied, fiddling with the engagement ring as was her wont. Seeing that this answer did not satisfy her host, she hastily added: "It is perfectly inconsequential."

"I must disagree. It has already had the consequence of keeping you from your repose."

The girl's cheeks flushed as she stood and walked nearer to the fire. From this position, she murmured,

"Sir, it is only an irrational feeling. I thank you for your concern, but it is unnecessary."

"Do you fear that I will laugh at your lack of sense? I promise I shall do no such thing. In all the months that you have lived under my roof, you have never spent your share of silliness, and I certainly will not begrudge you a small withdrawal now."

Anne smiled half-heartedly and yielded. The invitation was wholly welcome, for she felt that if she spoke of her apprehension openly, it would lose its firm hold on her soul. Thus, she allowed herself to break out in a low voice,

"I simply *cannot* understand it!"

"What is so difficult to comprehend, my dear?" Mr. Bennet echoed.

Miss Edwards sighed and returned to her chair. Entwining her hands, she gathered her courage for an uncharacteristically long and somewhat impassioned explanation.

"It happened during the wedding rehearsal today. At first, I was delighted, for everything was going along flawlessly. Mary played the organ exceedingly well, the plans to decorate the church with ribbons and flowers suited me, and I was beyond grateful that you, sir, consented to give me away. I was never happier in my life than during the thirty seconds that the two of us practiced processing down the aisle. And then...as soon as we reached the altar and you gave George my hand...the most illogical, inexplicable emotion seized me. As the Reverend expounded on the ceremony, I could not shake the feeling that there was...something...*wrong* about my being there, standing next to George before the altar... Oh, I know that it is all ridiculous!" she concluded with a forced little laugh.

The elder occupant of the room, for once, did not make any witty comment at another's distress.

"Most likely, you simply realized how conspicuous you would be at the front of the church, and due to your reserve, began to feel uneasy."

"I thought so too, in the beginning." Anne's hesitation was akin to that of a guilty child who is ashamed to confess its failing. "But when George was called away for a minute by Mrs. Bennet I felt a great deal more composed, even though I remained standing in the same prominent position. As soon as George returned, the insufferable illusion gripped me again."

"Have you ever felt so before?"

"No, I have always been perfectly happy in George's vicinity. Although...," Anne shook her head agitatedly and, abruptly rising, paced to the fireplace once more.

"What is it, Annie?" Mr. Bennet coaxed, his solicitous eyes becoming more anxious by the minute as they observed these novel affectations. For the first time in months, paternal indignation engulfed the indolent Master of Longbourn.

If Mr. Wickham has in any way caused the uneasiness I am now observing, he thought angrily, *I will personally throw the young scamp out of the house the next time he has the audacity to visit!*

But Miss Edwards at once pacified him and perplexed herself by responding,

"Today's sentiment was...again, in some odd way...kindred to the feeling that I often experience whenever I find myself playing that disconcerting improvisation on the pianoforte. I do not know how those two vastly different scenarios could produce such similar emotions, but they did." She tried to burrow her weary little forehead into the hard mantelpiece. "I feel positively ludicrous! Here I am, destroying what ought to be the loveliest days of my life, worrying about unreasonable emotions whose roots I cannot even begin to trace!"

"Annie....Annie," Mr. Bennet soothed, rising and slipping an arm around her shoulders. "It seems to me that you are merely suffering from a traditional last burst of nerves. Nearly everyone who is scheduled to visit the altar panics as the hour draws near and starts imagining all sorts of reasons why marriage is a foolish idea. You should have seen me the last night before my wedding, Annie! I would pour a glass of analgesic, stare at it, and then change my mind and pour it into the fire. I wasted an entire decanter of fine brandy in this manner! Then I went outside for a short walk to clear my head. The next thing I knew, the sun was coming up over the horizon and I was on the boundary of Hertfordshire and Essex. Thankfully, there was a laborer driving a wagon in sight. A frantic plea and a couple of shillings bought me a hasty ride back to Longbourn, amid ten crates of fruit. I only had half-an-hour to change and substitute the smell of cologne for that of peaches before the ceremony!"

Despite herself, Miss Edwards laughed. Pleased, the elderly gentleman gave the slight shoulders a gentle squeeze and recommenced in a more serious manner.

"I suppose one could argue that it would have been for the best if that wagon had never come along to fetch me in time. But Anne, would you care to know a little secret?" Enthralled, the young woman nodded. "Despite my domestic felicity being in an unusual form, on the whole, I do not repine. Had I married anyone else, Elizabeth and Jane and the rest of my daughters would never have been. Furthermore, as you have often taken pains to remind us, Fanny does have her good points, particularly as a mother. And," Mr. Bennet chuckled, "if some aspects of her character do grate on one's nerves, I have no one to blame but myself. Do you know that her chatter was one of the things that first drew me to her? Back then, it seemed to be a mark of good humor, and the occasional lack of tact I took for frankness. I did not foresee that it could become tiresome. But, be that as it may, *you* have nothing to concern yourself about! I see nothing in your fiancé's temperament which could misfire. George Wickham is a fine man, and I am sure you will do well together. He has sacrificed many plans and dreams for your sake, Annie. You have blossomed as a result of his attentions, and he has become a steadier sort of fellow since he met you. Depend upon it, this time next month you will be the happiest of women and will have a good laugh whenever you recall the absurdity of your present emotions."

Anne forced a little smile.

"I think you must be right."

"Of course I am. Now go upstairs, without any foolish novels to confuse you further, put that pretty head on a pillow and commence sleeping! If any silly feelings begin haunting you again, ignore them. Alright?"

"Yes," Anne replied softly, turning away from the mantel and taking the candle which was held out to her. "Goodnight, Mr. Bennet. And thank you."

"Goodnight," her benefactor echoed. He slipped back into his armchair, and she out of the library.

Miss Edwards glided through the downstairs hall and, doing her utmost to minimize the creaking of the wood beneath her slippers, began ascending the stairs. Halfway up, she paused and glanced back down towards the library door.

Mr. Bennet's words were extremely reasonable, she readily acknowledged. All her strange emotions were simply fancies. Anyone with sense would find it to be so. She loved George; he had made it very clear that he loved her. There was absolutely no reason to feel anything but pure elation at their upcoming nuptials.

Decided, Anne renewed her ascent. And yet, when she reached the landing, a brief memory of Mr. Wickham and Mrs. Younge intruded upon her consciousness, and immediately a hundred butterflies inexplicably swarmed about in her stomach. True to her resolve, Miss Edwards clenched her hands, concentrated, and pushed the contrary feelings away. When they were vanquished, she forced a triumphant smile at the upstairs walls, and went back into the bedchamber.

Chapter 36

The carriage travelled along at a rapid pace, for the coachman had been asked to hurry, but the beating of Elizabeth's heart far outpaced that of the horses' hoofs against the road. She could not believe what their destination was, despite the fact that she had been the one to decide upon it.

For the past two days, she had been convincing herself that so long as she did not go *there,* her journey breached neither etiquette nor sense. An English young lady was not expected to avoid the home county of a gentleman she had refused. But every tenet of propriety decreed that she avoid his house, unless expressly invited.

Then why had she, being in possession of a sound judgment and mind, looked up at the driver less than half-an-hour ago and said the word '*Pemberley*'?

Earlier that morning, Miss Bennet had gone to the shops, hoping that some cunning remarks would purchase her a bit more information about Miss Darcy's demise. That approach got her a little more than she bargained for, but not in the way she had hoped. No one had any further information about the drowning, and no one in Lambton had been at or heard any details about the lady's funeral. But each time she brought up the subject of the Darcy family in general, in order to ease into the topic of Miss Darcy's death, every shopkeeper or his wife had some unsolicited tale to relate about Mr. Fitzwilliam Darcy's exceptional goodness and generosity. Within a span of two hours, Elizabeth learned that her former suitor had twice forgiven the wine merchant his rent when lumbago kept him abed, purchased new clothes and plentiful provisions for a family of seven when their widowed matriarch was unable to do so, and, as a man of twenty, had actually risked his own life and limb to save an orphan boy from a burning livery stable.

Elizabeth received these voluntary reports with a grain of salt and as much patience as could be mustered. The first few stories about Mr. Darcy amazed her, until she recalled Harriet's comment about him owning half of Lambton. Surely, the businessmen and their wives were only looking out for their own interests, which were doubtlessly best served by staying in their landlord's good graces. By the time Miss Bennet's fourth conversation of the morning took such a detour, she was far less interested in hearing Mr. Darcy's praises than in scuttling the dialogue along and forcing it to center upon Miss Georgiana.

When all the prying came to nothing, Elizabeth went out onto the street, found a solitary bench put up against a tree, and sat down, torn by indecision. A great part of her wanted to go back to Longbourn, acquiring her own amnesia along the way, and celebrate Anne's wedding as if nothing had happened. But how could she? If she had been unsettled before by Anne's resemblance to Mr. Darcy, she was positively frantic now. How could she abandon her mission when it seemed more possible than ever that the wild ideas which had entered her head a few nights ago were true? Would she ever be able to sleep again without knowing for certain who Anne was, or was not?

But sweet repose would cost a pretty penny: her pride.

In the past five hours, the maid's answer that Mr. Darcy was probably absent from Derbyshire rankled in Elizabeth's mind, and muttered with increasing volume that there was still one last avenue of getting at the truth. One quick walk through Pemberley, like any curious wayfarer, and all would be made as plain as day. The servants *there* would certainly be aware of their little mistress's final resting place, and even if they refused to speak on the matter, they surely could be persuaded to say something about Miss Darcy's appearance. The moment that they declared the deceased girl as dark as her brother would be the moment of Elizabeth's immense relief.

Reminding herself one last time that by all accounts Mr. Fitzwilliam Darcy was *not* home for the summer, the young woman had taken a deep breath, called all her courage, and hired the carriage she now rode in.

It is for the best, she silently attempted to convince an uncomfortable conscience as they journeyed. *I am almost certainly mistaken, but my intentions are as pure as they could possibly be. Besides, Mr. Darcy invested a great deal of trust in me when he forewarned me about Wickham's character despite the great risk to his sister's reputation; and that does endow me, I daresay, with a duty to act if I ever suspect that particular lieutenant preying on a lady of my acquaintance!*

Her musings were suddenly cut short by a loud creak and violent lurch of the carriage. Flailing out her arms, the girl managed to grasp the side of the coach with one hand and the cushions behind her with the other as she was lifted a good inch and a half into the air. Landing down upon the seat so hard that breath was momentarily squeezed out of her lungs, the bewildered young woman glanced back at the road, expecting to see the culprit lesion which had interrupted her guilty internal monologue. The path behind them, however, was pristine and smooth.

"Beg your pardon, miss," the coachman said, turning around. "That is the second time that has happened to me today. When we reach our destination I shall take a look at the carriage and see if I can find what has been causing those horrid knocks."

Elizabeth murmured her appreciation and forgiveness, and redirected her attention at her surroundings.

They passed a large, open gate, and the coachman informed her that they were entering the estate. Expecting the house to come into view directly, Miss Bennet looked around curiously, only to be thwarted for another quarter of an hour as they traversed numerous groves and woods. It was only after they had passed hundreds of the finest trees in England that the stone mansion came into view.

It stood on an expansive green lawn. A large, gleaming lake prefaced it, and formal gardens could be glimpsed in the back of the edifice. Elizabeth was delighted. She had never seen a place for which nature had done so much, or where natural beauty had been so little counteracted by an awkward taste.

And of all this, I might have been mistress!

Recalling, however, that the mistress of Pemberley would necessarily be bound to one of the proudest, most disagreeable men in the country, it was easy for Elizabeth to refrain from remorse.

The coachman turned around again and said,

"I will drive you to the servants' entrance, madam. I mean no disrespect, but I find that visitors who try the side door often gain admittance more quickly than those who attempt to enter by the main one. Most likely, it is because there are more servants on hand to answer the doorbell, that wing being nearer the kitchen."

Elizabeth smiled politely.

"Then, as expediency is one of my primary concerns today, let it be so. And, anyhow, those archways in the front of the house look far too intimidating to be crossed by a mere sightseer!"

The coachman laughed at her wit, as Harriet had done the night before.

179

"I am afraid that you will have to cross them anyhow, milady, on your way out, as well as the courtyard behind them. The staff always has visitors leave by the front."

"Is that so?" Elizabeth murmured, trying to appear interested in such paltry matters, while the carriage came to a slow halt.

Chapter 37

Legs shaking, Miss Bennet fiercely clutched the sides of the coach and then the coachman's hand in order to descend.

O, what am I doing?

Especially here!

Steeling her nerves, she walked to the side entrance. As she rang for admittance, another moment of panic and a preposterous delusion seized her: what if Mr. Darcy himself were to answer the door?

Elizabeth Bennet, have you lost every grain of sense which you ever had? The man you think of would never even darken a servants' entrance, let alone heed the bidding of its bell! And anyhow, he is absent from home now.

She heard the faint sound of footsteps – feminine footsteps, it seemed – coming nearer to the door. And, indeed, when the lock clicked and the door swung open, she found herself looking at a maid of about five-and-twenty.

"Good day," Elizabeth began breathlessly. "I come from another part of England, and as I travelled through Derbyshire I heard about this great estate. Is it open to uninvited visitors at present?"

"It is, ma'am." The maid dropped a curtsy, but not a smile, and stood aside to let her pass. "Please come in; I shall fetch the housekeeper for you."

"Thank you," the lady replied, and hesitantly, crossed the threshold.

When the door had been closed again and Elizabeth was temporarily abandoned in the hall, an even greater feeling of discomfort alighted upon her. At first, she trained her eyes upon the carpet, feeling that it would be too great a crime to inspect the house whose command she had spurned viciously a few months ago. Recollecting at length, however, that information about Miss Darcy's fate would probably not be engraved upon the oak floor or woven into the carpet, Miss Bennet slowly allowed her pupils to rise and look about the corridor.

It was magnificent! The servants' entrance put Longbourn's main one to shame. A staircase with a gleaming wooden railing spiraled above her. The rug on which her feet were planted was the softest, largest she had ever seen. A decorative statue stood in one corner, and an exotic species of plant in another. And it was all dustless. It reminded Elizabeth of Mr. Darcy: handsome and pragmatic.

The sound of a hem dragging across the floor caught Miss Bennet's ear. Craning her neck, she was attempting to glimpse its owner, when that personage came into the hall.

"Good day, miss," said a soft, doleful voice. "You wish to see the estate?"

"Yes, if it is no inconvenience," Elizabeth replied, shocked. By first impression, the woman before her could be judged to be about five-and-eighty, and she was stunned that Mr. Darcy trusted his house to such an old and feeble woman. But, as the housekeeper came closer, the girl realized that her true age was nearer to five-and-sixty, and that the extra lines disfiguring her countenance were of melancholy rather than of maturity.

"No, it is no inconvenience at all," the woman said civilly. "I am Mrs. Reynolds."

For an instant, Elizabeth bit her lip, wondering whether she ought to risk giving her real name or be cautious and fib lest the housekeeper had heard of a Miss Bennet before. After a moment, she decided upon honesty, especially as her surname was a relatively common one.

"And I am Miss Bennet," the younger woman rejoined.

"Delighted to make your acquaintance," the servant said without any particular ceremony, and curtsying, began the presentation which she had made hundreds of times. A brief overview about the architectural style of the building, a concise summary of the number of rooms, and they were off, touring the famous Pemberley.

Despite the fact that the apartments were lofty and well-fitted up, with furniture that inspired her admiration and approbation, Elizabeth noted it to be a very somber home. A deep melancholy seemed to hang in each chamber, and lingered in Mrs. Reynolds' spiritless tone. Going from room to room, the housekeeper flatly related the size of the rooms and the price of the furniture. Even several fascinating stories, including one about how Pemberley had hosted Charles the Second when that king had been detained in Derbyshire by floods, were told without a single spark of excitement or pride. All the maids and menservants whom they passed in the hall possessed the same downcast eyes and lines of sorrow which marred the countenance of their superior. Elizabeth silently empathized with them, and wondered, angrily, what sort of master Mr. Darcy had to be in order to instill such an atmosphere of hopelessness in each and every inhabitant of his house.

Overcoming her antecedent shyness and growing bolder each minute they walked through the mansion without encountering its proprietor, Miss Bennet put her private opinions away and began to scour the halls for any clues about the life and times of Georgiana Darcy.

For a long time, they eluded her. Therefore, the instant she spotted a display of miniatures she went over to it with as much haste as would be unsuspicious.

Inspecting them, she dwelt energetically over each one representing a feminine countenance, and gratefully discovered that they were all foreign to her. Smiling, she asked the housekeeper who they were of, and whether any of the faces imprinted by the painter's brush belonged to the immediate Darcy family. To her surprise, a shadow of displeasure fell across Mrs. Reynolds' worn face at this inquiry, and it was with quite a bit of reluctance that she came forward and said,

"Almost all are of the family or of their close connections. These are the aunts of the late master, who died some five years ago; that one is of his dear wife. And this one is Miss Georgiana, taken when she was about five years old."

Elizabeth sharply turned back to the last indicated miniature, one which she had all but ignored before, and scrutinized it thoroughly. A mere child was characterized on it, a little girl with plump cheeks and big eyes, and with tresses rather darker than she remembered Anne's being.

"Miss Georgiana seems to have been a charming child," she said cautiously. "We are discussing the sister of the present Mr. Darcy, are we not?"

"Yes, madam," Mrs. Reynolds replied.

"Is this a faithful representation of her at five?"

"In most respects, yes, but everyone was of the opinion that the artist could have mixed his colors better when painting her hair. It was lighter than that."

"It must have been completely blonde, then," Elizabeth confirmed uncomfortably.

"Yes, miss."

"Did it darken as she grew?"

"No."

Elizabeth swallowed and nodded. Unsure of how to proceed, and unwilling to single out Miss Georgiana's portrait further lest the housekeeper grow quizzical of her curiosity, Miss Bennet turned to the right, where a few male profiles were represented.

"And these?" she asked, doing her utmost to feign interest in the answers.

This time, Mrs. Reynolds paused for so long that Miss Bennet wondered whether she would comply with the request at all. But, finally, the older woman began pointing at the various miniatures and saying in a quiet voice,

"That one is of Mr. Wickham, the son of my late master's steward. And that...," her finger moved to point at the next miniature, and suddenly acquired a slight quiver. Her voice, likewise, became unsteady and broke off. The housekeeper drew in a deep breath, as if to collect herself, and repeated, "And that, is...my present master...," before her voice once again faded into silence. The stillness lasted for a mere second before being shattered by a deep, profound sob.

Startled, Elizabeth whirled around. She found Mrs. Reynolds putting her hands over her face, and shedding generous tears.

"Ma'am!" Miss Bennet exclaimed. Her sense of compassion was thoroughly awakened, and gently taking the elder woman's arm, she managed to steer her shaking form to a pair of chairs stationed nearby. Depositing Mrs. Reynolds in one, she tentatively took the other, and asked,

"May I call someone? Do you feel ill?"

The housekeeper shook her head, fruitlessly attempting to stem the tears which flowed and hold back the sobs which punctuated them at frequent intervals. At a loss, Elizabeth grasped her own handkerchief and offered it to the servant, who took it with embarrassment.

"Pray tell me, what is the matter? Might I be of any assistance?" the girl pressed, her heart overflowing with sympathy for the poor woman.

These questions went unanswered, but slowly, the housekeeper began to regain some control over herself. She set about wiping her eyes with the handkerchief.

Desperate to solve the conundrum, and hoping that she could somehow remedy whatever had caused the stoic housekeeper to burst into such profound grief, Elizabeth ventured to make a guess which seemed, to her, very reasonable.

"I do not mean to pry, but it is quite plain that Mr. Darcy's miniature upset you. Has…has he been unkind to you?"

Mrs. Reynolds' countenance abruptly rose up from the handkerchief, and her eyes regarded the guest with horror.

"Mr. Darcy, unkind!" she exclaimed, as if it were a sin to utter those three words in the same sentence. "He has been nothing of the sort! I have never had a cross word from him in all my life, and I have known him since he was four years old."

Elizabeth drew back, stunned. Wondering if satire had any place in the housekeeper's forceful defense of Mr. Darcy, she led the subject on by remarking,

"There are very few people of whom so much can be said. You are lucky in having such a master."

This capitulation gratified the faithful servant, and she replied in a softer, more talkative tone,

"Yes, madam, I know I am. If I was to go through the world, I could not meet with a better. But I have always observed that they who are good-natured when they are children are good-natured when they grow up; and he was always the sweetest-tempered, most generous-hearted boy in the world. Being a stranger in these parts, you cannot know that there is not one of his tenants or servants but will give the master a good name." Mrs. Reynolds wiped away the remainder of her tears, thus allowing her pupils an unobstructed view of Elizabeth's shocked expression. Swallowing guiltily, she continued in a low voice, "I apologize, Miss Bennet; I have clearly dismayed you with my outburst, and owe you an explanation. My behavior has been insupportable, and I must admit that the master's miniature was the cause of it, but for a much different reason than the one you supposed. The truth is, I am a foolish old woman, and…I have avoided looking at any likeness of Mr. Darcy of late. Why, I have even taken to turning my head away from his portrait whenever I pass through the gallery upstairs! Consequently, when I looked at the miniature just now, every feeling which has been…avoided… repressed…for so long erupted forth."

The contradictions and mysteries contained in this vague reply naturally awakened every curious fiber in Elizabeth's being, and longing to hear more she asked,

"What sort of feelings?" Recollecting herself, Miss Bennet hastily added, "You need not answer me if you do not wish it, Mrs. Reynolds. I am well aware that my inquiry was meddlesome and that answering it may cost you your position."

The housekeeper studied the worried face before her. Decades of serving gentlemen and gentlewomen had made her extremely proficient at distinguishing true concern from ulterior motives. It was an indispensable talent when dealing with the likes of Miss Bingley! Therefore, a mere moment of observation was sufficient to convince Mrs. Reynolds that Miss Bennet genuinely wished to offer comfort and to understand her relationship with Mr. Darcy, and was not just fishing for an interesting piece of gossip to spread abroad. Hence, she dared to apprise the girl of the partial truth.

"It is difficult to see the confident, youthful countenances which are depicted on those canvases, madam; the contrast with the grave face, which is now all too familiar to us at Pemberley, is too stark. Have you heard that Mr. Darcy's younger sister was recently killed in a carriage accident?"

Elizabeth shook her head, frowning at the discrepancy.

"I understood that Miss Darcy drowned."

"That is accurate as well, I suppose. The horses bolted, crashed the entire carriage into a stream, and the current swept it and its occupant away."

"How dreadful!"

"Aye, it was. Miss Darcy was beloved by everyone who knew her. And so accomplished! She used to play and sing all day long, and was the handsomest lady that was ever seen."

Although they were on the subject which was her avowed purpose for coming to Pemberley, Elizabeth found herself becoming slightly frightened that the conversation would permanently turn and preclude her from ever discovering the other information which she was suddenly restless to know. Extracting further details about the lost gentlewoman would probably prove effortless, considering Mrs. Reynolds' obvious fondness for her former young mistress, while learning about Mr. Darcy's queer effects upon his servants would be hopeless once the redness dissipated from her companion's eyes. What praise was more valuable than the praise of an intelligent servant? Could all that the tradespeople in Lambton had said about Mr. Darcy be true? Hoping to redirect the dialogue, Elizabeth commented carefully,

"And yet…it was not Miss Darcy's miniature which caused you to lose your composure."

"No. We cried enough for her sweet sake, but the dear child is almost certainly in Heaven, and happy. The master, on the other hand, is not."

"Considering his loss, that is understandable," Elizabeth replied softly, remembering how amiably the gentleman used to speak of his little sister. "No one should have to bury their sibling at so young an age."

Mrs. Reynolds wiped away another tear which had slipped out from under her eyelids.

"The treacherous waters denied the poor master even that," she sighed. "They combed the tributary downstream, but never found anything to bury. No funeral, no last embrace - nothing to ease one's sorrow even a little."

Every fiber in Elizabeth tensed.

"You mean she was never recovered?" she whispered fearfully.

The housekeeper shook her head.

The visitor's heart wrenched painfully, as every suspicion harbored within it intensified. Reason strove to unknot the twisted organ, murmuring that it was far more probable that Miss Darcy was presently resting on the murky bottom of the sea rather than sitting in Longbourn's parlor with Mr. Wickham by her side. But in the face of so long a string of coincidences, even it was tempted to surrender. Trying to keep up the conversation while most of her attention was directed to her private thoughts, she remarked,

"But it is early yet - it has been but a few months. I am certain that eventually your master will come out of this melancholy."

"I certainly hope so, but each time death pays him a visit it leaves less and less inducements to entice him back into the world of joy. It first crossed his path when he was but sixteen, and stole away Lady Anne, his mother. Master Fitzwilliam was downcast for a long while, but he clung ever closer to his father's side and to his sister's little hand, and tried to substitute as much as he could for that which was lost. Do you know what that dear boy did?" Elizabeth, intrigued, shook her head. "It so happened that shortly before Lady Anne's last illness she had been teaching Miss Georgiana the pianoforte. Miss Darcy's small, plump fingers were just beginning to play. And then suddenly, a fever carried Lady Anne away. The poor little mistress

187

was disconsolate, and refused to touch the instrument for weeks. It was a pity, since even at that age it was apparent that she possessed a knack for it. Dear Master Fitzwilliam, in particular, was extremely anxious that she take it up again. Without telling a soul what he was about, he began to lock himself in the music room every evening for hours on end. Then one day, he left the door open. To the surprise of all, but particularly of Miss Georgiana, one of Lady Anne's favorite and most complicated melodies resonated throughout the house. The little mistress dashed into the room and found the brother who had never touched any instrument but the violin before playing as well as their mother had, if not better. The happiest of smiles upon her face, the child ran forward, leapt upon the bench, and joined Master Fitzwilliam."

"He certainly was a good brother," Elizabeth murmured, finding herself tempted to weep at the scene which Mrs. Reynolds painted. "I confess that I do not know another man who would teach himself to play the pianoforte simply to please his little sister."

"It was always his way, ma'am. Whatever could give his sister pleasure was sure to be done in a moment." The housekeeper sighed. "And then his father went too, about five years ago. That was even harder on him, I believe, for mountains of responsibility alighted upon his three-and-twenty-year-old shoulders the moment the old gentleman breathed his last. But nothing can compare to this last tragedy. One expects to outlive one's parents, after all. Very few expect to see the death of a sister ten years their junior, especially when the girl is but sixteen."

"Very, very true," Miss Bennet sighed compassionately.

Collecting herself, Mrs. Reynolds pressed the handkerchief against her eyes one more time and then quickly rose to her feet.

"O, what are we doing? You came to see the estate, ma'am, not to hear the useless moaning of an old domestic. Come, come along, there is still the upstairs gallery to see. There are many fine pictures there."

Though unwilling to abandon the conversation, Elizabeth obediently stood and began to follow the housekeeper to the marble staircase. They had just put their hands on the banister in preparation for ascent when a door in the corridor opened and a young maid rushed through it. Approaching her superior, she said breathlessly,

"You are wanted in the kitchen immediately, Mrs. Reynolds!"

Weariness took over the housekeeper's expression, and she asked as if she had been forced to make the same inquiry too many times in recent days,

"What is the matter?"

"One of the gardeners criticized the midday meal, saying that he would rather have a slab of boiled meat rather than the fancy dishes which the cook has been feeding us servants these last weeks. Predictably, this sent Mrs. Comtois into one of her tempers and she snapped that she had been hired to prepare the finest dishes from her country and not English peasant cooking. You can imagine the argument which this spawned."

Mrs. Reynolds gave an exhausted nod, and remembering Elizabeth, turned to her with embarrassment.

"I am afraid that we are all a little frazzled, madam," she said apologetically, clearly ashamed that the private disputes of Pemberley's servants had been aired in such a public fashion. "I cannot express enough regrets, but I am afraid that I must leave you and see to this. If you have no objection, Ellen will finish your tour. May she?"

"Yes, of course," the guest replied hastily. "It was a pleasure to make your acquaintance, Mrs. Reynolds."

"Likewise, Miss Bennet, likewise." For an instant, the older woman moved her hand as if she were going to overstep boundaries and place it upon the gentlewoman's, but caught herself in time to avoid taking the colossal liberty. In its stead, she simply gazed gratefully into Elizabeth's eyes and said, "Thank you," meaningfully.

"Thank *you*, Mrs. Reynolds."

The housekeeper gathered her skirts in her hands and hurried off to quell the tempest. Miss Bennet was left alone with the young maid, who during the leave-taking had been rethinking the manner of her entrance and come to the conclusion that she had committed a *faux-pas* in front of the visitor. Sheepishly, she now tried to vindicate her fellow servants' behavior by murmuring,

"I apologize for depriving you of Mrs. Reynolds, miss, for she is a much better guide than I, but she is the only one who can soothe Mrs. Comtois' feelings. The cook means well, for she is excellent at and takes great delight in her work. Pleasing the master's palate was usually enough for her, but with Mr. Darcy - ," she suddenly paused and then quickly continued. "Recently, she has started preparing novel meals for us as well. I find them absolutely delicious, but am

189

afraid that some of the men's stomachs are unaccustomed to French dishes."

Elizabeth civilly replied that it was very natural for men to crave hearty meals and assured Ellen that she would be glad to see the rest of Pemberley with her.

The maid, therefore, led her upstairs and into the gallery. There were many beautiful pictures there, but it was only when the lady noticed a large representation of Mr. Fitzwilliam Darcy that she halted.

Standing before his gently smiling portrait, Elizabeth began to review all that Mrs. Reynolds had said, and found her opinions of the man softening. He had earned the highest commendations as a brother, landlord, master. So beloved was he, that his sorrows were his servants' own. Surely, this was not the likeness of a tyrant. His manner of expression during his proposal and during his forays into society could doubtlessly stand some improvement, but on the whole, the gentleman who had offered for her several months ago was good and honorable. For the first time, Elizabeth felt honored and grateful that she had merited Mr. Fitzwilliam Darcy's attentions.

After a prolonged while, during which a soft smile unconsciously crept across her face, Elizabeth tore her eyes away from Mr. Darcy's portrait and glanced at the one hanging to the right of it.

Anne's gaze arrested hers.

Chapter 38

As if in a trance, Elizabeth stepped closer to the painting and touched its frame.

There was not the slightest possibility of a mistake. The young woman gracing the canvas was familiar - far too familiar. From the golden curls falling at the sides of her shy, uncertain face, to the dark blue ring on her right hand, Elizabeth knew her!

Miss Bennet's mind began to tumult, recognizing what this meant. In the brief instant it had taken her to behold a simple portrait an entirely new set of challenges, which she had never allowed herself to fully consider or catalogue before, had arisen. Continuing to finger the metal which encapsulated the image of the fateful bride-to-be, and the black ribbon hanging on its bottom, she noticed Ellen looking at her askance. Realizing how odd her proximity to the portrait and distressed countenance must appear, the visitor obtusely inquired,

"And who is this?" as if she did not know.

"Miss Georgiana Darcy, the late sister of the present master, miss. She died most tragically a few months ago, hence the dark ribbon there."

"I see," Elizabeth muttered, stepping away from the wall and willing herself to walk away.

Ellen pointed out a few more curiosities in the gallery and mentioned that the tour was complete, but the girl who ought to have been her listener heard nothing at all. With burning eyes and a pounding heart, she desperately began to deliberate on what had to be done. Should she ask someone of the Darcy household, perhaps Mrs. Reynolds, to return with her to Hertfordshire and collaborate her identification of Anne? But then again, she knew how strange such a story and request would sound to the housekeeper. Furthermore, she knew nothing about how privy Mrs. Reynolds was to the events of Ramsgate, and without enlightening her she could scarcely explain the absolute necessity for speed and tact in dealing with this new courtship. Assuming that the servant was ignorant of his earlier plotting, confiding so much in so new an acquaintance would be extremely ill-advised, particularly as the housekeeper's own master had strongly emphasized that Elizabeth's secrecy would be appreciated in the matter. And even should all this proceed flawlessly, Mrs. Reynolds was not at liberty to abandon her post at Pemberley for days on end. Shaking her head as she followed Ellen through the halls as the latter showed her out, Elizabeth discarded the complicated idea. No, there was a single reasonable course of action: returning to Longbourn on her own, confiding in her father, and begging him to stop the nuptials.

One thing was certain: time was of the essence! The wedding was set for ten o'clock on Thursday morning, and it was already early Tuesday afternoon. Even if she were to catch the fastest posts, she would only reach Longbourn around daybreak on the wedding day. Thus, every minute was precious. As soon as they reached the front door she hurriedly bid Ellen good-day and exited the great house without delay.

Nearly cantering through the courtyard, Elizabeth rushed through one of the archways and gained the drive, only to stop short.

The hired carriage was missing.

In its place was its coachman, a closed umbrella in his hand, waiting patiently. Turning around at the sound of her trotting footsteps, he bowed.

"Where is the coach?" Elizabeth gasped, glancing up and down the long, curved drive.

"I am sorry, madam. While you were within the house, I noticed that the front axle of the carriage was cracked. It would be unsafe to proceed any further in it. However, one of Pemberley's grooms noticed my dilemma, and took the coach to the stables for repairs. They are working on it now."

Miss Bennet blanched. Of all the times for a hired coach to fail! It was five miles back to Lambton. Walking was out of the question, even for her; it would take at least three hours, and the last post-carriage was scheduled to leave the village in two. If she were not on it, Anne - *Georgiana Darcy* - was as good as married to Mr. Wickham.

Concealing her fear and frustration, she asked in a voice of forced calmness,

"How long will it take?"

"We do not know, milady. If all goes smoothly, the axle may be repaired within the hour, but there is also a possibility that other problems may be discovered in the meantime."

Elizabeth nodded.

"If you will allow it, miss, I shall go to the stables and check on their progress, and then report back to you."

"Yes, pray do that," the lady said breathlessly.

"I suggest that you stay under the archway, madam, and take this with you should you choose to venture out," the driver continued, offering her the umbrella he held. She accepted. "The sky has become very clouded in the past half-hour. I will be back as soon as I can, but everything is larger on these estates, including the distance from the courtyard to the stables."

Elizabeth managed to nod and dismissed him.

As soon as the liveried figure disappeared from her sight, however, Miss Bennet leaned the umbrella against the middle of the stone passage, shed all restraint, and commenced pacing wildly within the darkened archway. Typically, she would have abandoned the edifice at once and taken advantage of the postponement to explore the fine gardens and majestic groves, but this time was determined to remain where she could be easily found by the coachman.

Is nothing destined to go as planned? What will I do if the coach is not fixed in time? Is there some way to get word to Longbourn to delay the wedding until my return?

The only idea which befriended her was that of an express, and it betrayed her almost immediately afterwards. Her funds for travelling were tight, and a large extra expense might make it impossible for her to pay her way home. Then again, Mr. Bennet believed her in London, and might consider a letter announcing her to be in Derbyshire and having uncovered so stunning a discovery the work of some clever forger. Worst of all, an express arriving at Longbourn was sure to attract every member of the family and staff to the front door. In such a case, it was entirely too probable that Mr. Bennet would read the missive aloud in front of Anne and Mr. Wickham, inducing dangerous confusion in one and possibly spurring the other into some desperate action.

A gust of wind howled through the courtyard, followed by the pitter-patter of raindrops. The latter exponentially increased in number until they constituted a veritable downpour. Miss Bennet watched the water seep into the gravel and into the grass beyond. Wet roads. Another unwelcome complication. In addition, fog rapidly shrouded the landscape until it was impossible to see more than fifteen feet into the distance.

Hopelessness overcame Elizabeth. Allowing her legs to go slightly limp, she permitted her right arm to come into contact with the hard wall as she stared out into the storm. Even nature was conspiring against her!

Perhaps instead of fretting and seeking nonexistent solutions, she would do better to come to terms with the fact that when she next stood under her father's roof, Anne would be an unhappily married woman. At this point, maybe it was more prudent to start devising strategies to lessen the poor child's sorrow as a matron, rather than plotting a way to avoid it altogether.

The sound of footsteps coming from the right of the drive roused her. Straightening up and craning her neck forward in anticipation, she impatiently waited for their founder to emerge from the fog. Surely it was the coachman, and perchance he bore news that the axle had been repaired! Her fortune, after all, was long overdue for a favorable turn.

Yet another disappointment followed. It was not the coachman. The figure which could be slightly traced through the fog was too tall to be the man who had driven her to the estate. Allowing herself a small sigh and leaning against the passageway once more, Elizabeth half-heartedly kept watching the shadow.

It was then that something about it struck her as very odd.

Despite being out in the cold, pouring rain, the figure was advancing very slowly, demonstrating no apparent haste to leave the elements behind. It seemed to be dragging its feet, walking at a pace slower than a stroll. Upon closer inspection, its shoulders were stooped, giving it the air of an old, defeated man withdrawing from the smoldering ashes of his village, without the slightest idea of where to go or to whom to turn.

The silhouette advanced a few more steps, lessening the impact of the misty veil. Its form became sharper and more detailed.

Elizabeth violently started.

Her wide eyes swept over the man who was approaching. So intent was she on observation that no thought of fleeing the premises or inventing excuses entered her head at that moment. Her mind, which generally gave credence to what her eyes saw and ears heard, was greatly doubting the information which those two organs were at present receiving.

No servant, but *Mr. Darcy*, was before her.

He wore no outer coat, only a fine white shirt and burgundy waistcoat, and walked with a hesitant, uncertain gait. His head and eyes were both bowed down towards the gravel. The forlorn man was as wet as if he had just taken a swim in the lake over yonder: the rain had already saturated his hair and clothes, and rivulets of water ran down his white sleeves before dripping from the tips of his dangling fingers. But, disturbingly, the victim seemed completely ignorant of the downpour's assault. He shuffled down the drive as if he had entered it by accident.

But he had some sense of direction, or at least a habit which had survived the death of his spirit, for, much to Elizabeth's dismay, he began to turn into the very archway in which she was standing!

For a single second Miss Bennet panicked. Then she noticed the gentleman's downcast eyes. Taking inspiration from them, the uninvited visitor hastily retreated a few steps into the darkest section of the tunnel and pressed herself up against the wall, praying that like the precipitation, she would remain unnoticed. During this maneuver, reason momentarily intruded, and informed her that it was foolhardy *not* to bar his way – this was, after all, the brother of Georgiana Darcy, who had even more reasons than she to ensure that Mr. Wickham's upcoming wedding did not take place. But no - she was unequal to facing him with so little preparation, and was certain that he would be infuriated to find a woman whom he must loathe by now upon his grounds, witnessing his pitiable state.

The drenched figure slowly entered the passageway and progressed through it in the same manner which had brought him across the drive. His head remained bent, and the dull, sloshing footsteps produced by the waterlogged boots came much further apart than one would expect. Elizabeth stopped her breath, and nearly her heart, as he drew nearer…a few more seconds - he was directly before her - and she could feel the edges of the bricks pressing into her back…there, he had passed her! She would only wait until he was definitely out of earshot before she exhaled; then she would watch him go into the house, and run away, and resume thinking of how best to save his little sister from the clutches of his former friend…and how best to eventually inform him of Georgiana's ongoing existence. A few more steps, and he would clear the archway -

Whump. Clash!

The forgotten umbrella, stationed at the opposite wall, had hooked the inattentive man's boot, and completely upset his balance.

The tall figure fell forward heavily, destined for a hard cushion of paved stones.

"Mr. Darcy!" she cried instinctively, springing forward.

The words were not fully out of her mouth before she vainly attempted to choke them back. But they rang out clearly, and even echoed through the passageway.

Her aghast voice succeeded where thunder had failed. The gentleman became aware of danger. He reached out and balanced himself against the wall. She wished to shrink away anew, but it was too late. Still braced against the archway, Mr. Darcy turned around.

His eyes, if so they could be called, met hers. As she stared into them, however, Elizabeth immediately saw that they were not the eyes of the Mr. Fitzwilliam Darcy that she had known but a few months prior. They were devoid of the slightest sparkle of his intellect, the smallest hint of the admirer and observer he had been. Instead, they were the eyes of a man whose soul has died, and whose body, although tarrying, inches towards the same end; they were sallow, flat, and expressionless. While they were fixed upon her, Elizabeth doubted that he actually *saw*.

Time seemed to have stopped. They stared at each other: he with that terrible, blank stare, she with a panicked, undecided one. She was afraid *of* him, as she would have been frightened by any ghost or madman who rose up before her; she was afraid *for* him, since she felt that it was just a matter of days before whatever he suffered from literally ended his life. And she knew not how to act. All tutoring in manners and proper conversation was useless when faced with such an unnatural countenance!

She thought of speaking, but was uncertain whether English words would bring him to himself, or merely resemble the sound of crickets to him. Worst of all, they might even move the man to some irrational, violent rage. Not being an expert in potentially deranged minds, Elizabeth decided not to take the risk. She merely swallowed, even though her mouth was as dry as beach sand at high noon, and remained still, allowing him to make the decision of how, or if, to proceed.

Neither of them ever knew that this protracted moment lasted only fifteen seconds. Towards the end of it, a faint tinge of perception and animation diffused into Mr. Darcy's eyes, clearly drawn from some deep, deep well inside of him where, against all odds, a cupful of life still flowed.

In a husky voice, which had obviously not been used for days, the gentleman gasped out,

"Miss Bennet?"

Still too much under the influence of the oppressive spell to think of a more original salutation, Elizabeth foolishly repeated,

"Mr. Darcy."

The sound of her own voice, however, jolted the lady back into reality and great embarrassment. She took on a very red color. Breaking away her gaze from his and casting it on the ground, she began to stammer,

"I, I…was informed that you would…almost certainly…not be home, sir. But the fault was entirely mine. I ought to have…inquired the same of your housekeeper, rather than relying on the report of a person in Lambton…I was just leaving."

At the word 'leaving', Mr. Darcy started anew and glanced to the right and left, looking for the despised conveyance or person who would transport Elizabeth Bennet from his sight. Finding none, he asked,

"How?"

Having collected herself somewhat, the young woman answered more evenly,

"I came in a hired coach which had a cracked axle. The coachman has it near the stables, and it will be repaired promptly, I am sure."

Mr. Darcy peered out at the drive once again, and for the first time, registered the state of the weather which he had just traversed.

"It is raining," he murmured, amazed, seemingly to himself. Turning to Elizabeth once more, he finally seemed to shake off the mental cobwebs which had woven themselves over his consciousness, and in a decisive voice much like his customary one, repeated, "It is raining. Have you been waiting out here long?"

"Not at all, sir."

"Pray come into the house."

Elizabeth knew not where to look or how to act. This piece of civility took her completely unawares.

"No, I thank you. It is very generous of you, but I am perfectly well. Please do not concern yourself."

"Miss Bennet," the gentleman coaxed, "there is absolutely no logical reason for you to wait in the chilly archway when it is in the power of an acquaintance to furnish you with warm, comfortable quarters. Axles take a long time to repair or replace, and even if it were ready at this very moment, it would be unwise to travel in these conditions." Glancing at the ground, he descried the umbrella which he had toppled. Reaching down, he picked it up, shook it out, and opened it. Holding it up over his head, Mr. Darcy extended his other hand to her, and uttered a soft appeal: "Come."

The young woman heartily wished that the cobblestones beneath her soles would loosen their connections and drop her gently into the crevice, but as they did not oblige she saw that she had but one other option. Rebuffing this earnest invitation and standing in the gale would make her look like a silly and stubborn child. She had brewed this strange-tasting tea; now she would have to drink it. Thus, she hesitantly walked towards Mr. Darcy, and consented to join him under the temporary shelter.

He carefully manipulated the arm holding the umbrella to ensure that none of the dripping water from his white sleeve would splash upon her dress, and they started off through the downpour. Halfway across the courtyard, the proprietor of the estate looked down at the lady next to him and asked kindly,

"Is anyone else with you? Do you have any friends whom we can also invite indoors?"

Elizabeth's face was completely coral with embarrassment as she answered,

"I came alone." Before he could make another inquiry, she made a statement of her own. "I was strongly reassured that the estate would be closed to the public if the family were in residence."

He acknowledged the truth of it, saying,

"Usually it would be. I have always closed it off upon my arrivals by a direct order. This time, I must have forgotten."

Elizabeth only nodded, unable to think of anything else to say. By then they had ascended the stairs which led to the front door. Two maids who had seen them coming threw open the heavy double doors to admit them, their eyes almost staring out of their heads. Mr. Darcy handed the umbrella to one of them, whispered a few words which Elizabeth did not catch but which sent the girls obediently scurrying down the stairs towards the kitchen, and then showed her into the grandest drawing room located in the anterior of the long corridor.

"Please make yourself comfortable, Miss Bennet," the Master of Pemberley urged. She turned around and politely thanked him, feeling ill at ease all the while. Giving his own clothes a quick, abashed gaze, he reluctantly murmured, "And please excuse me for a few minutes."

This Elizabeth did willingly.

"Of course, sir."

When he had gone back into the hall and drawn the door shut after himself, she had never been more relieved to be alone.

Chapter 39

Fitzwilliam Darcy bounded up the main staircase three steps at a time. For the first time since the fifth of May he had a definite destination - his chambers - and a clear purpose – dressing - in mind. The senses of sight and hearing, which had lay half-dormant since that fateful day, had been jolted into full awareness by the vista of Elizabeth Bennet and the sound of her soft voice. Darcy's eyes and ears were once again perceptive, noticing every detail of the banister his hand grasped and mindful of the dull thumps his soaked boots produced. More importantly, his thoughts were no longer fixated on the past, but concentrated on the present and the future. Once he reached the landing, he saw his valet and a maid conversing in the hall. It had been months since he had recalled their names, much less spoken them, but as he flew by the astonished attendants, he gasped out,

"Olivia, good day. Fredrick...come along, man! I need you - urgently!"

As soon as these words reached the servants' ears their employer disappeared behind the doors of his private apartments. The valet and maid turned and stared at each other, dismayed, for it did not occur to them that the spectacle of a drenched, frenzied Master of Pemberley dashing through the corridor was a foretoken of amendment. Instead, Fredrick wrung his hands and exclaimed bitterly,

"He has gone mad at last!"

Olivia nodded, tears springing to her eyes.

"But it was to be expected," she replied tremblingly, reaching for a handkerchief. "Not sleeping, not eating, crushed by melancholy...any mind, however strong, will eventually give way to mania under such a strain! The question is, what shall we do now with our dear, dear master?"

Fredrick took a deep breath and rallied himself before answering,

"One thing is certain: we will not abandon him. When he was well he often did us a good turn when he did not have to, and now that he is broken the least we can do is demonstrate our gratitude by tending to him tenderly. Go and tell Mrs. Reynolds to send for the physician, perhaps there is something he will be able to do. I shall go to Mr. Darcy, and try to calm him as best I can."

Olivia murmured her assent, and began the descent downstairs. The valet, for his part, took a brief detour before hurrying to the master's suite: he stepped into a room which housed a medicine chest and retrieved a small bottle of laudanum. Concealing this article in his closed hand, the faithful servant then made his way to Mr. Darcy's chambers.

Within, he found a most unnerving scene. Wet apparel was scattered about - on the bed, the chairs, and even on the floor. Fredrick's employer had apparently relinquished hope of obtaining the tardy valet's aid and had proceeded to attire himself in dry breeches, shirt, boots and waistcoat. He was presently standing at the full-length mirror, frantically tying his cravat. But, by far, most frightening was the fact that the formerly steady and composed man was speaking excitedly to his reflection. To an attendant who was unaware of the happenings in Kent and Pemberley's courtyard, Mr. Darcy's fitful words seemed the epitome of delirious ramblings.

"She is here! And she consented to remain, for a little while at least. But what do I...what should I...dare hope for? I was such a brute to her...if only I can somehow manage to mend months of atrocious, unpardonable behavior with a few minutes of heartfelt hospitality! If she leaves here with slightly less repugnant thoughts of me than when she arrived, I shall be satisfied!"

With much more certainty than he felt, Fredrick advanced and laid a hand upon his employer's arm.

"Sir," he coaxed, "pray sit down and rest awhile."

The Master of Pemberley turned and regarded his valet as if *he* were the madman.

"Sit here and rest when she is in my drawing room? Fredrick, what nonsense you speak!"

"I am sure that *she* will wait," the servant pleaded, not having the least idea of who or what he was referring to. "Come now, sir, do lie down. You must be very tired."

Darcy shook his head as he darted away from the mirror towards the closet.

"No, I barely managed to convince her to stay as it was. Every moment I am absent is one when she may change her mind and leave, never to return, never to be seen by my eyes again!"

The valet watched as his master flung open the wardrobe's doors and recklessly pulled out several coats and threw them to the floor in a desperate bid to find a forest-green one which would match his waistcoat. In the process, he also knocked his elbow on the door of the closet, but appeared to spare the pain no thought. After a moment, unable to bear any more, and foreseeing a far greater injury if the gentleman were left to himself, Fredrick crossed the room to a table where a decanter of brandy and a few glasses stood. Glancing over his shoulder to ensure that Mr. Darcy was still occupied by his quest for a suitable coat and would not notice what the servant was about, he stealthily poured a glass of liquor and, uncapping the vial of laudanum, mixed a few drops into the drink.

Who would have thought, merely earlier this year, that I would be reduced to slipping the master drugs in order to quiet him and protect him from himself?

Approaching Mr. Darcy anew, Fredrick held out the concoction imploringly.

"Sir, you have been out in the elements. Pray take something to warm yourself."

The younger man gave the proffered glass a disinterested and fleeting glance as he threw his arms into the sleeves of his favorite green coat.

"Thank you, my man, but I will eat and drink in her company…I ordered the downstairs maids to provide her with refreshments before I ran up," the aristocratic voice said, as its owner agilely buttoned the recently-donned outer garment. And before Fredrick could invent anything further to say, his master stood before him no more. The servant was left standing in the empty bedroom with a brimming goblet in his hand, listening to the sounds of a well-built man of eight and twenty galloping through the hall and then cantering down the stairs.

Chapter 40

Shaken, Elizabeth had sat down, unable to support herself. Looking down, she realized that her hands were trembling uncontrollably, and she clasped them in her lap in an effort to stop their erratic motions.

The shock of finding the Master of Pemberley at home…the embarrassment of her being there, uninvited…these emotions, which would have been paramount under any other circumstances, paled in comparison to what she had felt when she came face-to-face with Mr. Darcy. The utter emptiness of his eyes during those first few moments continued to haunt her even as she sat in Pemberley's comfortable drawing room.

How grossly Mrs. Reynolds had underrepresented his torture! The man was not merely unhappy; he was sunken in despair. That he knew not what was happening around him was certain, that he cared nothing for the world was evident. How acutely he must have felt the supposed death of his little sister! And yet, if that was the sole cause of his anguish, why had the sight of *her* instantly restored some of his faculties?

Could it be? My heartless refusal…given just a fortnight before his sister's presumed demise…could it have contributed to what I saw in that drive?

A shudder swept through Elizabeth's entire body. She had long realized how uncharitably she had acted during his proposal, but until now she had never considered the possibility that her words might have had a significant or abiding impact upon him. Frankly, she thought her suitor devoid of every proper feeling, and had been certain that his affection would be expunged faster than the footprints of the mount which took him out of Kent. She had even privately laughed at him when she told Jane about his unexpected proposals! And now, for the first time in her life, she saw what words could do: destroy a man, tear apart his spirit, and consign him to a premature death. Words…her own words…could kill.

The double doors of the chamber opened. Elizabeth shakily stood, expecting Mr. Darcy to enter. Instead, a procession of servants filed past her, bearing cold meat, cake, and a variety of all the finest fruits of the season. Elizabeth awkwardly remained standing, grasping the back of her chair, and returning the deep nods which were delivered in her direction before the food was deposited on the table. She wondered if they knew of the impropriety of a Miss Bennet being there.

If the people before her were aware of her history with their master, they gave no indication. Their countenances were perfectly respectful. Completing their task, the servers left as orderly as they had come in, leaving her to her solitude. The girl sank back into the chair and stared at the tempting mounds of nourishment. Could they possibly be meant for her benefit? Or was it simply a custom at Pemberley to have a bit of fare brought into the drawing room at that time of day? Surely Mr. Darcy would not go as far as offering her refreshments!

The door opened once more. Elizabeth half-heartedly looked up, expecting to see one of the domestics bringing in some platter which had been missed before, but instead laid eyes on the Master of Pemberley. He was attired in dry clothes, his head was held high and his shoulders were straight as of old. Anxiety could easily be traced in his features during his first glance about the room, but it was quickly replaced by relief when his eyes found her. Elizabeth rose. The faintest of smiles came to his lips, and he stepped forward.

"Thank you for waiting for me, Miss Bennet," he said in a most genial and grateful tone. "And please accept my regrets for my appearance when I welcomed you to Pemberley. I -,"

"Mr. Darcy, please," Elizabeth cut in. She could not bear it. Here he was, apologizing, when she was the one who was entirely at fault. "You were unaware that anyone besides your servants and tenants was present on the estate this afternoon, and regardless, it is your right to walk about the place in any apparel of your choosing and in any weather."

The gentleman thanked her for her understanding, and then, before she could offer some more apologies of her own, gestured to the overflowing table and pressed her to take some refreshment with the utmost politeness. She declined. He insisted, and after glancing at the clock behind her to verify the time, pointed out that it was still too early in the afternoon for her to have taken tea, but certainly late enough for her to feel hungry. Outdone, afraid that continuous refusals might be perceived as a slight to her former suitor's ungrudging hospitality, Miss Bennet slowly walked to the table, took up a light and fine china plate, and covered its painted designs with two kinds of cake and one of the sweetest peaches afforded by

Pemberley's extensive orchard. Guided by Mr. Darcy, who also took something for himself, she brought the bounty back to a small round table which only had two chairs stationed next to it. She took one, he the other.

The lady bit into the peach, praised it, and likewise sampled the baked goods. When these preliminary forays into eating were completed, she wiped her fingers upon an embroidered napkin and offered the assurance which she longed that the gentleman hear again:

"Mr. Darcy, let me once again apologize for intruding on your privacy. I would not dream of encroaching on this part of the world if it were not for some urgent business which I needed to dispatch."

For a brief moment, these words sent a sharp stab into the gentleman's heart. Did Elizabeth mean that she despised him so much that only the utmost necessity could propel her in the general direction of his dwelling? A scrutinizing glance cast over her lowered eyelids and blushing cheeks, however, soon cued him to the truth: the poor darling thought that he would fault her for coming hither since they had not parted on the best of terms! Desperate to comfort her, he replied in the kindest of tones,

"Miss Bennet, please be assured that your presence at Pemberley is no inconvenience. I am elated to have your company. It has been far too long since I had the pleasure of conversing with you."

Elizabeth stared at the cakes before her in amazement, unable to meet his eye. Who *was* this generous man? Mr. Darcy was certainly not the person she had thought him. At length she demurely murmured,

"Thank you, sir."

After an awkward pause, Mr. Darcy spoke again.

"May I ask if your business has been concluded satisfactorily? Might I be of any assistance in the matter?"

This was truly Providential! She had been agonizing over whether it was the right time to inform him of the ongoings in Hertfordshire, whether his mind was sound enough to bear such extraordinary news, and whether she would be able to persuade him of Anne's identity, or if these undertakings would be failures and only delay her own departure for Longbourn. But now that he had asked, in so rational a tone, she knew that she had to tell the truth. The man possessed every appearance of sanity, and had every right to know of the crisis. And thankfully, he had even provided a beginning.

"I did think my errand fulfilled, Mr. Darcy," Elizabeth said slowly, "but I am more than willing to discuss it, particularly as I suspect that it might be of some interest to you."

Mr. Darcy nodded. He could not fathom what sort of business Elizabeth was about to disclose, but one thing was certain: if his beloved wished to speak to him about anything under the sun, he would attend with unwavering concentration.

The lady took a deep breath, pressed her lips together, and reached for her pocketbook. Opening it, her fingers probed the interior of one of its compartments. They soon found and extracted a small circlet, and tightened reflexively around it. It would be her key to beginning the disclosure.

"Mr. Darcy," Elizabeth said quietly and very gravely, "could you tell me if you have ever seen this object before?"

He extended his arm to receive whatever he was supposed to identify. Elizabeth, likewise, reached across the table. For the slightest instant, her hand hung a centimeter over Mr. Darcy's; she could feel its radiating warmth. Then her fingers released their jeweled burden.

Her companion, who had been hoping that their hands would touch during this action, was briefly disappointed when hers withdrew without so much as brushing his. But anxious to oblige the lady, he swallowed his regret and hastened to examine the mysterious item.

The twinkle of a dark blue gem caught Darcy's eye. It was closely followed by the shimmer of diamonds. He blinked, focused on the source of the rays, and felt his mouth dropping open as it had not done since he was eight years old and had been presented with a long-desired, adorable pony on Christmas morning. Why - he held Georgiana's sapphire ring, the very one which he had given her for her fourteenth birthday!

His breathing and heartbeat became rapid and disordered. *How can it be?*

The jeweler commissioned to create the piece was a reputable tradesman, and had given a tenacious assurance that it was the only one of its kind in all of England. Georgiana had been so delighted with the gift that it had never taken a hiatus from her finger. Thus, the circlet ought to be with his sister in her watery grave, and not lying safe in his palm.

Elizabeth watched apprehensively as Darcy fingered the ring, angled it so that it caught the daylight which streamed in from the windows, and stared at it fixedly. It was clear that it was an item familiar to him, and that its reintroduction into his life was causing agitation. She only hoped that it would not bend the gentleman's fragile mind in an unfavorable direction.

Finally, Darcy glanced up and managed to gasp out,

"How…where?"

Elizabeth, cognizant of the cruelty of keeping him in uncertainty any longer than necessary, replied at once.

"It was on the hand of an unconscious young lady whom my father found on the side of the road several months ago, and brought to Longbourn."

"What did she look like?" the gentleman inquired eagerly.

"She seemed to be about sixteen, with a fully formed figure, and long golden tresses."

Just like Georgiana!

Darcy clasped the ring and held back tears of joy. And yet, he had been forlorn and hopeless for so long that he did not dare - nay, it did not even occur to him - to perceive that the sapphire ring and Elizabeth's information meant that Georgiana lived. Instead, Darcy thought that Miss Bennet wished to inform him that his mortally injured sister had been found and transported to Longbourn, where she passed away soon after. After months of unspeakable grief, however, it was a sweet consolation to know that Georgiana had perished in the midst of tender and caring people, instead of drowning in unrelenting waves. Perhaps his little girl's hand had been encased in Elizabeth's as she took her last breath! Wishing to verify these musings, Fitzwilliam Darcy startled the guest by whispering,

"How did she die?"

"Die?" Elizabeth cried out, shocked. Collecting herself, she realized what he was thinking and continued hastily, "Mr. Darcy, I am afraid you have misunderstood me dreadfully. The young lady of whom we speak did not succumb. On the contrary, within a few days she regained consciousness, recovered, and lives to this day."

There was an unforgettable quiver in the gentleman's voice when he echoed,

"She is *alive*?"

"Yes sir!"

Fitzwilliam Darcy fell back in his chair, looking at Elizabeth and the article in his hand by turns, waiting for the awakening from this beautiful dream which was sure to come. It was too much. How merciful could God be? The appearance of Elizabeth Bennet on his doorstep was miraculous enough, but to hear her beautiful voice saying that Georgiana was still upon this earth was beyond unbelievable. However, the ancient clock on the mantel kept ticking, and the nymph sitting at the opposite end of the table continued looking at him, without any intention of melting away. Another minute passed, and Darcy was forced to give credence to the idea that he was truly awake.

"How is she?" he finally gathered enough courage to ask.

For the first time since they had begun the conversation, Elizabeth hesitated and took a long moment to formulate an answer.

"I believe a *casual* observer would conclude that she is as healthy, intelligent and well-mannered a young lady as they ever saw."

Mr. Darcy instantly noticed the eccentric emphasis and wording of the response, and pounced upon it.

"And a more particular observer: what would he say?"

Compassion pooling liberally in her eyes, Elizabeth replied quietly,

"Once they had a chance to meet and speak with her, they would find that the dear girl remembers nothing of her life as it was before the accident which brought her to Longbourn. Indeed, they would realize that she was introduced to them as Miss Anne Edwards not because that is the name which was bestowed during her christening and the surname of her parents, but because it was the alias she and I liked best when discussing what she ought to be called."

Mr. Darcy closed his eyes. Joy was once again clouded by a mist of anguish, although not as much as it had been for the previous three months.

"Amnesia," he murmured, clearly pained.

"Yes, that was the apothecary's opinion," Elizabeth softly stated, surprised that he had heard of the rare condition.

Another pause ensued. The gentleman opened his eyes at the end of it, caught the lady's curious and amazed look, and gave her a sad smile.

"I read a book on the subject of amnesia some time ago," Mr. Darcy explained. "Little did I then suspect that its thieving hand would touch me or mine! If I remember correctly, very little can be done?"

"I am afraid so," Elizabeth acknowledged. "At the beginning, we did attempt a few remedies, but they all failed. Anne never noticed any improvement. You can imagine," here she glanced down at the tablecloth once more with a wry smile, "how this circumstance has made the tracing of her friends and relatives rather challenging. Even now, when I believe that I may have an inkling of who they are, I owe the dawn of my suspicions mostly to others."

"Yes, I can well imagine the difficulties involved, but I am euphoric that they have at last been overcome. May I inquire to whom I am indebted for sowing the seeds of suggestion in your mind as to Miss Edwards' former life, Miss Bennet?"

"You are scarcely indebted to those people, sir!" Elizabeth snapped, almost forgetting that he did not know who they were discussing. The abrupt fury in her usually pleasing, laughing voice took her companion aback and filled his face with consternation. Seeing this, she drew breath and composed herself before resuming in a terse tone, "Forgive me for my outburst, but your feelings, I am afraid, will soon mirror mine. I repeat, you are not indebted to the scoundrels, for they purposely concealed their superior knowledge of the poor child as they shamelessly plotted to use her affliction for their own gain. Only accidentally did I comprehend what was happening." Elizabeth forced herself to meet Mr. Darcy's aghast eye, and said very deliberately, "When I returned to Longbourn from an absence about a month ago, I found that Anne had been courted by, and had become engaged to – Mr. Wickham. They are to marry on Thursday. He has not involved Anne in any disgrace; he is too clever and was too closely watched by us for that – but you know him too well to doubt his motives. Until two days ago, I regret to say, even I missed seeing the obvious, for, believing Anne to have no money or connections, I thought that nothing less than deep love tempted him! And he played the part of a repentant sinner well enough. He would never see her without a chaperone present. Alas, I became convinced that he loved her and cherished her virtue."

Mr. Darcy jerked up from his chair, nearly upsetting it, and turned abruptly on his heel. With rapid steps he walked to the mantelpiece, stared at it, and remained still and silent for the better part of a minute.

The pause was, to Elizabeth's feelings, dreadful. Slightly trembling, she studied him.

Eventually he answered in a steady, albeit low, tone.

"I am grieved indeed. Grieved – shocked." He drew in a deep breath. "I almost want to ask if it is absolutely certain, but, what a nonsensical question that would be! You have been there all the while, and have seen all." Turning towards where she sat, he went on in a louder and more purposeful voice: "You said that the wedding is to be on Thursday...and today is...," Mr. Darcy stopped abruptly. He glanced around bewildered, looked at the clock, and then turned towards the windows. These could tell him the time of day and the season of the year; the date and day of the week, which he precipitously realized he did not know, remained mysteries.

Seeing his disorganization, Elizabeth offered,

"It is the twenty-second of August, sir; a Tuesday afternoon."

"Tuesday...and they are to marry on Thursday? Not *this* Thursday?"

Elizabeth shut her eyes, pained, and replied reluctantly,

"Yes, sir, this Thursday. There are but four and forty hours before the wedding. My discoveries came at a most inopportune time."

The gentleman took several quick inspirations, and asked without a shadow of condemnation, but as one who sincerely seeks guidance,

"And what do you judge to be the best way to recover her?"

"I wish I knew; until less than an hour ago, I hoped that my suspicions were delusions, and refused to consider what it would mean if they were grounded in reality."

Mr. Darcy abandoned his station by the fireplace and came back to the table, but did not sit down. Placing a hand upon his former chair, he leaned forward and, with entreaty in all his looks, said,

"Miss Bennet, I believe that it is unnecessary to convince you that this marriage must be stopped, if at all possible. I cannot do anything from here. Suffer me to accompany you back to Longbourn, and to do whatever I can to wrench my sister out of that tyrant's grasp."

The gentleman's quandary was obvious. Here he stood, before a woman who had told him five months before that she found everything about him repulsive, asking her to enter into a collaboration with him. If she refused, his hands would be tied; in order to form a good offense against Wickham in the short time left before the wedding, it was necessary to have the input of an expert on the battleground. Guessing and acting blindly would be disastrous. If

Elizabeth accepted, however, it would probably be out of onerous duty, and he would be the means of subjecting her to some of the most unpleasant moments of her life.

The young woman, however, did not waver. Regardless of what she felt about being in an alliance with Mr. Darcy, she immediately said,

"I would think very ill of a brother who asked anything less. Your intervention may be what turns back this hopeless tide. I love Anne as dearly as I do Jane; I would do anything to save her from pain."

"Thank you." The young man allowed himself a sigh of relief. "The latter is obvious, Miss Bennet, clearly stated by your journey here!" He seemed to be on the point of saying something further, but halted himself. Sensing his discomfort and indecision, Elizabeth took it upon herself to ask,

"Is there anything else, sir?"

Mr. Darcy took a deep breath.

"I was going to inquire whether it would be well-received if we involved Colonel Richard Fitzwilliam and Charles Bingley in this business. I am sure you remember that the Colonel shares Georgiana's guardianship with me. As for Charles – he has no interest in my sister's case beyond that of friendship, I assure you – but his reoccupation of Netherfield would put us in a better position to enter the neighborhood casually. That is, unless you think that his arrival in Hertfordshire would upset the…peace...of the county."

Despite the tactful generalization, Elizabeth immediately comprehended that Jane was in his uppermost thoughts, and honored him for his delicacy. She did not need long to decide upon her answer. Any suggestion which could make her elder sibling happier than she had been for the past eight months would be met with eagerness.

"I believe I can safely assure you that I know of no reason why Mr. Bingley should not enter Hertfordshire. His presence will be very welcome to myself, as well as to my connections."

This reply seemed to please and relieve Mr. Darcy a great deal. He expressed his thanks again, and glancing at her plate, urged her to finish her refreshments. This time, Elizabeth was stronger in her negation, and in about half-a-minute, managed to convince him that her appetite for sweets and cakes had disappeared, and was only whetted for action. Likewise yearning to begin, he helped her up from the table, and gently putting a hand on her arm, guided the lady towards the double oak doors.

There was a manservant passing through the hall.

"Harry," Mr. Darcy said as he and Elizabeth swept along, "go to the stables. Have the new coach prepared for departure. Hitch the four white thoroughbreds to it. You can also tell the coachman who brought Miss Bennet here to transfer her belongings to our coach, and pay and dismiss him. Would that be agreeable to you, madam?"

"Yes, I thank you."

Mr. Darcy quickly uttered a few more instructions, and continued escorting Elizabeth down the corridor, as the servant hastened to do his duty.

Chapter 41

At the end of the hall, he showed her into a beautiful room which she had not seen on her tour with Mrs. Reynolds. In the first moment, Elizabeth mistook it for another library. Two walls were completely covered in bookshelves. At least a thousand volumes had to be present there. Near the windows, a comfortable ivory-colored sofa was stationed. Two portraits, depicting the old Mr. Darcy and Lady Anne, hung close to the door. But the crowning jewel of the room was the large mahogany desk.

It was to this magnificent workspace that Mr. Darcy tended after depositing the lady tenderly upon the sofa. Pulling out and sinking into the chair which stood behind it, he shook his head at the mountains of paper which his steward and butler had been piling on the desk against the day that the master's melancholy would lift and he would take interest in life once more. Looking through them, he soon realized that they were organized into three stacks: transactions which his steward had undertaken on his behalf, other business records, and personal correspondence.

Reaching for the eighteen-inch-tall assemblage of personal letters which had gone unanswered, most of them for months, Darcy began to earnestly search through it. Due to the height of the pile, the exploration was lengthy. Elizabeth watched it intently from a distance, until he caught her gaze.

Trapped into speaking, she commented,

"Any good fortune, sir?"

"You mean besides finding you under the archway today, and hearing your news?" he rebutted wittily with a smile, before replying more seriously, "I am looking to see if I can find any recent epistles from my cousin or my friend. It has been weeks since I knew their whereabouts."

"Is there nothing I can do in the meantime?" Elizabeth inquired. "I dislike being useless when time is so short."

"If you are truly bent on being helpful, perhaps you could assist me in sifting through these letters. There are many of them, as you see." He held out a handful.

"I should be glad to, if you are certain that you would rather not keep them private."

The gentleman shook his head.

"From you, I have nothing to hide," he said softly, continuing to hold the letters out. Inexpressibly touched by this expression of trust, Elizabeth came forward and took the bundle from his hand. Sitting down upon a chair in front of the desk, she placed it in her lap, and began to flip through the stack. "If you should happen to find an illegible one, set it aside. It is probably from Charles Bingley."

A laugh escaped Elizabeth. Even Mrs. Bennet, at the height of her hope that he would marry Jane, had been unable to expound favorably upon the subject of Mr. Bingley's penmanship. The poor scribe claimed that his ideas flowed so rapidly that he did not have time to express them – resultantly, his letters sometimes conveyed nothing at all to his correspondents. And indeed, within a few seconds, Elizabeth came across a badly-scrawled address. Handing it over, she received confirmation that it was one of the letters which they were looking for. Mr. Darcy soon found an epistle written only days before by Colonel Fitzwilliam, and opening both, found to his delight that his friend and cousin were presently in neighboring counties, and ones which he and Elizabeth would pass through on their way to Hertfordshire. Informing the lady of this, the Master of Pemberley instantly set to writing the responses which had been neglected for so long.

As pen scratched against paper, Elizabeth took the opportunity to take a turn about the room, peer out the window, and explore the bookshelves. Halfway through her survey, she heard her companion's voice again.

"I am asking," Mr. Darcy said, glancing up, "Bingley and Richard to meet us in the south of Bedfordshire tomorrow at noon."

"At noon!" Elizabeth exclaimed, bewildered. "Sir," she continued, more gently, recollecting that information about travelling times and distances might be another item which three months of sorrow had muddled in the man's head, "I would consider it fortunate if we managed to make Bedfordshire by suppertime tomorrow. It is very far away, and it would be dangerous to travel by night."

Undaunted, the gentleman continued to write.

"We shall certainly stop at dusk, Miss Bennet, and still make Bedfordshire by noon," he returned. Looking up once again, he kindly and confidently concluded, "The horses will manage."

Understanding at last, Elizabeth nodded and played with her necklace while he turned back to the correspondence. Of course. The thoroughbreds which would be hitched to their conveyance would provide a brisker pace of travel than she had ever known. Barring any unexpected delays, they would reach Hertfordshire on the eve of the wedding rather than ten minutes before the ceremony. She exhaled with relief and contentment, blessing the moment when Mr. Darcy had tripped over the carelessly-placed umbrella and noticed her.

The rustling of skirts was heard in the hallway and was followed by a knock at the half-opened study door. Mr. Darcy invited the visitor in, and Mrs. Reynolds entered.

Elizabeth was struck by the woman's appearance. Sometime in the last hour she had shed twenty years at least: her eyes sparkled, her movements were full of purpose, and when she beheld Mr. Darcy sitting at the desk and writing as of yore, the corners of her lips curved upwards into a delighted smile.

"Sir," she said in a voice brimming with thankfulness, "the carriage is almost prepared, and Fredrick and Mary will be ready within ten minutes. The basket of refreshments which you ordered has already been packed. Will there be anything else?"

"No, that will be all, Mrs. Reynolds, unless you can spare a prayer for a safe and successful voyage."

"Oh, indeed I can, and will!" the woman murmured with feeling.

"Thank you." The Master of Pemberley rose, came around the desk, gently took her arm, and in a low tone which was designed to miss Elizabeth's ears, said, "And thank you for putting up with me all these weeks. I am ashamed of having caused you such distress."

"Pray do not apologize, sir! The staff and the tenants felt but an echo of your pain, and we only suffered because we love you. It was dreadful to see you digging your own early grave, master. I am very glad that you are improved, and I beg you never to go down that road again. As I dared to tell you once before…Miss Georgiana would not wish it."

Mr. Darcy chuckled sorrowfully.

"I confess that I do not remember you taking that liberty, madam, but then again, I remember very little of the days during which I was completely engulfed by my own thoughts. However, you have my word that from this day forward, I will be engaged in more fruitful pursuits than regretting the past. Good day, my dear Mrs. Reynolds."

"Goodbye, sir," the housekeeper replied. She curtsied, and departed.

Elizabeth, who for the duration of the audience had feigned great interest in the contents of the bookshelf, closed her eyes and attempted to reconcile her impressions of Mr. Darcy with the dialogue which, despite the participants' best efforts, had reached her ears. Mr. Darcy's comportment towards the housekeeper was extremely touching, but his admission of weakness was infinitely more so. This man, who but a few months before had been unrepentant about interfering between Mr. Bingley and Jane, had just apologized and felt guilt over burdening his own, well-paid servants!

Making sure to school her countenance and pretend to have heard nothing of the latter half of their conversation, she turned around to face him once Mrs. Reynolds had departed.

"Who are Fredrick and Mary?" she inquired as the gentleman walked around the desk to regain his chair.

"Fredrick is my valet, and Mary was Georgiana's maid. I have arranged for them to sit with us in the coach," replied he, reaching for the wax and sealing the letter. Once his signet ring had left its impression upon the hot, viscous liquid, Mr. Darcy stood and walked closer to her. He recommenced in a hushed tone, "They number among Pemberley's finest and most trustworthy servants, but I would rather that we not discuss my sister's affair in front of them. To no creature, except one, were the ongoings at Ramsgate revealed where secrecy was possible. I know you understand my aspiration to keep as many people as we can in ignorance."

"Yes, of course."

"But rest assured, Miss Bennet, that I long to hear every detail with which you can furnish me about the preceding three months. It will be difficult during so expedient a journey to find time for private conferences, I fear, but perhaps we might take a turn together while the horses are being changed, and when we stop for the night."

Elizabeth shrugged uncertainly.

"We might, but I doubt that so short a span of time will allow me to even begin to tell so long a tale. And an abbreviated version will scarcely add value to what I have already told you."

Recognizing the truth in her statement, Mr. Darcy checked a sigh and replied,

"Whatever the cost, your comfort comes first, madam."

Elizabeth started slightly. Studying his countenance, she suspected, correctly, that he was quite discontented with the restrictions which propriety was placing on their travels. And in all honesty, so was she. They would be enclosed together for hours on end, wasting time either in silence or by talking about some paltry matters, and only address the most important topic in a hastily whispered conversation. To say nothing of inconvenience, something would surely be forgotten, and the omission might turn out to be grave enough to bring all their plotting and trouble to naught. Therefore, praying that he would not think her completely mad, she hesitantly deigned to say,

"Mr. Darcy...this affair is very complex. I shudder to think of you being unpleasantly surprised at some critical moment simply because I did not have time to enlighten you." Casting her maidenly eyes down at the floor, she forced herself to continue, "I am grateful that you have considered my comfort, but I think that you would agree that in such cases as these, there are other priorities. If you have...asked Mary and Fredrick along only for my convenience, and not because of your own good pleasure, I...I believe that I will be able to bear the deprivation of their company in exchange for license to speak freely."

As expected, the Master of Pemberley stared at her in disbelief. However, his was not the gaze of an offended man; on the contrary, there seemed to be a good deal of elation in his dark pupils.

"Do you mean to say that you would not be opposed to being alone in the carriage with me?" he asked, incredulous with joy.

 Still gazing at the expensive carpet, Elizabeth blushed profusely.

"Considering the important business which must be transacted, I see no harm in it, just this once." Tentatively raising her eyes from the floor, she was a good deal relieved and emboldened to see a small smile on the gentleman's face, just like the one his portrait in the gallery wore. Inspired by the expression, hoping to compensate the poor man somewhat for her abominable behavior at Hunsford, she quietly added, "I trust you, sir."

Darcy could have seized both her hands and covered them with kisses at this unexpected, endearing profession. Interested, however, in preserving her trust, he refrained. Instead, he warmly said,

"Thank you, madam," and looked at her for a long moment before turning back to his desk.

Chapter 42

A mere hour after Mr. Darcy had spoken those fateful words: 'she is *alive?*', he and Elizabeth made their way down the front steps of Pemberley. The rain had ceased in the meantime. Two messengers had already been dispatched on fleet horseback to the Colonel and Mr. Bingley, and now it was their turn to hasten to the meeting place.

They walked across the courtyard, under the archways, and to the sleek, large coach stationed on the drive.

"Miss Bennet."

She turned toward the speaker, and saw Mr. Darcy holding out his hand to help her up. Taking it, she used its steadying tension to safely hoist herself unto the step and then into the carriage.

Sitting down and settling in, Miss Bennet looked about her new milieu, shocked. The interior of the coach far exceeded her expectations. Accustomed to Longbourn's plain, serviceable conveyance and now to post-carriages, the elegant soft seats on both sides, the wide windows, and the silky drapes surrounding them filled her with awe. She had been unaware that such luxurious travel conditions even existed.

Mr. Darcy, after giving a few last instructions to the coachman, leapt into the coach. Careful to preserve Elizabeth's faith in his gentlemanly behavior, he made certain to sit on the opposite side of the carriage. This, at least, granted him an ideal vista of her beautiful, bonneted head. He smiled at her slightly, a favor which the lady returned. With that, the coach began moving and they were off!

Despite the fact that they were closeted together to speak of Miss Edwards and Mr. Wickham, Elizabeth could not tear her gaze away from the Pemberley grounds which they were passing for the first few miles. They were departing via a different road than the one by which she had come, and it was equally enchanting. There were groves, there were meadows, and there were fields and fields of wildflowers. She watched the passing scenes eagerly and only hoped that her admiration would not be perceived as something like regret.

Such thoughts, however, were far from Darcy's mind. All he saw was his beloved enjoying herself, and he was desirous of increasing her pleasure. Thus, he began to name the species of trees which composed the groves and the parts of the world in which they had originated. Seeing Miss Bennet's interest in his elucidating, he continued speaking, and soon found himself pointing out the meadow in which he had learned to ride a pony and the section of the lake into which Colonel Fitzwilliam had dived when he was a lad of nine only to realize, to his great horror, his inability to stay afloat in its current.

"The old Mr. Wickham had to jump in and bring him out," Darcy said, chuckling for the first time since Elizabeth had rejected his offer of marriage. "My cousin was quite embarrassed by his deficiencies, as you might well imagine. He spent countless hours practicing in safer waters, and by the end of his visit to Pemberley, he went in at the very same spot and swam for a mile."

Elizabeth laughed at the tale, commenting that the Colonel's unwillingness to let such matters rest probably contributed to his success in the militia. Darcy agreed with this pronouncement, and continued instructing her in interesting particulars about the estate until they passed its main gates.

Turning her attention to the interior of the carriage, Miss Bennet found her companion caressing his sister's indigo ring.

"It is sapphire and diamond, is it not?" she asked quietly.

"Of course," he replied, with a look of surprise.

Elizabeth smiled sadly.

"We always thought it was cut glass. So certain were we all that it was not of value that we never bothered to have a jeweler appraise it. Wretched, wretched mistake!"

"Neither you, nor any of your family are to blame, Miss Bennet. Most young women of consequence are sought out by a veritable troop if they go missing. But, as I am sure you have gathered, I thought my sister dead, and thought searching unprofitable." He turned the ring to the light and watched it catch the rays and sparkle. Glancing from it to his companion, he asked, "Might I inquire what sort of pretense you used to borrow it from Georgiana's finger for the duration of this journey? For I presume that she does not know of the true reason for your absence and that this would be potentially used as proof of her identity?"

Miss Bennet sighed.

"Even Jane is in ignorance of where I am today. But, as much as I loath to cause you pain, sir, I must confess that I did not need to speak any falsehoods to coax that ornament from your sister's finger. She ceased wearing it weeks ago. I simply fished it out of my jewelry box as I was leaving, and doubt that she will miss it."

There indeed was injury in the look which sprang to Mr. Darcy's pupils, but it was combined with a tint of self-discovery.

"She claimed to adore it when I gave it to her," he said, without bitterness. "Therefore, either the accident changed her tastes, or, what is more likely, she was never much taken with it and only claimed to be overly fond of it in order to spare my feelings. I have often wondered, of late, what fraction of her exuberances at my kindnesses were real and which were exaggerated by her affectionate heart. As difficult as some lessons are to learn, it is always advantageous to know one's own character as it appears to others."

Elizabeth's cheeks took on the color of beets.

Is this meant for myself? she wondered. The look on his face tore at her heart. Quickly, she said,

"I disagree, sir. Sometimes people judge us on mistaken premises and come up with illegitimate conclusions. It would be destructive to take their opinions to heart. And in this case, both your presumptions are incorrect. Anne spoke of it as a pretty ring, but Mr. Wickham convinced her that it was an unnecessary reminder of a hidden past and would be best disposed of."

Mr. Darcy looked sharply at the circlet he held.

"I should have known!" he muttered. "I take it that Georgiana is as eager as ever to bend her will?"

Elizabeth replied that she was unable to answer that question in full due to her limited knowledge of the Miss Georgiana Darcy of a six-month ago. She was thereupon begged to tell what she did know of the present Miss Anne Edwards. She immediately complied, and expounded on the subject until the day showed signs of waning.

Chapter 43

'Hampton Village', the sign on the side of the road said.

Elizabeth read it with a sigh. To her travelling companion, she remarked,

"It is a great pity that we must stop with half-an-hour of good daylight left."

Mr. Darcy, who had temporarily lapsed into his own thoughts as he pondered how best to deal with Wickham, regarded her with a startled look.

"Stop?"

"Yes," Elizabeth replied, surprised in turn. "Are we not stopping here? From what I remember of the road, Hampton's inn is the last one for at least five and twenty miles."

"That is true, but I had not planned upon stopping in this village. If we press on, there is another place in about five miles where we may spend the night. Of course," he studied her with a compassionate and attentive gaze, "if you are tired we may easily stop at Hampton Inn. You must be greatly fatigued, travelling for days on end."

Fully aware of how great a sacrifice the gentleman was graciously willing to undertake for her comfort, Elizabeth rewarded him with a most affable glance and shake of her head.

"I am rather tired, but I could never forgive myself if our early recess today cost us a timely arrival in Hertfordshire. If you know another respectable lodging place, I humbly yield to your superior knowledge of the road."

"Are you certain, madam?"

"Quite, sir."

The carriage, therefore, passed Hampton Village and continued on. Curious as to what sort of accommodations to expect, the young woman inquired,

"May I ask if we are going to spend the night in a boarding house, or…?"

"No," Mr. Darcy promptly answered. "It is an estate called Menston Hall."

This was not quite the answer which Elizabeth expected. She slightly paled, thinking of the possible embarrassments which might be in store for them at so prominent a destination. She had been given questioning looks and double-takes enough during her solitary travels as she travelled into Derbyshire, and had already been dreading those reactions which she and Mr. Darcy would surely get when they entered an inn as unmarried and unchaperoned persons. But this? To seek out quarters from respectable people who already knew Mr. Darcy, and might cross paths with herself again in the future? How risky it would be, to have members of the English gentry knowing about her improper escapades! Hoping to give the man second thoughts about the questionable plan, Elizabeth asked in a most serious tone,

"Are you quite certain that we will be welcome at this Menston Hall, sir? I should hate to inconvenience your friends."

Darcy regarded her with a singular expression.

"Yes, I can guarantee that the Master of Menston will be delighted to have you under his roof, Miss Bennet," he said, apparently amused, for he wore a smile upon his face. "And furthermore, I can also ensure his and his servants' silence on the matter of our travelling together, something which I could never ascertain if we were to spend the night in a more public location."

Pacified by this response and reasoning, Elizabeth was able to look out the carriage window with a good measure of interest and anticipation when Mr. Darcy swept aside the curtain and mentioned that Menston Hall was coming into view. The house she beheld was a little smaller and from an earlier architectural era than Pemberley, but it was almost as handsome. Much to the young woman's liking, it was surrounded on both sides by a lovely forest.

The carriage entered a long drive, drove for another mile, pulled up before the mansion, and stopped. The footmen opened the door, and seemed vastly pleased when Mr. Darcy energetically alighted. Then their master turned to lend aid to Miss Bennet.

Taking the hand he held out, Elizabeth allowed herself to be guided down onto the firm pavement. Exhausted after the events of the day, she glanced at the retiring sun and hoped that she would soon be able to follow its example. However, before that could be, she would have to meet the residents of Menston Hall. She prayed that these friends of Mr. Darcy's were less pompous than Miss Bingley and the Hursts, for she did not feel equal to dealing with condescension after all she had recently been through.

Unwillingly, but for the sake of propriety, her companion released the gloved hand he held, and they made their way silently towards the front door, leaving the servants behind to unload the coach. When they reached it, Mr. Darcy rang the doorbell. Then they stood and looked at one another.

Fortunately for the weary travelers, the wait was anything but protracted. Within a fraction of a minute, the click of the lock was heard, and the door unbarred. A maid appeared, surrounded by the gentle glow of lamps in the entry hall.

"Why, Mr. Darcy!" she exclaimed, confounded.

"Good evening, Grace," the gentleman answered, and without further ado or invitation, gestured for Elizabeth to precede him into the building. Elizabeth, seeing no alternative, obeyed. Within, they found a very surprised older woman standing in the vestibule.

"Mrs. Corbridge," he acknowledged.

"Good day. We were not expecting you, sir," was the matron's reply, her befuddled pupils darting between him and his friend.

"I am aware of that," Mr. Darcy answered matter-of-factly, his tone devoid of a single note of apology. Turning to Elizabeth, who was by now blushing furiously, he continued, "Miss Bennet, may I introduce Mrs. Corbridge, the housekeeper of Menston Hall?"

Elizabeth murmured the servant's name, and by her nod and conciliatory smile, attempted to convey the remorse which Mr. Darcy had no interest in expressing. Mrs. Corbridge, for her part, respectfully murmured a proper phrase about it being a pleasure as she dropped a low curtsy.

The young man stepped behind the lady. With infinite gentleness, he helped her doff her travelling coat. Handing it and his hat to Grace, he once again faced the housekeeper.

"Miss Bennet and I will be staying the night. Pray have my usual room put in order, and have the chamber at the end of the hall prepared for Miss Bennet. We will take dinner as soon as the cook is able to prepare it." All these words were spoken with an air of command and instruction.

Elizabeth, employed in removing her gloves, was grateful that the occupation gave her an excuse to keep her eyes cast down as her cheeks redoubled their mortified flush. During the preceding hectic hours, throughout which Mr. Darcy played the parts of a magnanimous host, amiable acquaintance, and concerned brother perfectly, she had begun to forget why she had once disliked him so. Now, listening to his appalling words, old feelings which she had never expected to feel again, surfaced and flooded every crevice of

223

her heart. Who did this man think he was? To swoop in suddenly upon a household at the dusk hour, and without inquiring if the master was home or even after that gentleman's health, begin ordering about his servants! Even if he had an open invitation from the proprietor of Menston to accommodate himself in the mansion at any time, he ought to at least express a grain of remorse about inconveniencing the staff, particularly when she, an uninvited guest, had been brought along. Outraged, Miss Bennet had begun to contemplate declining the hospitality which Mr. Darcy had ordered for her and spending the night in the stable instead, despite any impropriety or discomfort which that eccentric idea entailed, when Mrs. Corbridge's response reached her ears.

"Certainly, sir. I shall see to the rooms myself at once." Turning to the maid, she mandated, "Grace, run downstairs and inform them that the master is here!"

Elizabeth became a stone statue. In this attitude, she watched as Grace nimbly ran off to the kitchen to fulfill her orders and as Mrs. Corbridge likewise excused herself to go upstairs. Finally, Elizabeth's attention rested upon Mr. Darcy, and found that the man was looking about the hall and the rafters with a possessive gaze, obviously checking whether everything had been kept in order during his absence.

Could Mrs. Corbridge truly have meant what her statement implied?! thought she.

Completing his cursory inspection, Darcy found the woman he loved staring at him as if she had never seen him before. While it was not Elizabeth Bennet's habit to be so indelicate in matters concerning fortune, in this instance she was so stunned that she could not help the expression upon her countenance or the incredulous exclamation,

"*You* own Menston Hall?"

The gentleman broke into a small smile at the violence of her reaction.

"I am afraid I must plead guilty to the horrendous misdeed." Seeing the young lady's amazement, he added in a softer tone, "That is why I could be so adamant in insisting that the Master of Menston would be delighted to have you under his roof, Miss Bennet. I thought that my assurances that we would be welcome at this estate would apprise you of the truth of the situation; but if they failed to accomplish what I intended them to do, I apologize, for I saw that you were indeed uncomfortable during your introduction to Mrs.

Corbridge." He paused, hoping that the lady would voice her forgiveness, and when she did not, he paled. Had he again proved himself something less than a gentleman? Did Elizabeth think that he had been amusing himself at her expense? Hoping to redeem himself, he meekly suggested: "Shall we go into the drawing room?"

Elizabeth nodded curtly, still too dazed to speak, and trailed Mr. Darcy through the hall to a set of double oak doors, one of which he opened. He stood aside to allow her passage into the apartment within. When she had entered the elegant room and he had followed, she was recovered enough to recognize her rudeness and to say,

"I hope you will forgive me for my indecorous outburst in the hall, sir. The news simply took me very much aback. While I, like the rest of Hertfordshire, was aware of your income before we were properly introduced, I was under the impression that your annual ten thousand pounds were the fruit of Pemberley alone. Clearly, I am no proficient at estimating the value of estates!"

During her speech, Mr. Darcy moved slowly but deliberately towards the mantelpiece and, despite his relief at realizing the true cause of her previous silence, uncomfortably fiddled with one of the objects gracing it. This position acquitted him from facing his beloved as he wrestled with an important dilemma.

Should I inform her? Our new friendship is so fresh, so fragile...will she think me a braggart? I could scarcely bear it if she had one more reason to think ill of me! And yet, if I remain mute at this juncture, and clarify not...she may accidentally discover the truth in the future, and think me a liar.

On the heels of these considerations, Darcy turned his gaze away from the mantelpiece and fastened it upon Elizabeth.

"I would not wish you to be deceived, Miss Bennet," he began. "The main estate of Pemberley, which you visited earlier today, *does* clear ten thousand a year at least. Society in general is well aware of my claim to it, and is also privy to the existence of Darcy House in London. However, very few know that both my grandfather and my father were heirs to the properties of several childless relatives, and that resultantly, Pemberley accumulated seven satellite estates, Menston Hall among them. It was all done very quietly at the wish of my predecessors, and thus these smaller properties are not included in estimations of my income. I, likewise, do not wish their existence to be publicly known. There are scarcely

225

any people besides yourself, madam, to whom I would dare make this disclosure."

Instantly understanding his concerns, Elizabeth assured him, "I give you my word, sir, that this will go no further."

Mr. Darcy nodded gratefully. Just then, the door to the drawing room opened, and another maid made her appearance. Curtseying, she addressed Mr. Darcy,

"Pardon the intrusion, sir, but Miss Bennet's room is prepared."

"Already?" Elizabeth returned with astonishment.

"Yes, madam." Seeing that the young lady still seemed to be having trouble believing her report, the servant added, "We always keep the rooms in order, whether or not the master is here to take advantage of them, miss. Therefore, all I needed to do now was to light the fire, for the nights hereabouts are always chilly, and to fill the pitcher and washbasin with water."

Elizabeth nodded her understanding, and Mr. Darcy cordially said,

"Pray go upstairs, if you wish, Miss Bennet, and refresh yourself. I daresay dinner will be ready in about an hour. Maybelle here will show you the way."

She gratefully accepted the invitation, and taking temporary leave of the Master of Menston, followed the maid out the door. As the twosome made their way upstairs, Maybelle leading, and Elizabeth following, the latter glanced about and noticed that the house was extremely neat and well-kept even though it was clear that its proprietor was but a sporadic resident. The picture frames and the small tables in the halls were all dustless.

Maybelle showed her into a large, femininely decorated bedchamber, and left.

Going to the enormous bed, on which her pitiful package of belongings had been placed, Elizabeth sat and closed her eyes and marveled.

Fitzwilliam Darcy owns not just Pemberley and a London townhouse, but seven satellite estates. Seven! How grossly underestimated the rumors of his wealth are!

However, it was not for mercenary reasons that Miss Bennet of Hertfordshire wondered thus at the size of Mr. Darcy's fortune. Ten thousand pounds had already seemed astronomically high to the maiden who was used to going several winters in the same coat. If those piles of income had been insufficient to incite her to avarice, these new seven estates could scarcely move her to awe. Had they fallen into her lap as her very own, she would have been unable to imagine what to do with so much money.

What was so captivating was how *he* regarded his fortune. Every other man in England would have openly published his worth and used it as a ticket for entrance into higher social circles. With eight well-managed estates, one could court and marry a Duchess successfully and almost be assured of the King's ear. And lo! He had chosen to keep his wealth secret, to befriend Charles Bingley, a tradesman's son, and then propose marriage to Elizabeth Bennet! Pride he certainly had, but it was not in proportion to his allotment. It was certainly not a disgusting kind of pride which flaunted every shilling its owner had for the purpose of impressing the world.

After half-an-hour of reflection, she approached the basin and splashed cold water upon her face and neck. It was time to put on a new dress and go downstairs. A very interesting, handsome gentleman was waiting!

Chapter 44

Elizabeth eyed the lavish table before her with a mixture of admiration and awe. It lacked nothing. A ham and a well-stuffed pheasant occupied opposite ends of the table, each encircled by five side dishes, all prepared by Menston's French cook. Nor had the decorations been skimped on: a beautiful bouquet of white and mauve flowers acted as a centerpiece, and two elegant candelabrums supplemented the light emanating from the crystal chandelier above. It was obvious that the man sitting at the opposite end of the table was apt at hiring efficient help who could deliver impeccable service at a moment's notice.

The meal was quiet, for most of the necessary conversations had been completed earlier in the day and they were both too drained to trouble themselves with inconsequential tête-à-têtes. Elizabeth smiled softly to herself, remembering times in Kent when silences between the two of them had stifled and confused her. But tonight, the lull was filled with a comfortable air of companionship. Their shared mission and improved understanding of each other had doubtlessly helped endow the quiet with such serenity.

It did Elizabeth's heart good to see Mr. Darcy enjoying his dinner with a healthy appetite in between the earnest, steadfast gazes he often sent her way. Stealing furtive glances across the table, she wondered how long it had been since he had truly eaten; if his hollow cheeks were an accurate barometer, the gentleman before her had not been particularly attentive to his fare for the past several months. It was clear that the poor man had been sunk in misery of the acutest kind. Elizabeth could not begin to imagine what he had gone through.

And how much he was currently undergoing! What agony, to learn that his own sister had lost all knowledge of him, and found love in her heart for his worst enemy! Moreover, *she*, Elizabeth Bennet, was partially responsible for the latter.

This consciousness of her own folly, combined with the guilt it produced, induced a state of agitation. She found herself longing for a walk - nay, a run - through the woods surrounding Menston Hall to dissipate it. But it was nighttime; going out was impossible. Elizabeth was forced to repress her inner turmoil, but unbeknownst to her, some of it slipped past her guard and directed itself into a series of small, fretful gestures. The generous slice of cake on the lady's plate was divided into at least twenty pieces before being consumed. Once the table was cleared and the servants absent, a certain chestnut curl at the nape of her neck was rearranged at least five times by fidgeting fingers. Finally, unable to keep still a moment longer, the young woman rose, went abruptly to the sideboard and poured herself a cup of tea, before unconsciously spending a full two minutes by the clock vigorously stirring a spoonful of sugar into the brew.

"Miss Bennet?" Mr. Darcy's concerned voice precipitously brought her back to the present, discontinued the clanging of the silver against the china, and provoked a crimson blush. "What is the matter?"

"Nothing of import, sir," Elizabeth answered as she took a deep breath, hoping that it would erase the rosy color from her cheeks. "Pray excuse me for disturbing you. I am afraid my mind wandered." Attempting to appear unperturbed, the girl casually turned from the sideboard, slowly made her way across the room, and stationing herself before the wall, pretended to admire a large painting.

The performance did not draw her perceptive audience in.

"Forgive me for contradicting you, madam, but something is clearly causing you distress." His tone brooked no further denial. When Miss Bennet made no answer, not feeling equal to one, the gentleman scrutinized her countenance before inquiring, "Are there any other troubling circumstances which I have yet to be made aware of?"

Elizabeth met his eye and saw his uneasiness. Yearning to reassure him, she replied directly,

"No, indeed, sir." She desperately wished that she could hold her tongue as to the rest, but finding herself unable to reign in her self-scorn, she was forced to continue passionately, "It is just that…I cannot help thinking that I might have prevented this. I, who knew what he was! Had I explained some part of it only - some part of what I learnt to my own family, to Anne! Had his character been known this could not have happened!" She paused, and pensively fingered the mural's ornamental frame, disgusted with her own blindness and folly. "But in the beginning, it never occurred to me that she could be in any danger from the deception. But when the engagement was formed, I *ought* to have been more reticent in giving my approval to the match. I *should* have spoken plainly to Anne, and told her all that I knew about her precious fiancé. It could have, perhaps, prevented her from falling more deeply in love with him each subsequent day, at the very least. How much heartache would now be spared her! After a few tests of his goodwill, however, I allowed myself to be persuaded that Mr. Wickham had truly reformed. In retrospect, I was enamored with the romantic notion that he had changed for love of her." Her next words were whispered bitterly, and spoken more for the sake of depleting her own ire than for Mr. Darcy's benefit. "What fools we women are! To think our charms capable of luring men from their vices, to suppose that their affection for us can alter their character! We possess no such sway over their minds. Oh, some of the opposite sex doubtlessly feign improvement, when the prize is deemed worthwhile, be it an extraordinarily pretty face or thirty thousand pounds. Most reveal the amendment to be a farce as soon as the trophy wears a wedding ring and is secure; some of the more thorough ones uphold the role for a while longer, but there never existed a man who truly improved himself for the sake of a woman!" Having said this, Elizabeth raised her teacup to her lips and took a sip, wishing that her remorse could be swallowed as easily as the hot liquid.

Silence took over the room, but it did not endure long. Elizabeth heard the scraping of a chair against the floor, and with great perturbation thought that it heralded his disgruntled exit from the room. Who could blame him? She had been a deplorable dunce, and a reminder of it could scarcely increase his desire to spend the evening in her company.

Expecting his departure, she only realized that his footsteps tended in her direction when they were halfway across the room. The next she knew, a hand was touching her shoulder and a gentle voice was speaking near her ear.

"You are too hard upon yourself, Miss Bennet." Elizabeth looked up at the gentleman standing next to herself, and found concern for her state of mind written all over his face. "From what you told me this afternoon in the carriage, you *did* question Mr. Wickham's conversion, and were given perfect, logical explanations in response. I might add that you are not the first to be taken in in such a manner. Once or twice, in my father's last years, I managed to tell him of Mr. Wickham's more flagrant breaches of propriety, and to incite him to challenge the wastrel. Each time, however, George Wickham offered such smooth clarifications that his godfather was unshakably convinced of his saintliness and would hear no more on the subject. If my own father, the wisest man I ever knew, was duped by this swindler, how could I expect more from yourself?"

"You are very kind, sir," the lady replied, overcome.

Mr. Darcy slowly removed his gentle pressure from her shoulder, and it seemed as if he were done speaking. But then, leaning slightly towards her, he continued, in an even softer tone,

"Furthermore, Miss Bennet, you must see the faultiness of basing these…newfound convictions about mankind…upon the model of Mr. Wickham, considering that nine and ninety men out of a hundred would consider him to be an embarrassment to our sex." Mr. Darcy's eyes caught and locked with Elizabeth's. "I swear to you, Miss Bennet, that there are men who will improve themselves for a woman. Finding an excellent lady, they will tear out of their character every vice which renders them unworthy of her, no matter what the cost. And when they seek to replace them with whatever virtues they think would please her, they do so not to defraud her, but that, should her favor turn in their direction, they might be a little more deserving of the pearl. I beg you, madam, refrain from consigning us all to the dregs because of a contemptible few."

There was something more in the plea than a mere philosophical reflection, and despite her preoccupation with Anne's situation, Elizabeth readily recognized it. An abstract musing would not warrant a lowered tone and a gentle bow towards her ear. Thrilling, she wondered if he could possibly mean to communicate that *he*, Fitzwilliam Darcy, was one of those men who would thoroughly transform themselves to be worthy of a woman, and that *she* was his inspiration.

Uncertain of the proper response, but knowing for certain that she did not wish to completely rebuff him, she moved her eyes from his face to his cravat, and said sincerely,

"I hope that you are right." Taking a deep breath, she glanced up shyly and gave him a small smile to assure him that she did not mind his proximity, but in the next moment, for the sake of decorum and ladylikeness, she walked a few steps past him before pausing and looking back. "If you have no objections, sir, I believe that I will go upstairs and retire," she said kindly, and slowly, careful to make it clear that she was not fleeing from him. Giving a meaningful glance to the bruises which sleeplessness of many months continuance had inflicted on the gentleman's eyes, she ended with, "And, if I may take the liberty, I would suggest that you do not tarry below stairs for long either. You appear to need rest even more than I."

Mr. Darcy's heart swelled at her concern for his wellbeing.

"I will follow your wise counsel, madam, and I thank you for offering it." Catching her eyes one last time that evening, he concluded with a gentle, "Goodnight!"

"Goodnight, Mr. Darcy," was the dulcet response, after which the young woman disappeared behind the doors of the dining chamber.

Left alone, Darcy sank into the nearest chair and put his hand over his eyes. How much had happened over the span of ten hours! Early that afternoon, he had taken advantage of the storm-darkened sky to wander outdoors and pay a visit to Pemberley's graveyard. He had stood at the resting places of his parents and wished with his whole heart that he were lying beside them, his course in this dreary, hopeless world done. And that same day had ended with caring words and a sweet 'goodnight' from Elizabeth Bennet, tying him to life more strongly than ever before. It was incredible.

Chapter 45

Elizabeth awoke in time to see the sun rise the next morning. Dressing for the day and going to the window, she gazed upon the mist-covered lawn and wood outside and again felt the desire to take a walk through them. Days of travelling had afforded her young, active frame with little of its customary exercise, and she strongly doubted her ability to keep still on a carriage's seat for another day without giving her legs some much-needed activity first.

Looking at her watch, she estimated that she had at least an hour before she could reasonably expect anyone but the servants to be up and about, and therefore decided to hesitate no longer. She snatched her bonnet from its hook, opened and closed her door as quietly as possible, and proceeded stealthily through the long, elaborate hall. She found the grand staircase which she had ascended the previous evening and descended it. Then, seeking and discovering a door which led to the back gardens of the mansion, she released herself into the morning light.

At first she walked through the dewy grass as became a genteel visitor: her hands neatly clasped in front, her gait brisk but proper. But finding herself absolutely alone, the girl soon began to act accordingly. Her boots began to leave the ground more and more often as their proprietress broke into a wild canter. Elizabeth's arms were raised far above her shoulders, and her fingers spread apart, enjoying the sensation of the wind rushing between them. Even her voice joined in the fun and began to loudly hum a lively dance tune whose beat fit perfectly with her skipping steps.

Miss Bennet ran along thus, up and down the lawn, for a good five minutes. The first signs of fatigue were just commencing when a mortifying discovery instantly quenched the song upon her lips and caused her to freeze like a statue hewn out of rock.

She had an observer.

Far off, on one of the balconies blossoming out from the back of Menston Hall, stood a man. His bearing and figure indubitably proclaimed his identity. His hands firmly rested on the marble barrier before him, and she knew that he was looking directly at the young woman who had just paraded up and down his lawn in a most interesting manner. Her face started to scorch, and her only consolation was that he was too far away to see it.

He was close enough, however, to note the general direction of her gaze, and realized that he had been discovered. Therefore, he lifted one of his hands and offered a decorous wave by way of salute. They were too far away from one another to speak a greeting.

Unable to avoid acknowledging him, Elizabeth hesitantly raised her own hand and moved it back and forth a few times. She fancied that he smiled at this answer, but whether it was due to him being pleased by it or simply because she had appeared ridiculous, she did not know.

After a moment, his arm moved again, this time beckoning her to come to the door several stories beneath his feet. She nodded, and half-eagerly, half-hesitantly, began to move forward. The gentleman watched as she advanced towards the house, but when she was about a hundred feet from the back door, he disappeared into the house himself with haste in order to run across his room and down the stairs.

When Elizabeth reentered, Mr. Darcy was already in the hall. Bowing, he said a tad laughingly,

"Good morning, Miss Bennet. Judging from your energetic morning walk, would it be lawful to presume that you slept well?"

Elizabeth flushed anew, but felt enough equability to reply,

"Yes, I did, sir. And, as you doubtlessly saw, this morning I discovered that Menston Hall boasts of many benefits."

The young man chuckled and boldly offered the lady his arm.

"The grounds are decent and expansive enough, if that is your meaning. But I suspect, madam, that you are far less fastidious with nature than you are with books or human society. If she gives you but one leafy grove or a small patch of wildflowers, your good opinion is bestowed straightaway," he replied as he steered her towards a breakfast room where the morning repast awaited.

"Perhaps," Elizabeth assented. "But then again, from my tender years I have been schooled not to expect too much of her. Hertfordshire is home and therefore fondly considered, but the small hills and meadows around Longbourn are nowhere as impressive or remarkable as the peaks of Derbyshire or the windswept beaches of Ramsgate, to my fancy at least."

"I must own that I agree with that assessment, Miss Bennet." He glanced down at the comely countenance next to him. "The county's beauties come from another quarter."

Is this meant to be a flirtation? Elizabeth wondered, coloring for what felt like the tenth time that morning. Feeling it injudicious to ask him to expound, in case it was, she turned the conversation by returning the civil inquiry of whether he had slept well. The gentleman replied in the positive, and she did not doubt him. The night's repose had melted away the remaining signs of his months-long despair: the dark circles under his eyes had vanished, the lines associated with them had smoothened over, and the man appeared as strong and young and handsome as ever.

They entered the breakfast parlor and filled their plates with delicious morsels. As they commenced consuming them, Elizabeth looked up and asked,

"Sir, have you thought of what exactly shall be done to deal with Mr. Wickham and Mrs. Younge when we arrive in Hertfordshire tonight?"

Mr. Darcy took a sip of his coffee before replying,

"I have thought of several different strategies, but hope to confer with Richard and Bingley before I fix on one."

The young woman nodded.

"That seems very reasonable. However, if I am dispensable in these plans and if it is not too much to ask, would it be possible for me to enter Longbourn and tarry there awhile before you act, so that my return and your arrival appear unrelated? In Hertfordshire we are not considered the most intimate of acquaintances, and many eyebrows would be raised by our close cooperation. Furthermore, there are surely some in my family and Meryton who will never be convinced of Mr. Wickham's dishonorable motives, and will find the part I played in bringing about the end of the match unforgivable."

"Naturally, Miss Bennet. Ensuring that your good name will remain unsullied is a central consideration in every course of action I have planned. My sister's maidenhood would cost too much if it were purchased at the expense of your reputation," was the artless response.

Relieved, Elizabeth somehow managed to thank him for his thoughtfulness, while marveling anew at the goodness of the man. Brother-in-law to Wickham. He would rather be that than tarnish the name of a girl who had abused him abominably to his face and had no claim whatsoever on him. Did it mean that in his eyes, her happiness was equally as important as Georgiana's?

They finished their meal, parted courteously from the staff, and returned to the coach to continue their travels.

Chapter 46

The modest watch said ten o'clock as the carriage swept into Bedfordshire's largest town, but its owner, who had thought noon too ambitious a goal, could not believe it. She was obliged, therefore, to ask the gentleman sitting opposite her to examine his watch as well. He did so immediately, and when he had confirmed the accuracy of her timepiece, she found herself in redoubled admiration for what a team of fine horses could do.

They halted in front of a stable, and both occupants of the coach descended. Mr. Darcy mentioned that he would go and inquire if the Colonel and Mr. Bingley had, by any chance, also made an early appearance in Bedfordshire. She released him with a slight curtsy and meandered near the coach, taking the opportunity to acquaint herself with the place. Joyfully Miss Bennet's eyes regarded the street before her and took in the variety of people who passed through it, as well as the shops which lined it. Judging from the items in their window displays, their selection rivaled that of London's warehouses.

London!

With a jolt, Elizabeth remembered that she had raised expectations of a wedding gift from London while arranging her departure. Up until that moment, she had utterly forgotten; climbing anxiety as one 'coincidence' followed another left no energy or time for shopping. But now, she realized that she would be at Longbourn within a few hours, facing questions from her family and Anne and…Mr. Wickham and Mrs. Younge…and she was empty-handed.

Seizing the current moment, which would probably be the last free one on the road, Elizabeth determined to deter disaster. Hurriedly turning to one of the footmen standing at the door of the carriage, she informed him that she would step into a few of the shops, and return shortly. That done, Miss Bennet struck out for the largest store, which would hopefully feature the broadest selection.

She chose well. The moment she pushed the door open, merchandise of every size and kind met her eye. Mindful that there were only a few coins in her pocket and that whatever she bought would have to be transported safely for dozens of miles, Elizabeth glided past the larger and more delicate items such as crystal vases. Seeing a long glass case in the front of the store, she walked up to it.

Perhaps it contained an elegant pen or dainty bracelet which she could imagine in Anne's possession.

The transparent cabinet was verily filled with jewelry. Miss Bennet's pupils roved eagerly over the necklaces, earrings, and other trinkets, but failed to notice any which would suit Anne whatsoever. She was on the point of taking leave of the case and preparing to move to another corner of the store when a red sparkle caught her attention and fancy.

Edging a few inches nearer to the object which shimmered so, Elizabeth smiled as she took a long look at it. The gleaming culprit was a golden hairpin set with red stones. About a quarter of her palm in size, it was large enough to be decorative but not flamboyant. It would not do for Anne, however; the gold would blend in too well with her locks and only leave a few crimson gems to be seen. But it would suit her own chestnut tresses remarkably well!

The more Elizabeth gazed at the piece, the more she desired it. Being an unmercenary girl, it was rare for her to take a very strong liking to an article of jewelry and to seriously consider buying it for herself, particularly when she was shopping for another; but something about that particular pin had her standing at the counter for several minutes, earnestly debating whether or not to decrease her budget for the wedding gift by treating herself.

The shopkeeper noticed her admiration and approached.

"The hairclips are very fine, yes, madam?" he asked persuasively.

"Yes, they are," Elizabeth replied, smiling. "I confess to liking the one with the red stones very much. Pray, how much is it?"

"Thirty pounds."

Miss Bennet drew back from the glass case as all hope of purchasing the trinket evaporated.

"Indeed?" she murmured, hoping that the man would take a hint and drop the subject. But the merchant was relentless.

"Yes, thirty pounds. They are very fine, large rubies, after all, embedded in the purest gold. Look at the way they are cut, madam, you will have trouble finding another stone like that anywhere! The pin was created by a master jeweler, and is a piece which can be enjoyed for years to come without fear of it ever tarnishing or becoming less brilliant. Would you like to try it on?"

The potential customer immediately shook her head.

"No, thank you, not today," she replied, and bowing slightly, walked away from the counter. Avoiding further contact with the proprietor, Elizabeth wandered about the store, wishing to discover at least one item which the pitiful sum in her pocket could purchase. It would be an additional blessing if the piece of merchandise would be in line with Anne's tastes, but the time for fastidiousness was past. Anything would be better than nothing.

Yet, for a moment, it seemed that both requisites would be fulfilled. A woodcarving in the shape of a quaint, miniature pianoforte caught Elizabeth's attention.

It was stationed in the middle of the store. It was only seven inches long, and was covered with beautiful, hand-painted pink roses. Anne would certainly rejoice over the darling decoration, and, considering its simplicity, it was probably very affordable.

Stepping forward, Miss Bennet eagerly reached for the price card which was attached to the item of interest. She looked at it. Her mind interpreted the number written on it, and her lips pursed in shock. Her first thought was that the merchandise was mislabeled. The second was that the shopkeeper had lost his wits. Dropping the card as if it were made of red-hot iron, the lady craned her neck forward and circled the table on which the pianoforte was displayed, trying to identify the feature which allowed the simple piece to merit one of the most outrageous prices in the store.

"It is a music box," an aristocratic voice informed her.

Whirling around, Elizabeth found Mr. Darcy standing behind her, wearing his top-hat, carrying his gloves and gentleman's cane, and looking very distinguished indeed. Advancing, he reached past her, and carefully lifted the top of the miniature pianoforte. Standing side by side, their coat sleeves merely fractions of an inch apart, they both gazed upon the hand-painted wooden object which, of its own accord, began to play a simple tune.

Enchanted and mystified, Elizabeth turned to her well-educated companion.

"How does it work?" she asked curiously.

"It functions on the same principle that causes clocks to chime. When one opens the top, it sets the fine machinery into motion, and causes the music to play. To silence the instrument, you simply close the cover." He did so. "These music boxes are novelties imported from Switzerland." His eyes shifted from the merchandise to

Elizabeth. "By the by, I believe that you left word at Longbourn that you were going to London to pick out a gift for the bride-to-be?"

Seeing the direction in which his thoughts tended, and being none too pleased with it, the young woman demurely murmured,

"Yes, sir, I said something like that."

He turned back to the music box.

"Do you think that Miss Edwards would like this as a present?"

"I am sure she would," Elizabeth returned decisively. "But it is utterly out of the question for her to have it."

Mr. Darcy's eyebrows rose.

"Why should it be?" he asked, a touch of bewilderment in his tone.

Miss Bennet stared at the wall behind him, wondering at the man's uncustomary lack of delicacy. Was he suffering from some sort of mental lapse? Anyone who had seen her father's small estate had to know exactly why a daughter of Thomas Bennet could not afford to squander so great a sum upon a mere plaything. She forced herself to look at him and said reproachfully,

"For the very good reason that I cannot afford it, sir."

Without hesitation, Mr. Darcy swung around and picked up the expensive commodity.

"But I can." Seeing the lady's lips opening in surprise and knowing that protest was inevitable, he continued emphatically, "Miss Bennet, I would never dream of saddling you with any further expense on Georgiana's account. You have done more than enough."

Taking a step towards the resolute man, Elizabeth attempted to dissuade him.

"Mr. Darcy," she began, in a tone that should have contracted no opposition, "are you asking me to give Anne a gift which you purchased as if it were from myself? Such a deed reeks of dishonesty."

The gentleman shook his head.

"There is no need to fib. Tell those who ask the truth: a secret friend and benefactor of the bride wished to express their affection by buying a present for her jointly with you. From what you have told me, there are many in Hertfordshire who are fond of Anne Edwards. George Wickham will never suspect who you actually mean, and your story will be as innocent as possible. Besides, we are due to meet my friend and cousin in a matter of minutes, and have no time to find something which you could personally afford; and even if we could, would it not appear suspicious that you went all the way to London to purchase something relatively inexpensive and commonplace?"

She was about to protest further, but the gentleman decided that the time for audiences was past. He turned on his heel and went to pay the shopkeeper. Elizabeth followed him. If the purchase were indeed to be a joint endeavor she would, as a matter of principle, pay for at least a fraction of the gift. She insisted on pressing a few pitiful coins into the shopkeeper's palm and hurried away from the counter before either man could return it to her. She deigned to walk outside, as Mr. Darcy pulled out his pocketbook and coolly laid out a sum of money which could have easily paid all of Longbourn's expenses for a year.

Standing alone in the hot summer air, her back to the shop which she had just exited, Elizabeth felt the uncomfortable pulling sensation of a stray curl entangled in some niche of her bonnet. Wishing to alleviate the annoyance, she doffed the headdress and smoothened her locks. Perceiving that the lack of a bonnet maximized her enjoyment of the gentle breeze, she kept it off for several minutes.

Just as she was about to don the restrictive covering again, Elizabeth faintly recognized another sensation: that of something relatively heavy, such as a large insect, alighting gently upon the side of her head. Frightened at the thought, she began to reach up to shake out whatever pest had decided to explore her hair, when she was again startled by a voice behind her.

"I do believe that is Bingley's carriage over there."

Elizabeth hastily glanced over her shoulder, and found Mr. Darcy carefully bearing a wrapped package in one hand while discreetly gesturing at the opposite side of the street with the other. Forgetting the insect, Miss Bennet followed his gaze and indeed saw a familiar coach pulling to the side of the road.

"And I concur with that assessment, sir."

"Shall we go and join them before they slip off in search of us?"

"Naturally."

With that, the young woman quickly replaced her bonnet, as one of Darcy's footmen advanced and relieved his master of the parcel. The gentleman offered his arm to the lady and guided her across the street.

Chapter 47

The two walked up to the carriage just as Charles Bingley and Colonel Fitzwilliam jumped out of it, and were spotted immediately.

"Darcy!" the Colonel cried out, infusing profound happiness and relief into the tone of his voice. He hurried over, grasped Mr. Darcy's right hand in his own, and engulfed him in an embrace before another word was exchanged. "You rascal, you gave me such a fright these last few months! Bingley and I were just agreeing that we had both thought that you had gone abroad, travelling the Continent like some lost soul!"

His cousin drew back and gave him a look of disbelief.

"Whatever gave you the impression that I was abroad?" he asked bewilderedly.

"What else is a man to think when he goes to his cousin's house five times in the course of several months, only to be turned away every time?"

"And what was I to think when twenty letters went unanswered, even as I became more and more careful to make them legible?" Charles Bingley rejoined, coming up behind the Colonel.

"I...forgive me, I was...preoccupied."

"As was I," Richard Fitzwilliam retorted. "But you never stopped to think that we could be preoccupied together, did you?"

"No, I just...," Darcy did not finish. His brow creased, and his thoughts went back to the time when he could not bear anyone, and yet began to feel guilty that he had denied his relation the solace of company.

The military man, seeing that his words had cut deeper than had been intended, reached out and squeezed his cousin's arm tightly with his hand.

"I did not mean to needle you so, Darce," he murmured. "A man has the right to mourn as he chooses. And, despite what I said just now, if I am to be completely honest, I spent many a day staring at a bottle of whiskey, alone."

Mr. Darcy nodded, looking at his cousin with compassion and understanding. Then he stepped up to Charles Bingley and the two shared another handshake and embrace.

Elizabeth stood apart from them during all these proceedings, feeling a little too feminine and foreign in the midst of all the brotherly feelings which were on display. She was, however, anything but forgotten, for as soon as the friends had finished the preliminaries, Mr. Darcy turned towards her and said to the other gentlemen,

"You remember Miss Bennet, of course?"

"As if I could ever forget the only woman who was able to best the debate maestro of Cambridge!" Richard Fitzwilliam boomed, bowing to the said lady with deference. "Miss Bennet, it is a great delight to see you again."

Elizabeth warmly assured him that she felt similarly.

"I second the Colonel's words," Mr. Bingley inserted. "I have oft wondered how you and your family were faring, Miss Bennet. Might I ask, are all your sisters still at Longbourn?"

Miss Bennet suspected that he only wished to know about the whereabouts of the eldest sister, but she would not torture him. Simply, she replied,

"Yes, they are all there," and saw relief rush into his face.

The Colonel saw that Bingley was on the point of speaking at length about his recollections of Hertfordshire and determinedly turned the conversation by remarking,

"Speaking of sisters, what is all this about new information on Georgiana's disappearance? How can there possibly be new hope after all these months? Are you certain that you are not being misled?"

"My source is highly trustworthy. All that I have been told fits perfectly. Even you, suspicious military man that you are, will be convinced. That I am sure of."

"And who is this source of whom you speak?"

"You greeted her just a moment ago."

The Colonel stared at Elizabeth.

"Miss Bennet?" he asked, surprised. "Is that why you are accompanying Darcy? He merely mentioned in his letter that he had met you in Derbyshire and that you would be coming with us to Hertfordshire. While I wondered at how you managed to be on such good terms after being almost deaf and dumb to each other in Kent," here he turned to smirk at his kin, "I never thought that you were to be the cornerstone of our mission! How has this come about? What do you know of my little cousin?"

"Miss Bennet will be glad to inform you, but we must stop dawdling," Mr. Darcy put in impatiently. "Bingley, leave your carriage here and have them put it up in the stables. We will all go in my coach." He reached for Elizabeth's hand and placed it on his arm, ignoring the broad grin which spread across the Colonel's face. He hurried the young woman back across the street, leaving his two friends scampering to catch up.

They settled into the carriage. Elizabeth noted that Mr. Darcy went to great lengths to suggest that Mr. Bingley and the Colonel should sit on the seat opposite her before he nimbly ascended the step and commandeered the seat next to hers. Only a few inches separated them.

She began to tell the story to the new arrivals just as she had the previous day told it to her lone listener. Beginning with the day that Mr. Bennet had brought the maiden home, she took them through her illness, recovery, and incorporation into Hertfordshire society. When Anne's first meeting with Mr. Wickham was mentioned, however, Richard Fitzwilliam began to fidget. He clenched and unclenched his fists, breathed heavily, and scarcely waited for Elizabeth to finish before he cried out, impassioned,

"He shall not be at her side for long after we arrive, depend upon it! The first thing I shall do is separate them, and this time I *shall* deprive that wretch of existence!" Seeing that his cousin was about to comment on this declaration, he hastened to snap out, "No, Darcy, *this* time I will not listen to your charitable speeches about mercy and the Fifth Commandment! I have had it with that reprobate! If you had not restrained me last summer and locked me in your study until I promised to forgo my plan of lodging a bullet in that blackguard, wildflowers would be growing over his grave today and none of this would have happened. I -,"

"Richard!" Darcy cut in. "*This* time, Georgiana does not know us!"

There was a catch in his voice towards the end, which forced the gentleman to turn towards the window and stare out sightlessly, striving to collect himself. Colonel Fitzwilliam, however, was too blind with rage to notice his cousin's feelings or to reflect on his words. Instead, he only retorted,

"What of that? *He* certainly will know who we are, and for what he dies!"

Elizabeth glanced at the gentleman sitting by her side. His breathing was agitated, and she fancied that it was due to repressed sobs. In any case, Mr. Darcy was clearly unequal to reasoning with his infuriated relation, something which had to be done sooner rather than later, before the military man became completely consumed with rage. Seeing that Mr. Bingley was unsure of what to say, she took the monumental task upon herself.

"Colonel Fitzwilliam," she began in a soothing, gentle tone, "I believe that what your cousin means to say is that your favorite course of action would be impolitic as well as immoral. Had you openly injured Mr. Wickham last summer, Miss Darcy would have soon forgiven you, for she knew that as a relation you had her best interests at heart. But now, tell me: do you wish Anne's first impression of you and Mr. Darcy to be that of two men who swooped in upon her happiness but a few hours before her wedding vows, and caused her fiancé's death? While I hope and pray that the sight of your faces, which were once so dear to my friend, will produce the miracle which nothing else has been able to effect, it is not an end upon which we can count. And I am sure that if you cannot have her for a cousin and sister, you would at least like to have Anne's friendship. Do I state your opinion correctly, Mr. Darcy?"

The man beside her turned from the window and nodded.

"Yes, Miss Bennet," he agreed softly, looking at her. "I could not have expressed it better."

For some reason, Elizabeth felt her pulse quicken as she returned his look. Breaking the mutual gaze, she glanced abashedly at her gloves, listened to the stillness which suddenly seemed to have filled the coach, and reflected. It was strange; she had perpetually misunderstood the man last autumn and spring, and now, but four and twenty hours after their unexpected reunion, she was well-acquainted enough with him to read his mind better than his own relations.

Her thoughts were interrupted by Colonel Fitzwilliam's somewhat subdued but still determined tone.

"You are perfectly right, Miss Bennet," he conceded. "I am ashamed that I did not think of that. But then again, *something* must be done. Wickham is not the sort of man who will walk away from so great a windfall easily!"

"Something will be done," Mr. Darcy's aristocratic voice declared. "But it will not be done in front of Georgiana. Miss Bennet, have you any insights as to how we may gain an audience with Wickham without alerting my sister to the same?"

Anxious to please him, for some reason, by coming up with a flawless scheme, Elizabeth bit her lip and deliberated in earnest for the better part of a minute. When her silent counsels were over, she hesitantly said,

"I am afraid that our anticipated late arrival today, with the wedding on the morrow, does not afford us many options. If I know Mr. Wickham, he will stay at Longbourn until late in the evening tonight, and return very early in the morning to await his bride. The only times that one could confront him without people about would be during his walks to and from Meryton."

"Walks?" Bingley interrupted, surprised. "Does he not ride?"

Elizabeth gave him a wry smile.

"The militia could not spare any of their horses when they set off for Brighton, and so during his leave he has gone without. I suspect that his habits do not allow him to accumulate sufficient funds to purchase his own mount."

Mr. Bingley shook his fair head in disgust, and fell silent as his friend took up the conversation once more.

"So much the better," Darcy mused. "It is much easier to stop a man on foot. Pray tell me, Miss Bennet: via which route does Wickham travel to Meryton?"

"He takes the path which cuts through my father's largest field of corn, sir."

Mr. Darcy looked at the Colonel.

"There is an open meadow along that road," he said quietly, half to himself, half to his cousin.

Something in his low, calculating tone made Elizabeth's blood run cold. She instantly thought of what open spaces were usually used for by gentlemen who felt themselves or a lady under their protection wronged, and felt her heart contract painfully. It had been clear from the onset that a duel was uppermost in the Colonel's thoughts, but she never thought that Mr. Darcy would condone such a measure. He seemed so nonviolent a man! Miss Bennet did not pity their prey; she would have gladly challenged the reprobate herself, so indignant was she about how he was using Anne - but somehow, the idea of Mr. Darcy facing an armed Wickham was highly loathsome. She dared not, however, probe further into his intentions by voicing inquiries or objections. After all, it was their right to make the final decision of how to deal with the blackguard who had imposed on their charge. Therefore, she only put in meekly,

"And Mrs. Younge; what of her?"

Colonel Fitzwilliam started.

"Is that malicious witch there too?!" he cried.

"I am afraid so. She is Mr. Wickham's particular wedding guest."

"The fiend!" the military man muttered. "I mean…I beg your pardon, Miss Bennet," he stammered, flushing profusely.

Elizabeth forgave him graciously. She turned once again to Mr. Darcy, who, when he was finished glaring at his cousin for disrespecting a lady's company, said,

"She shall have to be accosted as well, lest she guess the reason for Wickham's sudden disappearance and confide some highly convoluted tale in Georgiana."

"Naturally," the young man in regimentals agreed.

Darcy leaned forward, putting his elbows on his knees and clasping his hands earnestly in front of himself. Staring at the carriage floor, he seemed to deliberate some point most carefully for all of five minutes. At last, he straightened up, and taking a deep breath, sighed.

"I cannot believe that I am saying this, considering that in general disguise of every sort is my abhorrence," the gentleman began, "but the following seems to me at present the best course. Returning to what Miss Bennet said before: it would be preferable for Georgiana and Hertfordshire society to be in ignorance of the part we play in Wickham's departure from the region. Suppose we were to enter the county secretly and remain there covertly for a fortnight? We can confront Wickham and Mrs. Younge tonight, and see that they are safely out of the village before dawn, and then retire to Netherfield. We could leave the county altogether instead, but I am loath to be far away from Georgiana in case we are needed. I am certain that with the help of my servants we will be able to stay at Netherfield undetected for a week or two at least. By then, most of the rumors and speculation will have ceased and we can announce our arrival, and make Miss Anne Edwards' acquaintance without raising any suspicions as to who was responsible for her intended's removal. That is, if you agree, Miss Bennet, and do not foresee any trouble which could arise for you as a result of this plan. I do not wish to put you in an uncomfortable position by any part of this affair."

Elizabeth waved away his concerns with a quick flick of her gloved wrist.

"Pray, think no more of me, Mr. Darcy," she exclaimed. "Your plan is a very sound one, and if Mr. Bingley is not averse to using his house as a hiding place, by all means follow it."

Gazing at her gratefully, Mr. Darcy softly expressed his thanks. From the opposite side of the coach, Mr. Bingley chimed in with a wholehearted and lively assurance that all were welcome to refuge at his dwelling. All important matters having been discussed, the party fell silent for the reminder of the journey, each busy with their own thoughts.

Chapter 48

Traveling as expeditiously as possible, they were on the outskirts of Hertfordshire by sundown. The coachman, following Mr. Darcy's meticulous instructions, drove into the county by way of the more obscure routes, to minimize the chances of the coach being seen and the crest on it recognized. The sky was completely black, except for the silver moon and stars, by the time that the conveyance paused a quarter of a mile from Longbourn.

"While I am aware that you are an excellent walker during the daytime, Miss Bennet, I am sorry for requiring you to walk so long a distance at night," Mr. Darcy profusely apologized. "I will be glad to have the coachman drive up a little further, if such is your desire - ,"

"Sir, there is absolutely no reason for regrets!" Elizabeth interrupted. "If we were to attempt it, the sound of the horses and the carriage would be certainly heard by those inside the house, and all our schemes spoiled. As for my walking, I beg you not to trouble yourself on that score either. I have wandered in this lane alone, oftentimes past the midnight hour, on the hot summer nights during which I could not fall asleep. Therefore, I am neither afraid nor inconvenienced."

Darcy caught his breath at the picture which her words painted: Elizabeth, ambling about the moonlit path, her beautiful dark curls loose and falling around her shoulders. He implored,

"At the very least, do allow me the honor of escorting you to your door, Miss Bennet. While I do believe the road safe, I would feel better seeing you going in with my own eyes."

Elizabeth considered, and capitulated.

"Very well, Mr. Darcy," she said. "Come to think of it, perhaps we might be able to gain you a quick glance at Anne. While I doubt that I have made a mistake, I would much rather have you personally identify her before you involve yourself in this affair."

The gentleman needed no other invitation. He quickly alighted from the coach, and reaching up, eagerly grasped his beloved's hand to help her down. The Colonel suggested accompanying them, but Darcy, persuasively reasoning that a larger group would be more likely to make an accidental noise or otherwise draw attention, stayed him in the carriage. And so, Elizabeth found herself strolling towards Longbourn alone with Mr. Darcy.

They walked quietly, ears sensitive to every sound the nightingales made, constantly fearing that they might hear a voice or a footstep other than their own. All was still, however.

They saw the house and began to approach with caution. Despite the calmness of the night, it was clear that the interior of Longbourn was filled with revelry. Every window glowed with light, and it was possible to hear the clinking of glasses and silverware and laughter through the thick glass.

Elizabeth and Darcy slipped up to one of the windows, careful to stay in the shadows. Then, they peered inside.

Elizabeth, who was far more acquainted with the room which they were viewing and Miss Edwards' habits in it, located the girl first. In the midst of Longbourn's residents and guests, Anne stood upon the hearth holding a teacup and saucer. In between lifting the brew to her lips and taking sips, she spoke to and smiled at Mr. Wickham, who was standing barely a foot away.

Lowering her voice so that it was almost inaudible, Miss Bennet murmured,

"There, sir, right in front of the fireplace."

She felt Mr. Darcy's eyes shift to the indicated place, and waited for the verdict.

The sound of a sharp breath drawn in at her side conclusively proved her identification correct. Glancing up at her companion, she found his countenance displaying a vivid mixture of joy, grief, longing and anger. By sheer force of will, it seemed, he was resisting an overwhelming urge to cast aside all their carefully-laid plans and to dash inside Longbourn at once to gather his sister into his arms and confront the evildoer who had lied to her for weeks. Desperate to help him overcome the temptation, she boldly reached out and laid a restraining hand upon his coat sleeve.

Surprised at the unexpected touch, he started and turned towards her. Locking eyes in the moonlight, they gazed at each other for a long, spellbound moment.

Coming to his senses, the gentleman took the gloved hand which rested upon his arm and steered its proprietress towards a side-garden which was even darker than their original location.

"Are you alright?" Elizabeth asked concernedly once they had stopped and faced each other again. "I know that it was a difficult thing to see."

"Yes, it was, but I thank the Good Lord and yourself that I saw it before the situation became permanent. I shall be perfectly well."

The lady expressed her relief, and stated that she felt it was time for her to go inside lest someone come out and they be observed. The young man handed her the few parcels which he had carried over from the carriage for her. Once they were all in her arms, he transferred Anne's indigo ring from his pocket to hers.

"Should you not like to keep it?" Elizabeth whispered.

"I have no need of it. Having a fresh image of Georgiana's sweet face imprinted upon my memory is all the consolation I need. Besides, I do not want you to have to answer for its disappearance." Taking a deep breath, he hesitantly laid his hand on her shoulder, and added, "Miss Bennet, in the very unlikely event that Wickham prevails tonight, do not, I beg you, blame yourself in the least. You have done all you can, the rest is up to Providence. If anything happens to me and Richard in this attempt, and the day comes that Georgiana remembers who we were, pray tell her the same, and that we loved her."

Elizabeth blanched at this request. Trying to disregard it, she whispered indignantly,

"How can you speak such nonsense?" Her voice trembled all the same. "It is three against one, not counting your servants. What can Wickham possibly do, startled and unprepared?" The thought of them speaking about the meadow again slipped into her mind, but before she could find a way to tactfully appeal that the field be left desolate and untouched that night, the gentleman put a little extra pressure on her shoulder and spoke.

"One can never tell how such cases shall end. Promise me. Please, Miss Bennet."

Unable to deny him the reassurance, she murmured,

"I give you my word." Glancing apprehensively into the dark pupils which were focused upon herself, she petitioned in turn, "And promise me that you will be as careful as possible, for Anne's sake."

"I planned on that from the start, and I pledge it now. I have every intention of seeing my sister, as well as her friends, many, many more times in the future."

Miss Bennet swallowed, and nodded.

All the words which would pass between them that night had been spoken, save for one 'Goodnight' which Mr. Darcy uttered as he withdrew his hand from her shoulder and bowed. He then went away through the shadows of the garden, but as soon as he reached and was partially concealed by the gate, he halted, turned, and slightly gestured at Longbourn's front door.

Elizabeth understood this to mean that he would not fully vacate the premises until she was safely within the house. While she would have infinitely preferred him to be at least half-a-mile away before she alerted the family to her return, she was far too intelligent to spend time staging a mimed debate on the topic. With a slight curtsey, she went where she had been asked to go. Lifting the latch, she glanced over her shoulder at the figure standing by the gate, opened the door, and entered the house.

Chapter 49

She lingered in the foyer for several minutes, slowly removing her coat and bonnet, giving Mr. Darcy ample time to make his escape. When she judged that enough minutes had passed, Elizabeth tucked the wedding gift under the crook of her arm, braced herself, and plastering a smile upon her face, joined the general assembly.

"Lizzy!" Anne's shocked but relieved voice rang throughout the drawing room. Before Elizabeth could answer the bride-to-be flew across the room and in front of everyone, threw herself upon Elizabeth's neck. "Oh, my dearest Lizzy, you have returned! I had almost given up hope - I thought that you had been irremediably delayed and would miss the wedding for certain! But here you are, safe and sound, thank God! Oh, thank God!"

"I already have thanked Him, you may be sure of that," Elizabeth murmured, returning the tight embrace. "I am sorry, Anne, for giving you such a fright. I never meant to stay away this long. A carriage's axle was broken, and...well, the rest does not matter."

They parted. Miss Edwards' curious eyes intently searched the face before her.

"I did not hear any carriage just now. Did you walk the two miles from Meryton to Longbourn in the dark?" the girl inquired anxiously.

"The distance is nothing when one has a motive," Elizabeth answered. Noticing that her father and younger sisters were on the verge of asking five hundred questions about her activities since leaving Longbourn, she immediately pulled out the elegantly wrapped package which Mr. Darcy and she had financed, saying, "Here, my dear, is a little trinket for you. Open it."

Anne took the parcel held out to her, somewhat unwillingly.

"Thank you, Lizzy, but you truly should not have gone so far for this. And I already have received the greatest wedding gift a girl could ever hope for - seeing her best friend come in time to be her maid of honor."

"I know, but I am a very selfish creature, and for the sake of giving relief to my own feelings, care not how much I may be wounding yours. I believe that this new, improved wedding memento will last longer and give you more pleasure than the meager token of a dress which I purchased first."

Expressing thanks again, Miss Edwards seated herself, placed the gift upon her lap, and proceeded to undo its ribbon and to remove the delicate paper.

"Oh!" she exclaimed when she uncovered the miniature hand-painted pianoforte.

"That is merely the beginning," Elizabeth laughed, as she stepped behind her friend and lifted up the top of the little instrument.

"What?" Anne cried out, startled and shocked as the sweet melody tinkered through the air. "It is playing music, all by itself! How is it possible?"

"It is called a 'music box'," Elizabeth informed her. "They are made by watchmakers in Switzerland. You are so fond of music, and I thought that perhaps you would like to have a way to play it constantly without exhausting your fingers. Do you like it?"

"Like it? Lizzy, it is the prettiest, most interesting thing I have ever seen! I shall treasure it forever! Mr. Wickham, what do you think of our wedding gift?"

Mr. Wickham, who had been observing his fiancée and her friend with slightly narrowed eyes, nodded his approbation at this prompting.

"It is absolutely charming. I have seen them in several London shops, and know how dearly they are prized. I suppose," he glanced sharply at Elizabeth, "that it must have set our good benefactress back a great deal?"

Interiorly, Miss Bennet panicked. This was precisely the sort of commentary which she had feared. Thankfully, Mr. Darcy's foresight and suggestions had allowed her to prepare for the remark, and now she straightened up, threw her head back, and exclaimed waggishly,

"Mr. Wickham, I am surprised by you!" Raising an eyebrow, she continued, "I thought that a gentleman of your breeding would have better manners than to pry into the price of a gift!" The officer blushed at this and bowed slightly in apology and agreement, but Elizabeth could see that he was not fully satisfied. Thus, she added, "Perhaps, there was a person with me who helped me choose it and gladly furnished the extra funds." She stopped here, letting the engaged couple and her family interpret the statement as they wished. Anne was the one who swallowed the carefully dangled bait.

"Your uncle or aunt, who live in London!" she cried, laughing, believing herself to have cleverly made the right discovery. "But they

254

have never even met me! They must be kindness itself, to pay for a wedding gift for someone who is not among their acquaintance!"

"I do not confirm nor deny your assumption, as your benefactor wishes to remain anonymous. But the Gardiners are generous souls indeed," Elizabeth responded, trying to pacify her prickling conscience by silently arguing that she was stating complete truths in actuality, and if those present were deceived, it was by their own erroneous guessing. "And they have met Mr. Wickham."

The intended bridegroom, whose curiosity seemed completely quenched by the aforementioned exchange, came forward and warmly spoke about his memories of Mr. and Mrs. Gardiner and their presumed goodness. He was finishing, and the subject was on the point of being dropped, when Lydia suddenly bounded to Elizabeth's side and cried out,

"It is so unfair!"

Her older sister turned to her, bemused.

"What is it, Lydia?" she asked in a tired voice.

"Why should *you* always get so much from Uncle and Aunt Gardiner? You are the one they always invite to town, or on holiday with them, and you always get the best presents. I am sure I do not know what you have done to deserve being such a favorite!"

"Obviously, you have only been half-attending to our conversation," Elizabeth rebutted with a bit of exasperation. "The miniature pianoforte is for Anne, not for me."

"And I suppose that Uncle's pocketbook had nothing to do with *that*," Lydia returned sarcastically, staring at Elizabeth.

"With what?" the older Miss Bennet asked, confused.

"With this," Lydia sneered, pointing to a section of hair about two inches above her sister's right ear.

Elizabeth gave the accuser a distrustful look, but condescended to run her fingers through the indicated tresses. To her amazement, her fingertips collided with something hard. Bewildered, Miss Bennet applied all her concentration to feeling and then to tugging the foreign object out of her hair. Succeeding, she brought it before her eyes, and was utterly astonished to find that she held the princely gold and ruby clip which she had admired in Bedfordshire!

For one wild moment she absurdly wondered if she could have somehow inadvertently stolen it. This preposterous fantasy was abolished by the recollection that she had never laid hands on the accessory before, having negated the shopkeeper's suggestion that he open the glass case and afford her a closer look at the merchandise. It was then that she remembered the mysterious sensation of heaviness alighting on her hair in the seconds before Mr. Darcy, who had surreptitiously stepped behind her in the meanwhile, pointed out his friends' arrival.

Forgetting herself, Elizabeth cried out in realization,

"He must have - I never even noticed that he saw me admiring it!" Glancing up, her eyes alighted upon Mr. Wickham's face. Instantly, she realized what words had just come out of her mouth. All the color drained out of her face. Her violent reaction would inevitably inform him that something was amiss; and perhaps somehow allow him to guess exactly which gentleman she had referred to.

It was Mr. Bennet who unwittingly saved her. *He* was still under the impression that they were discussing Mr. Gardiner's generosity, and thus he coolly said as he unfolded a newspaper,

"I declare, that brother-in-law of mine spoils you girls to no end. If he continues in this vein, you will soon be clamoring to take up residence with him rather than continuing on at Longbourn with your stingy old father!"

Overflowing with relief, Elizabeth grasped at the opportunity and hastened to assure him that that would never be the case. As she spoke, she slipped the expensive trinket into her pocket, and afterwards fended off Lydia's rude questions about where the gift had been purchased and whether the younger Miss Bennets could expect to get similar hairpins the next time they saw their relations.

About an hour later, Mr. Wickham bid his bride-to-be farewell. For most observers it was a touching scene. Mr. Wickham reverently kissed Anne's hand, straightened up, gazed into her eyes, and then bent again to whisper a few words into her ear. These his apparent beloved received with a smile and a gentle blush and, at last, murmured her own tender adieu.

But to her who had been enlightened, the entire scene was the epitome of duplicity. There was a light of anticipation in his eyes, yes, but on closer inspection it was tinged with greed; he looked at Anne as a man would look at a stuffed pocketbook which was on the point of being bequeathed to him. The expression which others mistook for happiness was properly interpreted by Elizabeth as triumph. She waited impatiently until he had released Anne's hand; then she seized the alabaster fingers in her own, and pulled Miss Edwards away, insisting that it was time that the bride get some well-deserved rest. Mr. Wickham agreed, and bowing went away alone, as Mrs. Younge had gone back to Meryton with Mr. and Mrs. Phillips.

Standing shoulder-to-shoulder with Anne and the rest of her family at Longbourn's front door, waving goodbye to the prospective bridegroom, Elizabeth's breaths tightened. While she hoped that he would never return, she prayed that the price of his going would not be too high.

Chapter 50

There was one tradition which Miss Edwards forewent: she had no intention of staying awake and engaging in nervous affectations the night before her wedding. A week of late hours and sleepless nights had exhausted her, Elizabeth's return had soothed her nerves and, taken together, these two circumstances caused Anne to collapse into bed and fall into a heavy sleep as soon as she donned her nightgown.

This spared Elizabeth much. The girl's early retirement saved her from probing questions about her travels as well as from feigning excitement for the morrow. She was free to move around the bedchamber quietly, unpacking, and attend to her own thoughts.

When her meager supply of clothes had been transferred back to the closet, Elizabeth decided to be sensible and prepare for sleep. As was her routine, her hands first dove into her gown's pockets to ensure their emptiness. Today, they brought out the ruby pin which she had owned for half-a-day without knowing it.

Fingering the beautiful design, she wondered why Mr. Darcy had gifted it to her, and in such a manner! Had he meant it as a form of compensation for her travelling expenses, and decided that deviously slipping a valuable ornament into her brown locks would be easier and less mortifying than pressing her to accept a monetary sum? Or had it been a friendly expression of gratitude for her trouble? Or…could it be an indication that the feelings which he had ardently proclaimed last spring were still ingrained in his heart?

She turned towards the window nearest to the fateful meadow. A duel! This was the stuff of novels, of tall tales which found their way to her ears after passing through dozens of lips. Never in her twenty years had she heard of a duel taking place in or around Meryton, and the newness of the ordeal frightened her even more. She had not the faintest idea of how many duels ended with death or terrible injury. The hardest part of all was that she was destined to know nothing more for several days at least! Of course, if Wickham presented himself on the morrow to claim Anne as his bride she would know that all attempts to stop him had failed and that her friends were most likely perished; but even if he did not, there would be no assurance that everyone had escaped unscathed.

An idea crept into her head. Elizabeth tried to repulse it. It came back. She shunned it again. It proved persistent. Even as Miss Bennet was thinking: '*I will not do something so foolish and unnecessary*', she found herself walking to the closet.

Throwing a dark blue cloak over her shoulders for the purpose of hiding, and shaking her head at the absurd resolution, Elizabeth slipped out of her bedroom, yet again, for a secretive purpose. Praying that the soft creaking of the boards under her shoes would not give her away, she held her breath until she had descended the stairs and reached the ground floor. Then, going to a side door, she turned the lock with infinite care so that even she had difficulty hearing its click, opened the door, and closed it behind herself.

Once out in the garden, she was scarcely less cautious. Knowing that her sisters or some servants might still be up and at their windows, she took care to walk in the shadiest areas, and felt immense relief when the field of corn surrounded her figure on every side and the stalks' height outcompeted her stature.

Hurrying down the path which she knew Wickham to have taken, Elizabeth nervously listened for anything which would indicate another human being in the vicinity. She did not know which she feared more: bumping against Mr. Wickham and having to explain her nighttime roaming habits, or unexpectedly meeting Mr. Darcy and feeling his displeasure at her espionage. All was quiet, however. That is, until Miss Bennet came into earshot of the meadow.

Then, the sounds of metal clashing upon metal were unmistakable.

Her heart in her throat, Elizabeth ran towards the terrifying noises as quickly as she could without allowing her footsteps to pound into the earth and herald her arrival. She was absolutely desperate to see what was happening.

The rows of corn thinned. She was out in the open once more. The meadow in question was a few feet in front of her, and only separated from her visage by several tall boulders. Veritably shaking, she approached one of them, rested her cold hands upon the rock, and then craned her neck to see beyond it.

In the center of the field were two men. Mr. Darcy and Mr. Wickham had laid off their coats and waistcoats, and were attired only in their white linen shirts. They each held a sword hilt, and by

259

the light of the moon and of the lanterns held by the other gentlemen and Mr. Darcy's servants, bashed the opposite ends together for all they were worth.

For the first two minutes, Elizabeth could scarcely support herself. It was necessary to grasp the boulder with both hands to compensate for trembling legs. Breathing went out of fashion. With every loud clang of the swords she blinked, and dreaded opening her eyes again lest they behold Mr. Darcy lying on the ground, mortally wounded.

But after those terrifying hundred and twenty seconds, however, she became a little more accustomed to the sights and sounds before her, and gradually, very gradually, relaxed enough to resume taking breaths. The battle seemed fierce, yes, and it was horribly protracted, but Elizabeth noticed something important: its contenders were very badly matched.

Mr. Wickham swung his weapon wildly, furiously. There was no doubt that he desired his opponent's death. However, as the lazy officer's greatest foray into combat had been with his fists during drunken brawls, his clobbering attacks never even came close to landing on Mr. Darcy's person. With elegant, slight flicks of the wrist, each one was efficiently parried. In contrast to the lieutenant's heaving chest, his athletic opponent was barely taking air more frequently than his usual wont.

In addition, the more skilled challenger also seemed to be fighting with a much different purpose in mind. There were numerous times when an opening so broad appeared that even Elizabeth's inexperienced eye detected it; a mediocre swordsman could easily have dealt a fatal blow during one of them. Each time, however, Mr. Darcy slowed and allowed Wickham to recover. The spying young lady was not the only one who noticed his excessive sportsmanship. Elizabeth could hear Colonel Fitzwilliam producing low hisses and dissatisfied grunts whenever his cousin, once again, spared the scoundrel.

The scheme behind Mr. Darcy's unusual tactics soon became clear. As the fight drew on, Wickham's attacks and defenses became clumsier and clumsier. His arm was languishing. For a moment, he actually took his left hand and joined it to his right one in clasping the hilt. Realizing that this strategy drastically reduced his range of movement, however, he loosened the newcomer, and dropping it to his side, attempted to continue on with the original arm.

That was his mistake. The sore right hand could barely keep hold of the weapon. Darcy, seeing this, mobilized his own, capable arm, and swashed his sword energetically through the air, contacting Wickham's with great force.

CLACK!

The blade dislodged from Wickham's hand and catapulted into the darkness. Stunned, the loser stumbled backwards, and fell upon the ground of his own accord.

"Do you yield?" Darcy demanded, pointing his sword in Mr. Wickham's direction.

Despite the obvious defeat, the scoundrel's tongue was unfinished.

"And if I do not?" he sneered. "Frankly, I do not think that you have it in you to kill a man, Darcy. Especially an unarmed one. Your precious sense of honor, or religion, or whatever it is, would never allow you!"

"Perhaps not," his conqueror replied readily, owning the alleged weakness as if it were a virtue. "But that same sense will not permit me to let you use my sister for material gain and revenge. But never mind this; there is no time tonight for studying each other's character. You have lost the duel, and we are hardly in need of your capitulation. Refuse to do what we ask; we will find alternative means by which to inform Georgiana of the change of plans. In the meanwhile, *you* will forfeit the choice of exile over imprisonment. I have kept all the receipts for the debts of yours which I have discharged, and half of them will be sufficient to keep you in debtor's prison until you are old and gray. Which will it be?"

Wickham gritted his teeth.

After a quarter of a minute, he spat out,

"I will write it."

"Good." Darcy withdrew the sword. The Colonel came forward eagerly. Grasping Wickham's wrist anything but gently, he dragged him from the grass, across the battleground, and forced him to sit upon a half-rotten stump near the carriage. A pen was pressed into his hand. Mr. Bingley stood nearby holding a bottle of ink. A small wooden board was plopped down across the miscreant's knees, and a piece of blank paper was put upon it.

Mr. Darcy brushed off his white shirt and rearranged the sleeves into a neater fashion. He then accepted the waistcoat and the coat proffered by one of the menservants. Watching every movement of his uninjured frame, Elizabeth's heart sang with joy.

Properly attired, the young man strolled over to where the sulking scoundrel was sitting. Wickham looked up at him and haughtily said,

"I do not know where to begin."

"Do you mean," the Colonel exclaimed, feigning disbelief, "that you are less proficient at writing confessions than you are at pouring sweet words into young women's ears? Who would have thought this of you, George Wickham?!"

On the other hand, Mr. Darcy regarded him with a sigh and said in a tone reminiscent of a schoolmaster,

"Then I shall help you, but if you can agree with all the words in it, you will sign the epistle. Will that suit you?"

"I suppose it must," the other spat out.

"The first sheet shall be the envelope. Address it to 'Miss Anne Edwards'."

With a grunt, Wickham bent over the paper and complied.

"Now take the next sheet, and date it with today's date." Anger flushed the lieutenant's face, but he wrote. Afterwards, supervising every stroke of the pen, Mr. Darcy slowly dictated the following:

"Be not alarmed, madam, upon receiving this letter, by the apprehension that any injustice or corporal harm has befallen me. It has not. As I write this, I am whole in body but am, and have been for many years, severely corrupted in spirit.

I will not spend time enumerating the vain particulars; suffice it to say that I have engaged in behaviors which are beyond the scope of your imagination. This conduct of which I speak does not belong to the distant past. Up to this very night, I have been selfishly trying to turn every situation which I encounter towards my greater personal gain.

Here we arrive at the point: you, too, have been a victim of the ruthless game I play. Rest assured that it was through no fault of your own that I fixed upon you, for your manner was always perfectly humble and correct. I, and I alone, am to blame. To own the whole truth, Miss Edwards, you are far from the first lady whom I have

262

trifled with. I do not love you, nor have I ever loved you. I have no excuses to offer for my behavior. Pray do not attempt to deduce why I act as I do; you shall be unsuccessful. The mind of a man like me cannot be fully understood by a respectable lady's intellect.

I leave Hertfordshire tonight, never to return. By the time you receive this letter, I shall be long gone. Although this is doubtlessly a painful piece of news now, it is better for you than the alternative. If tomorrow was our wedding day as planned, you would forever regard it as the worst day of your life. Adieu."

When Mr. Wickham finished writing, Mr. Darcy gave him a sharp look and asked,

"Would you like to add an apology, a plea for forgiveness, or good wishes to the postscript?"

"Absolutely not," Wickham snapped.

Although irritated, Mr. Darcy reined in his anger and stated in a collected voice,

"Then I will not make you put in insincerity. Are you able to agree with the rest?"

"Yes," the other man sniffed.

"In that case, sign it with your customary signature."

When Mr. Wickham had done so, Mr. Darcy reached over, took the letter and the envelope, folded them up, and handed them over to Mr. Bingley, saying,

"Keep it safe for now, Charles, until we are able to get a hired messenger to deliver it to Longbourn." His friend obeyed, and pocketed the missive.

The Colonel, who in the meantime had retrieved some ropes from the carriage and was standing nearby, said at this juncture,

"Do you need his arms for anything else, Darcy?"

"I believe that we are finished with them."

"Perfect!" Seizing Wickham, the Colonel dragged the man to his feet. Pinning the blackguard's hands behind his back, he bound them with the rope, snarling, "The carriage doors will be locked from the outside, but these fetters should ensure that you do not conceive any creative notions on how to leave it. You useless cad! If Darcy would let me I would tie you so tight that gangrene would set in before you boarded the ship."

"Richard, pray do not stoop to his level," his relation interjected. "Following his lead scarcely reflects well on your own character."

The Colonel scowled, but Elizabeth saw him slightly loosen the bonds which held Wickham.

As his cousin continued to secure the prisoner, Mr. Darcy motioned to his coachman. That man left his companions and came towards his employer, who steered them both in the direction of the boulder behind which Elizabeth was hiding. She shrank behind the rock. Fortunately, they stopped in front of it and did not think to look behind it.

In a whisper, Mr. Darcy murmured,

"Have you any questions concerning your instructions?"

"No, sir. They are simple enough. I am to drive Mr. George Wickham to London, pull the carriage up to the docks, and see him aboard the ship. Between myself and the two footmen, there should be no trouble."

"The Captain should recognize you straightaway, having seen you with me on several past occasions, but in case he should have any qualms, give him this." He withdrew a letter from his coat. "It contains everything he needs to know. However, I would appreciate it if you would emphasize to him to *not* give Wickham any indication about who the proprietor of his ship is. If he knew that I owned the vessel which was transporting him to America, I would not put it past that man to upset a candle upon the wooden decks in order to burn it into the ocean."

"Duly noted, sir."

"Also, once you return from your mission, do not attempt to bring the carriage into Hertfordshire with you lest it be seen and recognized. Leave it at my townhouse in London and come back by post yourselves, wearing inconspicuous outfits and under no circumstances your livery. Bring along a trunk of food. Slip up to Netherfield House by night and knock five times upon the front door. We shall be watching for you."

"Very good, sir."

"That is all. Godspeed."

"Thank you, Mr. Darcy."

The gentleman and servant turned and went back to the others. Colonel Fitzwilliam was finished securing the blackguard, and the time had come to bid him farewell.

"So long, Wickham," the military man hissed behind the prisoner's ear. "If your pathetic existence means anything to you, stay in America. Should the news that you are in England again ever reach me, I *will* find you, and Darcy or no Darcy, my prize for the hunt shall be your life." Then he unceremoniously shoved the shackled man at the servants.

Mr. Bingley, whose acquaintance with Mr. Wickham was extremely limited and based on a few interactions the preceding autumn, merely touched the brim of his hat and bowed slightly to take his leave.

The last gentleman took his cue on how to act from neither his cousin nor his friend. Instead, he came forward, and stood about three feet away from Mr. Wickham and the footmen who were holding fast unto him. For a long moment, he looked at his childhood companion with something like pity. At length, he spoke.

"Wickham, harken to good advice," Mr. Darcy said in a low, firm, but not unkind tone. "In the Americas you will be a stranger, unknown to all. Start afresh. Cast off the sinful tendencies which have clung to you since you were fifteen, and find that old, well-mannered George who used to fish with me at Pemberley. Get an honest job, do good work, and act respectably. It is much more satisfying to gain a fortune by one's own merit than by lies and schemes." Seeing that Mr. Wickham was bent on remaining silent and glaring resentfully, the gentleman concluded, "You will have several weeks at sea to decide how to act; think upon it." With this farewell, he went away towards the others once more. A slight, aristocratic gesture of his hand ordered the footmen to take charge of the prisoner and guide him into the carriage. They obeyed, and Wickham was soon secured inside with the servants. The coachman respectfully nodded to Mr. Darcy, ascended to his customary seat, and taking up the reins, briskly commenced removing the cad from Hertfordshire.

Mr. Darcy watched the carriage disappear with relief. Suddenly, he was interrupted by a gentle touch on his shoulder.

"Are we forgetting something, cousin?" the Colonel asked.

"If you refer to Mrs. Younge, then I certainly remember."

"Then let us get on with it. Are you certain that she should not have been sent away with Wickham?"

"As I said, it would have been awkward for my men to manage a woman's imprisonment; it would make for a spectacle as they boarded the ship. Besides, Mrs. Younge is only loyal to

Wickham if her own interests are met. When she was trying to save her position at Ramsgate, she willingly poured out all his secrets and unleashed the full force of her tongue upon his name. I highly doubt that she will try to avenge him when she is informed that all hope of her profiting from Georgiana's marriage is over, especially if we make it clear that we will be at the dear girl's side from now on."

"Very well, cousin. Forward, then?"

"Forward."

The trio of victors began to walk to Meryton, on foot. Their horses had left with the carriage, and the short span of time between leaving Elizabeth at Longbourn and meeting Wickham on the road had made it impossible to procure any extra mounts. Elizabeth saw them go with empathy; while slipping into Meryton would doubtlessly be easier on foot than on horseback, they would have to walk a half-mile there, and then march four miles to Netherfield, all preferably before dawn. She dearly wished that it were in her power to make the journey easier for them, but as it was not, she too turned, in the opposite direction, and left the meadow. Going back through the field of corn, she regained Longbourn and her own bedchamber, where she lay down next to Miss Edwards and succumbed to sleep.

Chapter 51

"Lizzy? Lizzy? Wake up!"

The slumbering brunette found herself being gently shaken awake. Opening her eyes, she found Anne standing over herself, wearing the broadest of smiles.

"Forgive me for waking you, my darling friend, but it is my wedding day! And the sun is shining! O, how I feared that it might rain!"

Elizabeth dragged her exhausted form up. Daylight was indeed streaming into the room, and the window had been opened, allowing a cheerful breeze into the room. Gusts of air playfully toyed with the wedding dress and veil which hung on the closet door, waiting to be donned.

Obviously, the news had not arrived yet. Anne flitted through the room in her nightgown, dancing and prancing, still under the delusion that in a few hours she would be Mrs. George Wickham. Seeing that she was beginning to eye the wedding dress and would soon begin putting it on, Elizabeth desperately thought of ways to forestall her. The last thing she wanted was for Anne to be peacocking in front of the mirror in her bridal white and imagining Mr. Wickham's eyes as he beheld her walking towards the altar when the letter arrived.

Seeing that a tray filled with delicacies had appeared in their room and was stationed on the dressing table, the older girl commented,

"I see that Mrs. Lane has sent up a few tidbits. Have you eaten? You should."

"Eat? Oh, Lizzy, I would like to oblige you, and it looks delicious, but I have so many nervous fluttering in my stomach, I doubt that I can!"

Elizabeth would have none of it. Coming up behind Anne, she resolutely put her hands on the bride's shoulders and steered her to the dressing table, then gently pushed her into the chair stationed before it. It was critical, Miss Bennet knew, that the poor child have nourishment before the letter was delivered, for it was all too possible that her appetite would be nonexistent for several days after the unhappy event. Besides, breakfast would delay Anne's toilette by a few minutes at least.

"Come now, we must have no fainting today! Onrushes of emotion and fasting are a very poor combination, and it appears you are to experience both in a matter of hours. I refuse to help you dress until you have eaten a sensible meal."

Anne laughed.

"Very well, Lizzy, I promise to do my best. Oh, how I shall miss you, my cherished friend...and if I may say so...my sister! George and I will visit Longbourn as frequently as his duties allow, for I cannot dream of being separated from you and your tender, motherly ways for long!"

Seeing an opening to soften the approaching blow, Elizabeth took the opportunity to remark,

"That is the consequence, you see, of being married. You must leave behind many of those dear to you, and hope that your husband's society will adequately compensate for theirs."

"Nothing will ever replace you and Longbourn, Lizzy," Anne replied warmly. "But I believe that I will be very happy with George. Everyone seems to think so, after all." This answer only caused Elizabeth's heart to ache all the more. She stood by quietly as her friend gaily picked up a biscuit and proceeded to take hasty bites.

There was a knock at the door. Immediately, Elizabeth knew who, or rather *what*, it was. Her mouth instantly became a parched desert, making the utterance of a single word impossible. She quickly retreated to the opposite side of the room and began smoothening the folds of the wedding gown, positioning herself during the task so as to hide her anxious face. It was Anne who called out,

"Enter."

The door opened and Mrs. Hill made her appearance. As Elizabeth had suspected, she held a letter in her hand. The faithful servant acknowledged Miss Bennet with a slight curtsy, and then approached Anne.

"Miss Edwards, this has just come for you." She held out the letter, which Anne took, and commandeered her attention away from the missive for one last moment by remarking, "In case I shall not have an opportunity to speak with you again today, madam, I just wanted to say that all of Longbourn's staff will sincerely miss you."

The young woman smiled, thanked Mrs. Hill, and waited until the housekeeper had retreated and closed the door before she turned her attention back to the letter. Elizabeth soon heard a slight gasp, and an exclamation of,

"Why, it is from George!"

Miss Bennet swallowed the lump in her throat and replied, "Indeed?"

"At the very least, it is addressed by his hand," Anne murmured, hurriedly opening the envelope. "I suppose he wishes to bestow one last tender act of courtship on me before we are man and wife…" Her voice trailed off as her eyes commenced scanning the paper.

The ensuing minute was sheer torture to Elizabeth. Her hands convulsively clutched the sleeves of the white gown and her heart throbbed. It was necessary to feign ignorance, even though every fiber of her being wished to be at Anne's side and clasp the girl in a compassionate embrace as she read the dreadful news. From the corner of her eye, Miss Bennet watched the scene at the dressing table, waiting for the heartbreaking scene which was sure to come.

Indeed, the air in the bright, sunny bedchamber was abruptly pierced by a quivering cry.

Elizabeth turned away from the closet just in time to witness Anne putting her hand over her mouth and falling back in the chair. Without delay, she flew across the room and gathered the darling in her arms.

"What is the matter?" she cried, as if she knew not.

Miss Edwards was incapable of coherent speech; she held out the fateful epistle, gasping a disjointed rejoinder of,

"Left…ruthless…trifled…never returning…George!"

Her friend took the proffered object and skimmed it. As expected, it was a faithful transcript of the words which Mr. Darcy had spoken the previous night.

"Oh, Anne," she moaned sympathetically, tightening her hold on the girl who felt that the world had caved in upon itself, and commenced rocking her back and forth, trying to assuage whatever she could.

Many, many long hours and unanswerable questions later, Anne half-lay, half-sat upon the bedchamber's window seat, still supported by Elizabeth's sisterly arms. Jane, who had also done her share of condoling that day, stepped out for a moment to procure some tea for the heartsick bride-which-would-have-been. In this moment of stillness and quiet, yet another distressing thought seemed to occur to Anne, and for the first time that day, she absentmindedly began to indulge in her contemplative habit. After fifteen seconds, however, she stopped with a jolt, realizing that she was twisting the engagement ring around and around her finger.

Sitting up, she stared at the piece of jewelry, and eventually deciding that it no longer had a place there, tugged at the band and separated it from her finger. Dropping the ring upon the window seat, she ran her thumb over the small piece of skin where it once had been. The sun had gently tanned every other part of her hand, leaving a pale, extremely noticeable circlet around her finger.

Elizabeth had a moment of inspiration. She reached into her pocket and brought out the sapphire ring which Mr. Darcy had returned to her custody the night before. Picking up Anne's bare little hand, she was attempting to reunite the ornament with its former owner when Miss Edwards shook her head and gently repossessed her extremity. She began saying something about the ring being Elizabeth's now, when she was silenced by a gentle finger pressing against her lips. Her hand was taken yet again and adorned with silver and sapphire. Mr. Darcy's claim upon his sister had been restored.

Chapter 52

Elizabeth shifted the heavy basket to her left arm in order to give her tired right one a rest. She had naively expected the three-mile walk to be an enjoyable one, especially since she had not had a breath of fresh air for four days together. Unfortunately, her calculations had neglected to add the burdensome weight in her arms, the dusty back roads, and the continuous recollections of Anne's sad face which haunted her even amidst the lovely woods and meadows.

But if the trip was difficult, she had nobody to blame but herself. No one had asked her to make it, nor to tote half of Longbourn's kitchen in a basket.

Noticing a stile directly ahead, Elizabeth walked up to it, carefully lowered the basket down on the grass on the other side of it, and then gingerly climbed across herself. Sometime during this process the moss growing on the wooden beams succeeded in applying its green coloring onto a small portion of her white skirt. Noticing its impertinence, Miss Bennet groaned and vainly attempted to rub the smear away. Her agitation about the minor imperfection was so severe that, for a moment, she actually considered turning back and completing the journey another day in a clean gown.

Taking up the package anew, she noted the apparent unreasonableness of her thoughts. Less than a year ago she had made the same walk, to see some of the same people, and had jumped over the same stile into what had then been boggy ground. Her petticoats had coated themselves six inches deep in mud, but she had not cared a whit. From where, then, came so fierce a desire to look pristine that a slight discoloration upon her hem made her feel terribly self-conscious?

After another fifteen minutes of brisk ambulation, the large mansion of Netherfield Park came into view. Glancing around, as she had done throughout the morning to ascertain that there was no stray farmer or other observer in sight, Elizabeth Bennet hastened down the hill towards the house. As she crossed the lawn, she admired the multitude of closed shutters and dormant chimneys; the gentlemen were doing a fine job of concealing their presence. She boldly climbed the steps leading up to the front door, rang the bell, and then positioned herself on the landing so that her person would be easily visible and identifiable to anyone surreptitiously peering out of the windows.

Fingering the wicker handle of her basket, she waited. She was prepared for a long delay, which was sure to take place as the servant who heard the ring would have to find his masters and ask what ought to be done about the young lady who was present on the steps. Elizabeth was stunned, therefore, when the front doors were precipitously flung open, and Mr. Darcy appeared in the threshold.

Before she could recover herself enough to speak, he exclaimed,

"Good day, Miss Bennet. It is a delight to see you. Bingley has allowed me to assure you of your welcome."

"Thank you, sir," Elizabeth replied, cheeks flushed and eyes brightened by exercise. "I hope that my ring did not alarm you?"

"It had no chance to unsettle us, for I caught sight of you as you entered the gate, and immediately informed Richard and Charles that we had company. Pray, come in."

The lady hesitated. She had not planned on actually entering the house. She had expected to give the basket and a short message to Fredrick or to one of the footmen at the door before leaving as quickly as she had come. However, she could not in good conscience give Mr. Darcy himself a condensed report, and if they were to take a turn out-of-doors together, they chanced being seen by an unwelcome passerby. Besides, what harm could a short visit occasion? Therefore, she darkened the threshold.

Darcy reached for the large basket.

"Please, let me relieve you -," he broke off as his hand was dragged downwards. "Gracious, Miss Bennet, did you carry this by yourself all the way?" he cried.

Elizabeth laughed prettily into his horrified face.

"Yes, I did, and by the by, you may keep all of its hefty contents." She watched as the surprised gentleman raised the basket, lifted the white napkin on top, and peered into the interior. Before he could reply, she explained, "In there are a few of the breads, meats and cakes which were prepared for the wedding breakfast. There is so much food in Longbourn nowadays that these items shall never be missed, and I thought that you might make use of them here, especially since I figured that you would be reluctant to have your servants going into the village shops where they might be recognized."

Mr. Darcy replaced the napkin and transferred the weight to his left arm so that he could offer his right one to Elizabeth. She immediately took it.

"As usual, you surmised our present situation accurately, Miss Bennet. We have avoided ordering provisions from Meryton thus far, making good use of the few fruit trees and other crops that can be scavenged from the kitchen garden. My footmen, bless them, are talented enough to make an edible stew in the evening, when there is the least chance that the smoke from the chimneys will be observed, but they have not even dared try their hand at baking. Your goodness will be very much appreciated, Miss Bennet, even though you should not have strained yourself by lugging this burden for three miles. Thank you."

"You are welcome, sir," Elizabeth said, as they made their way down a hall she remembered tolerably well. In a more confidential tone, she added, "And please forgive me for intruding upon you so. I know that I ought not to be here, for several reasons, but I could not rest easily knowing that you were but three miles away and completely ignorant of what was transpiring with your sister. When Anne began to express her guilt for keeping me indoors so long, I seized the opportunity to ease both your minds."

"And I thank you for it. I would ask you to begin speaking on that score right now, but I do believe that Richard would never forgive me if he were not fully included. He has almost worn through the dining room carpet with his pacing. Bingley and he are in there now."

"That is fully understandable," Elizabeth acknowledged. Lowering her voice further, she continued, "While we are alone and unable to speak of your sister, I will use the time to thank *you*, in turn, for the lovely ruby pin which you gifted me. How surprised was I! While it was not necessary, sir, I must admit that I was delighted by it."

An elated expression filled Mr. Darcy's face, and in the tone of a self-satisfied schoolboy who wishes to know all the aftermath of a successful prank, he inquired eagerly,

"Might I ask when you discovered it?"

"Lydia found it for me, a few minutes after I entered the drawing room."

The gentleman's smile instantly vanished.

"Was it mentioned in front of the others?" he asked nervously.

Elizabeth glanced at him, attempting to decipher what, precisely, he feared about that particular scenario. She answered slowly,

"Yes, it was. For a moment, I confess, I was taken a bit aback and almost let the truth slip."

"Gracious, Miss Bennet!" Darcy exclaimed, ashamed and horrified. "Please believe me: I never dreamed that my little mischievous trick could place you in any danger! After you informed me that your family had thought Georgiana's ring cut glass, I assumed that they would mistake rubies for the same and not even bother remarking on your new adornment. Indeed, when you failed to notice its presence in your locks for the duration of the afternoon and evening, I thought that you would not find it until you were retiring for the night. Knowing Wickham and Mrs. Younge to lack knowledge of fine jewels, I had no apprehension on that score, either. I never suspected that you would be pressed to answer for its appearance!"

The lady pressed the arm entwined with hers reassuringly.

"Trouble yourself not, Mr. Darcy. My reputation is intact, and Anne is safe from the plotting of that malicious man for good, I believe."

With one last apologetic look, the gentleman allowed the conversation to be thus redirected, replying,

"I certainly hope so. That was our design in shipping him off to America."

"Were you successful in that regard?"

"Yes, very. After we had him write the letter which Georgiana received, we sent him to the docks via my carriage. The footmen came back with the report that he had been put on a ship which sailed out of port without incident."

"And Mrs. Younge? How did you dispatch her? I heard something about her leaving in the dead of the night without even collecting her belongings, but was unable to piece together anything more from the shreds of gossip which reached me."

"I allowed Richard the lead on that. He put on a worn coat and threw a scarf over his face in order to disguise himself. Looking every inch a windblown messenger, he rushed into the Meryton Inn and announced to the innkeeper that he had an express for Mrs. Younge, and thus gained entry to her apartment. Once they were alone, he removed the covering from his face, causing Mrs. Younge to blanch as white as snow. He informed her that all hope of Wickham marrying

Georgiana was over. He also strongly hinted that if she remained in Hertfordshire any longer, the London authorities would take an interest in investigating the ongoings in her new boarding house. According to Richard, she did not even ask to pack a trunk. She simply reached for her coat and followed him out, pausing only to give the innkeeper the address to which her belongings were to be forwarded. The midnight post-carriage to London was just leaving, and we saw her on it."

"I am glad that it came off so well. How easy it is to exercise control over one whose actions are corrupt! Who would want such a life?"

"They are first lured by the illusion that crime and deceit will lead to prestige and riches more easily than honesty. But as you said, sooner or later it becomes a terrible slavery."

They reached the dining room. Mr. Bingley and the Colonel sprang to their feet at the sight of Miss Bennet, and bowing, offered their welcome. The lady greeted both warmly, asked how they were faring, and took the seat which Mr. Darcy pulled out for her. Once she was comfortably settled, Elizabeth said,

"I am afraid that I do not have long before I must return home. Let me tell you something of Anne, as I am sure you are eager to hear it."

"Indeed we are!" the Colonel exclaimed.

With three interested, apprehensive faces turned towards her, Miss Bennet fixed her own eyes upon Mr. Darcy and undertook illustrating an accurate picture of Anne's recent mannerisms and feelings.

"The morning of the wedding was the worst, as expected. She was very confused upon receiving the letter, and came as close to irrationality as I have ever seen her. The poor thing wanted to personally run to Meryton to see if Mr. Wickham had indeed left the county, and it was only with great difficulty that we managed to persuade her to have Mr. Hill go instead. When he returned, bearing the news that Mrs. Younge had disappeared along with the missing bridegroom, the reality and finality of the situation settled upon her. She burst into tears. But these were dry relatively soon, and, while understandably heartbroken, she began to exert herself. Anne assured me that she was well and actually apologized about the waste that would ensue because of the cancelled wedding, even though no one had even thought to offer any reproaches on that score. Since then, she has talked very little, and prefers to keep to our room. She always joins the rest of us for meals and pretends to peck at whatever is set before her, but I am certain that she only ventures downstairs in order to not inconvenience anyone. All this, however, I expected. There is but one eccentricity which gives me great concern - she cannot bear the sight of sunlight. When she comes down to eat, she chooses the darkest seat at the table and turns her face from the windows. In our bedchamber, the curtains are drawn day and night. It worries me, for the light never troubled her before, and she insists that these newfound preferences are not due to headaches."

Mr. Darcy ran his fingers through his dark locks, and sighed.

"It pains me to hear of her avoidance, but I believe that I can safely assure you that for Georgiana, it is not extraordinary. It was the same after Ramsgate. She remained in her room with the curtains perpetually drawn for a week, and would scarcely permit enough candlelight to see by. At last, after untold hours of wondering whether it would do her good or be cruel, I picked her up in my arms and carried her out to Pemberley's sunny courtyard."

"Which did it turn out to be?" Mr. Bingley inquired curiously.

"The former. She blinked a few times, adjusting her eyes to the brightness, and then commenced pouring violent grief out upon my shoulder. Either my decisive action or the relieving tears cured her of the strange affection." Mr. Darcy's thoughts appeared to trail off, and he stared past Elizabeth at the very light which they were discussing. In the absentminded tone of a person who has forgotten themselves and their present company, he murmured, "I did not understand then, however, why illumination was so dreadful to her. Surely it could not trigger more memories of the blackguard than the sight of flowers, or any number of objects? But now, I comprehend. For one crossed in love, sunlight, with its brilliance, its *life*, contrasts harshly with the darkness and despair within. The jar is too great. Unable to reconcile the two, there is but one feasible solution: to shut out the light." His voice faltered.

The Colonel and Mr. Bingley looked at each other, trying to fathom the source of Darcy's newfound knowledge and emotion. Elizabeth, for her part, desperately wished to take his hand and press it. *She* knew why he had learned. Any remaining question of her own culpability was answered. She had played a great role in causing his extreme melancholy.

Her visit ended shortly after the aforementioned question and answer. Miss Bennet thought about jesting that they had no gentleman or manservant strong enough to carry her friend out to Longbourn's garden, but the humorous remark died at the bottom of her throat in view of Mr. Darcy's sad face. She was only able to offer a few further facts about Anne's current condition, and was profoundly relieved when the conversation turned to when the gentlemen could visit Longbourn.

They settled upon an approximate date, and Elizabeth said, a little unwillingly, that it was time for her to be going. Mr. Darcy, reanimated by the previous conversation, saw to it that the emptied wicker basket was returned to her, and accompanied her to the door alone.

Pausing in the entryway, he turned towards the lady and said, "Thank you again for your visit, Miss Bennet. While it is difficult to hear how Georgiana is suffering, it is a consolation to know how things truly stand rather than having to rely upon our imaginations, which usually paint a picture far more grotesque than the reality."

"There is no need to thank me. I am glad to be of service, especially after feeling helpless for much of this time."

"There is one more thing which I have forgotten to mention," the gentleman said. "Miss Bennet, would you please advise me on how I can gain an audience with your father in the coming days? I wish to inform him that it is my sister's life whom he saved with his generosity, and to assure him that he will be amply recompensed for his trouble. Of course, I will not mention your journey into Derbyshire unless you expressly give me permission to do so."

This request was vexing to Elizabeth for more reasons than one. In her answer, thus, she sought to put an end to every entreaty of the kind.

"With all due respect, sir, I am certain that such a proposal will be unacceptable and even offensive to my father. He regards Anne as his own daughter. The idea of being paid for hospitality and affection would be highly repugnant to any gentleman of honor."

"Quite so, Miss Bennet," Mr. Darcy agreed, but nonetheless firmly continued, "I never dreamt of compensating your father for love, no matter how grateful I am to him for bestowing it upon my sister in such abundance. However, Georgiana is, and for many years will be, in need of things more tangible than tenderness. She needs clothes and board, which must be paid for somehow. Your family has expenses of its own, and ought not to be burdened with the costs associated with my sister, particularly as I am perfectly able and willing to cover her debts." Seeing Elizabeth's abiding skepticism, he almost pleaded, "You must excuse this bit of manly pride, Miss Bennet, and allow me to provide for the young woman with whose guardianship I am entrusted."

"I have long been inclined to forgive you all your pride, sir," Elizabeth replied, and was slightly shocked to see that he paled from emotion. Feeling unequal to continuing this topic, she hastened to add, "But I must continue to insist that you desist from explaining the case to my father for a few weeks at least."

"Why?"

Elizabeth flushed. How she hated telling him anything which revealed the poor state of her family's life! However, the confession was necessary for Anne's good.

"I fear that if my father learns who Anne is, he will be unable to continue fancying himself her parent out of respect for her true family. And Anne needs him now more than ever before. He is the one who solaces her best nowadays, sir. You see…he knows what it is like…to fall in love with someone only to find yourself deceived."

By sheer force of will she kept her eyes locked with his as she said this, resisting the temptation to look at the polished floor all the while. No condemnation appeared in Mr. Darcy's countenance, however, only understanding. He nodded and surrendered.

"It shall be as you counsel, Miss Bennet."

"Thank you, sir."

She sank into a curtsy, he bent into a deep bow. Reaching for the handle, he opened the door and released her back into the fragrant breezes of the day. Looking to the right and left, for any unwelcome observers, she ran away from Netherfield, only looking back at the ajar doorway thrice. Hurrying back the entire way, she was able to take her place at Longbourn's dinner table promptly at five o'clock, amid loved ones who were completely ignorant of her calling schedule that day.

Chapter 53

"Does our poor Anne keep her state above stairs this morning?"

"Yes, Mama," Elizabeth replied softly, glancing up at her teary, pouting mother. "As you well know, she has yet to come down for anything besides meals and visits to Papa's library."

"The heartbroken child! How is she faring?"

"I believe that she may be a bit better. She has been occasionally going to the window, parting the curtains for a brief moment and glancing out, but I fear that it is never for long."

"My dear, dear girl," Mrs. Bennet murmured, bringing the handkerchief she clutched up to her eye and patting it against her face dramatically. "My poor little Anne! I think you are wrong, Lizzy, in saying that she will get over this. She shall die of a broken heart, I am certain! And when Mr. Wickham hears of it, *if* the scoundrel ever hears of it, *then* he shall be sorry for what he has done. It is the only comfort to be had in a case such as this!"

"Certainly, Mama, it is exceedingly consoling to imagine the naughty Mr. Wickham hearing such a report," Elizabeth returned sarcastically. "And what a small price the remainder of us shall pay in order to extract that possible twinge of regret from him!"

Missing the point of her daughter's reply, as usual, the older woman heaved a sigh and turned towards the door with the order,

"Do tell Hill to bring Anne some tea and cake, Lizzy. It is several hours until dinner and she must keep up her strength! I am determined to do all I can to care for her properly, even if it will all likely come to nothing. If anything happens, it will clearly be that jilter's fault, and not mine!"

Taking advantage of her mother's turned back, Elizabeth moved her lips vigorously, silently petitioning Heaven to grant her a small drop of the patience with which Jane and Anne's natures were amply infused. The prayer was heard, and instead of saying something which would have sparked Mrs. Bennet's ire and a daylong strife, the chagrined daughter was given the grace to say,

"I am sure that Anne will appreciate your kindness, madam."

The Mistress of Longbourn nodded in agreement, and took care to inform her daughter of her plans for the day.

"I am going into Meryton to see my sister Philips, for I simply cannot bear to sit at home and watch dear Anne's distress! It tears my heart to pieces. And I must look into the shops and see if anything new has come in since yesterday - Kitty might have need of some new clothes soon, I daresay!"

Elizabeth wished her mother a pleasant trip, and Mrs. Bennet betook herself to Meryton in the highest of spirits. Her second-eldest daughter was left to the stillness of the drawing room. She began untangling a messy ball of leftover threads, hoping that there would be a few which she could salvage and begin a new piece of work with. The project required much more finesse of the fingers than of the mind, thus allowing her thoughts to dwell upon the blessings which had sprung from the overthrowing of Mr. Wickham's schemes. One of the most unexpected ones was Mrs. Bennet's full and fervent acceptance of Anne as a sixth daughter. Anything which had remained unconquered in her mother's heart after Miss Edwards' demonstration of concern for the poor lady's nerves had fallen as soon as Mrs. Bennet was certain that the wedding had been called off. Anne was still unmarried; she had not outdone any girl of Bennet blood. The influx of would-be guests into Meryton, however, was well-received by the Mistress of Longbourn, particularly when one of their number, Captain Carter, commenced dropping hints that the ladies of Brighton could not compare with Catherine Bennet. The wonderful officer seemed on the point of asking for a courtship, and in Mrs. Bennet's mind, her second-youngest was as good as married. Equally important, the scandal surrounding Anne's almost-nuptials had greatly elevated Elizabeth's mother in the eyes of every Meryton gossip. The busybodies vied with each other in inviting her to tea, to hear a firsthand account of the events at Longbourn that sorrowful day. Taken together, these benefits had induced Mrs. Bennet to feel and express sentiments identical to the ones which she had articulated after Jane's unsuccessful love affair.

Tugging at a stubborn blue thread, Miss Bennet smiled to herself at the thought of Jane. Although her sister did not know it, Anne's disappointment could very well be her good fortune. It had brought Mr. Bingley back to Netherfield, after all! The young man would certainly call with his friends, he would see Jane again, and even a languid imagination could easily envision a very happy ending to the months of sorrow and suspense.

But it was the thought of Mr. Bingley's friend which was, once again, beginning to confound Elizabeth's feelings and vexing her. During their travels together, Elizabeth had realized that she was grateful for their renewed acquaintance. She had been glad for the chance to make amends for her abominable behavior towards him. Likewise, she was happy to have been the means by which some hope was restored to his world. Those emotions were simple and rational enough. However, they had been joined by some complex and impenetrable ones shortly after her covert visit to Netherfield. Without any logical cause, the face of Mr. Darcy would often insert itself into her consciousness. Elizabeth had ceased counting the number of times she had recalled him standing on the balcony at Menston Hall or reaching out his hand to help her alight from the carriage. These episodes usually caused her lips to stretch themselves into a broad, unplanned smile which was resistant to obliteration, leading Miss Bennet to spend great amounts of concentration and energy on reasoning with herself and slowly forcing the corners of her capricious mouth down.

Even more disturbingly, the man had begun to invade her dreams as well. Just the previous evening, her sleeping mind had been transported back to Pemberley. In the nighttime vision, the magnificent house had been bathed in sunlight, and she had been taking a most pleasant stroll in the gardens surrounding it. The meandering brought her to a rose garden, full of red and pink and yellow and white and orange blooms. She longed to reach out and pick a few, but did not dare to take such a liberty, so she stood in the midst of the fragrant flowers, trying to content herself with merely looking at them. While she was thus employed, she heard the soft sound of boots brushing against grass behind her, and turning, saw Mr. Darcy walking towards her with a gentle smile on his face. He reached out and plucked one of the red roses from its bush, and coming to a stop six inches from her, he slipped it into her hair, securing it in place with the gold and ruby clip.

She had then awoken, and for some reason, felt quite disappointed at the brevity of the night.

While she was still thinking about the dream, footsteps sounded in the hall; someone was approaching. Elizabeth took a deep breath to erase the blush which had appeared upon her cheeks, and prepared to face the newcomer.

To her absolute astonishment, it was Miss Edwards who entered. Giving the seated girl a gentle nod, the younger woman said,

"Good morning, do you mind if I join you?"

"Of course not!" As an extra welcome, Elizabeth jumped up from the couch and went to the windows, with the purpose of drawing some of the drapes. To have Anne in the drawing room was a great improvement, and despite what Mr. Darcy had told her about its beneficial impact, she was not ready to risk overwhelming the heartbroken soul with sunlight and tempting her back to the darker areas of the house.

"No, Lizzy, leave them be." Meeting Elizabeth's stunned countenance, she softly added, "If you were going to close them on my account, pray do not. I mean to start a new piece today, and needlework is best done in ample lighting."

Miss Bennet curiously studied Anne's face, and then obediently turned back and sat down. She cautiously remarked,

"You seem better this morning, if you do not mind my saying so."

The other girl nodded.

"I believe that I am. This…affair…has given me much to think of, but I have finished mulling over the vast majority of it. While I do not expect to be in perfect spirits anytime soon, I am resigned, having come to the conclusion that what happened was for the best. And so, this morning, the sunlight outside Longbourn reminds me that time moves forward and gives me hope in a happier future."

Their conversation was halted by Lydia's abrupt intrusion. As soon as her sister opened the door and stepped across the threshold, Elizabeth checked her reply and continued untangling in silence, for it was common knowledge in the Bennet household that anything discussed in front of its youngest member had the potential to be known on the streets of Meryton by the following day.

Lydia bounded into the room, her sewing basket and a bonnet in hand. Throwing everything down on the table, she grumbled something about the maids' inability to clear the tea service in a timely manner, furtively looking at the others in the room all the while and hoping that the annoying complaints would inveigle them to clean the area for her. When the wise girls showed no signs of taking the bait and moving from their present positions, however, the youngest Miss Bennet condescended to put the empty plates, cups, and saucers back onto the tea tray herself, albeit producing much more clattering than would normally be expected from that operation. Once the table was hospitable to a great number of sewing supplies, she emptied her basket and reached for the scissors.

"Lydia, what are you doing?"

Elizabeth glanced up, and found that Anne had lowered her own work and was watching her sister's distrustfully.

Lydia held up the bonnet.

"I am going to pull this to pieces and make it up afresh. I have been wearing the same headdress to church these last three months together and I am dreadfully bored of it. I yawn every time I put it on."

"But, Lydia, that is Jane's favorite bonnet," Miss Edwards said, laying a slight stress on the word 'Jane's'. "Did you ask her if you could have it?"

Unabashed, Lydia lightly answered,

"Why should I bother to ask? I know she has another, and I do not."

"Her other one is far too worn for church, and anyhow, it does not match her Sunday dress at all. Perhaps you could ask her for the old one and do something with it."

"The other would make me look like a mushroom! I like this one, and once I trim it properly it will be just right for me."

The order 'give Jane back her bonnet, Lydia' was already rising to Elizabeth's lips when Miss Edwards suddenly laid aside her embroidery, rose, and walked to the table with measured, deliberate steps. Gently she took the bonnet from the thief's hand and firmly said,

"I am sorry, but I cannot allow you to use this bonnet unless you receive Jane's permission first. I am sure that Jane has need of it. Alter yours or save up your pocket money to buy yourself a new one if you simply cannot stand to wear it any longer."

The redheaded maiden stared up at her counterpart in shock. *This* was one obstacle which she had not considered. For the first time in many months, Miss Lydia Bennet blushed. But she was so used to having her own way that it was impossible for her to surrender easily. Thus, regrouping, she replied slyly,

"I should love to trim my own, Anne, but I cannot change its form, which is the dullest part of it! And anyhow, if Jane were to deny me the bonnet she would be very selfish, for I will look better in this one than she ever could."

Miss Edwards proved inflexible.

"Who would look better in it is immaterial considering the fact that Jane would look positively ridiculous going to church bareheaded. I am afraid that you both must look a little unfashionable in order to both look respectable. No, Lydia, say no more. I shall not change my mind."

After this determined statement, Anne walked away from the pouting girl, and went back to her former seat. Placing the disputed bonnet securely at her side, where Lydia would have to lurch across her to get it, she picked up the embroidery hoop anew and reapplied herself to the delicate work.

Lydia comprehended that she had been overruled. Having never been gracious in defeat, however, she grunted fiercely, threw the scissors which she still held across the room, and stomped out into the hall, snarling over her shoulder as she went,

"You are becoming just as bad as my sisters, Anne! You are all envious of my superior beauty, and will stoop to anything to make me look shabby!"

Neither the taunt, nor the door slam which followed it, caused Miss Edwards to pause in her stitching or give any other indication of being unsettled. Only awareness of Elizabeth's shocked gaze induced her to look up.

"What is the matter, Lizzy?" the younger lady's calm voice asked.

Staring steadfastly at her companion, pointedly pronouncing every word of the serious communication, Elizabeth asked,

"Anne, do you realize what you just did?"

"What did I just do?" the addressed maiden returned, with the first, slight smile which had graced her face since the moment that the seal on Mr. Wickham's letter had been broken.

"You just confronted Lydia, withstood her manipulation, recouped a wrongly taken possession, and stood firm even in the face of violence and insults! Last month, you would have let the same girl eat the last piece of cake off of anyone's plate without a peep. This is an Anne I have never seen before."

Anne halted her needle, turned her pleased eyes onto the wall opposite her, and gave it a knowing smile.

"And yet, it is an Anne who was born at least six weeks ago, and simply wished for the courage to surface since then," she informed Miss Bennet, still gazing straight ahead as she made the confession, as if she were reflecting on some complicated matter and did not wish to be distracted from her thoughts by looking at a more changeable object. "You would be very surprised to know how often such speeches have come to my lips of late. But always, at the critical moment, my old timidity would reappear and push them down again."

"Might one inquire what finally conquered the shyness and strengthened the mettle?" a highly gratified Elizabeth asked.

Anne turned to her with an even broader and more heartfelt smile than the one the inanimate wall had received.

"One certainly might, especially if one happens to be a dear friend and adopted sister. But in all earnestness, I must give credit for my improvement to my near-brush with matrimony." She paused, and watched Elizabeth's expressive face take on a foreseen look. "I see that you are all astonishment, Lizzy, but attend to me, and I will explain my meaning to your satisfaction."

"Please do."

Becoming grave, Miss Edwards put the needlework down next to the rescued bonnet, clasped her hands upon her lap, regarded them, and proceeded to expound upon what had occurred in her head.

"I have always formed my own ideas on subjects, as you know, dearest Lizzy," she commenced softly. "But I never felt that I could rely on my own judgement. I was so young. I knew so little of the world. Surely the opinions of my elders and the more experienced were superior to mine! Thus I was unwilling to voice my sentiments, unless someone like Miss Elizabeth Bennet of Longbourn stubbornly drew me out, and I was ever ready to conform my judgments to those of my betters. Despite your efforts to make me act otherwise, I fancied that such humility served me well, and I suppose it did, until the evening that Mr. Wickham brought Mrs. Younge into the Philips's parlor." Looking up and locking her staunch gaze with Elizabeth's, Miss Edwards continued emphatically, "I *knew* from the moment he introduced me to her that something was not right. To this day, I cannot fix upon any phrase that they uttered or upon any unspoken communication between them which put me on my guard, but throughout that entire evening I felt a heavy aura of aversion settling about me. A similar, distasteful sensation was experienced when Mr. Wickham and I stood in the church, mimicking the actions which we were to have taken just a few days later. You laughed at me; Mr. Bennet attempted to talk me back into my senses, and although I yielded, I remained uneasy. And then, after I learned of Mr. Wickham's treachery - I realized that I, *I*, Anne Edwards, who never travelled outside the neighborhood, who only read a fraction of the books which you and your father have perused - had been correct all along! For the first time I truly believed your assertions that sometimes, just sometimes, Anne Edwards knows best. And if I know best, is it not my responsibility to speak and to act upon my convictions?"

"Of course it is!" was the enthusiastic answer. Elizabeth hurried to seat herself by Anne and engulf her in a strong embrace. When the two drew apart, the older girl smiled and looking directly into her protégé's eyes, wholeheartedly declared: "I am proud of you!"

Chapter 54

Everything came off remarkably well.

The neighborhood never knew that Mr. Bingley had any design of returning to Netherfield until the day, about a fortnight after the cancelled wedding, that his coach paraded through the main street of Meryton. Everyone gawked. Some of the more curious sent their servants to Netherfield directly to either make some ludicrous inquiry or to merely walk past the building as if by happenstance. These poor men and women returned with the news that Mr. Bingley and two other gentlemen, one of which seemed slightly familiar, had disembarked at the front door along with many mahogany chests, and seemed determined to stay awhile.

And then the moaning began at Longbourn. Mrs. Bennet shed tears, pleaded, and did everything in her power to convince her husband to call on the long-lost neighbor. However, the man stood firm.

"You forced me into visiting him last year, and promised, if I went to see him, he should marry one of my daughters. But it ended in nothing, and I will not be sent on a fool's errand again," was his curt response before he collected Anne and the chessboard and took both to his study, leaving his wife to continue her crying and hand - wringing.

Two and seventy hours passed in this manner. Finally, when Mrs. Bennet was quite exhausted, a marvelous sight caught her eye through the window: Mr. Bingley, seated upon a brown horse, riding into Longbourn's garden in the company of two other gentlemen.

The voice which had been all but lost was suddenly recovered, and every daughter and servant was hastily called to the drawing room to share in her joy.

When the reason for the summons became apparent, Jane turned very pale. She had spent the past three days promising Elizabeth and Anne by turns that Charles Bingley's return to the neighborhood did not trouble her in the least. But as she glimpsed his dear face through the window, her twisting heart privately informed her that for once in her life, she had been a liar.

Elizabeth, for her part, quickly reached up and began examining the state of her own brown coiffure. Halfway through patting the rebellious tresses into submission, she started. What was she doing? The tenant of Netherfield was coming to see Jane, and his friends would only have eyes for Anne. Instead of caring for her own appearance, she ought to be helping improve Miss Edwards'!

Dutifully, she took a look at the fair maiden. The golden locks were pinned up in a neat bun and needed no help; thankfully, the dress that Anne wore was one of the better hand-me-downs. She would have liked it if the girl had been wearing a nicer pair of house slippers, but it would look very peculiar to send her to exchange them for the sake of a mere morning visit. Elizabeth allowed herself one last stroke of her own tresses, therefore, before sitting down on the sofa.

"There are two gentlemen with him!" Kitty exclaimed as she hung out the window, watching. "Who can they be? One looks familiar – like that man who used to be with him before. Mr. What's-his-name. The tall, proud one!"

"Mr. Darcy! So it is! Well, on account of his being a friend of Bingley's I suppose that I shall not ask him to leave the premises. Other than that, I hate the very sight of him."

Anne caught these words, and Elizabeth saw her brow creasing with curiosity and confusion. Panicked that this unsavory comment would be the only introduction which Anne received to her long-lost brother's character, she hastily inclined her lips to the maiden's ear and fervidly whispered,

"Do yourself a service and completely disregard what Mama just said. Mr. Darcy is a very good man, who once expressed an opinion which was not well received. Indeed he has no improper pride. He is perfectly amiable. It is hard indeed, that a man has a slip of the tongue in what ought to be a private conversation, is overheard, and the entire neighborhood turns against him forever."

Pacified, Miss Edwards nodded, and Elizabeth withdrew. Two seconds passed, and the door of the drawing room opened, and Mrs. Hill came in. With a curtsy, she said,

"Mr. Bingley, Mr. Darcy, and Col -,"

Mrs. Bennet sprang up from her seat as if she were Lydia's age.

"Oh, sir, how good it is to see you!" she cried, interrupting Mrs. Hill. "We were afraid that you were never going to come back again! People *did* say you meant to quit the place entirely at Michaelmas. Pray assure us that it is not so! How forlorn the neighborhood seemed without you!"

The tenant of Netherfield managed to get enough words in edgewise to assure Mrs. Bennet that he had no fixed plans in that direction. She then spoke again, this time to direct him to a comfortable chair stationed only half-a-yard from Jane's. He took it with as little awkwardness as could be expected, and was straightaway engaged in further conversation by the Mistress of Longbourn.

In her impetuosity to secure Charles Bingley as a son-in-law and in her dislike of one of them, Mrs. Bennet had left his two friends by the door without even speaking a word to Mr. Darcy. More astonishingly, she also failed to seek an introduction to the gentleman who was unknown to her. At that moment, the prospects of her eldest were more important than finding a husband for her other single daughters. Here was a man who had eluded her grasp for over eight months; he would be ensnared now, if Fanny Bennet had anything to do with it! Others could wait. Jane tried to do her part, and sent the two gentlemen a welcoming nod and smile, but that was all that she could do before her mother required her to say something to Mr. Bingley. The Colonel, perhaps forewarned by his cousin, had had the good sense to forgo his regimentals for the visit and was dressed in more inconspicuous attire; together with Mrs. Hill's unconcluded introduction, the omission spared him, for the time being, Kitty and Lydia's attention.

Highly abashed, Elizabeth nonetheless rose, took Anne's hand, and endeavored to make what she could of the occasion. She led the girl to her brother and cousin.

"Mr. Darcy, Colonel Fitzwilliam," Miss Bennet said in a civil, friendly tone. "It is a pleasure to see both of you again. Welcome back to the neighborhood, Mr. Darcy."

"Thank you, Miss Bennet."

"May I present my friend, Miss Anne Edwards? Anne, this is Mr. Fitzwilliam Darcy and his cousin, Colonel Richard Fitzwilliam. They are friends of Mr. Bingley."

The gentlemen slowly bowed. Looking up, they fastened their eyes upon Anne, eagerly hoping that their presence would remind her of all the days they had spent together talking, riding, laughing! Elizabeth watched every twitch of Anne's countenance and form with comparable suspense.

Miss Edwards, however, did nothing close to extraordinary. She simply curtsied and murmured,

"Delighted to make your acquaintance, I am sure." The girl ventured no further remarks, looking to Elizabeth to continue the conversation. Three hearts sank.

In as natural a tone as she could manage, Elizabeth invited the gentlemen to be seated. Colonel Fitzwilliam meekly obeyed and took a chair, and Miss Bennet placed herself and Anne on a sofa stationed opposite him. There was another armchair available for Mr. Darcy, but that gentleman delayed his use of it. Saying that he had noted some recent alterations to Longbourn's garden as he and his friends had come indoors, he went to a nearby window as if he wished to study the placement of the anemones when, in reality, he needed a few minutes to recover from his disappointment.

Staring at the silent Colonel, Elizabeth felt all the awkwardness of the situation. Every idea failed her; there seemed to be an embargo on every subject. At last, she recollected that it was a very fine day outside, and made a slight comment on it. This managed to rouse the Colonel, and they talked of fresh air and cloudless blue skies with great perseverance. If Anne was surprised by the lack of substance in Elizabeth's conversation she gave no indication, but silently attended to the chatter without attempting to join in it.

Two persons distracted by their own thoughts cannot sustain a sensible discourse for a prolonged period of time, however; after a few minutes the dialogue trailed off and failed to resume. The still air was unfortunately very conductive to the sound of Mrs. Bennet's voice, and its shrill tones were quick to fill every crevice in the room.

"There have been some changes here since you went away, Mr. Bingley," the lady of the house was saying. "We acquired Miss Anne Edwards last May, and she has been staying with us ever since. You see her there, seated on the sofa beside Lizzy. Dear Anne was almost married to Mr. George Wickham, but what do you think? The reprobate jilted her the very morning of their wedding! Practically left her standing in front of the altar waiting for him. Everything indicates that he has left Hertfordshire for good, and I do not suppose there to be the slightest chance of him coming back for her now. I shall always say that he used my Anne very ill indeed!"

Anne's head bent quietly towards the rug as the Mistress of Longbourn continued to describe her feelings as to the dissolution of the betrothal. Elizabeth, mortified by the lack of tact which her mother was displaying, reached out and stroked the soft hand which rested upon the sofa beside her. The sensation caused Anne to look up and notice Elizabeth's discomfort.

"Dearest Lizzy, pray do not distress yourself," she whispered. "I know that Mrs. Bennet means well, and that this is her way of voicing compassion for my situation. Never having been crossed in love herself, she cannot know that it is painful to hear the affair retold."

Before Elizabeth could answer, Mr. Darcy strolled into their vicinity and seated himself in the armchair next to the Colonel's. Elizabeth suspected that he had tailored his return to serve as a distraction from the monologue which was still proceeding from Mrs. Bennet's lips. This impression was supported by his immediately remarking,

"That is a fine English foxhound of your father's, Miss Bennet."

Elizabeth followed his glance to where the puppy lay stretched out contently upon the rug, wagging his tail.

"I must agree that he is as lively a hound as I ever saw," Miss Bennet agreed, "but you are incorrect in presuming him to be my father's possession. Farley belongs to Anne."

Mr. Darcy raised his eyebrows, clearly taken aback by this piece of information. Looking at the golden-haired maiden, he asked,

"Does he?" He hoped that his inquiry and gaze might coax a small monosyllable from his timid sister, and thus grant him the privilege of once again hearing her sweet voice, if only for a fraction of a second.

Miss Edwards smiled proudly and replied,

"Yes, he does." At the sound of his mistress's voice, the puppy gathered his plump form up off the floor and bounded towards her feet, letting out a pleading whimper. Anne bent down, took the creature into her arms, and lifting him onto her lap, commenced scratching his ears energetically. Glancing at Mr. Darcy over the furry head, she continued, "Mr. Bennet saw me admiring and playing with Farley at Lucas Lodge during a party. When Lizzy and I returned to Longbourn that afternoon, I found that he had purchased him for me from Sir William. I own that I was never more happily surprised in my life. Mr. Bennet is so very good to me; I do not deserve such generosity."

Mr. Darcy fell slightly back in his chair, speechless. Elizabeth, noticing his amazement, straightened her own shoulders triumphantly.

He was undeniably stunned by his sister's maturity and easy conversation, and she could not help inwardly claiming some of the credit for Anne's blossoming.

Gathering himself, however, the young man soon answered,

"I am sure that you do, Miss Edwards. Although I cannot profess to know Mr. Bennet very intimately, he does not strike me as the sort of man who would bestow a favor unworthily."

"He is indeed considered a man of sense by myself and by all his acquaintances, sir. However, as by your own admission you know Mr. Bennet little and me even less, how can you possibly pass a fair judgment on whether I am deserving, or on whether he is excessively kind?"

Most observers would have said that Mr. Darcy remained perfectly stoic upon hearing these sentences. But Elizabeth noticed his eyelids flicker as if his heart had been surreptitiously pierced by a sharp object. Indeed, it was an excruciating moment for the man: to hear the sister, whom he had cradled in his arms when she was two hours old, whom he had indulged and played 'Tea Party' with by Pemberley's hearth when she was four years of age, whom he had comforted through the death of two parents and Wickham's first attempt at Ramsgate, declare lightheartedly that he knew next to nothing of her! Hiding his pain, he answered in an even voice,

"In that case, time will be the remedy. I am certain that as I come to know you better, Miss Edwards, I will not change my opinion; but I hope that you will become more willing to recognize its truth." When Anne only smiled dubiously in response, he turned the subject and remarked, "Returning to Farley, how do you find his temperament? By breeding, he was meant for a life quite different than the one I see he has. I always supposed that it would be nigh impossible to completely abolish the hunter in a foxhound."

Miss Edwards looked at the dog in her lap, and replied,

"As long as he is provided with ample time out-of-doors, I believe he is very content. I have never seen him chase a bird or a squirrel. He wishes to run free at times, that is true, but gives no other indication that he longs for the hunting grounds."

"He *does* have a bit of that streak left, Anne," Elizabeth interjected. "He simply prefers a different kind of prey." Looking over at the gentlemen, she laughingly informed them: "Farley is quite a helpful creature when it comes to locating lost objects. We have lost count of how many ribbons, handkerchiefs, and other accessories he has tracked down from behind sofas and other crevices in the house! Some have been lost since the time that we were children."

"Oh, dear me!" the Colonel burst out laughing. "You should have avoided telling us that, Miss Bennet! We shall soon be begging to borrow Farley every other day or so on Bingley's behalf! How many trifles *he* has lost in the last few months! See that watch-chain he wears? Since last autumn, it had a resting place behind a curtain in the front hall of Netherfield and was only rediscovered by myself yesterday when I went to look out the window. When I presented it back to him, he looked shocked and mildly commented that he had wondered where his father's watch-chain had gone!"

"And I suppose that you never misplaced anything yourself?" Elizabeth teased.

"Certainly not! In military life, you only leave behind that which can be a detriment to the enemy. Misplace and leave a musket at the site of your old camp; you have just given the enemy another weapon. Everything must be in perfect order and come with you when you march on."

"I had almost forgotten that you were a Colonel, sir," Miss Edwards said at this. "Where have you been stationed? Have you ever been abroad?"

"Alas, no, madam. I would welcome the adventure, but my father's position as an Earl has earned me a rather boring existence. I simply train regiments of soldiers within the boundaries of England."

"While a gentleman's and a lady's opinions might well differ on the topic, I would think that to be very agreeable. You have all the benefits of travelling and seeing the country, with very little peril involved," said the Anne who, in her own mind, had never left Hertfordshire. Traveling to different parts of the kingdom had been another dividend upon which she had counted back in the days when she planned on becoming Mrs. Wickham. "Pray, where have you been?"

The foursome spent the remainder of the visit on the subject. Colonel Fitzwilliam listed all the towns and villages in which he had fulfilled his duties and mentioned his impression of them. Mr. Darcy revealed his own perceptions on those which he had had the pleasure of visiting. Between the two of them, and occasional questions from the ladies, the conversation carried on. Anne enjoyed it as much as any morning visit. The other participants of the bittersweet tête-à-tête, however, were continually haunted by how much more meaningful it *might* have been.

It being a beautiful day, and everyone being eager to show Mr. Bingley every civility, the entire family saw the gentlemen out. Charles Bingley spoke to Jane even as they were walking outside. Mrs. Bennet gathered Lydia, Kitty, and Mary into a neat little group to keep them out of Bingley's way. Elizabeth and Anne escorted the other two men towards their horses, but then Farley demonstrated with a series of yelps that he was ready for a run. Miss Edwards apologized for his interruptions and was forced to take her leave prematurely. She took the foxhound into the gardens, and watched him dash back and forth, expending the energy which he had built up. This left Elizabeth alone with Mr. Darcy and the Colonel.

Looking at Anne's distant figure, she whispered,

"I am sorry that it did not go better. I hoped that by meeting you, the veil would be removed from her mind."

"So did I," Mr. Darcy murmured. "But I shall not provoke the Lord by complaining. To see her, to speak with her, is enough! By the way, Georgiana was much less of a conversant than the Miss Edwards we met today. Is there any hope that her ease with us stems from some unconscious recollections?"

"I hate to disappoint you, but I doubt it. She would have the same conversation with anyone nowadays. If you visit frequently enough, you shall be able to observe that for yourself."

"Hopefully, we will have that opportunity. We are planning to stay at Netherfield for as long as possible."

"Knowing Darcy, he will probably buy an estate in Hertfordshire ere long," the Colonel said with a grin as he boyishly elbowed his cousin in the ribs.

"I might," Darcy acknowledged. "The temptation to find a good piece of land and a house hereabouts gets stronger every day."

Elizabeth laughed.

"I am sure that you would make a delightful neighbor, sir."

The smile which crossed Mr. Darcy's face seemed brighter than the light of a hundred candles.

"I would certainly try my utmost to be an agreeable one, Miss Bennet. But in all seriousness, since I cannot watch over Georgiana every moment of the day, I am infinitely grateful that I can leave her in your capable hands. Her genteel demeanor always gave me much pride and joy, but now she has become a true lady, capable of making easy conversation and expressing herself dexterously. Thank you for all that you have done for her."

"You are very welcome. In all honesty I am the fortunate one, for she is a magnificent soul and a wonderful friend."

Mr. Bingley finally managed to tear himself away from Jane and approached them. Elizabeth dropped a curtsy and stood aside to allow the men to mount their horses. After they had ridden off, she went to join Anne.

"What did you think of our visitors today?" she asked Miss Edwards as they meandered through the garden.

"They were pleasant," Miss Edwards replied without any symptom of particular regard.

Chapter 55

The three gentlemen paid another call the next day, and the next. Charles Bingley grew blind and deaf to anyone besides Jane Bennet. The youngest Bennet girls soon discovered Richard Fitzwilliam's proper title and occupation and commandeered every second of his time, an intrusion which the military man bore with good humor and kindness. These arrangements left Elizabeth, Anne and Mr. Darcy in a little trio more often than not. Although Mr. Darcy's status as a common acquaintance to Anne did not permit many intimate dialogues, the subjects of books, plays, and travel kept them all sufficiently amused. Elizabeth struggled quite a bit in these moments. Despite realizing that she ought to forward every attempt at conversation between the brother and sister, she spent a good deal of time engaging Mr. Darcy's attentions to herself by entering into spirited debates with him. Thankfully, the gentleman did not seem to mind, but answered her challenges with smiles and strikes of his own.

To her surprise, however, he himself struck up conversations which, in days of old, he never would have willingly had. He occasionally answered Mary's burning questions about archaic literature and conversed pleasantly with Mr. Bennet if that gentleman happened to be in attendance. He was extraordinarily patient with Mrs. Bennet and even complimented her on her fine needlework. These civilities could be attributed to his gratitude towards the family who had kept his sister alive. But it was harder to find a reason for his newfound interest in inquiring of Sir William Lucas whether his entire family, including Charlotte and Mr. Collins, were well. His forbearance towards the vulgar Mrs. Phillips was likewise puzzling.

On the fourth day of such visits, Mrs. Bennet invited the gentlemen over for a luncheon, and then, eager to afford Charles Bingley more time alone with her eldest daughter, suggested that the young people make a picnic out of their noonday meal. Mrs. Lane gladly wrapped up some of the dishes she had prepared and putting them in a basket, sent them up.

Charles Bingley took the parcel in one arm, Jane in the other, and led the procession through Longbourn's grounds. Mary meandered after them and read a book while walking. The Colonel, flanked by Lydia and Catherine, came next. At the very end came Mr.

Darcy, who had offered his left arm to Anne and his right to Elizabeth, and had been accepted by both.

The Colonel and his companions were the only ones who did much talking or laughing during the journey; the minds of the others were too full. Jane and Bingley were thinking of each other. Mary's mind was saturated with Plato. Anne watched Farley sprint in circles around the group, and Elizabeth, for the moment, wondered if there was anything more she could do to lure her friend's memory back. Mr. Darcy, for his part, marveled at his happiness. He was surrounded by two women for whom he had the highest regard.

Looking for a spot on which to spread their feast, they all wandered through a short wooded path which led past a small meadow. As they neared the clearing, a most unusual sequence of sounds began to float to the ears of the party. First, there was the *twack!* of an axe splitting a piece of wood, then a profound sob, followed by another *twack!*, before a deep, quivering breath was drawn. This unusual cacophony repeated itself several times and became louder as they neared its source.

In the middle of the aforesaid meadow there were a few logs, a chopping block, and a growing pile of firewood. There was also a small, lean boy in attendance. He was certainly not older than twelve, but he wielded the axe like a man. In between swings of the tool, however, he produced shuddering sobs. Upon closer inspection, it was possible to see glistening tears running down his cheeks and mingling with the sawdust upon his little face.

"The poor soul," Elizabeth sighed. "My heart simply breaks every time I see him. How dearly I wish that something could be done!"

"Who is he?" Mr. Bingley asked softly.

Jane answered the question.

"His name is Joe Harper, and Papa hired him to do odd chores around the estate. A little over a month ago he had the great misfortune of losing his mother to a terrible bout of pneumonia. Ever since then the little creature has been inconsolable. His father is a good man, but he has his farming to attend to as well as Joe's three little sisters to look after; I am afraid Mr. Harper simply has neither the time nor the energy to commiserate with his son after the work is done. Lizzy and I have tried to comfort him, but the child invariably tells us, in the sweetest, most civil, and most despondent way, that we do not understand the matter, for our Mama is still living. 'Tis true, I must own. I have often been at a loss for words when speaking with Joe."

"So have I," Elizabeth added in a low tone, which was accompanied by a sad smile. "As a result, I think that we will all be in agreement that it must be a difficult case, indeed!" Darcy and Miss Edwards imitated her half-hearted expression, the former quite pensively. He stole another glance at Joe Harper. "However," Elizabeth continued, detaching herself from Mr. Darcy's arm, "I am determined to try anew. The two of you go on with the rest of the party and further your acquaintance; I shall be there before long."

"Certainly, Lizzy," Anne replied. As Elizabeth went off, she noted with satisfaction that Mr. Darcy had turned to his sister and begun speaking to her. Hopefully, Anne would soon regard him as one of her most intimate friends, the highest position to which he could ascend as long as her memory remained suppressed. In the meantime, she had to think of something original to say to Joe. Elizabeth was adept at consoling young ladies like Miss Edwards, but this man-child who felt a grief she had never known was an unsolvable enigma.

As she was standing silently by the edge of the meadow, taking inventory of all the strategies by which she had already attempted to comfort the little Mr. Harper, movement in the periphery of her vision caught her attention. To her stupefaction, Mr. Darcy was drawing near, sans his hat and outer coat. These lay behind on a boulder, and turning more completely and gazing into the distance, she saw that Anne had advanced to Mary's side and was disappearing from sight along with the rest of the party.

Looking back at the man who was by this point within five feet of her, she heard him ask the quiet question,

"May I join you?"

"Of course, if you are certain that you wish to," Elizabeth said, still surprised that he had given up the opportunity to have his sister to himself for half-an-hour at least. What did he hope to gain by standing in the meadow instead? All he would see was herself struggling to be of use in a sad situation. Thinking that he might simply be loath to leave an unaccompanied lady in the woods with an impoverished tenant's son, she said, "Anne may miss your company. Joe and I are well-acquainted, and I know him to be a very good sort of boy."

"Georgiana released me from her side very generously when I asked to take my leave, mentioning that she had long wished to ask

298

Mary to expound on a few passages from Plato and felt that today's walk was as good a time as any for that conversation. I shall stay with you, Miss Bennet, unless you would rather that I rejoin the rest."

Elizabeth murmured her acquiescence to this plan, although she dearly wished that she could blunder through another session with Joe without a witness. Mr. Darcy turned his countenance to the center of the field, and looked fixedly at the meadow's smallest occupant. Looking much less formal than usual in his waistcoat and linen shirt, the gentleman began to stroll leisurely in Joe Harper's direction.

Although she had yet to formulate something sensible to say to the crying boy, Elizabeth fell into step with Mr. Darcy. They halted about seven feet from the young lumberjack. Joe, startled, noticed them and lowered his axe, simultaneously choking back his laments.

"Can I help you, Miss Bennet, sir?" his trembling voice respectfully asked.

"I just wished to see if you were well, Joe," Elizabeth replied.

"I am well, ma'am," the boy said at once, but the glistening tears in his eyes belied his statement.

"Oh Joe, you need not conceal - ," Elizabeth began, before she was stopped by the sudden gentle pressure of a hand on her arm. Breaking off and looking at the tall gentleman standing next to her, she saw a look of warning on his face and a slight shake of his head. Abruptly, she realized that the exhortation she had been about to voice would be useless and even offensive to a lad of twelve. She bit her lip and cast her eyes down to the ground, unable to think of a way forward.

So that Joe would not realize why he had suddenly reached for Elizabeth, Mr. Darcy used the arm he held to guide the lady to sit down on a smooth tree stump nearby. Having nothing wiser to do, she complied.

Then the gentleman wandered to the pile of ready firewood and, taking up a piece, seated himself on another wide stump. Fingering the wood expertly, he smiled at the mystified young boy.

"This is as good a job of logging as any. These blocks are split so neatly that there is barely a splinter on them. And you are working quickly, without sacrificing quality. A grown man could not do better."

"Thank you, sir."

The gentleman looked down at the timber he held before ending his remarks with the soft statement:

"Your parents must be very proud of you, young man."

Joe Harper's small head bowed down towards the ground.

"Papa never says anything about it…and Mama cannot say anything. Dead people do not talk."

Mr. Darcy nodded sympathetically.

"Unfortunately they do not, no matter how much we feel that we need their kind words. But I am sure that she knows of your hard work, and is very proud of her son. Your father likewise must take great joy in having a dependable young man to help him take care of the family in her absence, even if he is often unable to find the words to express himself."

Elizabeth felt her eyes widen. Had he left his sister and rushed to her side to be of assistance in comforting a boy covered with sweat and sawdust? Had his gentleman's accessories been doffed to negate, as much as possible, the difference in status between him and the wood cutter?

And, indeed, Joe let the axe touch the ground and curiously stepped nearer the gentleman, feeling a kindred soul near.

"I…I hope so, sir."

Mr. Darcy fingered the block again before rejoining,

"Have you any brothers or sisters?"

"Three sisters."

The gentleman shifted upon his seat and vacated a few more inches of the wide trunk. He gently gestured to the bare wood beside him. It would be difficult to determine who lived through a greater jolt at this invitation, Joe or Elizabeth.

However, the former, after due consideration and hesitation, accepted.

"May I ask how they are coping without your mother?" the older man inquired once the young one was seated.

"Sarah is too little to understand, Rachael cries all day, and Lisa tries to cook."

"Tries?" Mr. Darcy echoed, lifting his brows.

The little Mr. Harper actually giggled.

"Yes, tries. Mama was teaching her, and I suppose it could be worse, but her soup is not the same as Mama's." The boy sobered. "Nothing will ever be the same again."

"No, it will not," Mr. Darcy said softly.

Elizabeth saw how profound an impact this simple acknowledgement had on Joe's countenance, and she realized that

300

that was where she, Jane, and all the tenants who had been trying to function as soothers had gone wrong. They had been insisting to Joe that things would become normal again, that everything would be alright. Clearly, this was one area where experience was priceless.

"Nothing will ever be the same again," Mr. Darcy repeated after giving Joe a moment to feel what the lad needed to feel. "But while life has changed, it will not always be so dark. It will take months and years, but eventually, memories of your mother will become sweet again. When your sister Lisa learns some more and one day manages to recreate the recipes properly, you will enjoy the food heartily and reminisce about older days with laughter. When your sisters become young women and you begin to see in them the very image of your mother, you will smile. It took many years before I could look upon the rosebushes which my own Mama planted in front of our house without feeling tears in my eyes, but now those fragrant hedges are my favorite place to walk during the dewy mornings."

Joe looked up at his new mentor with big eyes. He knew enough of the world to shy away from asking the aristocratic figure questions, but he had caught the entirety of the communication and by itself, that was enough. Hope infused itself into his pupils. This great man had lived through the same tragedy, and had come out on the other side, intact. He, Joe Harper, might have less money and consequence, but he was every bit as much a man. He, too, would survive. He would be happy again.

The two carried on the conversation for a while longer. Elizabeth said nothing, for she knew that her presence was completely unnecessary. Instead, she sat and stared as the grandson of an earl inquired, and learned, that Mrs. Harper had been exceptionally gifted in the art of making blueberry jam, that Lisa's last batch of bread had come out as tough as brick, and that Joe had learned to read and write but was no longer attending the local school because his days were now taken up with errands. He listened to all these tales with supreme interest, and Joe chatted away rapidly and confidently.

At length, the time came for them to part ways. Mr. Darcy actually extended his hand to the tiny lumberjack, and shook the sweaty palm which was placed in his with considerable warmth. Elizabeth grasped her wooden seat with both hands to prevent herself from falling backwards at the sight.

Joe thanked his benefactor, and rose to go about his work. Mr. Darcy likewise boycotted their bench and came over to Elizabeth. She took his arm, and together they tarried for a little while to watch Joe position a log and bring down the axe upon it smoothly. They observed while several more perfect blocks of wood were created, and by the time the two began to withdraw, a sound besides that of the axe filled the meadow. Joe was humming a quaint little lullaby.

Chapter 56

Elizabeth allowed herself to be led from the field. Mr. Darcy's arm was a most welcome guiding force as she contemplated the man to whom it belonged. He had surpassed her expectations many times in the previous weeks, but this last event…as much as Elizabeth prided herself on her eloquence and way with words, it escaped description.

For herself she was humbled; but she was proud of him. Proud that in a cause of compassion, he had been able to get the better of himself. In that touching scene with Joe, he had proven himself more a gentleman than he ever had been in his formal evening attire or by owning Pemberley. For what was more genteel and indicative of good breeding than showing kindness towards those less fortunate in society? She remembered all the praises which his tenants in Lambton had heaped, unsolicited, upon his head and for the first time, believed each and every one of them.

They walked to the place where Mr. Darcy had abandoned his coat and other possessions. He took them up and donned them, offering his arm to Elizabeth anew when he was through. They were well-advanced upon the path when the gentleman finally said,

"You are very quiet, Miss Bennet."

"I believe that I have spoken as much as most marveling women would," Elizabeth replied seriously. "I congratulate you, sir. There are few things which awaken admiration as readily as seeing someone succeed where you yourself have failed. I can scarcely believe that you are the same man who once said that he was ill-qualified to recommend himself to strangers, and that he lacked the talent of conversing easily with them. Either you disparaged yourself overmuch, or have improved uncommonly quickly."

"I deserve neither such praise nor such censure. I was in earnest when I spoke those words in Kent. Truth be told, I have always felt more at ease with children than I do with my equals or superiors in age, although I interact with them but rarely. Most children have yet to acquire the art of hypocrisy or of hiding their feelings. Befriending them is much simpler."

"All the same, I thank you, sir. You did Joe a great service, and spared me another failure."

"You are welcome, Miss Bennet," was the response, accompanied by a smile.

At this juncture, they rejoined the others to find most of them engaged in a lively game of Blind Man's Bluff. Anne and Mary alone were engaged in a more sedate manner, by reading.

While Elizabeth was not over-thrilled to see that her younger sisters had once again breached propriety and doubtlessly suggested a game which ought to have been played only in feminine company, Mr. Darcy's and her arrival had the advantage of interrupting it. Lydia hurled herself upon the picnic blankets as soon as she saw them.

"Gracious, Lizzy, where have you been? Mr. Bingley and Jane would not let us begin until you returned. I am famished!"

"Yes, Blind Man's Bluff is a perfect form of repose for young ladies whose knees are too weak to hold them up," Elizabeth replied dryly.

The others gathered around and all began the repast. Mr. Darcy seated himself between Elizabeth and Anne. Partway through the meal, Mr. Darcy looked at the two women and asked,

"Do you come here often?"

"Tolerably often," Elizabeth replied. "Although, we prefer the view from Oakham Mount for our morning walks. Also, the dwellings of some of my father's tenants are just beyond the next set of trees, and if one walks around here they must be prepared to occasionally meet some of them, as you have seen. If we are engaged in pouring out our hearts to one another as young ladies are wont to do, we rather not stumble upon an audience even if they be kindly people."

"That is completely understandable, Miss Bennet," Mr. Darcy said; however, a particular light in his eyes betrayed that he would dearly like to know what sorts of confidences were exchanged during these sessions.

"We shall probably walk here more often when the weather gets colder and ice makes the steep paths of Oakham Mount treacherous," Anne put in. "Lizzy says that this forest is very beautiful during the wintertime when soft snow falls upon it. I have not yet had an opportunity to visit it during the colder months, having arrived at Longbourn somewhat precipitously in May!"

The carefree way in which she alluded to the beginning of her stay in Hertfordshire seemed to take Mr. Darcy somewhat by surprise. He did not reply for a long time, and searched Elizabeth's face for cues before he proceeded. The lack of panic in her features proved that they were not on the verge of entering a dangerous topic, and after a minute he slowly said,

"Miss Edwards, you need not answer if you do not wish to, but there is something which I should dearly like to ask you. I have heard from other sources that your presence at Longbourn came about in a…rather unusual manner. I assumed that you would wish to avoid the subject altogether, but you touched upon it in your previous statement. Does it generally distress you to speak of it?"

Anne smiled reassuringly and openly informed him,

"At first it did. Despite all the care I received at the hands of Lizzy and everyone else, the first several weeks were dreadful. I was recovering from injuries which I never remembered sustaining, and I was learning what my own countenance looked like in a mirror! When I finally ventured out of the sickroom and into the world, everyone looked at me as a curiosity rather than as a young woman. They spoke of events which I had never even heard of. I felt like quite an outsider, and only the kindness of Lizzy and her kin made it bearable!" Mr. Darcy gave Elizabeth a look overflowing with gratitude. "Now I am able to speak of it easily, as you see. People have become accustomed to me and my situation. Most conversations are about balls and assemblies which I have attended. Occasionally someone mentions something in the distant past, but I do not dwell on it and am not bothered by it. I look upon it as a child thinks upon events which it was too young to remember. You may speak freely about anything you wish in front of me, sir."

"Thank you," Mr. Darcy replied. "I am very happy to hear that you have managed to make a life for yourself despite the trying circumstances."

"As am I. It might have ended very differently for me, as you may well imagine."

A breathless 'Yes' was all the acknowledgement which the gentleman managed to give to this statement.

Elizabeth, sensing that Anne was going too far in her ignorance, skillfully changed the subject of the conversation.

Chapter 57

The repast ended and the plates were put away. Mr. Bingley, for reasons of his own, kept looking at Mr. Darcy, and seemed extremely satisfied when he received a series of nods in response. Thereupon, he appeared extremely anxious to have Jane and the picturesque meadow all to himself. Miss Edwards sensed this first, and withdrew into the wood with Farley and a book. Elizabeth followed her soon after, hoping that Mr. Darcy would join them ere long. As she was departing, Colonel Fitzwilliam insisted that the three youngest Bennets show him a nearby stream which flowed between Longbourn and Netherfield.

The second eldest Miss Bennet had a difficult time locating her protégé in the vast forest. After about ten minutes of searching, she at last descried Anne sitting on an old bench along the path, reading. She was about to draw nearer to accost her when she heard a rustling of leaves which was too loud to be caused by the wind.

Turning around, she saw that Mr. Darcy had indeed left his friend and Jane to their devices and had chosen the forest as a refuge, as had the two ladies before him. He was several dozen yards behind her. Elizabeth was waiting for him to come up to her when yet another sound disrupted the peace of the forest.

"Miss Edwards, Miss Edwards!" called the voices of little children. Four or five youngsters, all about six years of age, came running out of the shrubbery. Miss Bennet promptly identified them as children of her father's tenants, whom she and Anne had met on several occasions. Not observing Elizabeth or Darcy, they crowded around the bench, pressing in on Anne, who smiled and laid aside her book.

"What is it, my dears?" she inquired in a motherly tone. She was promptly answered by a cacophony of distressed cries:

"Our kite!"

"Stuck!"

"Our pretty kite!"

"It is so high!"

"One at a time, one at a time!" Anne exclaimed. Turning to an adorable girl, she soothingly asked,

"Maggie, could you tell me what happened?"

"We were playing. Tom flew the kite too high. It is in a tree."

"In which tree is it?"

"Come, I will show you!" Maggie replied, grasping Anne's hand and pulling with all her six-year-old might. Miss Edwards immediately rose and allowed herself to be led deeper into the wood, the other children following at her heels. Elizabeth followed them at a distance and Mr. Darcy at an even greater one. Miss Edwards did not notice the other adults during the short procession.

Very soon, the children abruptly stopped and a pouting Maggie pointed at the branches of a tall pine.

"There!" she proclaimed, giving Miss Edwards a very unhappy gaze.

Indeed, enmeshed in the needles at a point at least ten feet off the ground, was a colorful kite. Darcy, already impressed by the maternal way his sister spoke to and interacted with the children, waited to see whether she would encourage them to call a servant to assist them or whether she would sympathize about the plight of their plaything and suggest another amusement.

Anne did neither. Instead, she approached the base of the tree, hiked up her skirts, and proceeded to expertly ascend the trunk. Within seconds, she reached the level of the entangled kite. A stupefied Fitzwilliam Darcy gaped as the usually ladylike girl walked nonchalantly along a thick horizontal branch, deftly freed the bright object, and let it glide gently to the ground, where it was welcomed with a chorus of,

"Thank you, Miss Edwards!"

Their possession restored, the children ran from the scene laughing gleefully. Anne retraced her steps along the branch, climbed down halfway, and leapt the remaining five feet to the forest floor. Straightening up, she brushed off her gown, readjusted her bonnet, and wandered deeper into the shrubbery, disappearing from the sight of her remaining observers.

Darcy drew his breath in sharply, relieved that she had descended safely. Even at a distance, Elizabeth could tell that his face was donning the stiff, unreadable expression which it had worn almost without pause the previous autumn.

What must he think of me! He has to know that his sister could never conceive such a stunt on her own without sufficient inspiration from elsewhere!

And, indeed, she was to blame. Early in June, she and Anne had been taking fresh air in Longbourn's garden when loud chirping alerted them to a nest full of distressed baby birds. Upon further inspection, they found the mother dead on the ground beneath the tree. Knowing that the small things could not survive long without nourishment, Elizabeth had determined that they had to be fed regularly and proceeded to teach Miss Edwards how to go about it. The two young ladies had dug up worms - Elizabeth blushed furiously as she recalled the state of their hands afterwards - and then ascended the tree. As usual, Anne had been very hesitant about climbing it, but her friend had urged and prodded, and provided through instructions about what kinds of branches to grasp and in what order. Soon enough, Miss Edwards was scampering up eagerly, and on several occasions ascended even higher than necessary so that she might admire the view. Elizabeth had praised her limberness profusely at the time, never dreaming that her particular skill might one day cause great embarrassment.

She watched as Mr. Darcy abruptly veered to his left, deliberately stepped off the path, and walked into the trees. Clearly, the man wanted time to think - or vent - and wished to make it impossible for anyone to find him until he was through. As she watched him disappear from sight, a great desire arose in Elizabeth's heart to pursue and intercept him, to excuse herself, to assure him that his sister had never knowingly made such an exhibition in front of polite company, to promise that she would speak to Anne about it at the earliest opportunity and ensure that it never happened again. In short, she wanted to say anything which would prevent the loss of his good opinion towards herself.

How often does one realize the worth of something only when it is threatened!

Gone was the need for Elizabeth to ponder her attitudes towards Fitzwilliam Darcy, to wonder why she enjoyed their conversations so much, to consider, piecemeal, what it meant to her that he was an excellent brother, landlord, master. All these qualifications united, and became the basis for her newfound conviction:

I love him!

Her fingers and toes began to tingle as the revelation engulfed her. She loved him!

She suddenly wanted to be alone as well, to think, to dream. But it was not to be. Just as she was considering which path would grant her the most solitude, an urgent summons composed of two different voices rang out through the forest.

"Lizzy, Lizzy!"

"Darcy, where are you? Come at once, man!"

"Lizzy, Anne! Could you come back, please?"

The eagerness and repetitiveness of the entreaties indicated that they would persist until they were heeded. Against her will, Elizabeth turned and went back through the wood.

At least a beautiful sight was her reward. As soon as she exited the forest, Elizabeth espied Jane and Mr. Bingley standing in the meadow with joined hands.

No words were spoken. None were necessary. She looked at Jane; Jane gazed at her. With a little cry of happiness breaking from her throat, Elizabeth flew towards the couple and enfolded Jane into the closest embrace of their sisterhood.

As they thus held one another, Elizabeth saw over Jane's shoulder Mr. Darcy likewise returning to the meadow. He, too, needed no verbal announcement of the new engagement. Walking up to Bingley, he extended his hand and said something which Elizabeth could not hear. When the gentlemen had concluded their ceremonies, Mr. Darcy walked up to Jane and offered his congratulations to her as well. He spoke well and warmly, and seemed genuinely pleased that she had consented to wed his best friend. The others soon joined them, and plunged the happy couple into a whirlwind of laughs, exclamations, and cries. Jane and Mr. Bingley thanked all profusely, offered handshakes and embraces where appropriate, and declared their certainty that they were the happiest creatures on earth.

The walk back to Longbourn was filled with every kind of emotion. Jane and Mr. Bingley, who headed the procession, were giddy with love and excitement. Lydia and Kitty's tongues wagged merrily, as the girls anticipated that they would finally be able to wear the gowns which they had purchased for Anne's wedding. Colonel Fitzwilliam walked next to them, the great grin on his face betraying the fact that he was dreaming up ways to torment the life out of Bingley before the wedding. Mary was thinking of all the beautiful prose she had ever read on the subject of marriage. Anne walked off to the side with Farley, reminiscing silently and sorrowfully about her own days of engaged glory. Mr. Darcy trailed a little after her, his eyes fixed on his sister. Elizabeth was glad that in his rumination he had not offered either of them his arm, for it would have been extremely rude to decline and even more confusing to touch.

She walked more or less at his side, but she ensured that there was a good five feet between them and that her face was turned away from him as she stared at the countryside with unseeing eyes.

She thought of Mr. Darcy with Joe, and wondered how the gentleman would act when surrounded by a brood of little boys and girls: children who bore a mixture of his features, and hers. She dreamt of what he would look like as a graying man, sitting in front of Pemberley's fireplace, and thought how much she would like to be at his side, her own curls powdered with white.

Glancing shyly to the side, she took in his stately form. Could there be hope for them yet? How much had he guessed about Anne's athletic habits? He was an extremely forgiving man, that much was obvious. But all men have their limits, and this time, she might have overdrawn her luck. Darcy loved his sister, and had taken great pride in her. During their last meeting before the accident he had doubtlessly parted from a lady, and now, lo! He rediscovered a wild child, one who recklessly put herself in peril for a plaything. Seeing Anne climbing the tree seemed to have induced a longer period of silence and contemplation than the news that she was to wed Wickham. How could he feel amiably towards the person who had induced the regression? For once in her life, Elizabeth was glad that she possessed two improper younger sisters. Although wishing her blame on another was highly dishonest, she could not help hoping that maybe, just maybe, Mr. Darcy would attribute Anne's peculiar skills to their tutelage, instead of her own.

Chapter 58

Everyone but the skies smiled upon Jane and Bingley for the next three days. Torrents of rain kept every resident of Hertfordshire indoors save for one ardent lover and his two friends who trudged to Longbourn before breakfast and never left before supper. This arrangement unfortunately closeted them all in Mrs. Bennet's presence for hours, and everyone went to bed with their ears ringing from her delighted shrieks. Needless to say, very little conversation was to be had in the drawing room during those three days. Elizabeth had to be content with sitting in the periphery of the chamber and sending occasional glances at a quiet man who sat on the opposite side with a book. He arguably spent more time observing the others than turning pages. She gloried in every action of Anne's which marked her good taste or commendable manners. It was comforting that he should know that she had learned a few things at Longbourn for which there was no need to blush.

And as for the rest, she tried to console herself that all was not yet lost. One small instance of impropriety, executed in the middle of a forest when Anne had thought her only observers to be children – this could surely be forgotten in time. In genteel company, he could see for himself, his sister was the model of respectability. In a few days, her embarrassment and hopefully his memory of the incident would fade, and they would return to building their friendship, and perhaps a romance!

On the third evening, the tide seemed to turn. The rains outside began to lessen, promising a fine day on the morrow. Around the same time, Mrs. Bennet grew hoarse. Seeing Mr. Darcy's gratification as he witnessed his sister ministering to the sore throat with patience and devotion, Elizabeth felt certain that her past imprudence was all but forgotten. She even allowed herself to hope that she might draw Mr. Darcy into a short conversation or two over dinner.

They went into the dining room. Elizabeth took her customary seat at her father's right hand, directly across from Anne. Mr. Darcy sat at Anne's left. Everything was on the mend.

And then Mary opened her lips. Since the engagement, she had been completely ignored despite having copious enlightenments to share. After Mr. Bingley made a remark about being the most elated man in the world, she pounced.

"My entire family and I are completely convinced of your sincerity, and rejoice with you and Jane upon this joyful occasion. But it must be remembered, sir, that happiness in marriage is far more a matter of the effort which is put in after the wedding vows rather than as a result of the feelings which preceded them. We all, I am sure, have had the misfortune of seeing some match which upon first impression was extremely felicitous, but with the passage of time and the fading of passion became a callous, shallow bond. One must never deceive themselves into thinking that because the rose is planted, it will bloom forever without water. Care must be taken with it, from the wedding till the grave…"

Mr. Bennet, who was thoroughly sick of hearing discourses on the subject of marriage, at first tried to swallow his impatience along with the contents of his wineglass. When four minutes went by, and Mary pressed on with the monologue, he interrupted her midsentence.

"My, my, that is an elementary reflection. A girl of ten could do better. But what could possibly be expected? You wake at dawn instead of rising early and applying yourself to serious study. You prefer to sing after dinner rather than sitting down with some philosophical texts. I always knew that you would never succeed if you only spent eleven hours a day poring over books. Go and find something truly edifying to read on the subject of matrimony instead of engaging in gluttony as you are at present." Mary, who had taken only a few bites of her meal, glanced down at her plate and up again at her father, searching for the smirk with which similar speeches directed at Anne and Lizzy were accompanied. This time, however, Mr. Bennet was serious. In a hard tone, he prodded, "Go. Now."

Mortified, unable to lift up her eyes, Mary rose from the table. She excused herself and departed from the room with the miniscule remains of her dignity. With her left all vestiges of sound. They all sat in uncomfortable stillness.

The speech that broke the silence at length was sweet, but strong and candid.

"I believe that you are too hard on Mary, Mr. Bennet," Anne said with the determination of someone who has been nettled by the *status quo* far too long and has decided, at last, to voice their disapprobation.

Longbourn's dining table was suddenly surrounded by ten shocked, still statues. In the middle of them sat Anne, her grey eyes calmly focused on the master of the house.

A few seconds passed in this manner. Mr. Bennet was the first to regain his animation, and clearing his throat, he challenged with an almost invisible twinkle in his eye,

"Kindly explain your meaning, Miss Edwards!"

Anne did not quaver.

"It is unfair to call her silly or berate her habit of constant study, sir. Mary longs solely for your approbation, and despite her valiant efforts to attain it, she receives satire. If you take closer note of her reading material, Mr. Bennet, you will find it, very often, to be something which you recently read, or praised. It takes but one quote of Rousseau's from you to spur her on a month-long quest to read every piece of writing he ever published."

This said, Miss Edwards casually consumed another forkful of potatoes, seemingly oblivious to Mr. Bennet's frown of feigned displeasure and the general stillness of the room.

On the other hand, Elizabeth was keenly aware of every movement, or lack thereof, at the table. She cast a diffident glance at her neighbors. Bewilderment had thankfully silenced her mother and sisters, but it was Georgiana's family, not her own, who perturbed Elizabeth the most. Colonel Fitzwilliam held his wineglass in midair, as if his muscles had frozen upon hearing Anne's words. Mr. Darcy, for his part, was eyeing his sister with unrestrained wonder.

It did not take long for Elizabeth to imagine their feelings. Anne had not only been bold; by the standards of any society, high or low, she had been abominably discourteous. To question an elder gentleman's management of his own daughter was hubristic for anyone, let alone an unconnected sixteen-year-old girl who already owed him a debt of gratitude. And if the statement itself were not rude enough, she had articulated it in the presence of guests!

Fortunately, Mr. Bennet was not truly offended. Indeed, he was so fond of Anne that he would have overlooked almost any impertinence, and his own conscience was prickling as he remembered Mary's face. However, he found it convivial to pretend himself affronted, and thus assumed a disgruntled expression. Elizabeth knew it was false, Anne knew it to be counterfeit, and Jane

313

suspected the same, but they were the only ones who could have enough insight into Mr. Bennet's character to perceive the farce.

As second after second passed without further sound, Elizabeth realized in desperation that something had to be said. For a brief moment she contemplated completely changing the topic, but was dissuaded from that course of action by the realization that it would only serve to underline Anne's imprudence, rather than tactfully draw attention away from it. Hence, there was but one way left: if she could not blot out the limelight which was shining on Anne, she would at least diffuse it by purposely attracting some of its infamy to herself.

Focusing on her father, consciously avoiding Mr. Darcy's gaze, Elizabeth took a deep breath and stated,

"I think that Anne may be correct, Papa."

Mr. Bennet swung his head in his daughter's direction and gave her the perfect imitation of a wilting glare.

"How so, young lady?"

"When Jane and I were very little, you would always take us into your library in the afternoon, read to us and have us read to you. As Mary grew, she would clamor daily to be allowed the same privilege, but she was always shooed away and informed that she was too young to understand our studies. One day, after emerging from our appointment with you, sir, Jane and I found Mary on the floor of the nursery, every single one of our primers and books opened and spread around her. She was but a child of four, but she demanded that we teach her the art of interpreting words so insistently that at last Jane took pity and taught her a few letters. Since that time, she and the schoolroom have been inseparable."

It was done. Anne was no longer the center of attention; that doubtful honor had passed to herself and her father.

"Humph! If Mary is studying philosophy today because she was denied access to my study a few times fifteen years ago, it proves that she is irrational."

"I think *persistent* would be a better choice of word, sir," Elizabeth replied, adding a bantering tone to the rebuttal via sheer force of will. Never before had she felt so disinclined to be lighthearted.

"Oh, have it your way, Lizzy," her father snapped, allegedly exasperated. "*You* are certainly persistent, whether or not your younger sister merits that classification. Eat your partridge and give me peace!"

The pause which succeeded Mr. Bennet's outburst was far less awkward and shorter than its predecessor, and was soon dispersed by Jane and Mr. Bingley, who resumed their conversation. Next, Kitty and Lydia took up their whispering and giggling where they had left off. The others returned their attention to their dinners.

Although her father had ordered her to consume the meat, Miss Bennet's appetite had fled. During the aforementioned discourse, Elizabeth had been painfully mindful that Mr. Darcy's eyes were upon her, and she did not dare to catch or interpret the feelings in them. If he had had any dubiety before about who had taught his sister to climb trees and contradict her elders, he could have none now. By echoing Anne's questionable contention, she had rightly incriminated herself as the culprit who had planted such notions in the formerly prim and ladylike mind. Everything was sinking, especially hope. All love must be in vain.

The meal ended soon after the disrespectful debate. As they retired to the small parlor and took up their customary evening pursuits, Elizabeth noticed that Mr. Darcy was spending an excessive amount of time staring at his sister, and only breaking his gaze to cast an occasional glance at herself or her father. She cringed as she imagined what he must be thinking. Nor did Mr. Darcy utter another syllable for the remainder of the evening. Offense seemed to have welded his lips together. Even as the gentlemen were taking their leave, he left Charles Bingley and the Colonel to issue the verbal adieus, and for his part only bowed silently before following them out the door. Seeing him thus depart, a section of his letter from Kent haunted her mind:

'The situation of your mother's family, though objectionable, was nothing in comparison to that total want of propriety so frequently, so almost uniformly betrayed by herself, by your three younger sisters, and occasionally even by your father.'

There was some meager consolation, however: at least one good occurred as a result of Anne's outspokenness that evening. When Elizabeth entered the library to bid Mr. Bennet goodnight, she found him discussing Shakespeare's *Othello* with Mary.

Chapter 59

Elizabeth slept poorly that night. Her constant tossing and turning was the reason that she and Anne found themselves present extremely early in the breakfast parlor the following morning, nursing cups of coffee as they waited for the servants to bring in the breakfast platters.

"My dear, I am so sorry," the elder girl said as she guiltily regarded the dark circles under her friend's eyes. "It must have been a very frustrating night for you."

Anne waved away the apology at once.

"Think nothing of it. I caused you at least a dozen sleepless nights after Mr. Wickham vanished into thin air. And besides, you chose a very good evening for your restlessness; my own mind was so busy that I doubt that I would have had a sound repose even under the best of circumstances. Lizzy - ," she paused to bite her lip, "it was rather rude of me to speak to your father as I did over dinner yesterday, was it not?"

Elizabeth sat back and closed her eyes briefly. If only the girl had recognized that sooner; preferably about ten seconds before she had spoken last night.

"It was." Seeing horror springing into Anne's face, she added a tad bitterly, "But it is over and done with, and Papa has forgiven you. Let us say no more of it."

Anne would have promptly offered further apologies, but the door swung open, and the family came in. On their heels were the three gentlemen who had arrived but a few moments before.

Elizabeth was not ready for them; she had not steeled her nerves enough to face any of them yet. Foregoing the prospect of breakfast, she quickly jumped up from her seat, curtsied in their general direction, murmured something about cutting flowers, and went out into the garden.

She located the shears, and taking them in hand, approached a rosebush. Grasping one of the stems, she thought of Mary's words from the previous night:

'One must never deceive themselves into thinking that because the rose is planted, it will bloom forever'.

Placing the shears about a foot from the petals, she squeezed them shut and freed the flower from the bush. How easy it was to cut off the sustaining water from the bloom!

"Miss Bennet."

Elizabeth turned around sharply and found Mr. Darcy approaching. He was hatless. His dark curls were caressed by the balmy morning breeze. The gentleman emanated a relaxed air. Her heart skipped a beat at his handsomeness.

"Mr. Darcy," she acknowledged before bending over and burying her face in the flowers as if she were inhaling their fragrance. In truth, she simply wished to hide her uneasiness. His purposeful strides forward announced that he had come into the garden to seek her out. Clearly, he wished for another private conference, and Elizabeth only hoped that its predetermined subject was not the previous evening's dinner conversation. If it was, at least she would be able to assure him that his sister had come to regret her outspokenness since then.

He stopped within three feet of her. Bracing herself, the lady removed her face from the petals and studied his dignified countenance. It was devoid of suppressed anger.

"Your flowers are beautiful, Miss Bennet," Mr. Darcy stated benevolently, his tone likewise free from enmity.

Has he come out here for a tête-à-tête, and not to reproach me for destroying his sister? Elizabeth marveled. Inspired by this prospect, she replied cheerfully,

"I would thank you for the compliment, sir, if I were entitled to it. But as it is, I cannot assume credit for nature's masterpiece."

"But I am certain that your pruning and care has added a few brushstrokes to her canvas," the gentleman said, smiling.

Elizabeth laughed softly. It seemed a very long time since they had had a lighthearted, witty conversation like this one, and she was surprised at how deeply she missed them.

"Perhaps a very few, thin lines," she said. "However, I am no genius like she; whenever I remove the blooms and attempt to create my own work of art indoors, their colors fade and their lines crumble within days."

"The elegance of your work amply compensates for its lack of endurance, Miss Bennet. The floral arrangements in Longbourn's drawing room are beyond lovely."

Elizabeth felt her face flaming once more. It was heavenly, to stand and converse with the man she loved, and to receive his commendations! If a miracle happened, and Mr. Darcy were to ask again, she would gladly spend the rest of her life filling every vase in Pemberley.

"Thank you, sir," she finally responded, busying herself with the shears.

Mr. Darcy bowed slightly, and pausing, assumed a more serious demeanor.

"Miss Bennet, my cousin and I leave for London the day after tomorrow."

This completely unexpected communication caused Elizabeth to start.

"Will you be gone long?" she asked casually, as if her entire existence was not hanging on the answer.

"Richard must rejoin his regiment, and so will be absent for some time. He hopes that he will be granted another leave in time for Bingley's wedding. I, however, will return in a few days after seeing to some business in Town." The gentleman hesitated. "Upon my return, I wish to apprise Mr. Bennet of the entire truth concerning my sister. I have been observing Georgiana, and I do believe that she is recovered enough to bear an alteration of her relationship with your father. Have I your permission to speak to him?"

He has been observing Georgiana, and wishes to encourage an alteration of her relationship with my father! Is this meant to be a commentary on yesterday's events?

Elizabeth looked past him into the distance and forced herself to state,

"I have nothing against you claiming what is yours, sir."

Mr. Darcy nodded.

"Thank you," was his reply. "I would feel much better if he were privy to the matter. It would allow us to cease shouldering the burden of orchestrating and holding these secret conversations."

He is burdened by speaking with me! He never hinted at being encumbered by the necessity before. Do I need to hear anything else? He has stated his feelings as plainly as can be!

Aloud, she simply murmured,

"Yes, I know."

"I am glad that you understand, Miss Bennet."

"Indeed I do," Elizabeth whispered, staring at the ground.

Feeling tears gathering in her eyes and preparing to slip out from under her lashes, she threw the few roses she held into the basket and bending down, grasped the handle of the same. She turned back towards the house, only saying as an adieu: "I must take these inside."

Without further delay, she proceeded to rush away from him into the house, relying more on memory than on sight, since that sense was obstructed by tears. Fumbling for the doorknob of a side door, she threw it open, rushed into Longbourn, and closed it behind her. Not wishing to go to her own room, where Anne had constant admittance, she instead slipped off to a small little chamber in which several pieces of unused furniture were stored against the day they would be needed again.

Locking herself in, she laid the basket of brilliant red roses upon the dusty surface of a desk. Crumpling into a nearby chair, she put her hands over her face and attempted to channel all the disappointment, grief and despair flooding her heart into the streams pouring down her cheeks. Could there be any other opinion on the subject? She had lost every shard of his esteem.

Why...how...has it come to this?

A few months ago the man had been in her power, and she had spurned him. Without a twinge of guilt she had informed the rejected suitor of her low opinions of his character, his honor...all based on mistaken premises. Yet, he had somehow forgiven her, and just when her heart had begun to beat for him, a new onslaught of complications, all of her own making, rendered her newfound fervent feelings worse than useless.

It would take a lifetime to forget him even if an ocean, five mountain ranges and seven thousand miles of moors separated them, but her situation was infinitely more hopeless. As long as Anne Edwards remained ensconced at Longbourn, her elder brother would be at least an occasional caller. He was destined to be frequently before Elizabeth's eyes, but always out of reach. Perhaps one day he would begin bringing his bride on these visits, and then she would have to endure seeing his adoring gaze fixed on another.

There was but one course of action. Pine she might, but *he* would not see or suspect it! He had to be heartily sick of women throwing themselves at him, and Elizabeth Bennet would not be among their pitiable ranks! Even if she died of a broken heart, it would be with honor. She would only speak to him when civility

319

pressed her to do so. She would assume a position next to his only when every other cranny in the room was occupied. Mr. Darcy and everyone else would forever think her perfectly indifferent, and would never know the deep pain she suffered every time she heard the sound of his voice or saw his handsome face.

Chapter 60

Steady to her purpose, Elizabeth spent the entire next morning out-of-doors, walking to Oakham Mount alone. Returning to Longbourn, she practiced great industry by tying together bundles of fresh herbs and hanging them up to dry in a little room below stairs. At dinner she commandeered the seat next to Mary, and while that scholar's long-winded philosophical insights made her head throb, the ache was infinitely preferable to sitting before Mr. Darcy's disapproving eyes.

After the meal, she joined most of the other ladies in the drawing room while the gentlemen remained behind to partake of brandy. Anne was the only one who was absent, having gone to fetch the book she was in the process of reading. Being in no mood to converse with anyone, Elizabeth took up her work and slipped into a window seat. When the gentlemen entered, she looked up for a brief moment, and hastily lowered her head anew before she had the misfortune of catching Mr. Darcy's gaze. She listened to Bingley's eager footsteps trending in Jane's direction, and to the soft creaks of the armchairs as his friends sat down. She was conscious of a great desire to go and start a conversation with one of them, but she made herself thread her needle instead.

I shall not force myself where I am not wanted, she thought firmly.

Before long, however, the crinkling of muslin made her glance up again, and she found Mary walking across the room to the table where the music books were kept. This stroll was also noticed by Lydia and Kitty, who instantly looked at each other, alarmed, and bounced up from the sofa on which they had been lolling. For an instant Elizabeth feared that, having never learned to play themselves, they would apply to her for a song in order to forestall Mary's concertos. Fortunately, at that moment, the door opened and Miss Edwards appeared. Lydia flew to her side, seized her arm and exclaimed,

"Anne, play for us! Any piece will do!"

"Oh yes," Kitty agreed, skipping to them and clasping Anne's other hand beseechingly. "A sonata, a jig, just not a concerto...or scales!"

Anne shook her head.

"I am sorry, but I am not in the humor to play right now," she declined. "Perhaps some other time."

"No, tonight!" Lydia screeched, glancing over her shoulder at Mary, who by now had selected a music book and was paging through it. "This instant!"

"Lydia, Kitty, I wish to read -," Anne recommenced persuasively. It was certain that she would have carried the point, but Elizabeth nonetheless took a breath and prepared to order the selfish girls to leave her in peace. She knew well that Anne had not touched an ivory key since the day she last saw Mr. Wickham: a fact which, no doubt, had escaped her less observant sisters. Just as the words were about to come from her mouth, however, she caught sight of Mr. Darcy. He was leaning forward in his seat, clasping his hands together, and eagerly attending to Lydia and Kitty's pleas. Rather than being disgusted by their behavior, he seemed almost grateful for their wayward insistences. Elizabeth realized that he was longing to hear his little sister play again, and found herself equally anxious to furnish him the pleasure. Therefore, she laid aside the embroidery, rose from the window seat, and walked up to the circle of young ladies. Taking Anne's hand, she gently drew her away from the clutches of Lydia and Kitty, and kindly petitioned,

"Anne, I know that you are enthralled by your book, but could you possibly delay your enjoyment of it just this once? It seems ages since you last played, and it is cruel of you to deny us the pleasure of hearing you. My dear, we only ask for a few short tunes, and we need not hear anything overly lively, either. Please?"

Miss Edwards looked down at the friendly hand which held hers. She was by now quite accustomed to refusing demands, but her tender heart had not yet mastered the knack of disappointing a dear friend. Furthermore, despite her own woes, she had perceived Elizabeth to be rather cast down of late, and wrongly believed that Lizzy's slowness to smile originated from worrying about her; this would be a perfect opportunity to ease her friend's mind.

Nodding, therefore, she gave Elizabeth the book she held and walked over to the instrument. Sitting down gingerly, she opened it and slowly fingered the keys without pressing them. Then, ruffling through the sheets on the stand, the musician selected one and began to play a slow sonata.

Elizabeth, who in the meantime had regained her former seat, slyly glanced up after the first few meters to see whether he was enjoying it.

Mr. Darcy was drinking the performance in. After looking at Anne diligently for some moments, he leaned back, closed his eyes, and listened with rapt attention. Elizabeth knew that he was fancying himself at Pemberley, at an earlier time, when his beloved sister knew who he was and when their future was much more ordered and certain than at present. The company on the other side of the room listened to half a song, and then resumed their conversations at a lower tone so that those who wished to listen, might.

Anne finished the piece, and immediately began another. Most people in the room ignored the transition, but for one man, it might as well have been a deafening thunderclap. Anne had barely reached the second meter when Mr. Darcy abandoned his leisurely posture and leaned forward in his chair, nearly gasping for breath. He stared at Anne's face, as if he expected to see something different in it, but eventually sat back, apparently unsatisfied in that regard. However, he took a deep breath, and rose, and advanced. His tread was decided and steady, but there was an element of tiptoe in it; it was plain that he deeply desired to avoid startling the performer. He walked up all the way to the pianoforte, placed his right hand upon the back of it, and continued regarding the musician with an intense gaze as the tinkling tune went on.

Anne looked up, noticed him, and immediately snatched her fingers from the keys.

"I am sorry. I know that it is dreadful," she murmured, blushing.

Mr. Darcy drew back from the instrument slightly, bewildered.

"Dreadful? It is nothing of the sort. It has been a long time since a performance gave me such pleasure."

"You are too kind, sir. I am fully aware that the last piece was sadly lacking."

"On the contrary, it was the crown of them all. Do you not agree, Miss Bennet?"

Elizabeth looked up from her work to discover the gentleman gazing at her and waiting for collaboration. Surprised at his drawing her into the debate, little suspecting that he had been longing to speak to her all day, she nevertheless answered at once,

"I do concur. However, Mr. Darcy, it would be wise of us to save our breath to cool our porridge rather than to lecture Anne further on the subject. Nearly every inhabitant of Longbourn, from my father to Mrs. Hill, has attempted to impress upon her the idea that the aforementioned melody is charming, but this is one instance where she has steadfastly refused to adopt our opinions. I am sure I do not know what she finds so ghastly in that piece."

"Lizzy overstates my feelings," Anne gently contradicted, smiling uneasily. "I never meant to imply that I think the song monstrous. It is just that whenever I play it, I feel that it is somehow…incomplete."

Mr. Darcy abruptly turned back to the lady seated at the pianoforte, and regarded her with an even more intense look than before. He remained thus for some moments, clearly struggling between desire and prudence. Eventually, the former won, and he remarked in a low tone,

"Miss Edwards, have you considered the idea that the piece may be part of a duet?"

Anne's eyes widened. Her lips pursed. Clearly, the notion had never occurred to her before, but it was apparent that she was receptive to it.

"No, that is one modification which I have not thought of," she slowly said, at length, pensively fiddling with her ring. "But a second part would fill in the void quite prettily."

Mr. Darcy reached for his own signet ring and began to move it around and around his finger. Neither he, nor Anne, nor anyone in the room save Elizabeth noticed the mirrored actions. Miss Edwards merely watched him politely, waiting for the next statement of the conversation.

Suddenly, Mr. Darcy ceased trifling with his ring, dropped his hands to his sides, and with a look which conveyed exasperation at his own uncharacteristic lack of restraint, he replied,

"Miss Edwards, I have a confession to make. I happen to be familiar with this piece, and it *was* written as a duet."

Anne's eyes resembled sparkling stars in the morning sky. Her tone overflowing with enthusiasm, she veritably cried out,

"Indeed, sir? How long have I wished for, nearly prayed for, someone who could help me with this piece! Oh, do tell me, what is its name?"

"It is untitled, unfortunately," Mr. Darcy said. Seeing Anne's face drop considerably at this, he hastened to add, "But I know where the sheet music can be found; if you so desire, I would be happy to procure a copy for you!"

"Thank you, sir, that would be most appreciated," Miss Edwards said, but the light in her grey eyes was significantly dimmed by the prospect of another long wait. Mr. Darcy saw this with pain; he loved his sister too much to bear it, especially when a faster remedy was available. He reached again for his ring and began to fiddle with it uncomfortably, since his next statement was certain to make him the center of attention, a position which he had always sought to avoid.

"Miss Edwards…while I will do everything in my power to expedite the arrival of the sheet music, its journey will still unfortunately take a few days. But I do believe that, even though I am sorely out of practice, I do remember enough of the other half of the duet to play it with you right now if you wish."

Anne instantly began to express her approbation of the idea and quickly slid to one side of the piano bench before he could change his mind. Mr. Darcy walked around the instrument and accepted the offer of a seat. At that moment, everyone else in the room who had not been attending to him hitherto stopped speaking mid-sentence and stared. Music-making was probably the last pastime on earth which they would have attributed to the stern Mr. Darcy.

But his back was to them, and he did not see their shocked countenances. He prepared for the task by adjusting his tailored coat sleeves and jeweled cufflinks. Then he looked over at his golden-haired associate, and instructed her,

"Begin as you usually do. I shall come in at the proper moment."

In a room where only Farley's breathing could be heard, Anne commenced playing the piece which had caused months of agitation. Elizabeth was unable to sit still any longer. Thrilling at this opportunity to learn something new about the man she loved, she left the window seat, dared to walk towards the instrument, and took up the same position which he had just abandoned.

A few meters into the piece, the gentleman took a deep breath, looked down at the keys, and began to play.

The tempo of his half of the duet was faster than Anne's and required extremely fine fingerwork. If this was him out of practice, then he could have probably put Mozart himself to shame during his better days. Even Mrs. Bennet let out an astonished gasp.

Elizabeth, glad that the performance gave her an excuse to fasten her eyes upon her former suitor, watched with admiration and flushed with shame, torn between marveling at Mr. Darcy's proficiency and recalling how many times she had plunked away at an instrument in his presence, fancying herself decently competent. If she had known the truth concerning their relative aptitude, she would never have consented to play in his presence, let alone direct saucy speeches at him over the music stand.

Since everyone in the room was watching Mr. Darcy, no one noted the changes which were occurring in Anne.

During the beginning of the piece, Miss Edwards spent most of her time looking at Mr. Darcy's fingers, an expression of pure awe on her face. She smiled as the simple melody intertwined with its complex partner. Closing her eyes, she drank in the sound of the finally completed masterpiece and allowed her imagination to wander over the beautiful daydreams it invoked:

A shady grove full of tall oak trees. There was the vista of a lake…and a grand house behind it. Next, she was seated at a hand-painted instrument, playing the same splendid tune upon it. Her song merged with another's. Together, they played…they played beautifully…

Towards the end of the piece, the fancies were suddenly abolished by excruciating pain. Her brains seemed on fire, tearing themselves apart in all directions. Anne crinkled her eyelids together; she bit into her lower lip. Only the most ardent desire to hear the completion of the duet kept her fingers moving upon the keys.

Dum, dum, DUM!

The final crescendo had sounded.

Mr. Darcy withdrew his hands from the instrument, offered the lady standing at the side of it a slight, self-conscious smile, and acknowledged the thunderous applause of the others with a small nod. He was turning back to Miss Edwards to ask whether he had played to her satisfaction when Elizabeth finally noticed what had escaped everyone for nearly half-a-minute.

"Anne!" she gasped.

Instantly alarmed, Mr. Darcy's head whipped to the left. He beheld his seatmate leaning her elbow upon the edge of the instrument and using the same arm's hand to support her heavy forehead. She seemed scarcely conscious.

The concerned brother reached out and touched her shoulder.

"Miss Edwards?" he murmured anxiously.

Slowly, the girl picked up her head and gazed into the distance with vacant, glazed eyes. Her expression was so peculiar and unreadable that none present were capable of deducing what she was thinking, or whether she was thinking at all. Frightened, Darcy repeated,

"Miss Edwards?"

Gradually, her neck rotated the ashen face in his direction. The blank pupils stared at him. The young lady's breathing was so disordered that even those seated by the fireplace, a good twenty feet away from the pianoforte, heard it. Mr. Bennet sprang to his feet, and then stood by his chair undecidedly, wondering whether to rush forward to render aid or to merely wait for what he thought was a fit of lightheadedness to pass. Colonel Fitzwilliam threw aside his newspaper and leaned forward in his chair, ready to ride for the doctor should Darcy or Miss Bennet order him to do so. The object of their attention, however, saw naught of this; her faculties were still overemployed, receiving and making sense of a series of mental images and sensations.

Almost at the end of his wits, Darcy entreated,

"Tell me what the matter is, I beg you, madam!"

A man's brotherly touch upon her arm…his gentle voice…the scent of his favorite cologne…his dark curls brushing his forehead as he bent towards her protectively.

As Mr. Jones had once informed a concerned Bennet family, no one truly understood the innermost workings of the mind. No one, not even its proprietress, ever comprehended exactly what passed on in Anne's head during those brief moments. But somehow, the stark similarities between her visions and reality spurred the delicate organ into action. It worked, it strained, it almost consumed itself with pain, but it prevailed. It insisted upon looking into storerooms which had been untouched for three months, pulled out the shards reserved there, and welded them together once more into the masterpiece called 'memory'.

The others in Longbourn's parlor were ignorant of the intensity and torture of this exercise. They only knew that the dear girl was in the clutches of some sort of ailment. After a good minute by

327

the clock, they were given the first signal of its resolution: Miss Edwards' white face regained some of its rosy color.

Then, regarding him with an attentive and intelligent gaze, the maiden inclined her head towards Mr. Darcy.

"*Fitz…Fitzwilliam?*" she whispered, trembling from head to toe with hesitation and anxiety.

The gentleman positively started. His eyes nearly bore into Anne; his ears were faintly aware of Elizabeth's sharp intake of air. He realized what this could mean. Trying to confirm his hopes, he likewise leaned forward, and addressed her breathlessly as,

"Georgiana?"

Every uncertainty vanished.

"*FITZWILLIAM!*" the young woman cried so loudly that the servants below stairs clearly heard every syllable of the name.

Without hesitation or reserve, she flung herself at him with such a velocity that Darcy scarcely had time to open his arms to receive her. He managed, however, and closed the same around the girl who was now certain of his identity and hers. And he pressed her to his heart with a force that fell just short of injuring her frame.

Fully aware of what had transpired, Elizabeth withdrew softly in order to grant the brother and sister a little more privacy. She went back to the window seat and sat down, hoping to be as inconspicuous as possible.

From this station, she saw Mr. Darcy clasping and cradling his sister for a long while, the two of them perfectly oblivious to the stares of the other onlookers. Georgiana was weeping with joy into his coat lapels, and at the end of two-and-a-half minutes, finally managed to gasp out,

"To think that I did not know you, to think that I treated you as a stranger!"

Mr. Darcy redoubled his hold and continued rocking her back and forth, unequal to speaking at that moment. After several seconds passed, Georgiana reached up to peck her brother's cheek. The instant after she did so, she drew back precipitously, met his eyes, and began to tremble like a leaf in the merciless autumn wind.

"And Wickham – I almost married Wickham!" The idea was expressed as a cry of horror, now.

Mr. Darcy hastily reached for his sister again and enfolded her once more in his arms, exclaiming decisively in his deep voice,

"It was not your fault. You did not know, you did not remember!"

Georgiana allowed herself to be comforted with this statement and embrace, and after a little consideration, sat up straight and said in a calmer tone,

"But in his parting letter he confessed his faults. Surely he had to feel some pricks of conscience or remorse to leave voluntarily before the marriage!"

"Voluntarily, my foot!" the Colonel sneered from his place in the middle of the room. "Darcy had to offer him the choice of debtor's prison or America for him to write that letter. And every word of that epistle was Darcy's – every single one."

Georgiana looked at the speaker, realization dawning anew in her eyes, and she exclaimed,

"Richard!"

Her seat was abandoned straightaway, and two eager feet ran across the room. She flew into the Colonel's waiting arms. He swooped her up as if she were a mere child, swung her around in a cousinly manner while bellowing with laughter, and at last set her and her spinning head back down.

"O Richard – you and poor Fitzwilliam were here all that time, and I never - ,"

"Shhh, little one!" the military man murmured, giving her a proper embrace.

"Would someone tell me what has happened?" Lydia's voice shrieked over the chaos. "Anne, what do you mean by throwing yourself at Mr. Darcy and the Colonel like that? You never even embraced Wickham when he was your fiancé, and now you kiss *Mr. Darcy,* of all people?"

As Lydia's voice startled the cousins and caused them to draw apart, Miss Darcy looked to the left and happened to see her best friend watching the fiasco with a blank expression upon her face. Taking this to be a sign of disapprobation, she took a step in Elizabeth's direction, clearly bent upon speaking to her before indulging the curiosity of the rest of the room.

With startling rapidity, Mr. Darcy intercepted her. He rose from the bench, came to his sister with hasty strides, possessed himself of Georgiana's hand, and escorted her to the other side of the room before she could make any more progress towards her friend.

Elizabeth saw this with exquisite pain.

Of course. Now that all necessity for interaction between myself and his sister is removed, he does not wish me to inflict any more damage than I already have. It is against his will that she should even speak to me in the midst of a crowded drawing room. Far be it from me to fault him for it, or to resist the well-deserved separation!

In the meantime, Mr. Darcy had stationed himself and the former Miss Anne Edwards in front of the Master and Mistress of Longbourn.

"Mr. and Mrs. Bennet," he said in a loud, confident tone, "please allow me to – finally - properly introduce this young lady to you. May I present *my sister,* Miss Georgiana Darcy?"

All were dumbfounded.

At length, Mr. Bennet shifted uncomfortably in his seat and looked at his adopted daughter.

"Is this true, Annie?"

"Yes, it is all true, Mr. Bennet!" Miss Darcy cried out, tears shining in her eyes as she gazed at her elder sibling. "This is Fitzwilliam, and I *know,* I *remember,* that he is my brother, and that I am Georgiana Darcy, more than ten years his junior, that we live at Pemberley in Derbyshire and spend our winters in Town, that Papa died nearly six years ago and Mama when I was barely five, and - ," she broke off, glanced behind Mr. Darcy at the instrument they had just been playing, and then back at her brother. "The song! *Mama's song!*" she exclaimed, clapping her hands. "Of course it was impossible to find the sheet music for it or anything like it – the only copy of it is at Pemberley, recorded in her own hand! It was this very duet which you played that day when you revealed to me and to everyone that you had learnt to play the pianoforte in her stead after she died!"

"Quite so, my darling," Mr. Darcy replied, reining in his own emotions by sheer force of will.

It was very obvious that further explanations would be necessary to satisfy the awakened curiosities of Longbourn's residents, and sounding gruffer than his general wont, Mr. Bennet invited the newly rediscovered siblings to sit down and begin talking. Elizabeth observed the touching scene from the corner of her eye. Mr. Darcy seated himself on the sofa at his sister's side, and put his arm around her shoulders protectively. Georgiana inched a little nearer to him, and gazed up with a look of fidelity and devotion.

A very strong desire implanted itself in and almost took over Miss Bennet's heart. She wanted to go to them, shoo Miss Darcy aside, take up her place by her brother, and be the one to feel his arm across her shoulders.

O, I am far gone! Elizabeth moaned silently, clenching her fists to forestall herself from giving into the peculiar temptation. *I am envious of the man's little sister, and this after he has given multiple indications that he cares naught for me! Could there be a deeper jealousy, or love?*

Nearly everyone in the room, with the exception of Elizabeth, hastily flocked to the fireplace and jockeyed for a seat near Fitzwilliam and Georgiana Darcy, so that no word of the impending tale would miss their ears. Elizabeth, seeing the rush and enthusiasm, realized that it would appear extremely odd for her to stay by the window, apart from everyone. Slowly, therefore, she followed their lead and commandeered a chair by the wall, next to the fireplace, so that her profile was partially hidden by the mantelpiece.

Mr. Darcy was the one who began. He briefly recounted how he and his servants had spent the fifth of May, and what he had been told of the travelling conditions on the fourth.

"Oh, yes, there was a dreadful storm," Georgiana murmured, chiming in, shutting her eyes tightly as she recalled the terrifying details. "Mrs. Annesley said that we had to leave the coach…she tried to see if it were possible, and accidentally fell out…then I noticed the chasm." Her brow contracted in distress and her breathing became labored. Mr. Darcy clutched her shoulders even tighter, and was about to assure her that there was no need to continue when she recommenced. "I was sure that the carriage would fall in…I closed my eyes…there was a crack…I thought the coach was breaking apart. But it was a merciful rumble of thunder, which frightened the horses so that they detoured and began to flee parallel to the chasm rather than perpendicular to it. I tried to do what Mrs. Annesley had attempted…I exited the coach, held on to the door…I remember clumsily losing my grip…I remember falling backwards, so rapidly! And then…I was at Longbourn, in bed, with Lizzy at my side." Opening her eyes, she sought out Elizabeth with them and sent a grateful, friendly smile her way, one which its recipient did not return. Suddenly struck with other ideas, however, Georgiana anxiously turned to her brother.

"Mrs. Annesley - is she well?"

331

"Yes. She sustained a few fractures, but recovered nicely. She is now the governess of Lord Markwell's daughters, I understand."

"Tom, Andrew, and James?"

"They came through with barely one scratch between the three of them. You were the worst casualty of that accident, dear," Darcy returned, a slight crack in his voice towards the last. Georgiana smiled sorrowfully and patted the hand which rested upon one of hers. "You know," the gentleman continued thoughtfully, "after you lost consciousness, the horses must have returned to the very place where Mrs. Annesley fell and made the jump which was spared you after all. We never knew about the detour, and thought that you had perished only seconds after she left the coach. Being insensate as soon as she reached the ground, your companion could not inform us otherwise."

Georgiana offered a few more words of comfort, and Colonel Fitzwilliam completed the storytelling by relating how he had been apprised of the awful news. When he was through, the general party, persuaded beyond any doubt of Anne's rightful identity, spent a long time clamoring, laughing, reminiscing, and moralizing about their enlightenment. Mr. Bennet and his second eldest were the only ones who remained silent.

Finally, the sound of the grandfather clock striking the eleventh hour was sufficient to quiet all nine tongues.

After the short pause, amid Mr. Bingley's jolly assertions that he had been completely unaware of the time, Mr. Darcy looked wistfully at his sister. When his friend concluded, he spoke,

"Georgiana, I am forced to remind you that Richard and I had plans to go away tomorrow, and we must unfortunately keep them despite this blessed turn of events. I trust that you will forgive us."

"Certainly, I shall! I know you well enough," she said with a doting look, "to know that you would never leave so if you could help it."

Mr. Darcy cleared his throat.

"Would you like to accompany us to Netherfield tonight and leave for Town with me early on the morrow?"

Georgiana smiled; it seemed that she had a clear preference in mind. But she glanced around nevertheless, to take into consideration the feelings of those who had saved her life and preserved her happiness for the past several months. Mr. Bennet and Elizabeth, those closest to her heart, were looking at the floor with carefully schooled, neutral expressions. Many of the others seemed eager to keep Miss Darcy at Longbourn, but did not seem to be desperate enough in this desire to change the lady's mind. She therefore said,

"I will go with you, Fitzwilliam. I love everyone at Longbourn dearly, but I have not been separated from them for a day since I awoke after the accident. On the other hand, it seems a century since I last saw you. Despite your presence for the past week, today is the first day that you are again something other than a mere acquaintance, and I feel that we have a multitude of things to discuss as brother and sister!"

"I could scarcely agree more," Mr. Darcy said, making no attempt to conceal his delight at his sister's decision.

The sector of the party which was to depart rose. Mr. Darcy relinquished his hold on Georgiana's shoulders to allow her a chance to properly part with those to whom they both owed so much.

The fair maiden first turned to the man who had taken pity upon her as she lay in the meadow, exposed to the elements, and given her a home when she could recall no other. She knelt by his chair, and placing her delicate hands upon the armrest, softly said,

"Mr. Bennet, I suppose a long speech ought to be in order, about how grateful I am, and how I will never forget your goodness. But I know enough of your character to know that my monologue would exasperate you before anything else. So I shall simply say 'thank you', and assure you that even though I now remember my own excellent Papa, I shall forever love you as a second father."

For once, Mr. Bennet had no ready repartee. He swallowed several times, trying to dislodge the lump in his throat unsuccessfully. At last, he only whispered,

"Annie," and caressed the alabaster fingers.

Mr. Darcy had followed Georgiana, and once she had finished speaking to the Master of Longbourn, he extended his hand to the latter.

"Mr. Bennet, words can never adequately express what a gift you have given me. However, I was hoping that while my sister takes her leave of your family, you and I might retire to your library to discuss a certain matter?"

Elizabeth knew what he was about. He was probably readying himself to leave Longbourn forever; why else would he pick this night, and such a moment, to settle his accounts? Her father also appeared to anticipate him, and asked plainly,

"Would your planned discourse, by any chance, have to do with the topic of debt?"

"It would," Mr. Darcy said slowly.

Buoyed by Georgiana's heartfelt declaration and stirred by his own feelings of love and loss, Mr. Bennet's courage was high. Although Mr. Darcy was the kind of man to whom he should generally never refuse anything which the former had condescended to ask, tonight the Master of Longbourn retorted,

"Then there is nothing to discuss. I simply cannot repay you." Before Mr. Darcy could recover from this complete turning of tables, Mr. Bennet added, "Your sister has enriched our lives beyond any monetary value. Even if I were thrice as wealthy as yourself, sir, I would be unable to shoulder the expense of recompensing one day of her company. You may rant and storm all you like, but nothing will be forthcoming from me." Turning to Georgiana, he ordered: "Run off now. And take your brother and this mangy mutt with you," as his fingers sneaked down and stroked Farley's shiny ears.

Mr. Darcy acknowledged defeat with a deep bow. He helped his sister rise from the floor, and they both left the elderly man in peace.

Miss Darcy next turned to Mrs. Bennet, who was clutching a handkerchief and had already taken the unprecedented step of standing to receive the farewell. Even more astonishingly, when Miss Darcy approached, the Mistress of Longbourn reached for her and pulled her into a close embrace. Holding her tightly, she cried with feeling,

"Oh Anne, whatever shall I do? You were the only one in this house who ever had any compassion on my poor nerves!"

"There, there, Mrs. Bennet," Georgiana murmured, stroking and patting the older woman's back. "I am sure that your own daughters, angels that they are, will always be of aid to you in your times of trial. Although I hope that those occasions are, for your sake, very rare!"

Hardly consoled, the matron continued lamenting into Miss Darcy's shoulder. As the two thus clutched each other, Elizabeth stole a sly look at Mr. Darcy to see how he bore the sight of his precious sister in the arms of a woman whom he had always disliked for her tactlessness and vulgarity. That he was surprised by the warmth and depth of the mutual affection was evident; but on the whole he seemed pleased by Mrs. Bennet's motherly expressions. He watched the touching scene with a small smile and without the slightest hint of impatience or disapproval.

After another half-minute, Mrs. Bennet relinquished the girl, and patting her cheek, let her go with one final, tearful declaration of,

"We will miss you terribly!"

Giving the woman a smile, Georgiana went over to give Jane an embrace and a peck on the cheek, say her farewells to Mary, and to promise Kitty and Lydia that she would write and send a full report of the latest fashions in Town.

During these proceedings Elizabeth shrank back into her corner, hoping to be forgotten. But alas, Georgiana's affectionate heart would never condone that! She hurried over, with outstretched hands, crying out,

"Last, but certainly not least, allow me to embrace you, my sweetest Lizzy, my dearest friend!"

Miss Bennet rose slowly, and was encased in Miss Darcy's arms. Embraced so strongly that she could scarcely breathe, ever conscious that Mr. Darcy's eyes were upon them, she slowly allowed her arms to encircle the younger girl, pressing as lightly as she possibly could. She did not want to be seen clinging desperately to Georgiana as a fervent friend. She wanted to communicate detachment.

Miss Darcy was too happy to realize that there was something amiss. She drew back, smiled, and then looked over her shoulder at her brother, signaling that she was ready for departure. He nodded, and disengaging his pupils from his sister's, fastened them upon Elizabeth.

Instantly, the sensation that she could not breathe clutched her anew, doubly as hard as it had when Georgiana had been squeezing her ribs. In what seemed to her a measured tone, Mr. Darcy said,

"Miss Bennet," by way of taking his leave.

She gave him a brusque nod, but as he persisted in looking at her, she was finally forced to verbally state,

"Sir." Then she quickly broke their gaze.

Georgiana had in the meantime approached him and now attached herself to his arm. He looked down at her, asked if she were ready, and when she uttered an affirmative answer, walked her out of the drawing room. Everyone followed. Elizabeth lagged several steps behind her family, and when the servants poured out from the door leading below stairs to wish Miss Georgiana well, she discreetly gestured that they should precede her and persisted in bringing up the rear.

In the foyer, after receiving the polite yet affectionate farewells of the staff, Georgiana was wrapped for the final time in Jane's old cloak. Wiping away a tear, she declared her undying love for everyone under Longbourn's roof, and then allowed herself to be led by her brother and cousin across the very threshold through which Peter had, months ago, carried her insensate.

The Colonel and Mr. Bingley entered the carriage first, followed by Farley, who jumped in energetically. Georgiana Darcy turned, offered a final smile and wave, and was helped into the conveyance by her beaming brother. Mr. Darcy was the last person to disappear into the coach's interior.

As the carriage drove away into the night, the young woman who stood furthest from it recognized, with an uneasy feeling, that she might never see Georgiana or Fitzwilliam Darcy again.

Chapter 61

The following days were tedious, lonesome, and altogether hard. The loss of Anne was felt keenly in every quarter: Lydia and Kitty spent more time in silence than in chatter, Mrs. Bennet wept and moaned for hours on end, and the servants wore frowns instead of their usual neutral expressions. The Master of Longbourn, to his credit, refrained from retreating into his library alone: he invited Mary to daily chess tournaments. His witty remarks, however, were few and far between. But none of them experienced anything akin to what Elizabeth suffered.

In all fairness, she was mourning the loss of two people instead of one. And, if she were to be completely honest with herself, she was mourning the gentleman far more than the lady. Ever since Anne had retrieved the kite for the tenant children, Elizabeth had felt rather ill at ease in her presence: she perpetually worried that she would thoughtlessly perpetrate some action which would later be emulated by Anne in front of Mr. Darcy and make her sink even lower in his estimation.

Walks did nothing to improve her mood, especially after she encountered Joe Harper during one of them and found out that a basket of reading primers, soft breads, and blueberry jam had somehow appeared at his family's homestead a few days after his conversation with Mr. Darcy. The best books were insufficient to hold her attention. Watching Jane and Mr. Bingley interact lovingly was exquisite torture. Finally, she took Anne's example and became a recluse in her own bedchamber for as many hours a day as she could without being missed.

During one of these stays above stairs, Elizabeth opened a small drawer in which she was accustomed to depositing her dearest treasures. In the recesses of its furthest corner lay Mr. Darcy's letter of last April, weighed down by the hairpin which he had bought for her.

She reached in and gently drew out both items. The letter she unfolded, read, and pressed to her heart. Laying it aside, at length, with a sigh and a tear, she next turned her attention to the prettiest of pins.

Filled with sorrow, she gently brushed her fingertips over its contours and the splay of rubies. Her love had, by his own admission, purchased this trinket to give her pleasure, back when he felt something other than disappointment…or anger…at her. Her right hand reached up and caressed the curls which his hand had grazed as he slipped it into her hair. How she wished that she had known what the sensation was when she felt it!

While she would never wear the pin again in his presence, she would cherish it until she heard of his betrothal or marriage. Then she would have to dispose of it - but even then she would never be able to sell it or destroy it. She would give it to some deserving soul who would not know its history and could wear it with a clear conscience. Until then, it was hers. Hers to hold, hers to dream over.

She moved to put it away, but it seemed to have affixed itself to her fingers like icy twigs to a wet hand. Elizabeth simply was unable to part with this last remnant of Fitzwilliam Darcy's bygone love for her. While it would be foolishness to put it into her tresses, there could be no harm in slipping it into a pocket where she could feel its weight and occasionally touch it. Therefore, she placed it into her gown's pocket, and slipping into a favorite chair, continued counting the hours since Miss Darcy and her brother had removed from Longbourn.

Chapter 62

A week passed without a letter from Georgiana or Mr. Darcy. And Mr. Bingley did not know when they were expected back at Netherfield.

What am I waiting for? Elizabeth raged within herself. *Am I naïve enough to believe that he will allow his sister to continue her acquaintance with me, and perhaps even offer me signs of friendship himself?*

One morning, as she was rising from her restless night, the young woman glanced around her bedroom and realized that reminders of Anne were everywhere. The girl's dressing gown hung on a hook near the door. On the writing table her sketching pad and pencils were neatly arranged. A book which Miss Edwards had been in the process of reading lay on the nightstand beside her. Determining that expunging these mementos would be more productive than another day of moping, Elizabeth set about it as soon as she was dressed.

The book was returned to Mr. Bennet's library. The sketching pad and pencils were put away. The dressing gown was sent down for laundering with a strict instruction that upon its return it was to go to the attic instead of her bedchamber. She had just extracted Miss Edwards' dresses from the closet in order to fold them and return them to Jane's possession when, without warning, the bedchamber's door swung open. This was doubly surprising since the entire family, with the exception of herself, had just departed for a luncheon at the Philips's. Elizabeth glanced up to ascertain who the discourteous intruder was, and laid eyes on her former roommate.

"Anne!" she exclaimed, stunned. Recovering herself, she quickly added, "I mean, Miss Darcy."

"You mean *Georgiana*," said the proprietress of that name, gliding forward with a heartfelt smile. Reaching Elizabeth, she wrapped her arms around her neck and pecked her cheek, as of old. And yet, the action was now performed with womanly tenderness rather than with childish exuberance.

"Yes, I suppose I do," Elizabeth managed, gently pulling away from the embrace. "I did not know that you had returned."

"We reached Netherfield late last night. I went to Meryton this morning to mail a letter, and on my way back I decided to stop by Longbourn to see you again, my dearest Lizzy!"

Elizabeth wondered whether Mr. Darcy would be displeased when he found out about the detour. Frankly, she could not fathom what the man meant by returning to the county and by bringing his sister with him, for it was obvious that he had already begun restoring Georgiana to her former status and ladylike demeanor. In lieu of Jane's hand-me-downs, a gown of the softest silk imaginable encased Miss Darcy's figure. An upswept hairstyle of the latest fashion had replaced the customary, quickly-done bun.

"You walked all the way from Meryton? Alone?"

The young woman regarded the speaker with a baffled gaze.

"Of course," she replied slowly, puzzled. "You yourself once said that the distance is nothing when one has a motive."

"I said many foolish things," Elizabeth murmured, wiping her brow and turning her attention back to the clothes. Shaking off her bewilderment at the previous dialogue, Georgiana stepped nearer to the bed and inquired,

"May I help you?"

"No. I am nearly finished. I was just going to put all of these things back in Jane's room, since I doubt that you will have any use of them henceforth."

The staccato in Elizabeth's tone again caused Georgiana to pause. She tentatively reached out and touched the older girl's elbow.

"Lizzy, are you upset with me?"

Miss Bennet shook her head quickly and attempted to make her next statement more amiable.

"No, I am not."

Miss Darcy, however, had already formed another conclusion. She caught Elizabeth's hand, and seating herself upon the bed, drew her friend down besides herself, exclaiming,

"Yes, you are, and for a very good reason. Here I am dawdling with embraces and pleasantries rather than immediately thanking you for everything you have done. My brother told me all as we travelled to London! Lizzy, I am perpetually in your debt. You saved me from a fate worse than death itself. Had it not been for your insight, your courage - I would be George Wickham's unhappy wife today! How little I suspected the true purpose of your sudden journey a few days before the wedding! I am sure that only concern for your reputation stopped Fitzwilliam from publishing the whole truth the night my memory returned, for the entire credit is your due."

Elizabeth rose and walked to the writing desk, which was stationed at the opposite end of the room, hoping to hide her discomfort. She noted that Georgiana had assumed, rather than had been informed of, the reasons for her brother's reticence, and Miss Bennet was certain that Miss Darcy was at least in part mistaken. In addition to being a gentleman, Mr. Darcy had probably abstained from mentioning their close cooperation because he did not wish to align himself with her in any respect. Thus, her back to Georgiana, Miss Bennet only remarked,

"Mr. Darcy is all discretion. I am much obliged to him, I am sure. And you need not thank me; I did only what any decent person would do."

"You are too modest, Lizzy!" Georgiana exclaimed. "You are the very best of friends! And as such, I have been thinking how jolly it would be if you were to come to Pemberley for two or three months next spring! I would ask you to come to us sooner, but this autumn you shall doubtlessly be busy helping Jane prepare for her wedding and settle into her new home, and travelling conditions during the winter are anything but ideal. But suppose you were to come to us next April? We would be able to spend Easter together, and watch all the different flowers which grow around Pemberley unfold their petals one-by-one. Oh, do say that you will come! I have been looking forward to your visit from the moment I conceived the notion."

The picture that her onetime roommate painted was extremely enticing. Miss Bennet, however, knew that this was a temptation which had to be resisted, and she set to opposing it.

"I thank you for the honor of your invitation," Elizabeth said. "But it is impossible for me to accept it."

Had she been looking at Miss Darcy's face, she would have seen it rapidly fall and then cloud over with confusion.

The perplexed question,

"Why, Lizzy?" was not long in coming.

Elizabeth gave the first reason which came into her head.

"Because I am needed at Longbourn."

"Is that all?!" Georgiana exclaimed, relieved, thinking that the frail excuse would be easily dissipated with a few persuasive sentences. "Of course you are needed at home, sweetest Lizzy; you always have and always will be necessary to Longbourn. But surely your family can spare you for a few weeks. They have before, you know. Everyone somehow managed when you were in Kent or visiting the Gardiners in London."

"It was different then. Kitty and Jane were not on the point of matrimony," Miss Bennet replied shortly.

"Have you not been listening at all, my dear? I am perfectly aware that it would be impossible for you to tear yourself away during this season of weddings! That is why I am trying to schedule your sojourn at Pemberley for *April*. God willing, all will be quiet at Longbourn then."

"Which is precisely why I must be here. Mama is incapable of sitting alone, and Papa, though he will never own it, shall be incredibly lonely with three daughters gone."

"Mr. Bennet will have Mary, and Lydia gets along beautifully with your mother." Seeing that Elizabeth was having none of it, Georgiana shifted tactics and added, "However, if you are concerned about abandoning them, let your parents and sisters, husbands and all, come too! You have seen Pemberley; it can hold twenty families with ease. And indeed, the rest of your family will be as welcome to me as yourself. Will that be suitable, Lizzy?"

Elizabeth had a brief vision of Mr. Darcy turning green upon hearing that his estate and privacy were to be invaded by a band of Bennets. Swallowing the knot lodged in her throat, the older girl retorted,

"No." Georgiana unclosed her lips again, but before a sound could proceed from them, Miss Bennet extinguished every hope by flatly declaring, "We cannot go to Pemberley in April or anytime in the foreseeable future."

Miss Darcy had reached her wits' end. She did not understand Elizabeth, but could see plainly that her friend's reasoning was operating on some information which she was unwilling to share. Though stung by the rejection of the invitation and even more so by the curt tone in which it was refused, she could do nothing but nod and hold her peace.

Averse to dwelling any longer on the topic, Elizabeth pulled open the top drawer of the desk before her and drew out a stack of papers. Trying to free herself from the fair maiden's company, she hastily continued,

"Here are the sketches you made while you lived with us. Would you care to have any of them?"

Georgiana rose and approached Elizabeth, saying,

"There are a few which I should like to keep, and many others which are promised to your father and sisters. I suppose I should go through and organize them accordingly."

"Yes, indeed you should," Elizabeth replied, hoping to separate herself from the girl before tears began to stream down her cheeks. "Let us go downstairs; there is very little room for the endeavor here." As they exited the bedchamber and proceeded down the staircase, she turned her pale countenance away from her companion.

How pathetically hysterical I am becoming! I am incapable of receiving and refusing a mere invitation without wishing to cry, I, who scarcely shed tears once a year, if that! Oh, if only I had never laid eyes on Fitzwilliam Darcy...and remained content with the prospect of being an old maid, destined for nothing more than visiting friends and making pretty things for my sisters' children!

They reached the drawing room. Walking over to the table in its center, Elizabeth put down the pile she had been toting.

"This is a good place to spread out the drawings and look them over in peace. I will leave you to it."

"I expected that you would help me," Georgiana replied, surprised.

Having foreseen this remark, Miss Bennet had a repartee ready.

"'Tis a task best accomplished alone, and anyhow, I have a letter which I must write," said she, going to the door.

Georgiana, most unwillingly, was forced to yield once again and murmur a temporary adieu.

Chapter 63

Elizabeth slipped into Longbourn's small library, and continued to rein in the desire to shed copious tears. Georgiana could follow her at any moment, and it would not do to alarm the girl with an outburst of emotion.

How I would love to go to Pemberley! Miss Bennet thought. *To spend a spring with Georgiana and Mr. Darcy, to run about those beautiful grounds and groves, to have a few more tête-à-têtes with the kindhearted Mrs. Reynolds and perhaps tease out a few more stories about Mr. Darcy's childhood from her…it would be marvelous! But how can I accept Miss Darcy's generous offer when the master of the estate despises me?* Despite her best efforts, a small sob escaped Elizabeth's trembling lips.

Remembering that she had to answer a letter from Mrs. Gardiner, she half-heartedly retrieved a sheet of paper and, sinking down into the chair behind her father's desk, opened Mr. Bennet's favorite inkwell. Then the young lady languidly penned a few lines of greeting.

While thus engaged, she heard the doorbell, but was far too melancholy to investigate whom it heralded. Mrs. Hill's brisk footsteps sounded in the hall, and were soon followed by the creak of the front door and the hum of indistinguishable voices. Elizabeth expected that the caller would be shown into the drawing room. There, they would encounter Miss Darcy, who, during her last few weeks as Miss Edwards had proved adept at entertaining Longbourn's guests; Elizabeth could tarry a little before making an appearance. Thus, Miss Bennet remained seated and continued dragging the pen across the paper.

Unexpectedly, there was a knock on the library door. Assuming it to be Mrs. Hill, Elizabeth called out,

"Enter."

The door opened, and no servant, but Mr. Darcy appeared.

Instantly, all breath was squeezed out of her lungs and the pen dropped out of her hand.

"Good day, Miss Bennet," the visitor said, with a slight bow.

"Sir," was all the lady managed. She remained seated, partially because she felt that assuming a more upright position would cause her to become faint, and partially because she thought that he would be gone from her presence so soon that it would be overmuch to undertake the formality of curtsying. Inhaling air and strength, Elizabeth regained some presence of mind and added, "I am afraid that someone steered you wrong. Your sister is in the drawing room."

Mr. Darcy's face showed the utmost stupefaction.

"Georgiana is here?" he exclaimed.

"Yes," Elizabeth returned. What was he at Longbourn for, if not to rescue Georgiana from the clutches of the ignominious Bennets?

"I had not the slightest idea. I thought she was at Meryton," Mr. Darcy replied. Elizabeth remained silent, waiting for him to back out of the door and go directly to the drawing room. Instead, he remained standing in the threshold, his hand resting upon the knob, surveying herself. "I came here with the purpose of calling on you," he said at length.

What could a young woman do now, but gesture to a chair on the opposite side of the library?

He let the door swing almost closed behind him, leaving a mere inch between it and the frame. Walking over to the seat which had been indicated, he took it and looked over at Elizabeth anew. At that moment, she realized exactly how far she had banished him; there were at least twenty feet between the two of them. Although she knew that moving nearer to him would only increase her anguish, holding any sort of conversation across the span of the room without raising one's voice was impossible. Therefore, she hesitantly relocated herself to a chair only five feet from his.

Watching intently as she made the transition, Darcy was struck with the idea that she seemed paler and thinner than she had been a fortnight ago. It was this observation which prompted him to inquire,

"Are you in health, Miss Bennet?"

"Perfectly so, I thank you," was the response. Thinking that it was her turn to offer a pleasantry, the lady dutifully remarked, "I trust that your journey to London was a good one?"

"It was. Georgiana spoke about you and your family incessantly." Becoming more serious, he continued, "Which brings me to the point of my visit. One evening, as we sat near our fire, she suggested that we invite you to Pemberley next spring."

So here it is. This is why he has dashed over to Longbourn so quickly - to give me a hint that Georgiana's fantasies of retaining me

345

as a friend are impossible, and that my declination of the invitation would be extremely appreciated.

"She also proposed the same to me," Elizabeth replied softly.

"Indeed, already?" the gentleman exclaimed, still stunned at how confident and sociable his dear little Georgiana had become.

"Just now, when we were upstairs. She said that she would be very happy to have me at Pemberley in April."

"And what was your answer?" Darcy asked with bated breath. This was a pivotal moment; in a matter of seconds, he would know whether Elizabeth Bennet would be willing to enter his house for pleasure rather than for duty. An acceptance of the invitation would mean that she had no objection to seeing him every day for a few weeks at least, while a rejection would indicate that her dislike was still so strongly rooted that even the temptation of Georgiana's company was insufficient to lure her under his roof. A silent prayer that the former might not be the case burst forth from his heart as he met her gaze.

Elizabeth saw the anxiety which crossed his face, and thought that she knew what it meant. Therefore, she forced herself to offer what she hoped would masquerade as an understanding and indifferent smile.

"You need not fret, Mr. Darcy," she said, endeavoring to keep her tone free from bitterness or, even worse, sadness. "I anticipated your feelings on the subject, and made it clear to your sister that she need not expect me at Pemberley next April, or any other time."

The gentleman drew back, pained and confused by her words.

She anticipated my feelings, and has refused Georgiana's offer as a result? Has she seen that my affection is as fervent as ever, and fears that I will pursue her during the proposed stay at Pemberley, much to her disgust?

Just as he was debating the merits and pitfalls of asking the lady to elaborate, she, desperate to redeem herself just a little, saved him the trouble.

"And since we have opened the topic, Mr. Darcy, I may as well take the opportunity to assure you that I am aware of the laws governing propriety, even if my family and I do not always follow them. I perfectly comprehend that with the return of her memory, your sister has been restored to a much different position in society. I do not mean to intrude upon her new – or rather old - realm in any way. Even though we were good friends while she was Anne

Edwards, that time is bygone, and I have no intention of degrading Miss Darcy by clinging to an intimate acquaintance. Your sister adores you, sir, and I am certain that if you plainly explain the case she will readily agree and cease issuing ill-advised invitations to Pemberley. By the by, I would like to apologize for the extra trouble I caused you by instructing her in impertinence. There is no excuse for my indiscretion, except for the fact that I never dreamt Anne Edwards to be so well-connected, and little thought that my teachings were encroaching upon manners which are highly prized by the *ton*."

There, she had said it. She had cut herself off from him and Georgiana forever. Even in the midst of the stabbing pain, however, a bitter pride crept into Elizabeth's heart for the strength which she had just demonstrated: she had put him and his interests above hers.

"Miss Bennet," Mr. Darcy replied slowly and sincerely, "why should I fault Georgiana for being nimble and useful and confident, or criticize anyone who made her so?"

Elizabeth openly gaped at him before exclaiming,

"Sir, you cannot seriously approve of such performances as the ones you witnessed!"

Darcy answered with a questioning look.

"I noticed no great gaffes. Pray, what exact instances are we talking of?"

Elizabeth briefly closed her eyes and exhaled. Was the man playing doltish in order to force her to name her sins, as some form of exquisite chastisement?

"I know, for instance, that you saw Anne climbing that tree the day of Jane's betrothal. I also know that you noticed the impropriety of her speaking to my father about Mary as she did. If you are being sardonic to punish me for teaching your sister such behavior, I beg you, pardon me."

"Punish you! I should not dream of doing anything of the sort. I was in earnest, Miss Bennet, when I said that you had made Georgiana nimble and confident. I admit to being surprised by Georgiana's prowess when she was climbing, yes, and perhaps a little concerned for her safety. Altogether, however, I do not think it so awful for her to engage in a little bit of spirited exercise once in a while. Actually, it pleases me. Georgiana was always far too sedate for her age. Had our mother lived, she would have instilled in her some youthful joy, but as it was, she grew up in a very somber, sorrowing house. Our father could rarely be prevailed upon to smile

347

after Lady Anne left this earth, and his daughter was wise enough to know that his broken heart preferred silence to childish laughter. Thus, she grew up shy and quiet, and in retrospect I am sure my own reserved character did not help the matter greatly. I am glad that she has discovered a more lighthearted, genuine world than that of the hypocritical *ton.*" He took a breath. "As for the way she addressed Mr. Bennet: yes, there was a component of impropriety in that. But she is still young, still learning, and anyone could see that what occurred was a slip of the tongue rather than the fruit of a perfidious nature. On the whole, I was far more impressed by the insightfulness of her comment than by its inappropriateness."

Elizabeth let out the breath she had been holding, and looked away, her countenance flushed with a mixture of relief and embarrassment. She knew not what to make of this extraordinary turn of events. Desperate for a diversion, she abruptly rose and went to stand by her father's desk. Unable to face him, she remained turned around and spoke while fingering the polished wood surface.

"I must say that I find your opinion on this issue very soothing, sir. I was certain that I was in for quite a reprisal! Not only have I displayed my own wanting manners to you on several occasions, I had now begun to corrupt your sister!"

"You have never been anything less than ladylike, Miss Bennet."

"Mr. Darcy, I did not think that you had so short a memory! What would you call my appearance at Netherfield last autumn?"

"Your motive for coming there was compassionate and sisterly, and therefore, most genteel. I far preferred your boots six inches deep in mud and your eyes brightened by exercise to all of Miss Bingley's posturing and pristine lace."

Elizabeth was much too abashed to say another word. She fell silent, and fiddled with the silver inkstand for all she was worth. Mr. Darcy took a look at her profile, most of which was hidden from him, but saw enough of it to know that she was flustered. Although remorseful for causing her distress of any sort, he felt gratified that his simple compliment had such an impact on her. Why was she so affected by a miniscule accolade? Could she possibly care for his good opinion?

He had not come for this. He had come only for a few minutes of her company, happy that he had a reason to call upon her. He had planned to offer nothing except a short sojourn at Pemberley. But

348

plans change as circumstances change, and as a hope which he had never known before began to beat in Fitzwilliam Darcy's heart, he made a desperate resolution.

He stood. With a measured tread he crossed the study and came to stand next to her.

"Miss Bennet," he said in a soft, tender tone to the woman who looked up, surprised, at being joined thus, "you are too generous to trifle with me. If your feelings are still what they were last April, tell me so at once."

Elizabeth absolutely started as she realized what he was saying. Undeterred, Darcy continued,

"*My* affections and wishes have only deepened. Your journey into Derbyshire to save Georgiana from a potentially loveless marriage redoubled my admiration for your care of those you love. Your tact and courage during the entire ordeal, during which you risked your own reputation a number of times, heightened my esteem. Being in the sunshine of your lively presence brought back into my life a happiness which I never thought that I would feel again. Thus, I am pleading with you to accept my hand and heart, and to return to Pemberley, not as Georgiana's guest, but as my wife." He paused for an instant, and then added, "But, one word from you will silence me on this subject forever. Your friendship with Georgiana is very precious, and I would never wish to make your interactions awkward by continuously forcing upon you unwanted sentiments."

Elizabeth could not speak. She wished to, but too many emotions welled up in her heart. Happiness closed her throat. Feeling, however, the great anxiety of his situation and being averse to prolonging his agony, she turned fully towards him. Noticing that the hand he had offered was slightly outstretched towards her, as if in supplication, the young woman took a small step forward, lifted her own soft hand and placed it in his. The spring of hope in his heart instantly overflowed at this simple gesture and reached the pupils which were looking at her.

Finally, Elizabeth's tongue was loosened, and she replied,

"During the period to which you allude, my feelings have undergone a great change. Today, I hear and accept your assurances with gratitude, pleasure, and a reciprocal affection whose strength, I believe, rivals that of your love for me!"

Within seconds, Elizabeth learned how well the expression of heartfelt delight became Fitzwilliam Darcy's face, and how much pleasure it brought her to hear him exclaim,

"Dearest, loveliest Elizabeth!" as he now did. "*My* beautiful Elizabeth!"

The smile which she bestowed on him was one that she had never given to any human being before. Its expressiveness and charm took his breath away.

Exerting a slight pull on the fingers which were laced with his own, Mr. Darcy drew Elizabeth into his tender embrace and buried his countenance in her chestnut locks. Trusting him implicitly, Elizabeth leaned her cheek upon his coat. How wonderful it was, to feel surrounded and protected by the arms of him whom she loved!

She presently heard his voice again, but this time, he was not directly addressing her.

"Thou are great, O Lord…" he was quietly quoting, "for thou scourgest, and thou savest; thou leadest down to hell, and bringest up again."

A tear escaped Elizabeth's eye and soaked into Mr. Darcy's coat. Her lips trembled. How much he had suffered! How little she had thought of him during those days when he was experiencing torment!

After he fell silent, she quietly lifted her head and looked at him. She meant to say something comforting, but found that he was already smiling again. Brushing back a curl which had escaped from her coiffure, Darcy murmured to his betrothed,

"You are the greatest gift that I have ever been given."

She articulated eight sweet syllables in response:

"As you are to me, Fitzwilliam."

At hearing his name, Mr. Darcy's head began to bend toward hers. Instinctively, her lashes drooped and her eyes closed. Before Elizabeth knew it, her lips were experiencing their first kiss.

Chapter 64

At length they pulled apart. Heads spinning, eyes shining, they felt as if they had sprouted wings and could fly if they so desired. The four walls of Mr. Bennet's study seemed too small to encompass their beating hearts, and conscious that they had many things to discuss, they made their escape through a small side door.

Walking hand-in-hand through the fields, they looked at the scenery, then back at each other, and smiled. The wind swept their garments and hair. The sun, too, shone full upon them, for they had left the house without hats. It mattered not, however. They were together, they loved each other, and if they became tanned because of their excursion, neither would think any less of the other.

"Elizabeth," Mr. Darcy said, caressing every letter of the beloved name, "I can scarcely believe that we are engaged. That you should love me, and wish to marry me, all seems like a happy dream. Ever since last autumn, you are the first person I think of when I rise in the morning, and the face which I envision when lying down to my repose is yours. Every room which you set foot in straightaway becomes palatial to me. I have treasured every moment I ever spent in your company."

Although she was beyond flattered that she was of such importance to him, the witty young woman was unable to let this remark pass by without comment.

"*Every* moment, Fitzwilliam?" Elizabeth asked with a raised eyebrow. "Do you truly treasure a certain quarter-hour which we spent together in the Hunsford Parsonage? I do not even wish to think of what I then said."

"Yes, darling, I will be forever grateful for that evening. What did you say of me that I did not deserve? My behavior to you at the time was unpardonable, I can hardly think of it without abhorrence. Your reproof I shall never forget: 'had you behaved in a more gentlemanlike manner'. You cannot conceive how those words have tortured me. I treated you like an object which could be purchased by my consequence. Had you accepted me then, our story would have been much simpler and our lives more miserable. You would have been bound to a man who disrespected you and yours, and I would have been a proud, disagreeable personage until I was eight and ninety. Already I have begun to look upon even the anxieties of the last several days with gladness. It will serve us both well if I continue to remember how much it took to win you."

"I was unaware," Elizabeth said, "that I had alarmed you of late. What exactly is your meaning?"

"I refer to your reticence over the past several days, my dear. I had not the slightest idea that you were uneasy over Georgiana's new nature, and thought that the change in yourself stemmed from a rekindled dislike of me."

"What reason could I have for detesting you now, Fitzwilliam?"

"In my frenzy I thought of several. Noting that you became withdrawn almost directly after Jane's betrothal, I thought it very possible that looking upon your sister's happiness reminded you of what my meddling had cost her for the better part of a year. I also wondered whether, upon deeper reflection, my stopping your conversation with Joe Harper and speaking to him myself had come off as very high-handed. I imagined you rereading the letter which I had put into your hands in Kent, and in anguish remembered some passages in it which could justly make you hate me. If I had been certain of the origin of your strange behavior I would have come and pleaded for pardon, but as it was, I feared making the situation worse by guessing incorrectly and appearing obtuse. All I knew was that one day we were making easy conversation and understanding each other perfectly, and the next you shunned my company as much as possible, avoided my gaze at all costs, and barely spoke. I will never forget what I felt the night Georgiana recovered her memory. When we went out and the carriage began to move, I became aware that I felt like an extremely ungrateful wretch. For how could I feel anything but the purest joy at the state of affairs? My supplications had been answered: Georgiana sat next to me, clinging to my hand, fully aware of who I was. We were in a comfortable carriage, both healthy and whole. And yet, every time I thought of you, Elizabeth," he looked at his love, "I was dissatisfied. After all the mutual prayers we had poured out, after all we had done to bring about this wonderful end, I expected something more from you at parting. A significant look, a warm handshake, a smile. Instead, I received only a nod, a curt 'Sir', and even Georgiana got nothing more than a half-hearted embrace. As I looked back at the lights of Longbourn, a dreadful chill crept into my spirit. I feared that your changed demeanor meant that you considered your duty done, and were washing your hands of both of us forevermore."

"That I was, but never dreamt that it would be taken in such a way. I thought you would be glad to be rid of me. How could one think otherwise when you called our interactions burdensome, insisted upon speaking to my father instead, and refused to let Georgiana talk to me five minutes after she remembered her identity? She was coming over to me, but you stopped her and redirected her to my parents instead."

"Gracious, Elizabeth! Forgive me – I never dreamed that those actions would be interpreted thus. My object then was to protect you, for Georgiana would have made you the center of attention as she laughed and cried and attempted to explain to you the revelation which had taken place in her heart. You would have been forced to feign surprise and disbelief, and I wished to spare you that, especially as I noticed that you seemed particularly tired and detached that day. As for calling our conversations burdensome, I only meant that if we were ever discovered conversing in secret it would cause a great deal of embarrassment and trouble and possibly harm your reputation. There was no hidden meaning in that communication whatsoever."

Overcome again, Elizabeth humbly admitted,

"It appears that my old habit of misjudging you remains. I trust that you will forgive me." Mr. Darcy warmly assured her that there was not the slightest reason for an apology. "But why were you so quiet after Anne released the kite from the branches and after her remarks to Papa?"

"Partly because you were grave and silent, and gave me no encouragement, and partly because I *was* stunned, although not displeased. Seeing Georgiana, who used to find giving orders to Pemberley's servants extremely effortful, engaging comfortably with her elders and in lighthearted pursuits dumbfounded me. I realized that I was no longer fully acquainted with my sister, and wishing to know more of her, began to study her actions and conversations. I know that some men are capable of learning amidst chatter, but I have always found that I am a better student when I attend silently."

"How unlucky that you should have a reasonable answer to give, and that I should be so reasonable as to admit it! There are few things, I believe, which cause as much misunderstanding and trouble as two unacknowledged lovers left to their imaginations! If it had not distressed you so, I could laugh at the supposition that I would fault

353

you for your intrusion between Mr. Bingley and Jane anew after seeing everything most happily resolved at last. Tell me, were you surprised by the engagement?"

"Not at all. When I left them to walk into the wood, I felt that it would soon happen."

"That is to say, you had given your permission. I guessed as much, when I saw how you nodded at him that day in the meadow just before he proposed."

"Given my permission!"

"Your approbation, then. Seeing you fix what you had broken only endeared you in my esteem, rather than working to your disadvantage as you supposed."

Mr. Darcy laughed and shook his head.

"I wish I could deny it, but then I would be denying the truth. Charles kept pestering me for my opinion on the matter even after I confessed my fault in separating him from your sister last November and then concealing the fact that she was in Town for the winter. He even wanted to know the most appropriate time and place for the proposal, and stared at me during the picnic until I gave him some indication. I finally gave in and recommended issuing advice, even though I scarcely felt comfortable about it. I feared that I should steer him wrong again."

"Even if you had, it would certainly not be the result of malicious intent. I confess that I once blamed you for what I saw as your interference into Mr. Bingley's life, but upon closer inspection I found that the fault, if any, was his rather than yours. He happens to be one of those men who trusts others more than his own judgment. If he is unable to make decisions on his own, it is far better for him to listen to you rather than to fall into the clutches of a man like Wickham."

Despite nodding at most of his fiancée's words, Mr. Darcy proved himself a loyal friend by readily clarifying,

"Bingley, however, does have most of his wits about him. He did not blindly fix upon me as a guide. Seeing that I had several more years' experience at managing landholdings than himself and was prospering, he thought that I would be a worthy professor as he strove to establish himself. Unfortunately, his great personal modesty and our close friendship led him to rely on me overmuch, even in sectors that had nothing to do with business."

"Does he know of your secret estates, or is he enamored with your advice simply because of the stature of Pemberley alone?"

"The latter. If Bingley knew that my income was forty thousand a year, I doubt that he would choose a coat in the mornings without consulting me."

Most women would have exclaimed at the sum which Mr. Darcy had dropped, but to the woman who loved him, it only became the subject of a lighthearted repartee.

"Whatever shall I learn about you next, Fitzwilliam? You hide thirty thousand pounds of your income and forgo further advancement in society, you slip rubies into the locks of unsuspecting maidens, and you duel without hurting your opponent, even if he be George Wickham himself!"

At this, Darcy turned upon her, astonished.

"How did you know that Wickham and I dueled?" the bewildered man inquired. "Did Bingley or Richard enlighten you as to the particulars of that night? I am certain that *I* never told you anything beyond the fact that we had forced him out of the country and sent him to America!"

Elizabeth colored prettily, and informed him,

"You need not blame them, for neither told me anything. I could not bear waiting at home, not knowing…I followed Wickham after about a twenty minute delay, and came upon the battle. I was behind a boulder for the latter half of it."

Her fiancé convulsively grasped both her hands, and drew her nearer to himself protectively, horrified.

"Elizabeth! How could you do such a thing? I had not the least idea that you were there - when I knocked the sword out of his hand, I could have just as easily sent it in your direction as another! Or, if we had been fighting with pistols instead of swords, a stray bullet - ," he could not finish. Clutching his beloved, Darcy trembled slightly and attempted to clear the lump which was barricading his throat. Hoping to comfort him and turn his mind into a different channel, Elizabeth reached up and gently cupped his face with her palm.

"But nothing of the sort happened; I am well, and Wickham has long been vanquished. Tell me, how did you begin fighting in the first place? With my own ears I heard you choosing the field as the point of confrontation, but hoped that a duel would somehow be avoided."

Taking a deep breath and loosening his hold somewhat, Darcy admitted,

"My primary objective in selecting the field was to make it difficult for the blackguard to slip away. After all the trouble we went through, the last thing I wanted was to have to pursue him through a field of corn or amidst trees. I hoped I would not have to physically battle him. But when we confronted him, he at first tried to deny knowing anything of Georgiana. Unable to convince us, he eventually tried to appeal to my sense of fairness by saying how wrong it was to startle a man in the middle of the night, on his innocent walk home, and offer him the choice of deportation or debtor's prison without any alternative ways to redeem himself. By that point, my patience was gone. Without further ado, I gave him another choice: pistols or swords. He paled at that. He seemed to think that I would retract the offer, but when I pressed for an answer, he was unfashionable for once in his life and picked swords over pistols. Why? I know not, but I suspect that he thought that I would be more incapable of injuring him from close by than from a distance."

"It is difficult to express how much I admired you at that moment, Fitzwilliam. The Colonel was acting exactly how a man in your situation would be expected to act, but your conduct was in stark contrast with his. I knew that you were as angry as your cousin, and on the matter of honor you had an even greater right to demand Wickham's life, being the nearer relation. And yet, your restraint during the duel and afterwards was impressive. Your parting words to him were charity itself."

"He is not completely bad. His companionship during my boyhood saved me from being very lonely, since Pemberley is far from other estates and my father would have never condoned my associating with the sons of the shopkeepers in Lambton. In those days, Wickham did have a rebellious streak, but overall was a decent child. His mother's extravagance, unfortunately, taught him to want for comforts beyond his means, and he made several poor choices of friends which drew him from the path of righteousness which his father walked.'

"Still, you are very kind to think so. Others would have considered his transgressions enough to merit the most gruesome death."

"How could I condemn another man to death, being far from perfect myself? It is not as if I have never made a mistake myself, as you well know."

She expressed her conviction of his goodness again, mentioning that she had seen it on full display during his conversation with Joe Harper, but Mr. Wickham was too painful a topic to be dwelt on further. After a few more minutes of walking, the gentleman spoke again.

"Returning to the ruby pin which you mentioned, I may safely assure you that you are the only young woman to whom I have ever given a piece of jewelry in such a manner. That adornment, too, caused me some distress, for I noted that you never donned it of your own accord. I am exceedingly sorry," Mr. Darcy said, "that my chosen method of gifting it caused so much embarrassment that you were never able to wear it again."

Elizabeth's fingers dove into her pocket, and brought out the object which they were discussing. Holding it up to capture the sun's rays, she explained,

"Lydia's lack of tact was not what kept me from using this beautiful hairpin. My own indecision regarding my feelings, and yours, was what kept it hidden."

"Do you feel that you would be able to wear it now, then?"

Elizabeth felt the moment was right to be flirtatious. Turning to him, she said with a slight flutter of her long lashes,

"My only present regret is that I missed the instant which saw it placed in my tresses. The memory would have been cherished."

The invitation was accepted. Fitzwilliam Darcy took the ruby pin from her fingers and threaded it into the locks which he loved. Then he kissed the silky brown curls for good measure.

357

Chapter 65

Eventually they fell to studying their watches, and realized that they had been out for over two hours. Although loathe to abandon their solitude, they knew that Georgiana and the servants would miss Elizabeth and worry about her inexplicable disappearance. Thus, they decided to direct their steps once more towards Longbourn.

While walking arm-in-arm, it was resolved that Mr. Bennet's consent should be asked that very evening. Soon afterwards, they were within sight of the house. Suddenly, the future Mrs. Darcy exclaimed,

"Fitzwilliam, I must say that I am disappointed in you!"

The muscles in her intended's arm instantly tensed. After Hunsford, he had determined never, ever to disappoint Elizabeth again, and now, two hours into their engagement, he had already failed her in some way. Worst of all, he was at a complete loss as to what had her offended, and was forced to say in a panicked tone,

"Forgive me for my shortcoming. What have I done?"

"After visiting Pemberley, I did believe that you had an elegant and agreeable taste in commodities. But apparently, sometimes even your judgment can err. Tell me, what possessed you to purchase that ostentatious carriage?" his fiancée concluded with a laugh, waving her free hand towards the drive.

Darcy's eyes followed her gesture, and noted the ridiculous conveyance stationed outside Longbourn's front door. The wheels of the coach were so high that they rendered it unsteady even on the best roads, and the bright paintings on its doors, which had probably been intended as decorations, were nothing more than eyesores. Relaxing, the gentleman rebutted,

"That hideous thing is not mine. I rode to Longbourn on horseback this morning."

"Now that I attend more closely, that is not your livery," his fiancée agreed apologetically. "But I could have sworn that I recognized the uniforms."

Darcy took another look at the coach and started.

"You do well to find them familiar," he said in a low, bewildered tone, "for that is Rosings' livery!"

"Rosings?" Elizabeth questioned, likewise staring at the monstrosity parked on her father's drive. "What could servants from your Aunt Catherine's estate be doing at Longbourn?"

"I know not, but I certainly intend to investigate the matter at once!" Darcy replied, hastening their pace. The beautiful woman at his side immediately matched his steps, and the two lovers dashed through the side door from which they had proceeded, into Mr. Bennet's study, and into Longbourn's front hall. Once there, their ultimate destination was decided by the sound of a furious, harsh voice emanating from the drawing room. Without hesitation, the couple hurried to it. The young man took hold of the doorknob, and, turning it quietly, swung the door wide open.

Neither of the room's two occupants noted the noiseless action. One of them was middle-aged, arrayed in gaudy travelling clothes, and wearing a most displeased expression. The other was Georgiana.

"How could you forget your name, your lineage, and your duties?" the older woman was inquiring incredulously. "I would never forget that I am a de Bourgh, or what my title signifies!"

Remaining the picture of patience and serenity, Georgiana took up a drawing from the table which separated her from the irate visitor, glanced over it, and replied coolly,

"If such be the case, you are indeed fortunate, Your Ladyship. I was under the apparently mistaken impression that all mortal beings were susceptible to incurring some damage to their memory or other faculties, particularly if they hit their head with great force."

"Humph! And speaking of which, what possessed you to fall head-first out of that carriage? I thought you had more sense, Georgiana!"

Miss Darcy put down the portrait she had been perusing into one of the neat piles which were forming on the edge of the table, and picked up another.

"It was not my first choice, Aunt. I am afraid that I was not particularly nimble due to the speed of the coach and the rough, muddy road." But the light note of sarcasm in her answer was lost upon Lady Catherine.

"Well, the next time you jump out of an out-of-control conveyance, make sure that you land upright, child! That way, you will not injure your head."

"I will do my best to follow your wise counsel, madam," Georgiana replied civility, despite clearly repressing laughter.

Witnessing this contentious scene from the doorway, Darcy's first instinct had been to promptly stalk into the room, station himself in front of his sister, and personally answer Lady Catherine's ludicrous accusations. But seeing that Georgiana was holding her own admirably and in no way in need of his protection, he remained at Elizabeth's side, and began to enjoy watching his sister expertly parry the attacks with wit.

The old woman looked about the chamber, and sneered,

"So this is the hut where you spent all those months! Just look at this room - the windows face full west. It must be a most inconvenient sitting room for an evening in the summer!"

"It cannot be denied that they are so, Your Ladyship, but I can safely assure you that the Bennets never sit here after dinner on such days."

"The Bennets! That is another matter which must be discussed. How dare they keep you here all that time, and force you into a sphere so decidedly beneath your birthright? I - ,"

Lady Catherine got no further. She was interrupted, for once in her life, by an angry feminine voice,

"Madam, that will do!"

Glancing up, startled, Catherine de Bourgh found that her niece, who until then had borne the interrogation with exquisite composure, had precipitously dropped the pile of paper she held, and was staring back at her, fire in her eyes. When Miss Darcy spoke, every syllable was fraught with deliberation.

"You may say anything you like about *me*, Your Ladyship, and I will bear it in a spirit of kinship and charity. However, I warn you that I will not tolerate any slanders directed at the Bennets. They preserved my life, and thus I, and anyone who claims to care for me, owes them a debt of gratitude which can never be repaid!"

"Gratitude! For what, pray? For concealing your whereabouts from your nearest relations? Or perhaps they should be praised for nearly wedding you to the son of your own father's steward?!"

With swift steps, Miss Darcy walked around the table which separated her from the visitor, and stationed herself fearlessly in front of it.

"There was no concealment. As soon as my identity was suspected, my brother was informed. As for the marriage, my engagement to Mr. Wickham was my own choice. I was the one who accepted his proposals. Mr. Bennet refused to grant formal consent, so cognizant was he of the fact that he held no authority over me. The family merely supported what I had already decided."

"Stop defending them, young lady! I am sure there was some great neglect on their part, for you are not the sort of girl to do such a thing, had you been properly looked after."

"Your Ladyship speaks as if the Bennets had turned a blind eye to an elopement or abetted some other scandalous action. They did nothing but accept a match which, at the time, seemed more than good enough for me, and which I yearned for." Georgiana's tone was becoming shorter and shorter, and her chin widened its angle with her neck.

Unabashed, the older woman continued in a most aristocratic voice,

"I do not believe that they could possibly be in ignorance of your position in life all this time. Mr. Bennet probably knew who you were the moment he laid eyes on you, for who would care to pick up an injured young lady lying on the roadside without some ulterior motive? Depend upon it, they kept you here and had that infamous scoundrel court you for their own amusement! I met Miss Elizabeth Bennet last spring, and I know well what sort of conceited, impertinent, disrespectful gal she is. Why, she would not even give me a straightforward answer when I asked her about her age! And with all five daughters out at once – they are no respectable family, the Bennets!"

This time, Georgiana's response was somewhat delayed. Before speaking, the generally amiable maiden was forced to take several deep breaths in order to regain equanimity. When she felt that she had achieved the appearance of composure, she broke the gaze between herself and her aunt. Moving swiftly to her original position behind the table, she commenced gathering up the artwork with an absorbed air which suggested the occupation to be far superior to further conversation with the noblewoman before her. Thus occupied, she spared the visitor these words:

"Your Ladyship is clearly not inclined to be reasonable, and therefore I see no sense in continuing to grant you a listener for your false and abominable accusations, or in attempting to dissuade you from issuing them. As such is the case, I do believe that it would be best if Your Ladyship were to depart from Longbourn at once. Mr.

Bennet is generally the essence of benevolence, but I am certain that he will not take kindly to finding an uninvited caller criticizing his goodness and his daughter. You had much better leave."

Lady Catherine gasped in disbelief at the resolute woman.

"How dare you speak to me thus, niece? Have you forgotten who I am? I shall certainly not go away until you have given me an assurance that you will have nothing more to do with this conniving family!"

"And I shall certainly never give it!" Georgiana returned forcefully. "I am not to be intimidated into something so wholly unreasonable. The Bennets are my adopted family, and they are some of the kindest and most generous souls in England. As long as I live, I will continue to visit and maintain an active correspondence with them. They will always number among my dearest friends, no matter what the world says about it."

"This. Is. Not. To. Be. Borne!" Lady Catherine bellowed, stalking wildly to the fireplace. Reaching it, she completed a rotation on her heel and came back towards her niece in a like manner. "It shall *not* be borne! You may choose to defy *me*, but upon my life, Darcy will set you straight! Where is your brother?!"

Georgiana was about to declare her honest ignorance of his exact whereabouts when the cold retort of,

"Right in the threshold," came.

Both women turned towards the doorway to find Elizabeth and Darcy standing in it.

Upon realizing that it was her sibling who had spoken, Georgiana turned slightly pale, wondering what he would think of her passionate defense. Nonetheless, she put her face up resolutely, clearly determined to hold fast to her points even if it meant a quieter disagreement with him.

Lady Catherine met their unexpected entrance with much more eagerness than her niece. Taking a step towards her nephew, she was about to open her lips when she half-noticed the proximity of his shoulder to Elizabeth's and the easy, familiar air between them. Something about the two of them struck her as odd, but still bent on punishing Georgiana for her defiance, Catherine de Bourgh pushed the very vague thoughts to the back of her mind as she made to speak.

Before her lips could utter any more vulgarities about the woman he loved or her family, however, Mr. Darcy flatly asked,

"I take it that you want my opinion on my sister's words?"

"Yes, I do! Tell her -,"

"Then you shall have it," Mr. Darcy interrupted. "I second everything your niece just said." Lady Catherine's face elongated itself to an extraordinary degree as she grasped his meaning. "I particularly recommend that you follow her suggestion of departing Longbourn at once. We have been having a wonderful visit with our good friends, the Bennets, and do not wish that the day be spoiled by foul humor and undeserved insults." Leading Elizabeth into the room, he vacated the threshold, leaving open a wide path for Her Ladyship's egress. Mr. Darcy held open the door for his elder, and concluded his remarks with a decisive, "Good day, Your Ladyship."

Lady Catherine paled, then flushed with anger, then blushed again, but was unable to recover the use of her tongue. The best she could do was to slam her shoes and cane on the floor with every stalking step towards the door, give her niece and nephew a poisonous glare apiece as she passed them, and point her nose perpendicular to the ceiling as she walked past the only Bennet in the room. The next moments heard her walking out of the front door and getting into her carriage. As the sounds of hoofbeats and moving wheels reached those remaining behind in the drawing room, a collective sigh of relief was heaved.

Georgiana was the first to break the silence with words. Looking apologetically at her best friend, she said,

"Lizzy, I can never tell you how sorry I am that you heard those hurtful things our unreasonable aunt said. She heard of last week's events through the Lucas's letters to Charlotte Collins, and rushed here to proclaim her unsolicited opinions as is her wont. She is the only one of our family, I assure you, who holds such notions regarding your family's hospitality to me." Glancing at her brother, the maiden concluded, "I daresay, Fitzwilliam, that your willingness to bear me out means that you are not too upset with my manner of speaking to our aunt. But if you feel that I went too far, I do apologize for grieving you."

"Not at all." He turned to Elizabeth. "This is a perfect example of what you have done for Georgiana. In times past, she would have cowered before Lady Catherine's forceful demands and given any promise exacted by her, even if it broke her own heart or offended her own sense of justice. I much prefer this spirited young lady to the quivering reed in the wind which she used to be."

Relief and pride swept into the faces of both ladies. In a much lighter tone, Georgiana remarked,

"Unfortunately, the student has not yet equaled the instructor, for Elizabeth still carries her point in almost all of our debates, even the ones which I would dearly love to win." Giving her brother a desperate look, she begged, "Speak to her, Fitzwilliam, and tell her how we were looking forward to having her at Pemberley next spring. She will not listen to me. Maybe your invitations will turn out more happily than mine did."

A slow, sly smile spread itself over Mr. Darcy's countenance, and he looked at the beautiful, dark-haired woman standing at his side as he spoke.

"What do you take me for, sister? We have already discussed everything; it is all arranged. The only trouble with your plan was the timing. Next spring, Georgiana? That is far too long in the future. Miss Bennet and I do not wish to wait that long. Do we?"

At Elizabeth's merrily shaking head, Georgiana undertook the hefty task of bundling her befuddlement, self-justification, and exhilaration into a few logical sentences.

"I am very, very glad, Lizzy, Fitzwilliam! I would have definitely offered an earlier date, but I was certain that Lizzy would not wish to leave Longbourn when one or maybe even two sisters would already leave it desolate, and she even insisted that she would be needed here next spring…but of course I will be very glad to have her at Pemberley even sooner!"

Ignoring his sister's rightful confusion, Mr. Darcy pressed forward and said,

"Miss Bennet, let us fix a date now. What do you say to the same day as Jane and Bingley's wedding?"

Georgiana seemed shocked that her brother would pick that particular point in time, and was even more stunned when Elizabeth replied,

"I have absolutely no qualms about leaving on that date, but for the sake of tradition and some old, girlish dreams of mine, I would rather have a little detour before arriving at Pemberley."

"How long a detour? A few weeks perhaps?"

"Yes, about four."

"That can be arranged. Where to? Spain? Portugal? Have you a secret hankering to see Rome or Venice?"

"I have heard a great deal of good about the latter two, but I suppose that a few stops in Spain and Portugal would be nice as well."

"We can visit them on our way home, but you realize all this might extend our tour well past four weeks, Miss Bennet."

Elizabeth pretended to consider, and said,

"If your business in England does not interfere, I do believe that I can relinquish that small part of my girlish fantasies which decrees that merely four weeks should lie between my residence at Longbourn and my sojourn at Pemberley."

"Done, then!" Mr. Darcy exclaimed, and allowed himself to place a proud and possessive hand upon her shoulder. Elizabeth rewarded him with a devoted look.

Georgiana, who had been watching the surprising dialogue with narrowed, suspicious eyes, slowly began to suspect the truth, and decided to force a confession. Sighing deeply, she dropped her shoulders as one disheartened, and murmured sorrowfully,

"Well, I see now that the two of you have merely been jesting at my expense. It is very cruel of you to toy with me thus."

The couple directed their gazes at the youngest member of the party.

"Come, now, Georgiana, that is an ungenerous assessment of Miss Bennet's actions and mine!" Mr. Darcy said jovially. "All these plans will benefit you as well. Many times during the past few days I have heard you refer to Elizabeth as your sister. While I fear that we will never make that true according to blood, the least we can do is to stand up in church alongside Bingley and Jane and make you sisters by marriage."

Having made the announcement, the betrothed couple now eagerly observed every twitch of Georgiana's face, waiting for an astounded reaction. In their minds, they were placing wagers on whether she would lose the power of speech for three minutes together or shriek in shock, when the girl simply laughed, clapped her hands, and went to embrace Elizabeth, exclaiming,

"I knew it!"

Wide-eyed, the older girl writhed out of her future sister-in-law's arms and stared into her fair countenance instead.

"You are not surprised," Elizabeth noted in a bewildered tone.

Georgiana laughed softly into her face.

"How could I be? I have been expecting, wishing this announcement!"

Elizabeth's bottom lip dropped significantly. She looked at her fiancé, fully expecting to find a broad smile indicating that Georgiana's insight resulted from a previously imparted confidence. All she saw, however, was an elder brother even more stunned and puzzled than herself.

Turning back to the beaming maiden, Miss Bennet stammered, "But...I gave no indication...how could you find us out?"

"You certainly did not, indeed! You have been very sly, very reserved with me, Lizzy! How little you told me of what passed during last autumn and spring! I ought to pay you back in kind and refuse to divulge a single hint about how I came to suspect the two of you, but unfortunately, my heart is dreadful at holding grudges and thus forgive I must!" Her smile grew wider, and in a softer tone, she explained, "Since they were restored, I have been spending a great deal of time alone with my memories, getting reacquainted with them as with old friends. About a week ago, I was thus engaged in my rooms in our London townhouse, when I precipitously realized that *your* name was interwoven with several recollections from last autumn and winter, Lizzy. For several minutes I was persuaded that my mind was simply clouded over with some remnant confusion, but the impression could not be shaken. Thankfully, there was documentation which could substantiate the claims of my head: I retrieved Fitzwilliam's letters of last October and November from my writing desk. And lo! There, written at least a dozen times upon various pages, was the name 'Miss Elizabeth Bennet'. I reread the pertinent passages, and found them all praising your intellect, or wit, or appearance! I nearly keeled over and fainted dead away upon the flowered rug beneath my feet. What a child I must have been, to have missed their implications during the original reading!" Elizabeth raised an eyebrow, already formulating teases on the subject of her fiancé's style of letter-writing. "And then," the brilliant Miss Darcy went on, "I had gathered that you had somehow known about the ongoings in Ramsgate, and it was this which allowed you to realize that I was Georgiana Darcy. Now, I suppose that it is possible that George Wickham told you of them, but it would be extremely uncharacteristic of him to freely impart something which made him appear so evil. Therefore, I was left with the conclusion that, for reasons of his own, my brother confided in you, meaning that he had to have the highest possible degree of trust in you. Fitzwilliam is not one to openly announce his sister's folly to the world. And then, meeting at Pemberley, a pretty, intelligent young lady entered into a conspiracy of good-doing with an eligible bachelor who had already expressed his admiration for her on more than one occasion. This could only end well!" Giggling at their rose-colored faces, Georgiana summed up her discourse with one last startling piece of information: "However, I feared that you had been too busy for the past few weeks discussing my case to talk about yourselves, so I cunningly suggested to Fitzwilliam that we invite you to Pemberley as my guest. He jumped at the bait like a starving man at a piece of bread, and laughing silently into my sleeve at him, I began to plot how I could encourage romantic outings and ample solitude for the two of you."

Elizabeth inhaled deeply, exhaled, and regained the use of her paralyzed tongue. Crossing her arms and looking over at her intended, she jested,

"Well, Mr. Darcy, I do believe that some of your statements appear to have been a little premature. How could we not regret Miss Georgiana's new wit – especially since she is now able to outwit us both?!"

The gentleman's only response was to laugh and to reach for the two women whom he loved in such different ways, and to press them simultaneously to his heart in one large, familial embrace.

Chapter 66

The evening was fraught with anxiety. The family returned around dinnertime and welcomed Georgiana back with exuberance. Little attention was paid to the two unacknowledged lovers who stood together in a corner of the room and watched the ongoings in silence.

Soon after dinner, when Mr. Bennet rose and withdrew to the library, Elizabeth saw Mr. Darcy rise also and follow him, and her agitation on seeing it was extreme. Georgiana, who had also noted the departure of the two men and realized what it meant, quietly came up and slipped her alabaster hand into her future sister's palm. Grateful for this support, Elizabeth squeezed her hand and let herself be comforted by the kind company.

They sat together until Mr. Darcy appeared again, and looking at him, they were a little relieved by his smile. Very promptly, he approached them, and while pretending to speak to Georgiana, said in a whisper to her companion,

"Go to your father. He wants you in the library."

Elizabeth was gone directly.

Her father was seated, impatiently tapping his fingers on his desk, looking grave and anxious. He glanced up as soon as she entered, and his eyes released her face no more. When the door clicked shut behind his daughter, he asked without delay,

"Lizzy, what are you doing? Are you out of your senses, to be accepting this man? Do you not see the war he wages on me?"

Miss Bennet started.

"I am sure I do not understand you, sir," she said slowly and fearfully. "I have never known Fitz – Mr. Darcy – to be aggressive!"

Mr. Bennet snorted.

"No?" In response to her violently shaking head, he elaborated: "The man is bent on stripping me of every sensible companion! First, he convinced his best friend to take Jane, then he claimed Anne as his sister, and now, just when I thought the worst over, he wants you as his wife! If this is not vicious battle, I do not know what is!"

Elizabeth's shoulders relaxed. This was a little better beginning than she had hoped for, but there was an expression in her father's eyes that kept her on her guard. Lowering herself into a chair across from him, she waited for the substance of his conversation.

Regarding her with a much more serious face, Mr. Bennet recommenced,

"I nearly fell out of my chair when he came in here earlier this evening and asked for your hand. My child, why have you accepted him?"

Blushing furiously, Elizabeth murmured something about him being a good man and a devoted brother, and about her affection for him.

"In other words, you are determined to have him. He is rich, to be sure, and you will have many fine carriages and jewels. But will they make you happy? As for him being a good man: I suppose deep down he is, for after Mr. Wickham's conduct towards Anne we cannot take his denunciations seriously. And Mr. Darcy treats his sister so warmly that he is obviously capable of *some* amiable feeling. But his merits as a brother do not mean that he will make a good partner in life. Consider, Lizzy, that he is still the same disagreeable man who refused to dance with you, and who can sit in a person's parlor for a quarter of an hour without opening his lips!"

"He refused to dance with me in what ought to have been a private conversation which I inexcusably eavesdropped upon, and I never knew that the goodness of a man could be measured by how well he rattled away in company!" was Elizabeth's warm defense.

"Neither did I," Mr. Bennet replied, a little dryly. "But be frank with me, Lizzy, and with yourself: does Pemberley seem like an inviting home because Anne will be there? Jane, and I daresay Kitty, are on the verge of removing from Longbourn; is it impending loneliness which entices you to follow in their footsteps?"

Elizabeth looked the concerned Master of Longbourn directly in the eye.

"Certainly not, sir. I would not be worthy of the confidence which you place in my reason if I were to dispose of my fate based on such preposterous logic. Yes, Georgiana will be at Pemberley for the present, but I am fully mindful that a girl of her warmth, beauty, and youth will be courted and wed in a year or two, and I will be left for a lifetime with her elder brother. It is on his account that I wish to move to Derbyshire, not on hers."

Mr. Bennet relaxed a little in his chair.

"Forgive me for suggesting that you might be such a terrible goose, but I am merely trying to make sense of this extraordinary turn of events. At first I feared that *he* was driven by the same sort of motivation - to make Anne happy - but on closer questioning that presumption of mine had to fall. I have never seen or heard a man so utterly besotted. He makes Bingley sound indifferent!"

Elizabeth smiled and coyly glanced down at her hands.

"He speaks very well indeed; I enjoy hearing him use words of four syllables."

"Particularly when he praises qualities which you did not even know you possessed," her father retorted cheerfully. "But be serious with me, Lizzy, I want to talk very seriously. I need to know how all this came about. How long have you loved him?"

Forgetting herself, Elizabeth laughed.

"It has been coming on so gradually that I hardly know, but I believe that I must date it from my first seeing his beautiful grounds at Pemberley."

Her father predictably started. Elizabeth shrank deeper into her seat. Having betrayed the matter, she had no choice but to tell him the entire tale. She admitted to having received a confidence from Mr. Darcy the preceding April, although she did not reveal the exact circumstances surrounding the disclosure lest it damage her fiancé in Mr. Bennet's eyes. She confessed that she had been nowhere near London the week before the wedding. She emphasized that she had thought Pemberley devoid of its owner, but once the opposite was proven true, she could not but take advantage of his assistance. Over and over she assured her father that Mr. Darcy had acted as a gentleman throughout their cooperation. Mr. Bennet heard her with amazement.

"This is an evening of wonders, indeed! So you and Darcy did everything – found the fellow out, broke off the wedding, expelled him from the country, and preserved Annie's freedom! So much the better. I always feared that the black-hearted scoundrel would return to Meryton for one reason or another, and cause more trouble somehow. I am considerably more at ease knowing him to be across the ocean. But I must own that I am equally surprised at your poor judgement, Lizzy! Instead of scampering to Derbyshire with meager funds and dabbling in half-truths which could have landed you in extreme trouble, it would have been infinitely simpler to come up to your old father and let him help you. Why did you choose the harder route?" Elizabeth knew that she could never answer that question honestly without hurting her father's feelings immensely. Thankfully, the second after the speech had crossed his lips, the elderly gentleman seemed to realize its absurdity and spared her the necessity of answering. "What a silly question," Mr. Bennet mumbled under his breath. "Why would you come to me with such a serious and extraordinary application? To be laughed at? To hear my quips on the business openly aired at the dinner table, even in front of Mr. Wickham, perhaps? You needed far more than the man of jest and negligence that I am: you needed a man of action. I should only be grateful that you found him in time, and will belong to him forevermore. He will do right by you, as I never have." Catching his daughter's stunned countenance, he continued, "Do you wonder, Lizzy, what finally made me see what an abomination of a father I have been? What, after three and twenty years, opened my eyes to the pitiful way in which I fulfilled my paternal duty?" Watching his daughter desperately try not to nod, he satisfied her curiosity anyhow. "It was Anne, Lizzy. When she came, for the first time in a long time I had someone who depended on my protection. Being woefully aware that the moment I ceased my vigilance would be the moment the defenseless girl was turned out-of-doors, I was forced to emerge from my library more often than ever before. And the more time I spent in the drawing room, the more I realized that Anne was far from the only one who needed me. As your mother's own children, you were in no danger of being thrown out of Longbourn's main gates, but nonetheless you still needed a parent who told you that you and your dreams mattered, that you were worthy of marrying for love, and who disciplined when necessary. Despite my strides, I have yet a long way to go, as evidenced by Anne's well-placed remark about Mary the other day. Breaking old habits at my age is difficult, Lizzy, and I am extremely sorry that further improvements will come too late to benefit you."

Elizabeth rose from her chair, and walking around to her father's side of the desk, took his hand in hers comfortingly.

"You must not be too severe upon yourself. I believe that I turned out well enough; and I never doubted that you loved me, sir."

"I am glad to hear that, Lizzy, but let me feel for once in my life how much I have been to blame. I am not afraid of being overpowered by the impression. It will pass away soon enough. At least Lydia did not take advantage of my horrid laxity to elope or get into some other incredible mischief!"

Elizabeth leaned down and embraced the old gentleman. He accepted the caress and pressed his lips upon her curly tresses. During these exchanges, he noticed the ruby pin in her dark locks, and straightaway recalled her embarrassment when Lydia had first mentioned it several weeks ago. With his usual good humor, he thereupon extracted a confession as to its true purchaser, and after laughing at her for some time, at last allowed her to go.

Chapter 67

The remainder of the Bennet family vacillated between awe and joy to hear that one of its members was engaged to a man whom they thought had ten thousand pounds a year. Elizabeth was obliged to recite her solemn assurances of attachment several times, mainly for Jane's benefit, before all were reconciled to the idea. Mrs. Bennet, as expected, went into paroxysms of happiness. Captain Carter, not to be outdone by Mr. Bingley or Mr. Darcy, paid Kitty a visit soon after her sister Elizabeth was betrothed and prevailed upon her to likewise resign the name of Bennet.

The ceremony which joined the three happy couples in holy matrimony was remembered in Hertfordshire for generations, partially because it was everything celestial, majestic and beautiful, and partially because Mrs. Bennet would not let anyone forget it. Georgiana, Lydia and Mary made a trio of lovely bridesmaids, attired in pink silk and smiles. Grand notes flowed from the organ and from the trumpets which had been hired for the occasion. The entire church overflowed with bouquets of flowers which the grooms had imported from London's hothouses; all went home with the scent of roses on their garments.

One by one, Mr. Bennet escorted his beautiful daughters from the back of the church towards the altar and towards the men to whom they were about to pledge their lives. Jane's Grecian profile glowed with joy. Kitty's lips were strongly curved upward and her steps were brisk and eager. Elizabeth and her Mr. Darcy, however, were the ones who captivated the majority of the attention and who were talked of the most when the event was over. There was something infinitely touching in the stately yet warm manner in which the satin-clad Elizabeth processed towards her groom, accepted his proffered hand, and took her rightful place at his side. While all the couples repeated their vows with due reverence and feeling, there was a depth in Mr. Darcy's voice that resonated with everyone present and made Elizabeth visibly thrill with happiness.

The two succeeding months were as a dream. Together, Fitzwilliam and Elizabeth Darcy toured Portugal, Spain, and Italy. After they had had their fill of the Continent, they came home to England and to Pemberley. All forty servants lined up in the courtyard when they heard of their approach, beaming. Mrs. Reynolds was at their forefront, smiling for all she was worth. At the center of the courtyard stood Georgiana Darcy, holding a bouquet of flowers which she presented with pride and delight to the new mistress of the house.

If Lady Catherine had been furious to hear that Georgiana would be visiting the Bennets, Mr. Darcy's letter which announced that a Bennet had consented to be his wife rendered her absolutely livid. She wrote both her nephew and niece a reply in language so abusive, especially of Elizabeth, that they burned the epistle and for a long time all interaction was at an end. After several months, however, Mrs. Darcy managed to convince them to seek a reconciliation. Lady Catherine refused their kindness at first, but after a while became reasonable and condescended to wait on them at Pemberley. Once she encountered Mr. Bennet during her visits there, and was good-natured enough to advise him to repaint the walls of Longbourn, for she remembered their colors as being quite drab.

Mr. Bingley and Jane remained at Netherfield only for a year. He then purchased an estate in Yorkshire, placing Jane and Elizabeth within thirty miles of each other. Of note, Mr. Bingley managed to buy new windows for his house without consulting anyone but his wife, causing Mr. and Mrs. Darcy to silently congratulate him.

Lydia found Longbourn exceedingly dull without Kitty. In time, she began to wonder whether she would be better served by tempering her immoderate laughter and forging ridiculous pranks in order to tempt her elder sisters into issuing invitations to their new homes. The scheme worked. By the time she was nineteen, Lydia was a respectable, albeit still lively young lady, who managed to catch the eye of one of Colonel Fitzwilliam's wealthy military friends during a visit to Pemberley and shortly thereafter became Mrs. Stevens.

The Master of Longbourn and Mary became extremely close companions, both during their time at Longbourn and their joint trips to Derbyshire, Yorkshire, and wherever Kitty and Lydia happened to be. For many years, it appeared that Mary would be an old maid, but at seven and twenty she met a well-read, affluent merchant who had headquartered himself in Meryton. As neither parent was able to part with their last remaining daughter, he consented to make Longbourn his residence after the wedding. A usual evening found Mary by the fireplace with her husband and father, discussing a work of literature. Mrs. Bennet sat with them, occasionally marking her deference for her son-in-law's opinion.

Georgiana blossomed into one of the most sought-after ladies of the *ton*. For three Seasons, she steadfastly rebuffed dozens of suitors, letting them sweetly know that she was very content to live with her dearest brother and sister-in-law at Pemberley and to be an aunt to their growing brood. But during the fourth Season, she laid eyes upon the Duke of Avon and her loyalty to the house of her ancestors was slightly dampened. With Mr. Darcy's, Elizabeth's and the Colonel's blessing, she and her young man wed in a ceremony large enough to encompass the bridegroom's noble connections as well as all her friends from Hertfordshire and Derbyshire.

Her military cousin also found happiness in the form of Lady Agatha. With her impressive dowry, they were able to travel through the Continent which he had always longed to see, and returning to England, buy a small estate which they made into a peaceful, cheerful home.

Of Wickham, very little was heard for a long time. Several days before the triple wedding came the welcome news that Darcy's ship had safely returned to its London port and that the crew had released Wickham on American soil without incident. Those in England breathed a sigh of relief.

Half a decade later, Darcy invited the captain of his ship to dinner at Pemberley to honor him for his longstanding service. After the meal, when all the servants had been excused and only Elizabeth, her husband, their three sweet children and the Captain remained around the fireside, the grizzled seaman offhandedly mentioned,

"By the way, sir, I am sure that you recall a certain man who you once sent into my care with the instruction to bring him to America, which I did?"

Fitzwilliam Darcy cuddled his two-year-old daughter to his heart gently before replying,

"Actually, I had been doing a good enough job of forgetting him. But I know to whom you refer; speak on."

"I am not sure if I ever told you all the details of that voyage. For the first several weeks, the man was impossible; he was constantly trying to sabotage the ship, cutting ropes and the like, to force us to return to England. Thankfully, the crew kept their eyes on him and placed him in a cabin whenever he started his tricks, and he did not know enough to do any true damage. And the language he used! I have heard enough of sailor's talk in my day, but that man surpassed them all. Halfway through the passage, however, we had a dreadful storm. Even I thought that we might lose the ship, for the hull was creaking and extremely tall waves were crashing down upon the deck. At the height of the squall, I looked in on Wickham to ensure that he was in his cabin and not causing mischief at so critical a moment. He was there, trembling and pale to the lips. Death was not something he often contemplated, I guessed, but he was clearly thinking of it now. Praise the Almighty, after a few hours the storm calmed, and – surprisingly – so did Wickham. He was extremely quiet and withdrawn for the remainder of the journey, and when he was put on shore and told he was free to go, he went without even a memorable word for those of us who had brought him to and were leaving him in a foreign land.

I never expected to see him again. But on my last journey to America, I went to a little shop near the docks to purchase a few things for myself before embarking for another two months at sea. A little boy of about three sat by the stove playing with a wooden toy. A pleasant-faced woman, his mother, was behind the counter with another babe in her arms. She was not particularly beautiful or fashionable, but she strove to please her customers and worked quickly. When I walked up and asked for a particular type of wine, she looked about, realized that she did not have it in the front, and called to her husband to bring it from the back. The instant he appeared in the doorway of the storeroom, I knew him. I doubt that he returned the favor as he gave no indication and my beard has whitened and grown long over the past several years. He gave her the wine she had called for and asked, in a tender tone, whether there was anything else she needed. She released him to go back to his work sorting merchandise, but as he passed the three-year-old boy the little one called out 'Papa!' and reached out with his plump hands. With a love which I would have never assumed that man capable of, Wickham picked up the child, put its soft cheek against his, and talking to him soothingly took him to the storeroom. Few things bring tears to my eyes after all the lands I have seen and all the dangers I have survived, but something about that entire scene caused me to wipe some moisture from my cheek. I never would have hoped for such a good outcome for that young man."

That was how they found out that Wickham had married in America and had taken Darcy's advice to settle down to work. And they were glad. Even Colonel Fitzwilliam grudgingly agreed that sparing the man had been a decent idea. In so many ways, good had come out of evil. Wickham's designs upon Georgiana had been the means of uniting Elizabeth and Fitzwilliam Darcy; and now his exile had become the seed of his restoration. It had all been worthwhile.

The End

About the Author

Monika Barbara Potocki is from Livingston, New Jersey. An avid daydreamer, bookworm and hopeless romantic since childhood, she began writing in her teenage years. Her hobbies include reading, watching nostalgic movies, and spending time with her family and friends.

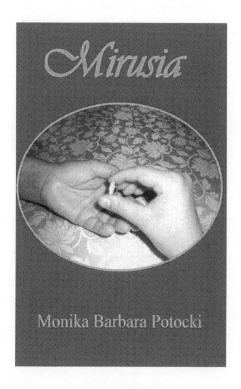

It's not Pride and Prejudice
Or even a Pride and Prejudice variation,
But there's still a young eligible bachelor,
A witty maiden,
And a timeless romance.

Enjoy a preview of *Mirusia* on the next few pages!

Preview

Dutifully, the following day John Robinson put on a suit and walked down the street to the town hall, whence beautiful strains of music came. He was met at the door by Mr. Drexel, one of those men who know everyone and who insist on integrating all outsiders into the mix as soon as possible.

"Good evening, Mr. Robinson."

"Good evening, sir."

"Why, where is your carriage?" the older man inquired in a surprised voice as he craned his head, looking around vainly for a conveyance.

"I walked, Mr. Drexel."

"Walked!"

"Yes. After all, I only live a few feet away from the town hall."

Mr. Drexel gave him a queer look, unable to comprehend why a young man of consequence and wealth would not wish to flaunt it before the whole town by arriving in an expensive rig, no matter how short the distance was. Putting the matter aside, however, he drew his arm through the guest's and steered him towards a group of people whom John vaguely remembered from summers past. They were reintroduced, and then Mr. Drexel, pulling him away, repeated the procedure with several other cliques which were standing or sitting about. Finally, considering his duty sufficiently done, he released his companion's arm and allowed him to survey the scene and make advances on his own as the orchestra prepared to strike their first chords.

John looked around. Everywhere, maidenly eyes glanced at him flirtatiously. Locks were tossed or smoothened; every figure was turned towards him so as to show its best advantage. Had he been a vain man, he would have doubtlessly enjoyed the attention. As it was, however, it made him feel like a fish surrounded by bait, none of it worthwhile. More than ever, he wished that he had not come.

Meanwhile, Mr. Drexel watched him expectantly, wondering what lucky young lady would have the honor of being his first dance partner that evening. John inwardly sighed.

There is no help for it, he said to himself. *I might as well pick one and prepare to make insignificant small talk for the next ten minutes.*

Trying to appear as interested as possible, he scanned the assembly. Nothing was in view but those silly, brightly bedecked girls. Then, as his glance momentarily and inadvertently fell into the background, he finally saw a very curious creature.

He stared for a moment, and then turned to Mr. Drexel.

"Sir, would you be so kind as to tell me - who is that lady standing by the windows near the lounge area?"

"That is Ms. Nellie Gordon," his guide said, nodding approvingly. Ms. Gordon, by virtue of her position as the daughter of a relatively prosperous tradesman and as the golden-haired town beauty, was widely considered the only proper match for Greenvalle's most eligible bachelor. And Nellie, in multiple conversations, had made it known that John Robinson was a conquest she was determined to prevail in.

"No, not the one in the green dress. The one on the other side of the windows. The one in navy blue," John replied.

Mr. Drexel stared at him as if he were a madman.

"Not the one with the cap?"

"Yes, that one."

"Err…I…*we*…don't know much about her. She moved in about a month or so ago into a little rental house on the outskirts of town. No one has ever called on her as far as I know."

"What is her name?"

"Her name? I don't know." He paused. Then, in a laughing tone, he added, "You…don't think her *pretty*, sir, do you?"

"Pretty? No, I…," John stopped short. Then he reddened, ashamed. "But I find her interesting."

"Interesting?"

"Something about her manner…I do not know."

Mr. Drexel seemed confused. Was this handsome, brilliant bachelor joking? John, immediately sensing the feeling, forced himself to take his eyes off the lady in navy blue and to place them on another. As they happened to fall on a blond girl in bright pink, he walked up to her and asked for a dance with as much enthusiasm as he could muster.

While he danced with the silly girl who continually chattered about the history of the family heirloom necklace she was wearing, he often and surreptitiously glanced at the girl in navy blue. Unlike every other eligible female in the room, she was making no effort to attract his attention. Instead, she watched the entire dance floor intently, and seemed particularly focused on the dresses of the women; this, however, without any show of envy. From her entire attitude, he suspected that she did not resent her situation as a wall-flower in the least.

Between quick responses to his dance partner, he also observed, as closely as possible from a distance, the girl's physical appearance. She was decidedly unattractive. Her features, as far as he could tell, were not grotesque, so it was impossible for him to call her ugly, although he later found out that many of the villagers did so. Her figure, however, was rather unsymmetrical and ungainly. It was completely encased in a floor length, navy blue dress of rather coarse cloth and a high waistline. The same had long, tight sleeves which completely covered her arms up to the wrists. Her collar was high and hid her neck. On her head, in dramatic contrast with all the other young ladies who tossed their soft locks at every opportunity, she wore a matching navy blue, unbecoming cap with a frilly border: no hair and very little of her ears showed. Underneath, a low forehead could be seen. Most prominent of all were the large, black-rimmed glasses. They covered a substantial portion of her face and made her look like a nerd and bookworm. Other than that, her hazel eyes (although glazed over by the glasses), lips and nose seemed somewhat decent; her eyebrows were covered too much by the glasses for him to make a fair pronouncement on their merit.

384

And yet, despite her appearance, she seemed amiable and pleasant, as evidenced by a small smile she wore and the air of intelligence which hung about her. The duality provoked John's interest. Besides, he felt something like pity for the poor creature who had resided in the usually companionable town for several weeks, in such utter desolation that one of the biggest town gossips did not know her name.

After several more reels, he could no longer contain his curiosity. Stepping off the dance floor, he wove his way through the crowd and soon found himself by the nearly deserted lounge area. She was still watching the floor, and did not seem aware of his approach. Trying to be casual, he strolled over to one of the windows and looked out for a minute at the star-studded sky.

"Lovely evening, is it not?"

She turned her head and glanced at him for an instant, but evidently decided that he must have been speaking to himself. She turned away.

John tried again.

"Do you not think that it is lovely, madam?"

This time he looked at her as he said it. She caught his eye and seemed quite stupefied for a moment. Then she quickly glanced over her shoulder, expecting to see the young lady to whom the remark had been addressed. But there was nobody there.

"Are you speaking to *me?*" she asked, looking at him again.

"Yes." John smiled. "Nice evening, isn't it?"

"Yes, very," she replied with a small smile and began to turn her head away.

"Are you new in town, miss?" John asked quickly, to prolong the conversation.

Again, she seemed quite shocked that he would favor her with his time. But she finally turned her whole body towards him and smiled warmly as she replied,

"Relatively new. I do not believe that you are, though, sir."

This engaged his curiosity even more. He had assumed that someone who sat in corners, was perpetually ignored, and dressed so shabbily would be a shy creature. Her friendly smile and confident tone, however, proved otherwise.

"You are correct, madam. I have spent many summers here, as I am sure you have heard," he replied, laughing a little. "But I generally live in Yorkshire - I suppose you have never heard of that town?"

"Actually, I have. I lived most of my life in Summerside. Yorkshire is less than twenty minutes away."

"Summerside?! I have driven through it often. It is very pleasant, very neighborly." John paused. "How long has it been since you moved here?"

"A little more than a month."

"Do you like it?" he asked. Then he reddened, wondering if he had said the wrong thing. How could she like it when everyone in town disliked and was rude to her?

But she surprised him. Instead of being offended, she laughed at his expression, having guessed what he was thinking. He marveled at the sound. Her laugh, just like her voice, was beautiful and musical. It seemed completely out of place with her unattractive looks.

"I find it very interesting, as you might imagine," the young lady replied with a smile.

"Yes. The customs here are quite different. It is like stepping back in time."

She laughed again and nodded in agreement

"Time travel does not only exist in science fiction books and movies."

After he had acknowledged this small piece of humor, a short silence ensued. To break it, he turned to her again.

"I am sorry, but you see, I do not quite know your name...Ms..."

"Jansen. Mirusia Jansen. If I am not mistaken, you are John Robinson."

"You are not mistaken," that gentleman said laughing, as they shook hands and sat down on the sofa to continue their conversation.

The tête-à-tête went on and on. Despite her strange looks, John found Mirusia incredibly easy to talk to. She was intelligent, and she was charming. Before he knew it, they were discussing the campuses of their respective *alma maters*, which soon evolved into a conversation about the Middle Ages and afterwards into one about *Jane Eyre*. John was scarcely aware of the numerous stares and glances which were sent their way from the opposite side of the room. Ms. Jansen did not seem to mind them either; if anything, they amused her. This captivated John, and awoke in him a deep respect and admiration for his companion. He knew many kind-tempered women, but none that would have suffered so many injustices and slights in amiable silence.

Her manner was also beguiling. While she was sociable, she was not bold: her air was sweet and virginal. No questionable or colorful word or phrase ever passed her lips. Everything about her was ladylike.

After a good two hours, which for him seemed like fifteen minutes, they paused in the conversation to catch their breaths. For the first time, they noticed how much the hour hand on the clock had moved and that the last dance of the evening was beginning.

"The Viennese Waltz," John remarked.

"Yes."

"I have always loved it. It is so spirited."

"It is one of my favorites, too," she replied.

"Really?" John smiled and held out his hand to her. "If so, may I have this dance?"

Ms. Jansen looked at his hand for a moment, and then at him. She evidently decided that he had made the offer on the spur of the moment and in forgetfulness of the circumstances. In order to save him the embarrassment of standing up with her, she shook her head and said,

"I am sure that some other young lady has already promised you this dance, as it is the last. You had better seek her out and keep your offer to her. Thank you for the talk, however."

387

John immediately comprehended what she was trying to do. Smiling and shaking his head a little he answered,

"No, I have no previous engagement. And I would prefer to dance this one with you, Ms. Jansen - unless- of course, if you do not want to."

"In that case," here she gave him her hand, "I have no objection."

They stood and hand-in-hand, walked to the dance floor. When they had reached it, quite a loud murmur ran through the crowd and numerous incredulous glances were cast their way. Ms. Jansen turned away from him slightly and looked at the floor, not in embarrassment, but to hide an extremely amused smile. They got into position, took their preparation step, and began sailing away on the strains of the Viennese waltz. Both danced well, and if it were not for the looks of his partner, John was sure that their litheness would surely have awoken much admiration. As it was, they were only rewarded with vicious whispers and shocked stares.

When the waltz ended, so did the evening. There was a bustle as the waitresses began to clear the refreshment tables and the couples began to wander out the door.

"May I see you home?" John Robinson asked Ms. Jansen as they slowly left the dance floor.

"If you wish to, yes."

"Yes, I would like to," John replied, half-laughing, simultaneously offering her his arm. She took it.

They walked over to the coat-room, where they retrieved the young lady's clutch and cloak, both made out of the same dull navy blue material as her dress. Afterwards, they stepped out of the hot town hall into the cool night air.

Made in the USA
Coppell, TX
03 March 2021

51220452R00229